FOR CHRISTABEL

"All they who live in the upper sky
Do love you, holy Christabel."

PREFACE

THE gentle reader is invited to approach this novel as if it were a historical romance, an, alas! imperfect but imaginative epoch, the memory of which is almost obliterated, an inquest into the causes and conditions that preceded and perhaps were partly responsible for its effacement. The scene is laid, mainly, in an English seaside town during the opening years of the twentieth century; and the story is as much concerned with this town as with any of the characters that move through its streets.

To understand how far that period with which we deal has retreated from us, it is only necessary to find a fashion-plate of twenty years ago and match it against a Cretan wall-painting in the Ashmolean museum. The distant, mysterious inhabitants of that lost world are infinitely nearer to us in their clothes, and probably in their outlook, than our own parents.

And then seaside towns are always silted up with the debris of the past century. The predominant note at Newborough, before the bombardment, was one of long settled comfort and confident respectability. The town faced the world with a Credo the grounds of which it refused even to examine. This belief in the inherent rightness and essential righteousness of the prevailing system was, in reality, but a sur-

vival of that Swiss Family Robinson attitude
toward life which the English had adopted at the
outbreak of the nineteenth century and had maintained until its close; and this belief it is which
throws so inexplicable a charm over the whole
period. Elsewhere, in the years in which our
narrative is laid, it may be that this confident
pose was breaking down, but as a wild flower,
imagined to be extinct, or an obsolete but un-
obtrusive wild animal, may yet linger on in a
remote Welsh mountain or wide Yorkshire moor,
so in this wind-bound, sea-pounded town, the
nineteenth century has been allowed to project
its heavy shadow across the opening years of the
young era. For it is a mistake to think that a
century ends everywhere at the same time, however clear may be the transition from one of
these artificially made periods to another. Mr.
George Moore has described exquisitely how the
eighteenth century lay hidden among the lakes
and woods of Ireland until the year 1860; and
no doubt the enthusiastic amateur of dead epochs
can still find the nineteenth century much poorer,
rather angry, but none the less sure and respectable, lurking in unobserved corners, in Parliament, in the Church, in a seaside hotel.

AMALFI.

CONTENTS

ix

BEFORE THE BOMBARDMENT

CHAPTER I

"When blood is nipp'd, and ways be foul,
Then nightly sings the staring owl,
To-who;
To-whit, to-who, a merry note,
While greasy Joan doth keel the pot."

THE tin tongue rattled on, high up under a dome. So loudly it clacked and racketed through the silence of this vast edifice that, surely, it must have pierced through the layers of cloud, at this season stretched like blankets, one over another endlessly, and must now echo through the ultimate blue imbecility beyond. This cerulean lining, however, was in the winter a thing utterly incredible; while the grey blankets above and beneath yet invited slumber, warm deep slumber. But on and on it cackled, this idiot tongue, trying to inform the sleeper of its monotonous and invariable message, slave to a slave. It seemed fearful of betraying a trust. Six o'clock, six o'clock, six o'clock, it hammered and ranted.

Through an unconscious cunning born of long experience, the sleeper was able to transform the brief moments which this metallic music occupied into the most lingering period of the entire day. While still fast asleep, she could calculate precisely the last second of the alarum, and only when the final syncopic death-rattle was strangled

13

in the clock's throat, did she, almost automatically, leave the sandy plains or issue forth from the aromatic summer pine-forests of her native northern Germany. Indeed the bell itself usually played some past in the dream, serving both to lengthen and end it. Now her withered limbs must lumber out of bed into the frozen air; she must switch on the light and tumble into her tousled, rumpled clothes lying on a chair and by a judicious, though not too protracted, application of brush and sponge arrange the wisps of flaxen, flocculent hair, the straight pale eyes, the long shapeless nose, the lump on the forehead above the right-hand almost invisible eyebrow, into their usual weekday perspective, imparting to them by this process a cohesion and sense of focus which they had lacked as she lay there sleeping. All these attributes which have been described now centred round a personality, and formed Elisa, the Prussian housemaid at a hotel in the North of England. Every morning she must pass through these extraordinary experiences and mutations which constitute getting-up and dressing in this part of Britain during the winter months.

Every morning it grew colder, colder and colder, and all for fourteen pounds a year! Ten years of it. She couldn't go on doing it for ever, really she couldn't, though it was better than that first place, at the Rectory! Angrily, dumbly, she shook out her body, turned off the light, and creaked blunderingly out of the room. Now she was wading through the familiar stillness, a silence infringed by a thousand crepuscular crepitations, of the hotel-corridors. As she

moved, these minute, crackling vibrations were
lost in the cascades of sound which her clumsy
feet unloosed to dash up against tiled walls.
Soon it would be light, she supposed; and, before
dawn came, there were the grates and the fires,
the stoves and the boilers, the floors and the staircase, to do: and, not properly, her work. It was
a man's work, but just because she was a foreigner, she must do it. She repeated to herself
the names of her hated enemies—the grates, the
fires and the stoves, the boilers and the floors and
the staircase. The lilt of the words gradually
formed in her mind into a Housemaid's Miserere,
to be repeated, rather meaninglessly but with a
sense of comfort. She would feel better by and
by. She must light the fires.

The flames were first born in a faint blue
flicker, and then swiftly growing lusty, purred
and coquetted at her from their iron cages. The
rhythm of their lithe and feline movements woke
the reflections that had been slumbering in their
nests, high among the overwhelming gold frondage
of cornice and capital, which had been overgrown in a breath by the bronze forest of the
darkness. Directly the light was turned off, the
forest overgrew all this splendour, as an Indian
jungle swallows up a city on the very instant of
its desertion. To turn on the light was, similarly, the excavation of a buried town. And now
the fire woke all these little reflections up in the
branches, making them stir and preen themselves,
and peep out of their dark high nests, as a wild
creature moving through a forest at night would
wake all the young birds, set them quivering and
twittering.

At any rate, Elisa said to herself, it would grow warmer now. But no sooner had she thereby attempted to instil life into her starved hands and feet than it became necessary for her to draw aside the heavy plush curtains and open the shutters. With an air of protest she threw these clattering back against the wall; immediately, the cold twilight poked and scratched at the window-panes with its sharp black claws, then moaned like a hunted animal that craves shelter. Blue frost flowers could be seen expanding and contracting on the glass, and the cruel wind squeezed through every crevice, and conducted a paper-chase high into the grey air of the open plot outside, while within the grates the flames for a moment shrank back, became sensitive plants that closed, opened and closed, their red petals.

Now there were the floors: no peace all day long, not a scrap of it (and the chilblains!). Bad enough in the summer, it was; but the visitors made it lively (though the other servants—being only "temporaries"—got all the tips, of course) and never even half a day's holiday. She might work her fingers right off her hand, she might, without anybody as much as minding. And nasty, too, because she was a foreigner. "Remember you are only a German," the manager had said. "German," indeed, and none the worse for that, she supposed? And she gave the shutter a real bang, as she thought of it, with the back of her brush; that would teach them, perhaps; wake them up. Tea for those Two at eight o'clock. A lot of tea she'd get, she shouldn't wonder. What had they come here for, in the winter? To give trouble, extra trouble, that was all, with

their tea and hot water bottles at all hours.
"German," indeed; and she struck the shutter a
second time.

The blow resounded up the stairs, through the
empty corridors and rows of vacant rooms.
"Good gracious, 'Tibbits,' whatever can that be?"
called out the deep, broken voice of Miss Collier-
Floodgaye, timid in spite of its rather masculine
tones. And the more experienced Miss Bramley
in the patient and effusive voice of a paid companion, answered, "Nothing, dear! It's quite all
right. It must be Elisa. She should be in, in
a few minutes now, with the tea. How did you
sleep, dear?" "But it's not light yet, Tibbits,"
the first speaker protested. "No, dear, but it's
nearly eight o'clock," and Miss Bramley could be
heard chinking the gold chains of her little watch,
as though she were hauling in a cable, hand over
hand.

These two visitors were quite unaware of the
intense nature of the interest, almost amounting
to a commotion, for which their presence in the
hotel was responsible. In these two rooms, and
in these alone, were to be found the rarest of
specimens, winter visitors. The other rooms lay
in empty rows all these long months, filled with
a bitter green light such as filters through into an
aquarium, waiting for their next denizens. The
other hotels in Newborough were equally guiltless
of visitors: for English seaside resorts had not
yet determined to inaugurate winter seasons with
that wild and continuous display of Christmas
hilarity, paper-caps, and any quantity of objects
in paper, wool or cardboard, to be thrown at
friends. The hotel managers had not yet grasped

the fact that to induce the famous Continental gaiety—that spirit of Carnival—which must always be their aim, in English hearts, two things and two things only were essential—incessant noise and a multitude of pellets, balls, bullets, rolls of paper and streamers with which the jovial guests could pelt one another. No, at the time of which we are writing, guests during the dark months were an unwanted treasure. In the summer the town was ready for them, but in the short cold days it did not welcome nor even solicit them . . . after all, it was a warm-weather place: and there must be something unusual . . . queer . . . about people who came to a hotel here in the winter. And the visitors could not have many friends, could they? or they would be spending Christmas with them? Then who were they, and why had they no friends? Newborough was intent on an answer.

CHAPTER II

THE DAWN OF FRIENDSHIP

"Here I am, an old man in a dry month,
Being read to by a boy, waiting for rain."

EVEN when Miss Collier-Floodgaye first came
to Newborough, she appeared to be in failing
health. Old, old with the strength and dignity
of an antlered oak, in the manner of that tree,
it seemed that—unless she was uprooted by some
sudden fury of a wind—her gradual decline might
extend over a considerable period. But her dark
figure was only, really, to flit for a few winters
across a darkening screen.

Her origin was, undoubtedly, an obscure one,
and in her conversation she never referred or gave
the most minute clue to it. In the build of her
gaunt body, though, in the sweep of her features,
in her large bones and stately stature, there
lingered, surely, something rustic rather than
urban. That deep, bold voice, which was her
most marked characteristic, still held, it might
be, the dying notes of a harsher, more Doric
music. A farmer's daughter, perhaps; but as-
suredly she was no tradesman's offspring. And
then, too, she was lacking altogether in the liveliness of the city.

Her dress was a suitable translation of her.
Sombre, with never a touch of colour, it enhanced
her personality, adding to it the aged, grape-
blown dignity of a raven. Never intricate, be-

wildering or bewildered, as was the apparel of so
many old ladies in Newborough, it yet conveyed
a certain battered and buffeted pride that was not
to be found in all their laces, shawls, frills and
brooches.   Her large hands were knotted and
veined, unexpectedly virile, the counterpart of
her voice. The few gold rings which adorned
them were rather unexpected, and she wore no
other jewellery. One ring in particular, remains
in the memory, a ring designed to represent intercoiled snakes, with ruby eyes that flashed a
piercing fire as she moved her bony hand. About
this there was a subtle atmosphere, as if it were
the testimony of an incident in the past, or would
be the witness of some event in the future. Her
slow gait, her halting step, the tapping of the
malacca cane which aided it, all enhanced the
difference between Miss Collier-Floodgaye and
the ordinary dweller in hotels, and endowed her
a little, even, with the air of the Wicked Fairy
who went unasked to the Christening—not that
any aura of evil emanated from her, but that
there was undoubtedly a quality of strangeness
clinging to her; which also raised her high above
any symptoms of silliness that she might display.
The whole effect, her very physique, the structure
of her face, her deep voice, strong grey hair, and
brown eye in which sometimes gleamed a brown-
red light, seemed indicative of the hovering, somewhere in the air about, lurking behind, or just out
of sight, ahead, of Tragedy. Yet she was ordinary
enough in many ways. Though not so well informed as numerous invalid ladies of Newborough
with regard to the constant crossing and recross-
ing genealogies of the county families, she, too,

could spend happy hours in tracing a lost stitch in one of these intricately knitted septs.

But, however much interested in them, it was clear that she had never met a member of these tribes in all her long lifetime. Had she, then, been a housekeeper to some rich man who had bequeathed her his fortune? No, for surely her fate had been more interesting, more cruel, even. She was possessed of a dignity that was inborn and ingrained, while her education was as good as that of any other lady of her period. Was she, perhaps, the natural daughter of a distinguished man? But this, again, hardly seemed a solution of the problem: for her life appeared to cover only the last fifteen years out of some seventy-four or five.

Once I thought I had discovered the secret . . . had she been married, fettered for life to lunatic or criminal? Might not such a history account for the fear—if fear it was—that was felt in all the things personal to her? She wore no wedding-ring, but there was not about her any suggestion of spinsterhood. In the end, this theory, too, was discarded; for it seemed impossible in face of many contradictory reports to reach any conclusion. She never explained where she had lived as a child, girl, young or middle-aged woman, nor did she ever allude to the part of the country from which she had sprung. In fact, she had apparently contrived to be born into the world without human agency, fully dressed in black, at the age of approximately sixty years. Her past had thrown no discernible shadows. She had no friends to whom she could refer; and no adventures which she could relate had befallen her.

She wished, it seemed, to be accepted as she was, the creature only of immediate past and present.

In disposition the old lady was, most obviously, kind, generous and amiable. Of this, there could be no doubt. Yet in all the long, accumulating treasure of her years, she had so far caught and made fast no friend except Miss Bramley, a paid Companion.

Now of all professions in this world, that of salaried friend is usually the most degrading, pernicious in its effect upon employed and employer: a declaration in common of their spiritual bankruptcy. For a poor woman to be forced to sell her friendship is infinitely more evil than, for her to be obliged to sell her body. The prostitution is at the same time more prolonged and more hypocritical. The avowed prostitute declares an infamous trade by her ways and appearance. But paid Companionship is a less obvious, more subtle betrayal of personality; a rarer, less robust vice of weaker souls: while for an old lady to have to descend into the "Agony" or other columns of the *Times* in order to buy friendship is as repulsive, surely, as the spectacle of an old man purchasing his love in the market-place. It is a vice unexcused by any inflammation of the senses: a form of slavery infinitely guileful, fatal and pathetic, alike to vendor and purchaser. It is a fraud committed by two undischarged and unrepentant spiritual-bankrupts, each intent on the deception of the other. Nor is the excuse of training valid, as it is in cases where Companion and Companioned are related. For example, the plight of martyr-daughter, of patient victim-niece, so frequently to be observed in seaside towns and health

resorts generally, may appear, at first glance, to be more tragic than that of the paid Companion, because the former reap no financial benefits, however slight, from their martyrdom. In reality, however, their ultimate reward is more certain. The niece bound to hypochondriac aunt, the daughter chained to invalid mother, is but passing through a severe apprenticeship, for the whole time she is learning the tricks of that intricate and difficult art which herself will one day be called upon to practise. Not the faintest nuance of malice, not the most delicate shade of ill-temper is wasted on her, since these are intended to be skilful weapons for future use in her own hand. Hereditary secrets and possessions are these, passed on from mother to daughter, from daughter to niece, from niece to daughter, for innumerable generations. In a lesser way, the preservation of these secrets, the loyalty which informs the entire body of such a society, is reminiscent of a mediæval guild. And further, since daughter and niece are supposed to be free agents, they garner an additional reward in the popularity of an imagined sacrifice ("She has been so good, given her whole life to looking after the old lady"), while the paid Companion is not pitied, because the public knows that she "is paid to put up with it." For those who are not parties to this particular bargain of mother and daughter, aunt and niece, refuse to recognise its existence. How are they, then, to comprehend that the brutal ill-temper of the elder woman, the mild reproach of the younger, the constant and maddening sequence of grumble from one, the patient and galling brightness of the other, are merely

so many essays in technique, like a prima donna's
rendering of scales?   They will not understand
that a properly constituted and hypochondriac
elderly relative takes years to manufacture; that,
like a Damascene blade, before being "turned-
out," she must be tempered by fire, plunged into
icy water, hammered by iron, submitted to countless tests, innumerable processes, constantly and
over a long period of years.   Fortunately those
who are privy to the bargain recognise its nature,
extent and obligations.   It would, indeed, be a
Wicked Aunt (infinitely more serpentine in evil
than the Wicked Uncle of the Babes-in-the-Wood)
who, in breach of unwritten contract, left away
her fortune—for to be as unpleasant as this it is
necessary to have substantial private means—a
very foolish Mother's Right-Hand, who, mis-
taking the educational nature of her cruci-
fixion, cast away all the subtle weapons of her
armoury—resignation, meekness, altruism and
abnegation—and packed her trunk.   But each
can threaten, as the climax of a series of
manœuvres that have extended over several
months, that she will do so, without endangering
her prospects or incurring the genuine displeasure
of the other: for each knows that such a pretence
is merely the most effective, final and dramatic
move in the whole pageant of this tactical display—the big gun which is held in reserve and
can never in reality be dragged up.

Alas, with a paid victim of alien blood, the
relationship between employed and employer is
beyond comparison more tragic, more devastating
in its effect on both.   If the Companion is free
at any moment to give notice of the severance

of her friendship at a given date, the whole basis
of illusion (the very thing for which she is paid—
the "goods" in fact) is shattered beyond repair.
It becomes, therefore, an understood, though undefined and unmentionable clause in the unwritten
contract of such employment that it is to continue
throughout the lifetime of the elder lady: the
agreement can only be terminated by her death.
For the Companion to die first would put her
completely outside the pale: it is a sin which
cannot even be referred to in the presence of old
ladies.

Similarly, to give notice would be "not to play
the game": for it might hinder the Companioned
one from venting her temper, giving rein to her
malice, or indulging fully that other fault, which-
ever it may be, that has hitherto prevented her
from making—or at any rate from keeping—
unsalaried friends. For the Companioned one
is, actually, paying a person to be her friend, in
order that herself may continue unchecked in
some particular line of vice so violent that no
friend unpaid would tolerate it. That is why she
has to pay.

And, in the case of a professional Companion,
there is another powerful financial motive besides
her ordinary emolument: a hope, never, alas, to
be a certainty, of a fortune to reach her as a
posthumous gift from the elder lady. Unfortunately the employer seldom feels bound to the
strict execution of this part of the unwritten
contract, seldom feels morally compelled to carry
it out, in the way that mother or aunt would feel
it incumbent upon them to provide for their
daughters or nieces. For mother and aunt learnt

their trade in the same hard school, and hold their
very worldly goods on the condition, however
undefined, that they enable their hereditary
secrets and family tricks to be handed on, like
the small blue flame of a sacred lamp in a temple,
from one generation to another. The unrelated-
companioned does not hold her possessions on
such easy terms. She does not belong to so strict
or haughty a caste. She must buy herself into
the companioned-class. Compared with mother
or aunt, she is what the Jewish profiteer who
purchases a country seat is to the old landlord
from whom he acquires it. She has no traditions,
and is bound by no sense of obligation. Further,
she knows that the gambling clause of the unwritten contract—that one which relates to her
will—often hovers in the mind of her Companion:
and this serves to summon up before the elder
lady what she most wishes to forget—Death!—
and accordingly irritates her the more, lashing
her into extremes of sulking and ill-temper. And
then, even at the end of these rather fragrant
moments of surrendering to her ruling vice, the
employer is again reminded, by the restraint and
forced "pleasantries" of her Companion, that the
latter dare not answer her back, or give notice,
for fear of alteration in her will—Death again!
Thus the jangling skeleton of the richer lady is
for ever dancing between them, clacking its
castanet-like bones with a ghastly grace: while
still alive, her own ghost dogs her and seeks to
envenom still further the relations between employer and employed.

Miss Collier-Floodgaye's motives, however, for
hiring a friend were rather irregular. No violent
temper or brutal fault marred her character. But

owing to events—of which it was possible for others to feel the existence, though not to conjecture the kind—she was sad (sombre rather than sad, perhaps) and lonely and rich: and, though undoubtedly courageous (for courage was a virtue that could be detected even in her mien) it appeared as though she were a little frightened, frightened perhaps only by the accumulation of her years. She did not wish to be left alone in a silence, a silence in which the few voices that spoke were those of the dead. It is doubtful if the old lady was frightened of anything more tangible than her own memories.

But she yearned for friendship . . . certainly she yearned for friendship: and since, through lack of charm, by a total deficiency in all social qualities, she was debarred from making a friend in the usual way, however much she longed and strove to do so: she was in the end obliged to buy one. When this purchase had been completed, she hoped, perhaps, by means of one friend, who would always be in her company, thus learning to understand and appreciate her, to make others. Miss Bramley, in fact, was in part decoy, in part interpreter; for the old lady needed some one who would translate and dramatise her for other people.

And it seemed to Miss Collier-Floodgaye that she had found what she wanted. So unused was she to the ways of a friend that she was able to accept the over-effusive ways of her new Companion as the genuine coin of friendship. She could not test this mintage by experience, discount it by previous disappointments, or in any way compare the genuine money with the counterfeit.

CHAPTER III

"Freeze, freeze, thou bitter sky,
That dost not bite so nigh
   As benefits forgot:
Though you the waters warp,
Thy sting is not so sharp,
   As friend remembered not."

MISS TERESA BRAMLEY'S life had been no easy one. From the beginning she had been given her full share of difficulties. She was one of the two daughters of Canon Bramley, of Torquay. Her other important relative was her father's aunt, Miss Titherley-Bramley, who for many years lived at Newborough. Both her father and this aunt were supposed to have private fortunes of their own.

At the age of twenty-six, Miss Bramley had found herself alone in the world, for her mother had died many years ago, and her sister, married to a former curate of the Canon's, was too busy child-bearing to be of very much use to any one. The Canon had been so distressed at his aunt's death—or rather at the unexpected fact that her estate had, so to speak, predeceased her—that he never really recovered from the shock of it, soon afterwards dying himself. After his own death, a discovery of a similar sort was made. Miss Titherley-Bramley had failed to leave any evi-

dence behind her of her long passage through
this world, while the chief proofs of the Canon's
travail here below were Miss Teresa Bramley,
Mildred (her married sister) and a few faded
photographs.

Miss Teresa Bramley was, therefore, left behind with no assets except her youth, a simple
country freshness, rather than prettiness, an
indifferent education, a naturally charming voice
unassisted by any training or knowledge of music,
a disposition, at once affectionate, religious and
extremely malleable, together with a few more
assertive, more tangible certificates of genteel
birth and upbringing.

Personal belongings are perhaps among the
most pathetic forms of human self-expression.
Nelson's pigtail at Greenwich Hospital, the cat
that once belonged to Petrarch, and stuffed now,
is still to be seen in his house, the giant turtle
in the Zoological Gardens which traditionally was
the pet of Richard III, King Alfred's jewel at
the Ashmolean, the tortoise-shell-veneered cane
that once aided Beau Brummell in his rather
unsteady walk, the tricorn hat which Napoleon
wore on his return from Elba—perhaps the most
remarkable resurrection of the last thousand
years—and now to be seen in the palace of Fon-
tainebleau, all these are infinitely more poignant
than the written stories of their illustrious pro-
prietors. It is these relics of vanished affection,
vanity or fashion, which portray the men who
owned them, summon them up before us much
more clearly than the most magic brush or the
finest pen. Miss Bramley's personal property
(net) and private treasures, after the Canon's

affairs had been wound up and his debts paid, comprised:

A gold watch, and fine gold chain, the property of her father.

Two silver-backed hall-marked hair brushes, once the property of her mother.

Three Indian silver boxes of intricate Oriental workmanship.

One Oriental Filigree box in Dutch silver.

One bit of brown bread, dating from the 1870 siege of Paris, made of straw and dust, the whole enclosed in an ornamental metal box, fashioned out of a Prussian shell-case, the gift of her former French Nursery-Governess.

Two Volumes, morocco-bound, of Hackett's "Sermons" (London, 1868) and an edition of "Tom Brown's Schooldays," unsold at the sale of her late father's effects.

One chasuble worked, and presented to the late Canon by the Lady Workers of Torquay and contained in a wooden casket, handsomely decorated with poker work.

A Christmas presentation from the inmates of the Torquay Workhouse and Pauper Lunatic Asylum, in grateful recognition of his services.

Two cut-glass scent bottles, a wedding present to Miss Bramley's parents, from their relative, the late Lord Liddlesfield (a valuable certificate, that one).

A coverlet of floral pattern, embroidered in grass-green, sparrow-green, ochre, salmon pink and rose-pink silks, by herself; and

A photograph in a Burmese cedar-wood frame of the late Miss Titherley-Bramley, sitting in her conservatory, feeding a large dog with one hand, and holding up a permanently-waved chrysanthemum of mammoth size in the other.

Besides these effects, there were her clothes,

some of them from her aunt's wardrobe, several
photographs of her father, and a miniature, painted
from a photograph, after her decease, of her mother
—a very good likeness, it was said, but Miss Bramley hardly remembered her.

Thus equipped, Miss Teresa Bramley was
launched on life.

. . . .

Luckily her sister had heard of an opportunity
for her, otherwise she really did not know what
she would have done. It appeared that an old
Miss Fansharpe, who lived in Wales, wanted a
Companion. A real piece of good fortune, they
thought. This venerable person, directly she saw
Miss Bramley, "took a fancy" to her. Miss Fansharpe was a great character, benevolent and fond
of good works. Having procured Miss Bramley,
she proceeded to persecute, and, at the same time,
to train her thoroughly. She acted the part of
hierophant in the mysteries of companionship.
As a younger woman, Miss Fansharpe had been
most active. For three or four decades she had
spent a part of each year in Cardiff, and had
then founded, in conjunction with her friend, the
Bishop of Llandudaft, a Rescue Home for
Women. The Bishop and herself were wont to
drive about in a brougham at night through the
more crowded streets of the city, and whenever
they saw a likely subject, swooped out of the
carriage and carried the poor girl off. So great
was the respect felt for them and their work that
no questions were asked. Once in the Home,
escape was impossible. Laundry was the task
imposed upon these slaves, who were, except on
Sundays, never to be seen again. An imagined

fall was sufficient passport to an eternal mangling,
in every sense of the word, of gentlemen's shirts.
The poor women had their revenge: the sexes
were engaged in an undying and sturdy warfare.
Perhaps thus, Eve obtained her revenge on Adam,
by compelling him first to wear clothes, and by
then proceeding to wash them herself.

As we have hinted, after their imprisonment
the inmates never saw the world except in its
Sunday aspect: for every Sabbath, but on that
day alone of all the days in the week, they were
allowed to go out of the grounds (an asphalt
yard) to church. Dressed in dark clothes, which
were made specially by the command and beneath the eye of Miss Fansharpe, so as to be
as ill-fitting and unbecoming as possible—to
lessen the chances of temptation for them—
stumping along in heavy boots, with their hair
pulled back under plain straw hats, their flashing
eyes obscured by blue spectacles, this sad croco-
dile of kidnapped syrens was to be seen every
Sunday, under the stern supervision of a Matron,
dragging wearily to Divine Service.

There was, indeed, one incident at the Home
that for a time focused interest upon it, and even
disturbed local opinion; but this was soon forgotten in the admiration felt for the personalities
and the work of both the Bishop and Miss Fansharpe. The Bishop's daughter, who was so intensely religious as almost to rank as a Saint and
Seer, and lived in constant expectation of the
Second Coming, was not surprised to notice one
night a star so radiantly illuminating that she
was able at once to identify it as the Star of
Bethlehem. This by itself created something of

a stir in the district, but when about the same time, several girls in the Home began to show obvious signs of an approaching maternity, which they were unable to explain by any natural causes, excitement knew no bounds. The one difficulty, the only thing, that puzzled the faithful was how to select from such an unexpected, such an embarrassing plenty.

Alas, soon after, it transpired that the flaming star which had been observed, was no new one but was in fact, our old friend Venus, which owing to some natural and recurrent phenomenon, was in a state of peculiar effulgence; while, when the inmates of the Home were given their rather infrequent baths, it was discovered, to the dismay of those concerned, that a youth had dressed up as a female and had then contrived to get himself carried off by the Bishop and Miss Fansharpe. For many months this recreant had lived in the Home without thinking it necessary to divulge his sex or identity. Indeed, even at the time of his capture the governing body had been surprised at the fervour and enthusiasm with which this girl—for such they had taken him to be—had sought to be incarcerated in the Home.

A time came, at last, when Miss Fansharpe grew too old to take any serious part in the management of the Home, though right down to the time of her death, the dear old lady still maintained an active and vicious interest in the vicissitudes of her involuntary wards. She was now more or less bed-ridden, and lived all the year through at her country home, Landriftlog House. After so energetic a life, she began to feel rather sad and lonely, no doubt missing the constant

excitement of her former career. She could not
read much now, and knitting and talking to her
Companion were her sole relaxations. With her
Companion, she had already, in a few weeks, developed a technique, which was little less than
astounding in one who was herself a novice,
hitherto companionless. Indeed if, as some think,
genius consists in an infinite capacity for giving
pain, Miss Fansharpe may be said as an employer
to have possessed genius. As Miss Bramley
became better and better trained, it naturally
became increasingly difficult for Miss Fansharpe
to goad her into a scene. Thus, while the quarry
grew ever scarcer, it grew yet more worthy of
an Amazon's skill. A moment was reached when
she found it impossible to trap her Companion
into contradicting her. From that instant, the
old lady altered her tactics, developing an extraordinarily ingenious new method, difficult to convey, except by illustration. The first thing to
do was to tire the Companion out, by fussing,
fretting and worrying her, in the manner of
Fabius Cunctator. The old lady would, therefore, begin by saying, "Teresa, I understand that
you wish to go into Llandumfniff. It's a very
good plan, I think. But there are three trains,
one leaving here at 8.47, another at 10.8 and a
third at 11.20. Which do you think would suit
you best?" This point Miss Fansharpe would
argue for two or three hours, Miss Bramley meanwhile warily refusing to commit herself. It was
a strain, though, for the younger woman, and
when Miss Fansharpe felt that she had thoroughly
fatigued her and worn her down, she would then
very subtly proceed to the next tactical point,

by pretending to let slip the information that personally she favoured the 10.8 train. Utterly exhausted, Miss Bramley would snatch at the possibility of agreement, for by now, she would have been willing to fall in with any definite view, however inconvenient to herself, in order to end the discussion. Miss Fansharpe knew this, and as soon as Miss Bramley had agreed with her about it, said very mildly, "So it's your opinion that the 10.8 is the best train of the three?" Miss Bramley thinking the whole matter over and finished, said, "Yes, dear." Then, like an angry lioness, the old lady would spring furiously on her prey, saying, "But what makes you think so—I don't agree at all. It's much the worst of them to *my* mind," and a terrific onslaught would develop. The miraculous part of this technique was its economy, for it ensured that one subject would yield sufficient ammunition for several severe battles, and at the same time it contained within itself the whole secret of perpetual motion; for the identical discussion could be turned inside-out, so as to appear different every time, while the mere mechanical action of turning it would precipitate what seemed to be another cause for war, though in reality it was the same one. So perfectly was worked out every possibility, every theme, that the whole display almost attained to the level of a great musical composition.

It cannot be said, though, that Miss Bramley disliked her patroness. On the contrary, though in awe of the old lady, she became really attached to her. Into the life of Llandriftlog, she entered with zest. She was, in fact, a born Companion.

And if there were difficulties, there were many consolations. Very often she was allowed to deputise as Lady Bountiful for the elderly invalid: and she was encouraged and supported in her village activities. She did "a great deal of good" locally.

It was interesting to note how the character of the younger woman became set in the mould of the elder. Perhaps a Companion must, as part of her duties, adopt to a certain extent the personality of the old lady to whom she is administering artificial friendship: perhaps she is obliged to take on little tricks of manner, vocal inflexions, gestures, a smile, habits of speech and thought, for by so doing she bestows upon her patroness a spurious life-after-death, an extra span of a generation or two. Thus a Companion becomes the counterfeit offspring of the companioned, an offspring more true in physical traits and mental colouring to her progenitor than would have been any children of that lady's own bearing.

At home, in the Rectory, Miss Bramley had been rather "Liberal" in her views: but now her political faith was inexorably Conservative. And it must be reckoned as a testimony to the altruism of human nature—though it is not so rare a phenomenon as might be imagined—that, from this time forth, the worse Miss Bramley was treated by Fortune, the more ardently she strove to support that very social order out of which she had gained so little, and from which there was now, for her, so little to hope.

In a sense it would not be inaccurate to assert that out of this conversion she did acquire something for herself. Gradually she transformed it

into a kind of asset, a spiritual certificate of
gentility, which was added to—and matched
beautifully—those other ones already enumerated,
while it possessed in addition the merit of being
more visible, more audible to the public. If some
one were to call, one could not very well rush
upstairs, and snatching a silver-backed hair brush,
return with it to the drawing-room, crying out
in the manner of a child, "Look at my silver-
backed hair-brush!" But from the lumber-room
of one's mind, it is always permissible to take
out a political creed, and give it an airing.

Miss Bramley's religious views remained unaltered, and these she was able to share with Miss
Fansharpe, a fact that brought great comfort to
the younger woman. Indeed she really enjoyed
the life at Llandriftlog, though it may be that she
was learning "adaptability" or the art of dis-
sembling her feelings even from herself. In order
to disarm the old lady, her manner became, at
first gradually, then increasingly, effusive. For
Miss Fansharpe could be "difficult"—yes "difficult" was the word. One could understand it,
Miss Bramley reflected, for how cruel it must
be after so active and so *interesting* a life, to be
confined almost entirely to your bed! And she
was so philanthropic, too, a dear old creature
if one only understood her ways.

Miss Fansharpe, on her part, often seemed
eager to make the younger woman confident as to
her future, was always seeking fresh methods by
which to let her Companion know that she had
been "remembered" in her will, that there was
a legacy. The transmission of such intelligence
is inevitably embarrassing, and the old lady, in

her tactful benevolence, even went so far as to
organise a slight skirmish with Miss Bramley on
some abstract issue, such as the home life of the
Prince of Wales (afterward King Edward) or the
precise meaning of the word "Primrose," in the
context of "Primrose League," in order· to hint
darkly that disagreement with her views would
incur the penalty of an altered will. This no
doubt was simply the old lady's delicate way of
letting her Companion know that there was a
legacy in waiting for her.

But Miss Fansharpe's constant anxiety to
reassure Miss Bramley about her future had for
the Companion another most awkward and perhaps not entirely unforeseen consequence. Tidings
of the old lady's new testamentary depositions
reached Colonel Fansharpe, her only nephew and
heir. How far the percolation of this news was
his aunt's intention is a matter that will probably
never be quite cleared up. But it did not seem
as though she was altogether displeased at the
leakage. Indeed, while her nephew and his wife
were in the house, she was always more than
usually affectionate to her Companion.

Formerly Colonel Fansharpe and his wife, Ivy,
had paid visits of barely three or four nights at
a time to their aunt, and these had only taken
place about twice a year. But, with the advent
of her Companion, their visits became more frequent and of longer duration. During these
family parties, Miss Bramley's life was apt to
become harassing. For Colonel Fansharpe did
not like her, and let it be known round about
that he regarded her as a "damned scheming
woman"—while he even went so far as to char-

acterise her singing, which generally endeared
her to all hearts, as "Another of That Woman's
devilish tricks," no doubt regarding it merely as
one of the devices by which she was endeavour-
ing to obtain and wield the mystic sceptre of
"undue influence." Both Colonel and Mrs. Fansharpe were ever on the watch. They bitterly
resented Miss Bramley's necessary adoption of
their aunt's mannerisms. Ivy, specially, contrived, though always with an air of courtesy,
a thousand subtle machinations for Miss Bramley's discomfiture, a thousand ways through which
she could allow her dislike and distrust to become
apparent, without committing any overt act of
war, on account of which the Companion could
have acted, demanding an explanation or taking
the matter before the old lady. No, there was
nothing positive: but Ivy could be seen counting
the silver spoons, or the umbrellas in the hall.
She was so bad at arithmetic, she would explain,
and always practised adding-up when there was
an opportunity. She would, in the presence of
the Companion, dilate on the iniquities of
"scheming" or would very humbly (and this was
the most irritating of her tricks) ask for Miss
Bramley's permission, in front of Miss Fansharpe,
to pick a flower in the garden. This little act
of courtesy served both to embarrass the Companion and, what was more important, to embroil
her with the old lady, who would become senseless
from rage if a single one of her proprietary rights
was in any way infringed.

It was difficult to escape Miss Fansharpe's
anger, almost impossible to cheat her of her prey.
Singularly free from prejudice, though only for

the duration of an argument, she would, in order to engage her Companion in single combat, change her views, normally so well-defined, with the circular spinning motion of a whirlwind, the direful force of a tornado. Useless was it for Miss Bramley to make any timid attempt to keep pace with the lightning make-up and quick-change artistry of such a virtuoso; absolutely useless; far better for her to face the storm, which would then, after a sharp will-altering climax, be followed by a scene of lachrymose and affectionate reconciliation.

In between these sudden squalls, in between these family visits, Miss Bramley's life was often peaceful. Moreover, she found it enjoyable. She formed the habit of writing to her married sister twice a week, and the letter reproduced below is one typical of her epistolary gifts in the latter period of her companionship, when she had already somewhat assumed the character of Miss Fansharpe's second self. Indeed, it is a letter such as might almost have been written by that old lady. Her use of underlining and capital letters justifies itself, for by it she was able to produce effects not to be obtained by any other means, to express a meaning not otherwise to be conveyed. It is a literary device, an important ingredient in her style.

LLANDRIFTLOG HOUSE,
LLANDRIFTLOG, N.W.
25 *Feb.*, 1900.

DEAREST MILDRED,

Your charming and serviceable gift of a pigskin pocketbook (most useful for Croquet-engagements in the Summer) was delayed in the post, and only

reached me yesterday. For here, we are having a Dear old-fashioned winter, and until yesterday there had been no post for ten days. But the old place looks so Nice and Bright and cheerful, with the snow outside, like a white carpet, rolled up to the dining-room window-sills—just the sort of house that Poor Papa dreamed of. He would indeed have loved it, with its pretty, Quaint Wellingtonias and Scotch firs in the garden—they always look so Picturesque under snow, do they not? Our only concern is for our dear little feathered friends: but we put out half a Coconut each day. Only this morning a dear little robin came and tapped at my window.

The prospect from the house is indeed, Wild and Picturesque, but within all is bustle and cheerfulness: and one never feels dull for a moment. Last week, for example (was it *Thursday*, or Friday, I wonder?—but now, dear, that I have your delightful and serviceable gift, I shall be able to remember more accurately) the Rector was coming to tea, and we had prepared for him, as a special Little luxury, some *Soda* scones (I wonder if you know them? so good and Economical). Unfortunately the Severe weather prevented his coming here. I forget if I mentioned him in my Monday—or was it Tuesday—letter? He is a Newcomer, and his name is the Rev. Bernard Broometoken. A most interesting man, *We* think him; but, unfortunately, *Afflicted*. It is a truly sad case. Owing, they say, to a shock received when young, he developed General Paralysis combined with St. Vitus's dance, which is said to be most unusual. In spite of it all, he is so gentle and *Unassuming*, and his Views on the Oxford Movement are quite unlike any I have heard expressed, even at the dear old Rectory; so original and wittily put. As a younger man he worked a great deal among the Romans, for owing to his affliction he was forced to spend

the winter at San Remo, where he officiated in the
English Church during the winter-months. It must
indeed have been interesting work; but he is convinced, as regards the Romish Church, that Reform
must come from *Within*. He is obviously a man
who thinks for himself, and should go *Far*. He is
a widower, and has now no help-meet to support
him in his distress, though his five daughters are
all nice girls, and devoted to their Dear Father.
Yet I fear they are not strong. Ruby, the eldest,
is unfortunately deaf, while Rose (and *so* pretty)
is, so they say, rather dumb. The other girls are
still children. There are only four sons grown up—
and these, though Dutiful, are, I fear, a Sad grief
to their widowed Father. Desmond and Wilfred
are both Afflicted, though very bright, and Percy
(Mr. Broometoken's favourite too, which makes it
so *Sad*) has inherited his Father's paralysis but
without the facial liveliness and Alert expression
that accompany it in his case.

The War, of course, overshadows all our little
joys and pleasures, and only our *admiration* of the
Dear Queen's Courage keeps us cheerful. The Behaviour of the Radicals (if they are Radicals, and
not simply Socialists) in Taking the part of the
enemies of their *Country*, in supporting *Bullies* and
Murderers, when they are at our Very Gate (for
that is what It amounts to) is past belief. Have
they no religion, no patriotism? Fortunately as
far as *We* are in a position to judge here, the Feeling of the Country is so strong that we doubt if
they will *ever* get in again. We must Trust Buller,
and remember that Right is Might. We may be
only a poor little island; They may be a Continent
crammed with gold and diamonds: but we have
faced worse things than that—and, besides, to
whom can they *sell* them? And then, don't you
feel, dear, as We do, that we are a People with a
Mission? let us pray that we shall not shirk the

Task imposed upon Us, and that, should it become necessary in the Best interests of the Natives (as Miss Fansharpe thinks it may) to annex the whole of Africa, we shall not Flinch or Turn Away. It is a duty. We *Cannot* leave the Natives alone.

Fortunately Miss Fansharpe keeps wonderfully well and looks the Sweetest Picture of an Old Lady (I wish I could send you a "snap") as she lies in bed with her White-hair and Lace-cap. But I am sorry to say she has been Troubled about one of the girls in the Home. The Story is a Real Tragedy—a second time, too, it appears.

Yrs. affectate sister,
TERESA BRAMLEY.

P.S.—Could you forward me a Copy of the "Absent-minded Beggar"; and then let me know how much I owe you for it, dear? Have you any news of Poor Minnie? Many messages of greeting to Harold and the children.

A few days after this letter was dispatched, Miss Fansharpe passed peacefully away in her sleep at the ripe age of eighty-seven.

After the funeral in the manner of a bygone age, the old lady's will was read by her solicitor. It was now discovered to the intense relish of Colonel and Mrs. Fansharpe that their aunt had not, after all, left an annuity to her Companion. They did not mind "the woman being remembered" in the will. That in a way was only right and just, and dear Aunt Henrietta was far too noble and sweet a character—they felt—ever to err except on the side of generosity. Still, they had to admit, she had shown a strong vein of common-sense, and had proved herself a Fansharpe through and through. Of course she had been far too generous—there were many gifts and

mementoes. All her religious books she left to
the Home, and each girl in it was to be provided,
free of charge, with a black band round her arm
and a stout pair of walking boots.

Instead of an annuity, then, Miss Fansharpe
had thanked her Companion for her faithful care,
and bequeathed her a seventy-year-old Broad-
wood Upright Piano (because her Companion
was so fond of music), a silver hand-mirror on
the back of which were represented in repoussé
the faces, sprouting wings instead of whiskers,
like so many bloated white-bats, of five angels
or cherubs, after a picture by Sir Joshua Reynolds
(because it had been a "little Christmas gift"
from her Companion) and ten pounds to buy a
mourning dress.

Thus Miss Bramley was given another chance,
launched on life for a second time with her possessions slightly augmented.

She was fifteen years older, and, as a Companion, rigidly trained in the best school. She had
now formally accepted as her creed the views of
an Impoverished Gentlewoman and her voice,
though a little frayed, was still charming. She
was able to add the silver mirror to the other
objects of vertu of which she was the fortunate
possessor (it went beautifully with the hair-
brushes and silver boxes) and besides the mourn-
ing-dress, she had plenty of good plain clothes,
and serviceable straw hats. And then there were
the photographs, of course!—enough things to
make any room look nice.

The upright piano Miss Bramley sold locally
for the sum of twenty pounds, in order to escape
payment of carriage and storage dues; and, with

her worldly fortune thus increased, left Llandrift-log for London. Colonel Fansharpe, though he still regarded her suspiciously, was civil, even kind, in his manner; but, as Miss Bramley drove away in a snowstorm from the door, she could see Ivy Fansharpe, in the brilliantly lighted rooms, engaged in a perfect hurricane of counting. One, two, three the umbrellas in the hall; one, two, three, four, five the best tea-spoons; one, two, three, four the ornaments on the drawing-room mantelpiece. It was sad leaving the old place and feeling one was not trusted. But one must be resigned to these things. It was the Lord's will . . . and He would provide—at least that was what her dear father had always said. . . .

CHAPTER IV

IN ROOMS

*"They are rattling breakfast plates in basement
    kitchens,
And along the trampled edges of the street
I am aware of the damp souls of housemaids
Sprouting despondently at area gates."*

LONDON seemed to have become rather overwhelming. It was many years since Miss
Bramley had visited it, not since Peregrine's
christening, she thought; and then she had only
stayed for a few days. It was so noisy, with all
those dreadful omnibuses and their swearing
coachmen; and then the four-wheelers and han-
soms and bicycles made it positively dangerous
to cross the street nowadays. Fortunately the
police were most kind and attentive, otherwise she
really did not know what she would have done!

The room in Ebury Street, which Mildred had
found for her, was quite quiet, at any rate. Perhaps a little . . . gloomy after Llandriftlog . . .
but then one couldn't have everything, could one,
and one mustn't grumble, must one?

The lodgings were kept by a fat, retired butler,
with a red nose, and his emaciated, whining wife.
She was usually on the doorstep, without a hat
on, pressing her fringe down on her forehead with
her hand, away from the clutches of the mis-
chievous wind, and deploring the days that were

past—days, apparently of an unimagined grandeur, spent as lady's maid in the houses of the great. Consequently she suffered from almost permanent neuralgia, which, again, aided her excruciatingly shrill lamentations. Her husband was not often in the house, but it was always to be understood that he would be back in a minute, back from some sudden and important mission. Miss Bramley's bed-sitting-room, on the third floor, was lined with a dark-red varnished wall-paper, which set off a gilt-framed and very fly-blown mammoth mirror that reflected back again, only more sadly, the wall-paper. On the mantelpiece there was a large, square black marble clock, like the old front of Devonshire House in shape, which was a very infernal machine for ticking and chimed every quarter of an hour; and, on each side of it, stood another candelabrum, its limbs hopelessly entangled in a dusty gauze cobweb, the object of which must ever remain a mystery. It looked as if it had been caught by the landlady in a butterfly net during one of her infrequent days in the country. The window curtains were of fringed green plush, and there was a portière to match. The place was perfect of its kind, even down to the perpetual, rather pleasant smell of roast mutton and baked potatoes, warring with the other, distinctive odour exhaled by the bathroom geyser, a scent composed, in equal quantities, of gas and hot copper. Recurrent trouble with this remarkable but truculent machine was a decided feature of life in the house. A singular contraption, it was the only method of warming the water and imparted an air of caprice and whimsicality to the

whole establishment. Sometimes when it was quite obvious to every one in the house that the gas was full on and escaping very freely, the geyser would refuse for hours even a flicker, however many matches were struck and applied to it; while, at other moments, it would light unexpectedly, giving a loud and festive pop, as though in sardonic mimicry of a champagne cork being drawn—perhaps a spiteful reference to the retired butler's habits—then proceed to give a spirited imitation of galloping horses, and, finally, within a few seconds, would explode with the report of a bomb, and flood the entire house with boiling water!

Of course Miss Bramley was a great deal in her room. Each day she must read the *Times* and *Morning Post,* studying the "Situations Vacant" column, or search the other headed "Situations Required" to see if her own advertisement had been entered. The worst of it was that putting in a notice became so expensive after a time. There seemed to be nothing, absolutely nothing at the moment. The War, no doubt. Everywhere, she heard the same thing. And, then, much of her time was spent in her room because, you see, she knew so few people in London. Of course Mildred, her sister, was most kind, very kind indeed, and asked her to lunch every Thursday and to cold supper on Sunday evenings. Mildred was now extremely prosperous, for her husband, Canon Hancock, a clergyman who believed in healthy, manly sports, holding that they helped true worship, had invented a contrivance, made of bamboo and watch-springs—like a mouse-trap at the end of a

fishing-rod—for the ferreting out of "ping-pong"
balls which had fallen under sofas, or bounced
themselves on to the tops of cupboards. "Ping-
pong" was the game of the moment, every country
house, London mansion and suburban villa resounded with its wooden chatter and repartee,
so that the clergyman's invention had brought him
in a substantial sum. It had helped him, too, in
his career, filling the church with ping-pong en-
thusiasts who could hear in his sermons, even,
some echo of the sound of their favourite and
fatuous recreation, and had heightened his fame
among his brother clergy, by singling him out
from them as a modern ecclesiastic; though some,
it may be, were envious.

There was nothing, Miss Bramley felt, like
brains. Oh, why couldn't *she* invent something?
But what a wonderful age of inventions we
were living in, with what Harold's "Ping-Pong
Picker"—as it was called—and that geyser; and
then there were phonographs, too, with their
funny little tubular brown records, smelling of
dark cardboard (Harold had bought one), and
pianolas, and those funny motor-cars (she would
be terrified of riding in one, herself) and everything. Really one felt quite proud to live in
such an age. Most interesting. And it was nice
to see Mildred so prosperous, though she told
Miss Bramley that she was really no better off
than before, because of "the numerous calls on
her income." Still, Harold's living was a good
one. They lived just behind Lancaster Gate, in
the Vicarage, which they had made so "pretty
and countrified." But, alas, Mildred was busy,
so busy—too busy, as she told Teresa, to see as

much of her as she would have wished . . .
but perhaps later . . . afterwards . . . but they
were both extremely kind, and always asked a
great many questions, and were, undoubtedly,
most helpful. Since her prosperity, Mildred
(though Miss Bramley had not analysed the
change in her sister) had developed a beautiful
new voice, especially for the discouragement and
intimidation of the needy—and, as she was inclined to think, needless poor—while at the same
time the firm certainty of its tone reassured the
nervous rich. It was the voice of a plump person,
a voice clear and cultured, impersonal yet emphatic—a real Charity Institution voice. By its
aid she could render poor as "poo-ah"—a sound
which contained in itself I know not what of
condemnation—and "dear" as "deahr." Every
day, through the absence of suitable situations,
the renewed failure of Miss Bramley's application, in the columns of the *Times* became more
poignant to her. And Mildred could hear of
nothing. It was dreadful . . . where was it to
end? She could not go on like this for ever . . .
the expense, too! . . . and then if one slept
badly and was depressed, one was less likely to
find a post. But though Miss Bramley realised
it, she could not help becoming more lost, by
day and night, in mathematical calculations based
on her bank-book.

．　　．　　．　　．　　．　　．　　．

One morning, after five weeks spent in search-
ing, she found what she had been seeking, and
felt that it was for her; "Elderly Gentlewoman
of Independent Means," she read, "wishes for
Refined and Well-Connected Lady Companion,

musical and accomplished." She applied for the
situation at once. A few days later, Miss Bramley set out, in her best clothes, for the Badminton
Hotel, there to interview her future. She did not
wear her mourning dress, for after careful consideration she was afraid it might give a bad
impression, or make the old lady melancholy.
When people were old, they did not like to be
reminded of death. One had to think of these
things, for so much depended on them. She put
on a blue dress, therefore, quiet in tone, but over-
inclined to fret and worry in detail, like a Gothic
cathedral; covered with cobwebby frills and
unnecessary though quite gentle and modest attempts at animation. However innocuous, these
tiny flowerings were irritating as the minute yet
quite distinct scratching of a mouse in the
night.

Alas, she was now no longer the Rector's pretty
daughter. The face was drawn and rather sallow,
and she had developed, as a defence, too much
charm. There was a little tightening of the
muscles round the mouth, which revealed itself
when she was agitated—a trembling of nerves
which were still expectant of an attack from Miss
Fansharpe. As long as Miss Bramley lived she
would carry this indelible memento of her dead
patroness, the only one which it had not been
within the power of that lady to put in or take
out of her will. This tremor she could, with some
difficulty, smother by means of a rather too fixed
smile. Though only a small thing, it might go
against her, prejudice the old lady whom she was
to interview, especially if at all excitable herself.
She must cover it up, therefore, and smile. She

must look cheerful and bright: it would never
do to appear timid. Her hands, now rather
shrivelled, were very cold. Nerves again, she
supposed. She treated herself to a final glance
in the fly-blown mirror, gave a slight tug at her
"toque," arranged her veil, and walked down-
stairs, and out into Ebury Street, which lay in
the afternoon light as brown, smooth and unpre-
tentious as a canal in a northern industrial town.

She beckoned to a four-wheeler—it looked less
"fast" than a hansom cab, she thought. In less
than thirty-five minutes she was at the Badminton
Hotel off Piccadilly, and was being ushered up
into a private sitting-room. Miss Collier-Floodgaye received her very kindly. They talked a
little about the War: the Boer atrocities were
past belief. Only a few days before, a Boer
farmer had taken deliberate aim at a band of
English soldiers who were trying to enter his
house, quite deliberately and killed two of them
. . . on the veldt, too, which somehow made it
so much more horrible . . . and then he made
out that they were trying to burn his farm! It
was said that several English children had dis-
appeared . . . one had been found, it was
rumoured, with its tiny toes cut off . . . foul
play, somewhere. What a terrible grief it must
be to the Dear Old Queen. But Miss Collier-
Floodgaye was more interested in the Princess
of Wales. There, she said in her deep voice, was
a really beautiful woman. And so young looking.
Now Miss Fansharpe had always taught Miss
Bramley to regard the Princess as rather "insipid-
looking," but she had the sense to see that one
must move with the times, and indulged in a

warm eulogy of the Princess, ending up with some
lines of Tennyson's:

> "Sea-king's daughter from over the sea,
> Saxon and Norman and Dane are we,"

she declaimed.

Nor can it be said that when Miss Bramley
delivered this encomium, she was insincere: for
whatever she said, she meant and felt . . . while
she was saying it. Now the old lady asked her
to sing, and sitting down at the piano, Miss
Bramley sang:

> "She is far from the land
> Where her dear hero sleeps."

Miss Collier-Floodgaye was so pleased with the
performance that she had to sing it again. A
sweet voice, the old lady thought, without any
airs or graces. That was exactly what she liked.
So many people became affected directly they
tried to sing.

And, in truth, Miss Bramley's singing, of its
sort, was at its best that afternoon. The little
trill which lay hidden in the upper register of the
voice, rose sweetly as a bird into the air, pecking
gently at the china vases on the mantelpiece,
fluttering softly round the walls and ceilings.
Miss Collier-Floodgaye was really moved by it.
Tea was brought in, and the Companionship
settled.

   .   .   .   .

It was an immense relief: though after living
under the martial law of Miss Fansharpe she
found Miss Collier-Floodgaye unusual . . . yes,

unusual. The elder lady never seemed to want
to indulge in a skirmish, never wished to bully,
seldom grumbled. It seemed so strange that Miss
Bramley wondered at times whether she could
go on with it. The Companion's nerves, from
habit, would be braced up periodically against
the coming of some terrific onslaught . . . and
since, now, one never developed, she would be
left with a feeling of expectancy, which she was
unable to interpret for herself, an intuition of
impending disaster. If Miss Collier-Floodgaye
had risen to the occasion, and had bullied her
thoroughly for half an hour, this feeling would
have been dissipated. But such was not the old
lady's way. Gradually Miss Bramley became accustomed to the calm tenor of her new life . . .
but, still, there was something lacking in her new
friend . . . she was not really (Miss Bramley
hated to say it, even to herself) such a lady as
Miss Fansharpe . . . and none of the little ways
. . . *you* know . . . not just those little ways.
. . . There was, always, something by which you
could tell, wasn't there . . . ?   What was it?
she wondered.

From the first moment of meeting her, Miss
Bramley felt that her new friend was failing,
but very slowly, imperceptibly; she might go on
for many years yet, with the same mode of life
that she was leading now. Her memory was one
of her weakest points. Occasionally she would,
for example, refer to events, of which her Companion could make nothing, in a manner sug-
gesting that she thought the younger woman
shared her memories; but she would never be
sufficiently explicit to give Miss Bramley any

idea of the actual sort of circumstance to which
she was alluding, and if questioned, it would then
dawn upon her that of course the Companion
knew nothing of such happenings, and she would
refrain from any further mention of it. It was
terrible, too, the way in which the old lady forgot
things! so inconvenient and gave so much trouble.
It was not just inaccuracy, it was real absent-
mindedness, so unlike Miss Fansharpe. Sometimes Miss Collier-Floodgaye would make an ap-
pointment with a lawyer or dressmaker, forget
altogether, and then maintain that she had kept
it! Or again, she would imagine that she had an
engagement, when she never made one at all,
and then be angry because the lawyer, or dressmaker, had not been ready to receive her.

The months telescoped themselves into years,
were folded up into packets and put down.
London in the summer months was delightful,
with its occasional ballad concerts, and concerts
every Sunday at the Queen's Hall. It was so nice
to be able to hear a little music, for though the
reign of Miss Fansharpe, being over, had attained
that golden varnished glow which accrues to old-
master paintings and to past scenes in one's own
life, it was useless to pretend that Miss Bramley
had been able to enjoy much music at Llandriftlog. But then Miss Fansharpe had not really
cared for music, did not approve of it . . .
though of course on the whole she had liked Miss
Bramley's singing. It had not been a mere
caprice, for it appeared that the old lady had
her reasons for such a prejudice. She had been,
it seems, the confidante of a sad story from a girl
in the Home, who was a Lady . . . so Miss Fan-

sharpe had said . . . and had once Trusted a
Man Who Played the Piano . . . but things were
different nowadays.   Miss Collier-Floodgaye was
genuinely fond of music, indeed of almost any
sound of any sort . . . but then, Miss Bramley
was forced to admit if Miss Collier-Floodgaye
lacked the strong *moral* tone that had inspired
Miss Fansharpe's every action, infused her every
word, all the same she was much more "artistic"
all round than the dead lady had ever been.
Everybody had their faults, the Companion supposed, and one must try to make allowances,
mustn't one?

Nearly every Sunday, too, they went to church
together, but often Miss Collier-Floodgaye would
walk out before the sermon.   This Miss Bramley
did not like—it was irreligious and at the same
time *conspicuous*.   The truth of it was, as the
Companion suspected, that the old lady really
liked a very High Church service.   But Miss
Bramley was nothing if not Evangelical and
would not give in: she *would not go* to places
where they indulged in "Romish frippery."

Life in London was very exciting.   On the 17th
of May, 1900, there arrived once more a solemn
moment in our national life.   To quote the leading
article of a popular newspaper the following day:

"Mafeking, after 216 days of siege and starvation
and bombardment, is relieved.   The last and third
of the besieged garrisons has been snatched from
the grasp of the Boer commandos, and the British
flag has been kept flying over the most sorely tried
of the three towns.   Deep, indeed, must be the
nation's gratitude to the Almighty Dispenser of all
fates for this issue; deep, too, its admiration, regard.

and thankfulness for the heroism, constancy and endurance of Colonel Baden-Powell and his memorable band. And in our congratulations, let us not forget the greatest of living English generals, the man who has turned defeat into victory, who has conquered the Free State, and is now marching with inflexible resolution upon the Transvaal. Lord Roberts, our Commander-in-Chief, promised that the relief should come by May 18. He has kept his word.

In this hour of joy, it is the nation's duty to express its thanks to those who have fought and suffered, not by mere acclamation, but by giving practical proof of its sympathy and regard. Let us all recall the work of the heroic women who chose to share the daily toil and torment of our soldiers, who ministered to the sick and wounded and rendered the last sad office to the dying. Let us think of them shunning the refuge of the women's laager and facing the terrors of the constant warfare—and what that has meant is not lightly realised. Let us remember them starving in silence with cheerful faces that they might keep their country's flag flying overhead; confronting death and a miserable death and preferring any fate rather than surrender.

And of the men who have fought under Colonel Baden-Powell, what shall we say? Only that they proved themselves worthy to be ranked with the greatest heroes of our race. For all time their fates will be remembered, their names will be an example, and the defenders of Mafeking will live in history as men of whom the greatest Empire in the world will be proud. Throughout the tragical events of December and January—those melancholy months of war—we can point to them with exultation. They were an inspiration to us, though they never knew it, for they, in that far-off isolated town, could not understand, with what anxiety and

growing admiration their exploits were followed at home. They were equal to every emergency; they committed no faults; they were never found wanting. Starving, and dying of hunger, they met and beat off the last furious onslaught of the Boers, with what grievous loss we have yet to learn. Many, too many of the heroic garrison have laid down their lives. "Dark to the triumph they died to gain," they did not repent the sacrifice, they gave gladly their all, and remembering their devotion we can say in the sacred words, "It is well," as we sorrow for them.

It goes without saying that when the news arrived, London burst forth into demonstrations of joy. Cheers for Colonel Baden-Powell, whose light-heartedness and resourcefulness have to a special degree won the regard of our race, and even the grudging admiration of the Continent; round the streets flags and demonstrations were everywhere. The event was an historical one. We have waited for the news in mingled confidence and apprehension, yet with the inner belief that the God of all justice was upon our side, and that He would not suffer defeat and humiliation to be the lot of this heroic band. We have not been disappointed. The nation, steadfast through defeat, merciful in victory, may well acclaim the steadfastness of the defenders of Mafeking.

London, indeed, did burst forth into demonstrations of joy. A prominent and respected judge ran out of his house into the streets of the Imperial City sounding his dinner gong, a vast bronze cylinder of Oriental workmanship. This was only one incident in a night filled with the pageant of empery. The streets were crowded and palpitating with singing, cheering and dancing patriots almost mad with joy at the defeat at

long last inflicted upon our ungenerous, unsports-
manlike and sneaking foe. Now at length they
would realise that it was not safe to hit some one
smaller than yourself. It was touching, our two
ladies thought, to observe the way in which grown
men went wild with delight, sang, danced and
even fell down in the street with emotion.

Before a year had gone came a moment even
more solemn. There was the alarming illness
and then the death of Queen Victoria . . . this
latter perhaps the most extraordinary event—at
least so it seemed at the time—since her birth.

The funeral procession for which all the foreign
monarchs came over was beautiful. To quote,
again, a celebrated morning paper of the next
day:

"The attitude of all was in keeping with the occasion. The city was a city of mourners. Black
and the Royal purple were everywhere, even the
humblest and poorest made efforts by their dress
to show their respect for the dead. History may
have its surprises, but never again shall we look
upon a mourning world. To those who knew it,
the experience will prove inestimable. No one could
attend so august a service as these last solemn rites
at Windsor and remain unchanged. The grandiose
simplicity of our English prayer-book seemed to
hush the ambitions and humble the purpose of all
the great ones of the earth there gathered together.
And then the memory pictured the Queen, whom
we so lately saw, and whose death assembled so
many monarchs, and memory lost itself in wondering respect. To her were consecrated the grandeur
and solemnity of the service; for her sake the whole
world was disturbed. Kings walked behind her
coffin in glad subordination to her wisdom and

nobility.   It is true that the majesty of death
always appals us; death falsely called the great
leveller ennobles those upon whom he places his
icy finger.

The world bowed its knee because it recognised
not only a majestic death, but a majestic life.   It
mourned the lady whose public virtues will long
remain, let us hope, a shining example.

Circumstances, too, conspired in the strangest
manner to introduce dramatic effects into these
great rites.   The setting of the sun as the Queen's
body entered Portsmouth Harbour was a coincidence, the dignity of which was felt by all.   It was
as though nature joined in the people's grief.

Alas! Miss Collier-Floodgaye and Miss Bramley were not able themselves to observe this
dramatic gesture on the part of Nature, but they
were able to enjoy—if enjoy is the right word—
the passing of the funeral procession.   The most
inspiring figure, the ladies agreed, was the German Emperor.   Of course he ought never to have
sent that telegram to Kruger, it was disgraceful
(what could he have been thinking of?   But
then foreigners are so funny in that sort of way
. . . do not see things like English people).   You
would have thought that Kruger's appearance
(what an unpleasant face that horrid old man
had—the last cartoon of him in *Punch* wearing a
top hat and fur coat, and holding an umbrella
was wonderfully good) would have been enough
for the German Emperor (did the Kaiser read
Punch? they asked themselves).   But then, whatever his faults, he was so quick, clever and
changeable—the artistic temperament that so
many foreigners possessed.   Not, of course, that
he was a foreigner entirely, for after all he was

the Queen's grandson: though he did not look a
bit English with his funny twirling moustachios;
but the artistic temperament was a queer thing.
They said he was almost a genius—though he
had a disease of the ear, a withered arm, and
cancer, and could not live long. How wonderfully
great men fight against misfortune!

Personally, Miss Collier-Floodgaye wished the
Tsar had been there. Such a good-looking man,
but not a bit barbaric or Russian in appearance.
More, she supposed, like the Duke of York
(would he ever come to the throne? . . . how
sad it had been about the Duke of Clarence . . .
and poor Princess May engaged to him). Miss
Bramley doubted whether the Duke of York *ever*
would come to the throne, though she admitted
that it was beginning to be credible now that the
Prince of Wales was King . . . (not that he was
crowned yet). She had never felt that he would
be King. (Not clever like the Kaiser.) His
subjects adored the Tsar; Miss Collier-Floodgaye
had been told that they called him the Little
White Father, but Russians were like that, so
loyal and religious. They would go through fire
and water for their Tsar. There was no doubt,
Miss Collier-Floodgaye affirmed, that they were
the People of the Future. Fortunately for him,
the Tsar had married the granddaughter of Queen
Victoria. She was sure to keep him straight and
see that he did not abuse his great power. Nothing much could go wrong while *she* was there
to look after him. All the same, Miss Collier-
Floodgaye was glad that she had not got to rule
over Russia—and now, as if they had not got
enough, they wanted India too. As for Miss

Bramley, she confessed that if she had been the
Tsarina, she would have been terrified of bombs
and those dreadful Nihilists . . . dreadful . . .
to go out and never know if you would come back
again.   Meanwhile, there was the King of Portu-
gal riding by, in his white uniform, quite an
imposing figure.

.   .   .   .

The summer passed, and there came round the
Coronation, the delayed Coronation of King Edward.   What an awful thing appendicitis must
be!   It came, so they said, from eating grape
pips—not of course that King Edward was in
the habit of eating grape pips, but he must,
they supposed, have swallowed one by mistake
(curious, though, that bullfinches never suffer
from it).   It was so very odd, though, that no
one ever had suffered from appendicitis when
Miss Collier-Floodgaye was a young girl.   What
had happened to our ancestors when they had
appendicitis?   However, the Coronation when it
came was magnificent.   Such lovely illuminations!
The Badminton Hotel was most comfortable,
and all the servants so *obliging*.   It was very near
everything, too; near the theatres.   They did not
go so often to theatres as to concerts, but they
went, of course, to see *San Toy*.   This was a real
success!   And they made a rule of going to see
any musical comedy in which Edna May was
performing, because she was so sweet and genuine
and unaffected, with a lovely voice.   They went
to see Beerbohm Tree's productions, as well:
Ulysses, all those wonderful poetic plays by
Stephen Phillips.   The scene in Hades was most

effective, though really almost too overpowering
and frightening.

But it was difficult to go out much to plays
in the winter, unless one went to a matinée, for
the old lady suffered severely from bronchial at-
tacks and a kind of asthma. Any foggy night
seemed to bring it on; and London, when one
could not get out, was rather lonely: though there
were always, of course, interesting people staying
in the hotel. But Miss Collier-Floodgaye was
too much inclined to talk to any one she saw, the
result of a life that must hitherto have been
lonely.

During the first few years, which they spent
in London and in short visits to seaside resorts,
Miss Bramley had become steadily more attached
to the old lady, though with this new feeling of
friendship other sensations mingled. But the two
ladies got on very well with each other. Miss
Bramley was privileged to call the elder lady
"Cecilia," while Miss Collier-Floodgaye called
the Companion by her Christian name—or,
rather, by a pet variant of it—"Tibbits." Miss
Fansharpe would never have done such a thing.
She had revelled in the sonority of "Teresa." But
there could be no doubt that Miss Collier-Floodgaye was kind, extremely kind. Yet it is doubtful
whether the amiability was in the eyes of the
Companion altogether a virtue. The truth is
that though Miss Bramley liked, indeed loved, her
new friend, she looked down upon her for her
kindness and affability. Was this because there
existed a stratum of intense and unexpected hard-
ness in the character of the younger woman, or
because she had been, as a Companion, rigorously

trained, fashioned by Miss Fansharpe into a
marvellous instrument, for any one with a temper,
possessed of a sensitive technique, to play upon,
and therefore despised Miss Collier-Floodgaye
for lack of virtuosity.   Contempt, certainly,
entered into Miss Bramley's affection for the old
lady . . . but, in spite of it, she was grateful
to her.

One day, after Miss Bramley had been in her
employ some years, Miss Collier-Floodgaye informed her that she intended to see her solicitor,
and make a new will—or rather add a codicil to
her old one—bequeathing to her Companion all
her property.   Often in after years the old lady
was to revert to this fact, as if to assure the
younger woman that she need have no fear of the
future.   And Miss Bramley, for her part—though
this tale was one she had heard before, and the
truth of which she must by this time have begun
to entertain suspicions—was once more inclined
to believe it.   For Cecilia was, she had to admit,
most kind and considerate . . . if rather difficult
. . . in small ways, of course.   And though she
was not aware of it, Miss Bramley had not until
now in her life received much kindness.   Thus
even if contempt mingled with her affection, she
was sincerely attached to the old lady.

This new emotion experienced by Miss Bramley, this feeling of friendship, was not, however,
without its disadvantages for Miss Collier-Floodgaye: instead of drawing her out, instead of
interpreting her to others, as the old lady had
hoped, the Companion was careful, as it were,
only to let her out of herself when they were by
themselves.   For   from   this   novel,   disturbing

sensation was being born slowly, painfully, another emotion, jealousy: and Miss Bramley was
frigid in manner to any one who displayed a
tendency to become intimate with the old lady.
Even upon the casual acquaintance of a hotel—
upon that pathetic over-dressed proportion of
England's surplus middle-aged females, which in
the short span between sunrise and sunset, birth
and death, finds an assurance of eternity in the
involute inanities of a conversation carried on
among itself, and thus lives by taking in its own
spiritual washing or occasionally washing its own
dirty linen—Miss Bramley turned a severe, and
then a threatening eye. Indeed it was the Companion who had turned instructress and was now
training the Companioned, the Companion who
was courageously cross and bad-tempered, fearing
no reprisals. In fact, under the genial warmth
of Miss Collier-Floodgaye's kindness, the character of the younger woman was suddenly beginning to sprout in new, unexpected, sometimes un-
desirable ways. It was as though the inexorable
system of restraints and restrictions responsible
for the gnarled, crouched, crooked growth of a
dwarf Japanese tree had suddenly been removed,
and long after one had imagined it set for ever
in its present mould, the tree had begun to thaw
its shape, to draw up and disentangle itself, to
sprout and bud and blossom, attempting a growth
to which it could never now attain, so that the
mere effort which this attempt entailed must spoil
the grotesque symmetry imposed upon it, without
hope of the compensating gain of that balanced
woodland beauty for which it strove.

Many persons must have attributed the mani-

festations of ill-temper in which Miss Bramley indulged, if her friend tried to make a new acquaintance, to the scheming nature of the Companion—for this is an attribute with which Companions to rich old ladies are invariably, inevitably credited. It was, no doubt, simply presumed that she was fearful of the financial consequences to herself of any new friendship upon which the old lady might embark. But this motive did not account to any great extent— at any rate not during this period of their intimacy—for the Companion's behaviour. A more reasonable, as well as charitable, explanation of it would have been that Miss Bramley was for the first time experiencing jealousy, that primitive symptom and complement of affection. She had never, it is true, treated Miss Fansharpe's friends in this manner; but then she had never really been fond of Miss Fansharpe. Her mind, however, had been so innocent of friendship up till now that she had not realised it during Miss Fansharpe's lifetime, and now that the old lady was dead, took her affection as established. Herself had accepted all the little tricks of disarmament, the effusive and gushing ways, which she had been forced to develop for her own protection, as the genuine expression of that mysterious thing, friendship. But now, suddenly, the counterfeit coin which she had been taught, been forced, to pass off had become genuine! Alas, so false was it still in appearance that strangers would not, could not, believe in its authenticity.

No, Miss Collier-Floodgaye had earned her affection and contempt. If any feeling at all connected with the old lady's will ever entered

Miss Bramley's mind, it was that a fresh codicil, as betokening new allegiances, new affections, would—however slight in themselves were the bequests—be painful as indicating that while Miss Collier-Floodgaye had once been so fond of her— and of her alone—as to name the Companion heir to the entire fortune, the old lady had latterly rated this friendship less highly and had permitted others to share with the Companion the final testamentary proof of it. It may be, again, that Miss Bramley was not even as much occupied as this with the pecuniary side of her friendship. As a Companion she had been rigidly trained, and had probably been taught to consider any surmise, even in her own mind, about a will as taboo—taboo in thought as in conversation. And a discipline such as that which Miss Fansharpe had imposed upon her takes many years of soft indulgence to break down entirely.

.   .   .   .

In the winter in London, Miss Collier-Floodgaye could not get out much, because of her asthma. Consequently she would sit—not in her own private room—but in the public sitting-rooms; and directly Miss Bramley turned her back, would begin a conversation with some visitor; would even tell them about her money affairs . . . inclined to be boastful, the Companion remarked. Then, if she did go out, a severe attack of asthma would follow—the fogs, no doubt. It was, therefore, Miss Bramley who conceived the idea of spending a winter at Newborough, Miss Bramley who first suggested it. Very nice people still lived there, she was told, though she had not visited it since, as a child,

she had stayed with her aunt, Miss Titherley-Bramley. It had been delightful. And Harold had been compelled to go there, two years ago, in connection with his work for the Ecclesiastical Rest Home (where he had installed a ping-pong table and founded a challenge cup) so he had decided to make a holiday of it, taking Mildred and the children with him. They had liked it very much, very much indeed. And all the Curates in the Home loved the place, they said. After all, if one did not care for Newborough, one need not visit it again, need one, dear? And then Cecilia liked being "braced," and Newborough was so bracing, whereas Torquay, as Miss Bramley knew, for she had lived there, was inclined to be relaxing.

CHAPTER V

FACING SOUTH

AN impression of gaiety during its season must always be the aim and attraction of a seaside resort. To produce this effect, Newborough relied even more upon the crowds that flowered with a brief radiance in street, avenue, and crescent, through the few summer months, than upon the bold gesture with which it stood, as if at bay, confronting the elements, or upon the clean, spreading gold pavements diurnally revealed and obscured by its burgeoning green tides that under the warm sun seemed to break into white petals as you watched them. And if the sea blossomed at these moments, how much more so did the town! Though of no one plan or pattern, it was a natural garden in which could be exhibited ever-varying human flowers, flowers beautiful or grotesque: and through these pleasances, summer flickered for a while with a northern fervour, with the intensity of an aurora borealis.

Essentially it was the crowds that gave life to the town. Newborough depended, in fact, for its characteristic air of vitality as much upon the fluttering mobs that in the season decked it, as an old tree counts for its adornment upon the yearly birth and unfolding of its buds. The town resembled an old tree, too, in that while throughout the winter it feigned death, in reality it was

merely hibernating, gathering to itself fresh
strength for the vernal effort that must ensue.
As through black and angular branches, the cruel
winds soughed and moaned through the empty
winter streets, or cracked their steel-tipped whips
at the street corners. Only the perpetual thud
and hammer of waves at the walls below
quickened the corpse of a town with a chafing
movement, as if, as a last resource, artificial
respiration were being applied to it. In addition,
the battering of the sea imparted a sense of con-
tinuity, of being in touch with history, and the
huge desert of time that lay behind it. All history,
which is life; all life—which meant to this town
death—had been brought hither over the backs
of these whale-like jostling grey waves that still
leap and plunge under the cliffs. Celt and Norman, Saxon and Dane, had followed the same
troubled and rebellious pathway. Beneath the
precipitous, broken wall of the Norman castle
up on the jutting hill, was hidden the foundation
of a Roman Camp. Occasionally this Castle had
notched the long stick of English history, with
the atrocious murder of a royal favourite, with
a barbarous slaughter of traitors, by the recep-
tion of a hunchback and assassin-king, or finally,
by harbouring the Roundheads, who from this
retreat carried out their raids for the destruction
of the few isolated works of art that blossomed
miraculously in this arid district, noticeable as
the plants that in the springtime flaunt their shrill
glazed cups among polar wastes. It was always
with a tragedy that the stick had been notched.
But now History appeared to have sunk into a
respectable, genteel old lady with a past into

which it were better not to enquire, while the town
depended for its present existence—as must all
health resorts—not so much upon the death, as
upon the continued ill-health or eccentricity of
its residents, who would, but for their being thus
afflicted, move to live elsewhere. The numerous
local doctors had banished as far as possible a
sudden or definite death, and had instead, developed their aptitude for inducing in patients a
subtle state of suspended animation, which cor-
roded the will and transformed the visitor, as if
by magic, into a resident.

Yet the breakers still thundered, foaming at
wall and cliff, eating them up ever so slowly. And
during the winter this sound communicated to the
sensitive a feeling of nervous tension that, in the
years of which we are writing, grew steadily more
acute. Something was beginning to stir again,
to move in the dark winter nights . . . something
was being prepared far away behind the curtain-
ing of the grey foam, the black rolling waves,
something sudden and disastrous . . . a pom-
peian fate was surely in store for this placid town;
but what could it be, since no volcano let her
feathers droop softly over these northern waters?
It was, in fact, History once again collecting her
pack of ghouls for another and more ferocious
attack. Death was once more to stretch, in concert with her, his cold bony fingers over the grey
wastes toward this town. With that occurrence
we are not properly concerned, but nevertheless
our story must be told to the monotonous accompaniment of waves beating like the drums of
gathering armies: an accompaniment so tre-
mendously out of scale that its very force adds,

as it were, a certain mad interest to the varying
trivial and human events which the tale describes.

.   .   .   .

When these splintering steel rollers thudded at
the town all day, and hammered, muffled by wind
all the night long, as though secretly preparing
for it a coffin, life in the borough became infinitely
local. Newborough reverted to being a small
country-town, except for its great proportion of
idle shops and voracious tradesmen. The old,
the white, and the asthmatic had installed themselves by this time in their upper rooms—which
by a respectable but quite useless convention, for
here all winter winds were equally withering, all
prospects similarly bleak—must face South. Between these numerous rooms of Southern aspect,
however, a never failing line of communication
was formed and heroically maintained in the very
teeth of the East wind, by an eager chain of
clergymen, nurses, doctors, masseurs and volunteers for gossip generally. In the manner of the
honey bee, these active workers sipped the gossip
of each flower, which, by a constant flitting and
droning from one blossom to another, they were
at the same time able to fertilise, forcing them
to bring forth a new crop of honey for them the
following year. Thus they were partly responsible for the sweet yield of each new flower,
each new scandal, by which they were to benefit,
and by passing on to the next flower, would probably cause to spring up a hundred more seeds
that would again flourish into new and lusty
scandals.

The genuine local magnates had either by now
taken shelter in their vast yellow cardboard man-

sions in the fog-bound squares of London—mysterious, almost invisible mansions whence they
conducted their annual winter harlequinade under
the flaring greenery, that suggested a swampy
forest in South America born of mingled yellow
fog and gas-light, gradually building up, in the
manner of coral insects, a whole mountain of
parcels for the coming festival—or had retired to
their frost-bitten seats in the countryside adjacent to Newborough, where, too, they prepared
for a riotously expensive and imbecile celebration
of Christmas. From these latter icebound and
isolated forts of ignorance, the garrisons of
pheasant-coloured country gentlemen, accompanied by their mates, sallied forth to slaughter
the birds of the air. The respect in which each
male of the herd was held altered every day,
moved up and down as by a sliding scale, in
direct proportion to the massacre he had achieved.
At midday, or shortly after, they would pause in
their slaughter and would hold a feast in the
middle of the shambles and would then again
return to their carnage. In the hamlets and small
towns which they dominated, the county families
continued to preserve the pure tradition of English logic by themselves rearing vast quantities
of birds solely in order to kill them afterwards,
while at the same time they were busily engaged
in collecting subscriptions for the establishment of
a "Bird Sanctuary" for "our feathered friends."
Or else they would preside one evening over a
concert in aid of the "noble work" carried on by
the "Society for the Prevention of Cruelty to
Animals," and then the next day they would
themselves ride out to hunt. More foxes would

be chased until they were finally exhausted and could move no more, until the little red-brown beasts would be torn to pieces, like Jezebel, by the expectant dogs, and those young members of the ferocious tribe, who were taking part in these rites for the first time, would have their cheeks anointed with the blood, yet warm, of the poor furry creature. On the way home, one of the hunters would stop to give a carter in charge for beating his horse.

It is here interesting to turn aside for a moment to note, and wonder at the fact, that it is always the horse these people protect. In England deer, foxes, badgers, otters and hares may be practically eaten alive, the dogs that worry them munching pieces of flesh that still quiver with life; rabbits may be put in sacks, and then ejected, a few yards from a varied assembly of dogs, to be bludgeoned with clubs by a mixed herd of male and female sadists, or they may, with general approbation, have their blood sucked by human-trained ferrets, who fasten cruel teeth on their unoffending throats. Pheasants, grouse, snipe, partridges and nearly any other bird can be shot at sight. Similarly, the English big-game hunter abroad seems determined on the extinction of nearly every animal except the horse. One can understand his wishing to cover his own tracks by attempted parricide, by wiping out of existence everywhere the man-ape, the gorilla, orang-outang, and chimpanzee, but why need he assassinate such wise and graceful creatures as elephant and giraffe? But who ever heard of a hunter out after the heads of the wild horse? The bull-fight, too, is taboo to these savages be-

cause, in the course of it, their pet, their darling, the horse may be injured. No pity is felt for the bull. Yet of all animals the horse, though occasionally beautiful, is the stupidest, is merely an obsolete method of locomotion, an animated, strong-willed and headstrong Stephenson's Rocket. By its slowness in the town, by its silliness in the country, it is surely responsible for more deaths in city and countryside than all the elephants and motor-omnibuses of the world heaped together. Not that any one wishes to see the horse, however low it may rank in animal life, maltreated or injured, but it is time that the creature was relegated to private collection or to museums and zoological gardens.

These logicians were, then, in the winter too busily occupied with their multifarious activities in death-dealing to visit the neighbouring towns. Newborough was now given over, except for an occasional shopping raid, to its all-the-year-round inhabitants; and the departure of the grandees in the early autumn was a signal for certain lesser figures to emerge from their summer hiding-places. Afraid of being overshadowed, these either went away for the summer months or, pretending that they had departed, remained in-doors. But directly Lady Ghoolingham left New-borough—for her exit was the maroon which sounded safety to them—they crept out from their several retreats, gradually inflating themselves to a due degree of importance, and at the same time aping in their manner, with much accuracy, the great who had just gone away. This latter trick was a fault in technique, because it at once suggested that mimicry of this kind must have been

founded on fairly close study, and that these winter-patricians must in reality have been very near the town all the time to observe so minutely small details of deportment, and to maintain such a successful impersonation. Mrs. Shrubfield, for example, would appear (as when a great actress is taken ill and an understudy plays in her stead) in the leading rôle, that of Lady Ghoolingham. It is true that in looks, in dress, they did not very much resemble each other, but in each case, the part was conceived, was interpreted, in the same way. The plump, pyramidal chest and head—for the neck was not obtruded on one's notice—of Mrs. Shrubfield, the shoulders draped in a black mantle, the face smiling and sur-- mounted in its turn by the double curving smile of a black wig, crowned with a bonnet (which never varied, for it was copied each year on the principle of "The King is dead, long live the King") was borne along in mimic state by two black horses. On the box sat a coachman and footman, both wearing in cold weather a short black fur cape, which repeated the pyramidal shape within, and imparted to the entire equipage a certain quality of poise, of rhythm, as it were.

Occasionally Mrs. Shrubfield's twinkling eye of jet, an optic carefully trained for such detective work, would track down a friend. She would tap the footman on the back with a folded-up fan, that together with an umbrella, the handle of which was carved and painted in imitation of a parrot's head, were part of the insignia of her hibernal office; without them she was never seen in public. The footman, having received this ritual tap, this accolade, passed it on to the coach-

man, who, knowing full well its meaning, immediately drew up without making any enquiry of his mistress, for it signified that Mrs. Shrubfield wished to have "a little chat," to "hear all the news." As a matter of fact, she was inclined to give more than she received. No sooner had the carriage drawn up, indeed, than a muffled oracle came forth from the depth of the great pyramid. But owing to veils, frills, and above all to furs, the limpid meaning of the prophetess was somewhat obscured. Always rather out of breath, as if after some tremendous effort, her first action, therefore, would be to disentangle the wolf, fox, skunk, stoat, squirrel—or whatever the dear little animal was—which, presumably indulging in a fit of local colour, aimed at impersonating the English whiting and so, thoughtfully clasping its own tail in its mouth round her billowy throat, now kept her warm. But the little creature was resolute and tenacious as well as kindly. At first it would spin round her neck playfully, chasing its own tail like a puppy. Then trouble would ensure with its teeth, which appeared to be snapping in death rigors. The struggle became titanic, resembling that of Hercules when he wrestled with the lion. Yet even when one first saw Mrs. Shrubfield, one felt that everything in the world was possessed of a purpose that could be explained, that, at the same time, there existed no difficulty that would not yield to a combination of firm courtesy and applied reason. Every roughness could, indeed would, be made smooth. And, sure enough, the minute though rebellious creature, was soon tranquillised, a triumph as much due to diplomacy

as to brute force. Beaming with good nature, in spite of her recent encounter with a wild beast, and with a wheezy geniality which was supposed to be not always unaided by artificial stimulants, Mrs. Shrubfield would now proceed to hand out little cosmopolitan clichés in French, German and Italian. Of these lingual accomplishments she was immensely proud, nor even in her most exhilarated moments did such gifts desert her.

This appearance of Mrs. Shrubfield in her winter rôle of Grande Dame was resented to an extraordinary degree by the invalid population, which was nevertheless, by its own edict, powerless to oppose. Others there were, however—Miss Waddington for instance—who, supported silently by the contingent that still bravely faced South in their upper rooms, strove to divide the sceptre with her.

CHAPTER VI

APART, then, from this local winter-noblesse, of whom Mrs. Shrubfield was a worthy, if not indisputable leader, apart from the gossiping tradesmen at their untrodden doorsteps, there were only to be seen in the streets at this season well-known figures, whose peculiarities distinguished them and were, as well, a source of continual, eager discussion. These unfortunates were often the wrack of some former remote tide of summer visitors, their wanderings now bounded by poverty and the sea.

There was, for example, Mr. Paul Bradbourne. It still remains doubtful which of many experiences, some of them in the end unpleasant for himself, and all of them tragic in their consequences for others, had finally deposited him upon this winter beach. But he must by this time have been nearly seventy years of age, and thirty of these, at least, he had spent here.

A sinister enough figure was this little apple-cheeked gentleman jockey and former friend of the then Prince of Wales, as he passed by in his woe-begone, well-cut checks, sucking an appropriate straw. In his hand he held a riding-crop, with a long, folded lash, and every few minutes he would smack with it his beautifully polished brown leather gaiters. Into this empty gesture he poured an intensity of feeling. It be-

came, as he did it, a symbol of sporting worldli-
ness. Half French by birth—for his mother had
been a famous French actress, who after a com-
plicated career, had married his father, a rakish
officer in the Life Guards—he had lived much
in Paris as a young man, but had never been back
to it since the fall of Napoleon III. Indeed the
last sound he had heard was the bull-mouthed
bellowing of the guns outside Paris in 1870, for
he was cut off from all auditory impressions of
the modern world. Only once more in his lifetime was any vibration exterior to Mr. Bradbourne to reach his consciousness.

But this disability did not much inconvenience
him, for few people attempted, few wished, speech
with this little old man. The truth was that there
were unpleasant stories about him . . . rumours
sufficiently unpleasant to outweigh in the minds
of the townspeople the proven facts of his former
friendship with the great. As he went by, the
plump, red shopmen, with their bushy, bristling
whiskers, eyebrows and moustaches, could be observed pointing him out, whispering, and shaking
with loud, lewd laughter, while, on the other hand,
the solidly dressed, stately wives of doctors,
lawyers and clergymen could be noticed flurrying
their young daughters past him, and commanding
them not to turn round. If the inquisitive young
demanded why they were forbidden to look back
at "the funny old gentleman," they were made to
feel that by this enquiry they had not only committed a grave impropriety, but had also probably forfeited for their parents the general esteem
in which they were held. Thus in many a schoolroom a breath of brimstone, an attractive aura of

ogreism lingered about this small, rather evil
figure. But himself was possessed by no such
scruples about turning round to stare, and as
though deafness had sharpened his eyes, out of
them darted, like a cobra's tongue, a forked grey
flame, which seemed to flicker lingeringly round
the flaxen pigtails of the young girls now receding into the perspective.

Paul Bradbourne had been rich in his time, but
having ruined himself as well as many others,
must live on a small allowance doled out by unwilling relatives. Still, it had been a great day
for them when they had finally succeeded in landing such an expensive reprobate alive in a small
red coffin at Newborough. This square little
house, with its few windows like over-prominent
eyes, had seldom been entered by any one except
its owner and his housekeeper, and was a point
upon which was focused an amount of local interest. But for the watchers nothing ever transpired. Yet out of all the town, only one or two
men from the Club, who excused themselves by
letting it be known that they "liked a good sport,"
were ever sufficiently conquered by their curiosity
to speak to him. These, when they encountered
him in bars by chance, would roar questions at
him about past racing days and dead personalities. If he answered them, his speech was that
of the deaf, hollow and impersonal, though often
he would make no reply—perhaps because he
could not hear, perhaps because he despised
them—merely allowing the grey fire of his eye
to scorch their faces. When, however, he was
inclined to talk, his lower jaw dropped, then
opened and shut rapidly, as if on a hinge, in the

abrupt manner and with the jerky rhythm of a
ventriloquist's dummy. Indeed he resembled an
automaton of the Second Empire, so small and
neat was he, his body thin, angularly elegant, as
though stuffed with straw, his movements disconnected and broken.

He perhaps comforted himself that, in as far
as his mind could interpret life, he had lived,
compressing as much adult experience as possible
into a small span. But, in reality, life had ended
many decades before death occurred. It was dull
enough now that his old friend had ascended the
throne. Nevertheless, though bankrupt in all
else, body, mind, friends, money and present
pleasures, there were yet in his possession things
of which it was impossible for any human being—
even a relative—to deprive him . . . his memories. These, by allowing no present sound to
obtrude upon the sanctity of the past, it is probable that his deafness intensified. He was continually, as he grew older, away from Newborough, in those Paris dance halls, cafés and
gambling saloons which had long ceased to exist
except in his own mind, continually in places
where he had been admired and well-known, a
general favourite. Once more he could hear the
peculiar leafy rustle made by the silken flounces
of the crinolines, while they rippled caressingly
past, while patchouli floated to him over the shrill
east wind, whose shrieking he could not hear,
whose sting he could hardly feel. Once more in
his empty conch sounded the languorous lilt, beating up into a furious storm, of the Hungarian
band, in their slung jackets and gaudy frogged
uniforms. Or, he was back in the fabulous spring

days of his youth, when May burnt with a steady
green flame now unknown, and, as though the
honeyed west wind had lifted suddenly a curtain,
every tree was revealed weighed down by blossom, from the formal, pointed flambeaux of the
chestnuts to the gold-flecked white foam of the
fruit trees, to the hedge of hawthorns that were,
at these moments, avenues of white-winged ships
in full sail across a green ocean. He was moored
in a punt on the Seine with beautiful companions
now dead, at his side, while under them the sleek-
maned river-horses played gently, softly rolling
and tumbling. He must be back soon for a first
night at a theatre; already the whiskered critics
were beginning to gather for their attack. And
to-morrow, there were the races, and, soon, would
sound again in the petrified shell of his ear, the
genial, rather guttural congratulations of the
Prince on a remarkable win.

.　　.　　.　　.　　.　　.　　.

Very different from Mr. Paul Bradbourne were
the two little Misses Finnis—the peripatetic Miss
Pansy and Miss Penelope—daughters of the mid-
Victorian artist of that name, portrayer of so
much pensive youth and beauty wilting amid
azalea and almond blossom. These sisters, so
pathetic in their half-hearted gentlehood, so kind
yet so badly made, were queer progeny for that
old laurelled æsthete who had for so long tyran-
nised over them. During their father's lifetime,
these slaves had been too busy, looking after him,
too busy cooking and tidying, atoning for his
extravagances, to have any spare minutes in
which to develop themselves mentally or physically. And now the great man, to whom it had

been their pride to minister, was forgotten by all
save themselves, and they must hurry past on
their short basset-like legs to give some secret
piano lesson to a child of vulgar parentage, to
instil in the right-hand of a rich tradesman's
daughter the requisite large flourish of a lady's
handwriting, or on a similar task of carefully
guarded opprobrium. A timid look of recognition smiled from those eyes of faithful, basset
brown, and they bowed tentatively. They
blushed as they did so, a cold heliotrope blush,
as the false brown fringe, with its regular curls,
seemed to be creeping downward over their fore-
heads in an amiable attempt to shelter them from
embarrassment. The odious nature of their task
was to be read in their kindly, furtive glances.
"Nowadays," one sister would remark to the
other, "the commoner you are, the more money
you have. It's dreadful," and would give a little
frost-bitten laugh. Their own comprehension of
the iniquity of their Judas-like dealing made
them more fervent in such protestations. For by
initiating these children into the mysterious accomplishments of a local lady, by divulging the
correct style of handwriting, the secret of scrap-
ing through with a water-colour or reaching home
safely after a piano piece, they were, they felt,
betraying the class to which themselves so tenaciously clung. Their action was equivalent to the
disclosure, for sake of money, on the part of a
Freemason, of the precious, closely hidden rites
of his society. And one day their treachery would
leak out (it was sure to do so) and they would
be exposed, ruined. What condign punishment,
what awful humiliation, would then be inflicted

upon them by the genteel but ferocious denizens
of square and crescent!

Fortunately, though, in their good nature, the
sisters were of the greatest use to the numberless
wealthy invalids of the town, who were therefore determined, however well-informed of these
lapses, not to notice—nor to relieve the circumstances that occasioned—them. On Miss Pansy
and Miss Penelope hurried, in their threadbare,
blue coats and skirts, iridescent feather boas tied
round their short necks, the whole effect crowned
with wide-brimmed, dark-blue straw hats.

They bowed, in passing, to Sir Timothy Tidmarshe, who could be seen walking very rapidly,
with an unusual but quite obvious combination
of pomposity and intense fright, down St. Peter's
Street—Sir Timothy was that proud possession of
every seaside town, a marine Baronet. In character he was consequential but amiable, eccentric, and above all, superstitious. Extraordinary
events would, really, overwhelm him occasionally,
so that it was no wonder that the poor gentleman
was a believer in good and ill fortune. One day
after lunch, for instance, he turned into an auc-
tion room, where a sale was in progress—for he
liked, he used to say, to see things going on. He
happened, an unusual occurrence in any case, to
fall asleep with his eyes open, and woke up to
find himself the involuntary purchaser of a diamond and ruby tiara, which he had never seen,
for £5,000. Further, at the moment, Sir Timothy
was singularly innocent of money, but, out of
pride he was obliged to buy, and not to dispute,
the wretched bauble, and out of fear to keep it
hidden from Lady Tidmarshe for the rest of his

life. He did not dare send it to the bank, for they might wish to know why, in the present state of his account, he had purchased such a thing, and as well, it might give a bad impression of his moral character. Every day he was in terror that the blazing-eyed creature might be discovered. One never knew, even if one locked it up, whether it was secure. And whatever was he to say to Lady Tidmarshe if she found it? He would have to explain, too, why he had not shown it her before; so that in a way, every hour that passed without her discovering it, would make the difficulty more acute when the dread day should arrive. She would be sure to credit him with some purpose in his wish for concealment. Why had he hidden it, she would ask?—women were so jealous. And he would seek reassurance by the consultation of a thousand auguries.

In the end the tiara was only found after the Baronet's death, at the bottom of a locked chest of drawers. Its discovery was the opportunity for much talk and many surmises, and caused great pain to his family, above all to his lady.

Lady Tidmarshe, though in constant care over her own precedence, had only one real anxiety in the world—and one that, luckily, she was able to share with her daughter—how best to "keep up Papa's Position." With this object always in view, she had, perhaps prudently by a kind of feminine intuition, decided never to be seen in public. Many years before, she had passed this dignified decree of voluntary self-confinement, comparable to the gesture of Pope Pio Nono after the loss of his temporal dominions. If she went out, she might "lower" herself . . . it might not

be realised who she was . . . and people were so
pushing nowadays . . . but if she remained in
an almost Papal seclusion, no one could fail to
yield her correct precedence to her. After all
nobody could attempt to get into the room in
front of her, if herself was already in it . . .
moreover, there was more in it than that . . . for
if she received no one, then how could any one
get in front of her . . . it was much wiser. She
consented, however, to receive one or two vassals,
such as the Misses Finnis; but for the rest she
remained in her own house, writing constant
letters of condolence (for her friends seemed
always to be losing their relatives) which she was
able to permeate with a wonderful atmosphere
of patronage, and sending an occasional bunch of
wizened grapes, with a card attached, to an infuriated invalid.

One curious consequence of her decree of invisibility was that in appearance Lady Tidmarshe
had really become almost invisible, non-existent,
a ghost in her own drawing-room—or rather, by
some modification of the fate that overtook Lot's
wife, she seemed to have been transformed, by a
sudden shock, into a pillar of pepper and salt.
Her features were not there . . . life was obviously extinct . . . there was only this colouring, as of an Aberdeen terrier. Her hair was
parted in the middle, while at the back she wore
it in a fossilised flat coil, in the form of an
ammonite. Extremely attached to dogs, her
movements were invariably accompanied by the
faint tintinnabulation of teaspoons and by the
deep roar of dachshunds in full battle—for of all
dogs, these have the angriest, most bass voices.

Whether it was this affection of hers which was responsible for her condescending affability to Miss Pansy and Miss Penelope is uncertain, but they were, except for relatives, a tame doctor and a pet freak-curate, almost the only people whom the august and self-immured lady would be sure to receive. To these two protégées she would descant on the past glories and lost beauties of their "place" in the country (why Sir Timothy had sold this Paradise, which like Lady Tidmarshe, was invisible to all eyes except those of the family, to settle in Newborough, remains a mystery) in much the same manner that the old Pope might have painted, for the benefit of the younger Cardinals, the forfeited grandeurs of Quirinal and Castel Gandolfo. Miss Pansy and Miss Penelope were, in fact, the authorised filters through which these stories of bygone splendour were allowed, encouraged even, to pass for the nutrition of the Monstrous Regiment resolutely facing South. To see Lady Tidmarshe, with Miss Tidmarshe, sitting in her silver-tinkling drawing-room, talking to the Misses Finnis, and surrounded by her guardian fleet of dachshunds was to be furnished with an alternative theory to the Origin of Species. This heresy would deduce a basset, instead of a simian, descent for mankind, for human could be seen blending down into animal by slow, imperceptible stages.

Sir Timothy, when not out walking, liked in his study, a room on the ground floor, lined for luck with Egyptian mummies and scarabs, with black cats (which battled fearfully with the dachshunds upstairs) pieces of rope from which notorious criminals had been suspended, lady-birds, old

horse-shoes, fragments of the human pelvis, pentagrams, swastikas, money-spiders, and a perfect meadow of four-leafed clovers. A great part of the year was spent by him in tapping wood and eating mince pies before Christmas, while, when the new moon swung a bright scythe through its golden harvest, the Baronet had to be led blindfolded to the window, for fear of seeing it accidentally through glass.

Meanwhile Miss Tidmarshe—a terrible castigation was in store for any one who should refer to her as Miss Evelyn Tidmarshe—sat in her room, pondering on her Position, drinking hot, black tea, and then telling the prognostic tea-leaves as though they were a Rosary, for she inherited the proclivities of both parents. Miss Tidmarshe, too, had adopted a Vatican attitude toward the outside world. As she hardly ever appeared, there were many legends, sedulously tended by the Misses Finnis, current about in the town, such as that she was that queer, illusive thing "Very artistic," and possessed of "a positive genius for the guitar." It was not until she was over fifty years of age, however, that Miss Tidmarshe, clad in glowing gipsy garment of red and yellow, a crimson rose behind one ear, but still sporting a fringe like that of Queen Alexandra, was induced to leave her room and give a special display at a local charity matinée upon her favourite instrument.

Poor Sir Timothy lived in abject terror of his daughter, who was apt to denounce him to her mother for his "want of natural dignity." But if the poor Baronet was afraid of Miss Tidmarshe, it was as nothing to the awe in which

he held his sons, a pack as ferocious and plentiful
as Lady Tidmarshe's dachshunds.   Paragraphs
were wont to appear in the local paper—written,
insinuated the ill-natured, by no less a person
than Miss Tidmarshe, so that the information
might be regarded as coming straight from the
Kennel—to the effect that the "fine old sporting
baronet, Sir Timothy Tidmarshe, and Lady Tidmarshe, his gracious lady, are at present staying
at their marine residence, where they are entertaining in addition to Miss Tidmarshe, their six
warrior sons."   No two members of this martial
brood held commissions in the same regiment, yet
this did not prevent the brothers from quarrelling
horribly among themselves; for the sextet appeared to be always on leave and all at the same
time, while now not only the question of personal,
but also of regimental precedence was able to
enter into their battles.   The only cause that
united them was the harrying of their father.
As regarded himself, Sir Timothy could always
count on their perfect unanimity.   They would
join up together, stamp feet, shout, shake fists
and demand money, while, in the background,
Lady Tidmarshe and her daughter would afford
them a silent support, enwrapping the Baronet in
a thick blanket of keenly felt but unexpressed dis-
approval.   Hence Sir Timothy's nervous way,
when out walking, of looking from side to side,
for his sons could often be seen in the streets of
Newborough, treading in different directions, all
with their elbows turned out at right angles, their
moustaches turned up imperially, while they perpetually dragged up and shot their shirt-cuffs
with a gesture of supreme personal dignity.

Sir Timothy would in the meantime be shuddering swiftly through the streets, praying for the continued obscurity of that tiara, turning his eyes from side to side in the hope of eluding his sons, tapping wood, taking his hat off to chimney-sweeps and piebald ponies, meeting funerals at the correct angle, dashing away after dropped horse-shoes, hurling himself impetuously in the flight of a sea-gull, or improvising a thousand little grotesque feats of balance on kerb and pavement—these acrobatics being part of a private system of omens which he had devised. Alas, soon he was to meet his eldest son, face to face.

.   .   .   .

Another frequent, favourite street spectacle was Mr. and Mrs. de Flouncey, the dancing instructors. Both of these prophets of Terpsichore were now grey and well stricken in years, but they could not afford to let this be seen. It might ruin them. Nor could they ever afford to be tired. They must always be gay, young and full of high spirits. A little hair still feebly feathered Mr. de Flouncey's head, and of these few flat strands he made the greatest use, dyeing them, then winding them round his bald forehead turban-wise. Mrs. de Flouncey, on the other hand, had come out boldly with a wig, over which was arranged a hair net to give an extra touch of realism. The teetotum-like gaiety in which this couple was invariably, inevitably involved, had imparted a look of severe strain. This look was covered over with twinkling smiles, rather full of teeth, but indicative of youth and engaging frivolity. Besides, no doubt, they still felt young, for it had always been understood that Mr. de

Flouncey's father had been a French Marquis, obliged to fly from his native country after one of those bouts of revolution, in which that light-hearted people engage from time to time. Revolution, and French people generally, were not much approved of in Newborough as yet; but still it had to be admitted that the French were different from English people, and this apocryphal ancestry helped Mr. de Flouncey's professional reputation and was, at the same time, felt to explain and excuse his almost painful "joie-de-vivre."

Mr. de Flouncey had champagne-cork eyes, and a moustache ending in waxed rat-tails. Mrs. de Flouncey was gnarled but mouse-like. Since they were always on their way to a party—and, unlike the reader and writer of this story, a party which they were paid to attend—they were continually in evening dress under full daylight. Mr. de Flouncey wore a long brown cover-coat as a shield to this glory, but it was short enough to reveal the end of his evening tail-coat. While this glimpse, combined with the overt grandeur of top-hat and white cotton gloves, allowed those passing to conjecture the existence of a hidden blaze—that radiance of buttonhole, gleaming white shirt front, flushing a deep crimson where a red silk handkerchief was tucked in to the beginning of an equally flashing waistcoat, jewelled studs, heavy gold watch-chain, gold fobs, and many seals that even now, as he moved, could be heard pealing their golden carillons, and that soon, when he danced, would clash and ring out in time to the music. Mrs. de Flouncey wore an antiquated velvet opera-cloak over a pleated tur-

quoise-blue crêpe dress, that suggested in tone and texture the coloured paper covers that are found encircling a pot of ferns or an aspidistra in a lodging-house. Both husband and wife were the stewards, wearing prodigious badges, of every charitable function, every Masonic dance, every entertainment, even, of Primrose League or local Liberal Associations. For, as the Monarchy is above politics, so did their calling place Mr. and Mrs. de Flouncey high above party feeling, while at the same time it bestowed upon them a political immunity unknown to the Royal Family—an immunity which enabled them to take part, without giving offence, in the celebrations of every sept. Moreover, apart from their prestige in the town this gay couple commanded the esteem of National Dancing circles—that is to say that they attended each annual meeting of the Dance Teachers' Guild or whatever may be the name of that association which is for ever attempting to foist unwanted new dances on the public, and at the same time complaining bitterly if the public adopts a new dance on its own initiative. Syncopated rhythms, which were to alter dancing out of all recognition, had not yet made their appearance in any English ballroom, but when they did arrive, they came unintroduced by the Association, and, indeed, much to its dismay. Alas, the tidal wave of ragtime, gradually rolling toward these shores from the New World, was to overwhelm Mr. and Mrs. de Flouncey, who were by that time too old to do anything but oppose it. Their God was a strange God called "Smooth Rhythm," though in reality their dancing was excessively full of jerks and contortions, each

step insisting too strongly on its own individual-
ity, refusing to give and take, disconnected both
from predecessor and heir. For this very reason
it was most difficult to learn dancing from the
de Flounceys, for each step was taught as an
object in itself—a conjuring trick—and it was impossible to trace or remember any connection between one of these isolated attitudes and the next.
Indeed so little transition had Mr. de Flouncey's
genteel rhythms, that even when static, in repose,
talking to a friend for example, he appeared to be
finishing an old step on the verge of a new one.
Every attitude he adopted seemed one suddenly
arrested from a figure in the "Lancers," as
though, in the middle of his professional services,
he had been afflicted with catalepsy and had
retained the graceful pose of that minute, but
frozen, made rigid. These sectional slices of the
dance were, in truth, but the stock-in-trade of the
other more mysterious art which he dispensed
professionally—deportment.

Beside being adept at polka, lancers and waltz,
the de Flounceys were the repository in which was
stored the secret of the correct practice of such
forgotten rites as Veleta, Albert Veleta, and High-
land Fling.

Alas, the flood of ragtime was approaching.
When it reached them, poor Mr. and Mrs. de
Flouncey, already old but still bravely struggling,
were carried out to sea and on to oblivion; she
sank completely, but his cork-like eyes could still
be seen popping up to the surface occasionally,
with a dazed, reproachful look in them. The
town was inundated with blue-faced side-whisk-
ered Tango teachers in their stead—Tango teach-

ers who earned annually twenty times the de
Flounceys' total capital, and spent the winter
teaching in Nice and Monte Carlo.

.   .   .   .

There were other persons, of course, more
noticeable than Mr. Bradbourne, the Tidmarshes,
the Misses Finnis or the de Flounceys.   There
were the two children of Alderman Worrell, who
would ride through the streets every day on their
way to the sands.   The boy was about seven, the
girl eight, years of age, and they suffered from
some rare disease, which made them enormously
fat, red and expressionless, as if carrying the
aldermanic tradition of their parents to its fur-
thest, fullest conclusion.   They seemed overblown
cupids as they passed on their ponies, with never
a glance or smile.   Equestrian exercise was a
necessity for their health, and therefore perhaps
pardonable.   Then there were the two Misses
Cantrell-Cooksey, now penniless but still painted,
and even yet clad in their extraordinary garments.
And, most exotic of all specimens, perhaps, there
was the Count de Bolmarano.   A rich, retired
local tradesman, he had purchased a papal title,
and had adopted a style of his own in clothes,
for he always wore a very tight-waisted frock
coat with an astrachan collar, and top hat, under
the front brim of which (for he was completely
bald) was attached a solitary row of curls, so
that, with an exaggeration of courtesy, he doffed
not only his hat, but also his hair, to any lady
of his acquaintance.   The middle of the road was
his chosen path, for in those days there was not
yet very much danger from motor-cars; and

down it he would walk with a smile of supreme satisfaction.

All that could be discovered, detected about such persons had long ago become the property of every citizen of Newborough. Thus the advent of an unknown personage in the winter months would be a happening of the first order, and one not easily accountable. The news would be repeated and magnified through the empty streets, as the volume of a speech is increased through an amplifier. It would be known straightway in every inhabited house, and, apparently, without human agency. There are mountain villages in India, it is related, where the last piece of political information is in the possession of the natives before it has reached the great cities, engirdled as they are with telephone, telegraph and wireless. The news is picked up by these sable villagers, these human receivers, as from the very winds. So it must have been, too, in Newborough.

CHAPTER VII

ON THE TRACK

I T was, then, into this winter atmosphere that
Miss Collier-Floodgaye and Miss Bramley
chose to precipitate themselves, though it is quite
true that at the moment of doing so they were
unconscious of the detailed and curious attention
which their every movement would incur. But,
if there was an arrival in the town at this season
of sufficient standing, wealth or eccentricity to
be noticed at all, the scrutiny, made sharp through
long practice, of a whole army of veterans in
ambush would be focused upon this one poor
mortal. The object of this interest would stroll,
all unconscious, down the grey-brick promenades,
the tawny stone terraces; in the upper windows
there would ensue a surge of white muslin curtains, that resembled the wash of a tidal wave,
but would recede unnoticed from below. In reality, however, the stranger might as well be lying,
properly set out upon a glass slide under a micro-
scope, for on this specimen would be concentrated
the minute and trained attention of a thousand
heads concealed behind blinds, curtains and glass
panes. Dear Old Persons, who had spent many
months, years even, in a bed-ridden condition,
would allow themselves to be wrapped in light-
pink woollen shawls and propped up comfortably
near the window, there to enjoy a rare but intense ecstasy of scientific observation.

There were, of course, at the head of this army of volunteer—if veteran—research workers, recognised experts of long standing. Such were both Mrs. Shrubfield and old Miss Waddington. Since her recent masterly handling of the Cantrell-Cooksey scandal, the latter lady, especially, had obtained an unrivalled influence over her followers. But Mrs. Shrubfield, too, had distinguished herself in many a nigh hopeless fray, and opinion in the town had been forced to add a wreath of laurel to that fringe of vine leaves with which it had already crowned her.

Unfortunately, since a certain amount of jealousy between leaders of the same rank, in the same profession—between Field-Marshals for instance—is inevitable, these two ladies did not, at this period, love, however much they might respect, each other. While equally distinguished, equally successful, their methods were different. But in times of grave emergency, old feuds are forgotten in the common cause. When, therefore, the monumental pyramid that constituted the upper half of Mrs. Shrubfield, was observed being borne past in triumph by black horses, and was then seen to relax and unfold on to Miss Waddington's doorstep, excitement knew no bounds. It was rightly felt in the town that only some matter of supreme, of almost national, importance could have been responsible for such a sacrifice of pride. Something, in fact, was on hand. The invalid rooms, high up in the air, were a-twitter with expectancy, like so many nests of young sparrows at sight of a succulent meal.

. . . .

Old Miss Waddington had been a little better

that winter, and was sitting up in her bedroom,
by the fire, reading a weekly edition, published
every Friday, of the local paper, and hoping to
detect a clue to some new mystery. She was
studying an account of the Hospital Ball. A
tame affair, it sounded—stupid and tiresome of
Ella (where can she be, by the by?) not going
to it. The papers never gave one an idea of anything. Probably something had happened, if only
one knew. She passed on to a new heading,

"FASHIONABLE BAZAAR
AT
GHOOLINGHAM HOUSE."

That sounded promising, at any rate. What a
relief to find something interesting. She read
further:

"With every augury of success a two days' bazaar
was opened by the Mayoress (Mrs. W. L. Bamberger) in the ball-room of Ghoolingham House,
which has been the scene of so many brilliant local
functions. The bazaar is in aid of St. Catherine's
Convalescent Home, where extensive sanitary altera-
tions and improvements are rendered necessary for
the health and well-being of the patients. A letter
was read from the Earl of Ghoolingham, expressing
his sorrow, and that of the Countess, his wife, at
being unable to be present in person. In an un-
ostentatious manner, however, they have once again
demonstrated, by their thoughtfulness and liberal-
mindedness, how thoroughly they make the anxieties
and needs of this Convalescent Home their own.
The ball-room lends itself admirably for the purpose of a bazaar. The stalls are arranged in a
circle, with the flower stall and newspaper stall
running down the centre. They are decorated alike

with white Indian muslin, with bunches of Scotch white heather placed here and there, and a bordering of ivy, the tasteful drapery being supplied by Messrs. Beamish & Sons. The effect is pretty, combining simplicity with neatness. In keeping with the surroundings, the stall-holders wore bunches of white heather, also from Scotland, tied with white satin ribbon. Appended is a list of those engaged at the various stalls.

City of Ebur Stall.—Miss Agger, Miss Gladys Anthracks, Mrs. Binger, Miss Bower, Miss Barbara Bower, Miss Bowyer, Mrs. Bitt, Miss Bite, Mrs. Darcy Doherty and the Misses Doherty, Lady Poole, the Hon. Hylda de Trifling-Sedbury and Miss Sedgewick.

East Riding Fancy Stall.—Mrs. Peddar, the Misses Peach, Miss Pansy Pipp and Miss Hermione Bartlett.

Newspaper Stall.—Mrs. W. L. Bamberger (the Mayoress of Newborough), Miss Beatrice Bamberger and Miss (Bobby) Berry.

Fruit Stall.—Miss Anthracks.

Confectionery Stall.—Lady Dombay, Lady Dinger, the Misses Doodle and Miss Delia Donner.

Parcel Stall.—Miss Thornfox.

Flower Stall.—Hon. Mrs. D. Richety-Rudyer, Miss Persephone Rudyer, Lady Racket, Mrs. Rolls, Mrs. Rump and Miss Ruby Rump. . . ."

Just at that moment Miss Waddington was startled out of the almost subconscious state into which the associations and rhythm of these assorted names had caused her to fall, by the sound of a carriage driving up to the door. A ring at the bell, and then—for by this time the dear old lady was already on the landing outside her bedroom—the name of Mrs. Shrubfield. (What could it portend? Was it, perhaps, connected

with some affair rising out of the second day of
the Bazaar? Could that be it, she wondered?
In any case she realised at once that here was
no moment for trifling or standing on one's dignity.) She could hear Mrs. Shrubfield's skunk—
or was it fox?—snapping its teeth briskly in the
hall below, and a mingled odour of camphor, wild
animals and port wine was wafted up to the
watcher at the top of the stairs. Soon a wheezy
cosmopolitan geniality made itself felt throughout the house. She must be talking to Ella. In
a trice—yes, that is the exact word for it, in a
trice—Miss Waddington had thrown another
shawl round her shoulders and was walking unaided—a thing she had not done for ten years—
down the stairs. Her energy was extraordinary,
for emergency called up all her latent powers
of leadership. Almost before she could have believed it possible, she was in the drawing-room.

"Ah, Miss Waddington, *Carissima Signorina*,"
Mrs. Shrubfield brought out in her melodious but
husky voice, *"Ca va bien?* How are you? *Va
Bene, speriamo?* (Why be affected at a moment
like this, thought Miss Waddington, can she never
be natural, like any one else?) *"Gibt es was
Neues?"* I felt I must come and see you now
that I'm back (where from, I should like to
know? What a mass of affectation!) How fortunate you are never to go away, dear lady. But
then, you know what it's like when one has a
lot of friends, I expect? Though I'm quite old
now, people still pester me, positively pester me,
to go to them. And then, it's so nice to come
back to Newborough, though it's altered a lot.
The town seems quite empty (and the bottle, I

should think, reflected Miss Waddington, port or
only hock?). Hardly any one in it . . . *mais si,
il y a quelques unes qui viennent d'arriver. Es
sind neue G'âste zum Superbenhof gekommen.* In
fact, *il y a de nouvelles arrivées á l'hôtel. C'est
drôle, n'est-ce pas? Molt' interessante.* At the
Superb (so that's it, why couldn't she say so before?) *deux dames qui ne sortent jamais. Molta
Vecchia, l'una.* The other one must be her Companion, I should think. (Miss Waddington had
now lost all feelings of anger at her rival's affectations: for one leader can appreciate the qualities
of another, without the question of like or dislike entering into such a purely technical matter.)
Do you know them, I wonder, *Carissima Signorina?* I've never heard of them before . . .
but the elder one does not look to me like a
Nobile Donna."

.   .   .   .

For many weeks after this dramatic "ren-
contre," as Mrs. Shrubfield would have phrased
it, the two Marshals were inseparable: a common
interest bridged the chasm between them, until in
the end a solid friendship was built miraculously
on the ever-shifting sands of such a mystery. In
future, when Mrs. Shrubfield called, Ella was sent
upstairs to read *Punch;* while Miss Waddington,
contrary to all her winter regulations, drove out
several times to have tea with her new ally, for
Mrs. Shrubfield even went so far as to send round
her carriage for the old lady. When, therefore,
the rank and file of the Monstrous Regiment saw
from their upper windows the familiar equipage,
with its two black horses, with its two pyramidal
figures on the box, bearing along at a stately

trot—not the expected greater pyramid of Mrs.
Shrubfield, not the two curves of the black wig,
and the completing black bonnet above—but the
frail, mauve-clad, asthmatic form of Miss Waddington, the aged head thrust forward and nodding as if already on the trail, the eyes, too,
slightly bloodshot to complete this conception, it
can be imagined how a thrill of wonder mingled
with enthusiasm and the blood ran hot again in
their ardent veins. Excitement mounted higher.
Telephone and front door bell rang continuously
and without ceasing. The bees were at work
again, flitting from blossom to blossom. Tea
became stronger and stronger, nerves ever more
taut. . . . Soon the news was out . . . a Miss
Collier-Floodgaye, it seemed, and a Companion
. . . at least so it was supposed . . . staying at
the Superb . . . in the winter too . . . Mr.
Spry, the framer, had seen them walking down
St. Peter's Street . . . no doubt about it, he'd
seen them himself, actually, and had told Clara
. . . you know Clara . . . about it . . . walking down St. Peter's Street . . . walking, too . . .
not even as if they kept a carriage . . . in the
winter, too . . . oh, odd, very odd indeed.

The next step, of course, was to ascertain
which doctor attended the two new arrivals. This
highly specialised piece of research work was en-
trusted by Mrs. Shrubfield to Miss Waddington.
But, to her dismay, she discovered that neither
Dr. Sibmarshe nor his rather pushing young
partner, Dr. MacRacket, had yet fathomed the
unknown with their stethoscopes. It was too bad
of them; *she'd* say "Ninety-nine to *them*, when
she saw them. After all, it was their business

to get new patients . . . what made it so extraordinary, too, was that Miss Waddington knew that the Management of the Superb always recommended one of these two doctors to their guests . . . fortunately there were other links and other methods. The matter could not be allowed to rest where it was.

John, the hall-porter at the Superb, of twenty years' standing, was a local figure of the first magnitude, and in direct communication with a countless number of invalid rooms, which moreover—however much he might despise them in his heart—he must, for the sake of pecuniary advantages, conciliate.

In the first careless rapture of two new arrivals, several old ladies who had confined themselves to their beds, winter after winter, were injudicious enough to clamber into the bath-chairs, and allow themselves to be trundled round—as though in the death-embrace of an overturned giant black-beetle, to the Superb. On arrival they would, rather wearily, ask John if there were any letters for them, a transparent manœuvre. They would then seek to engage him in a talk, which beginning with a general application would swoop mercilessly to a particular instance. The use of such tactics was incorrect and injudicious. These old ladies, however enthusiastic in the cause, had proved themselves mere amateurs, and John, contemptuous of their technique, would divulge nothing. Even Lady Tidmarshe, to whom the news must have penetrated through the two little Misses Finnis, went so far as to send her maid to John with a bunch of the famous withered and

mildewed grapes, which looked as if they had
spent the previous night in her parrot's cage, and
ask him to come and see her one day. John,
however, was determined to let no information
escape him yet awhile, though he saw a moment
when information would reach a premium, and
therefore collected assiduously what there was of
it. In order to find out further details about the
two visitors, he refrained from bullying Elisa (the
"German Sausage," as he had wittily christened
her) and even sought to pacify and please her.
But she came of a warrior nation, and would
have none of it.

Miss Waddington's subtle expertness was in a
category altogether different from the bungling
attempts we have described. Deliriously, day
and night, she knitted a red woollen comforter,
"nice and warm for the winter," as a gift to
John's youngest son. The moment came when
the scarf was finished, and she was able to send
for the child's mother to receive it. By this
method, every detail (alas! there were but few)
was soon in her possession, and could be served
out as a treat, after any slight skirmish, to her
attendant niece.

She rang the bell. "Emily, I am out except to
Mrs. Shrubfield. I must have a talk with Miss
Ella; please send her up to me." A sound of
feverish, but mousy, footsteps on the stairs, and
Ella rustled into the room, anxiously, but still
striving to look bright. What could she have
done now, or was Aunt Hester preparing for
something, an asthmatic tornado or a hurricane
cold? "Yes, Aunt Hester, did you want me?

I hope you're all right, dear? Do you want another shawl or anything?" But at this instant the
old lady exuded amiability.

"No, dear, it's only that I should like a little
chat . . . a Miss Collier-Floodgaye . . . yes . . .
rich and elderly . . . oh, the name sounds all
right, dear, of course it does. But then it would,
wouldn't it? Oh, that you may depend upon.
. . . All the same, I don't know it. Of course
there's Canon Floodgay at St. Saviour's, and
though very High Church—indeed almost more
than that—he came originally of good family
. . . at least, so they say. But then why, dear
child, need he be so theatrical . . . Anthems and
Rubrics and things. And that awful picture!
. . . *in* the church, actually . . . and not in the
least bit *like* Our Lord! At any rate, it's not *my*
idea of Him. With eyes like that, oh no, dear!
I wouldn't trust the Canon, not for an instant
. . . what with all those Rubrics and Anthems
and things . . . it would never surprise me if, in
the end, it was discovered that he went in for
incense. What did I say, dear? Yes, incense.
Never surprise me. And they say that he gives
Mrs. Floodgay a lot of anxiety. But, in any case,
he is Floodgay, not Collier-Floodgaye; and Mrs.
Floodgay, you'll remember, dear, happened to
drop in to tea here yesterday. Absolutely no
relation, she said to me. None whatsoever.
Alone in the world we are, she said, with the
Canon and Cécile. Pretty, bright little thing,
she ought to know if any one did, oughtn't she?
I really like that little woman . . . besides, they
spell it without an 'e' . . . but a Miss Collier-
Floodgaye is, without doubt, staying at the

Superb (don't fidget, dear!) with . . . (andante)
. . . (and then allegro) her Companion. (There,
that will give you something to think about for
a change, fidgeting like that," the old lady
thought to herself, and brought it out suddenly,
sharply, like a smack. "That will surprise you!)
Oh, yes, she must be a rich woman, Leeds, very
likely; I shouldn't wonder if that was it . . .
rich, of that there can be no doubt. Always
dresses in black—a stiff knee, too; and walks
with a stick . . . and walks with a stick, always
walks with a stick. Louise Shrubfield saw her,
herself. ('Of course,' I said to her, 'the stick
may only be her *affectation,* I do so like people
to be *natural.*') A mystery somewhere . . .
dressed all in black, oh odd, very odd, very odd
and queer, indeed . . . dressed all in black, with
a stiff knee . . . and a *stick* . . . you know.
And I've heard, too, that she's short-sighted . . .
I told Louise Shrubfield . . . I said to her,
'They say she's blind . . . in the best sense, of
course . . .' She didn't like that, I can tell you,
Ella. But really she had been so affected . . .
still, there's a lot of good in her . . . and so well-
informed. . . . What was I saying? Oh, yes,
dresses all in black, with a stiff knee and a stick,
and short-sighted. Lives in London in the summer, so they say. In a hotel, so I hear . . . yes,
a hotel . . . oh odd, very odd, indeed! A *Companion* . . . and a stiff knee . . . dresses in
black, and always leans on a walking-stick. Oh,
so odd. The *Companion* sings beautifully, so
they say, with real expression (that's what I like.
That's what I like, expression.) Not so much
what she sings, they say, as the way she sings

it . . . and what makes it prettier still, plays by
ear! Quite natural, with a sweet little voice and
no training. She sings, you know, that song by
the Italian . . . you don't, dear? . . . of course
you do! . . . you know, this one (and here the
niece was treated to wheezy, wintry variations on
Tosti's 'Good-bye'). Very pretty, with a lilt to
it. A lilt to it and much feeling! I often wonder,
dear, why you don't sing. It's such a help to
girls, I think . . . a Miss Bramley, the Companion . . . and seems to know more of the
World . . . a niece, it is supposed, of old Miss
Titherley-Bramley, who lived for years in the
large-white-house-next-but-one-to-where-Mrs.-
Sibmarshe's-mother-lived-before-her-daughters-
married. But surely you can recognise it from
that, can't you? (I never liked that house . . .
something about it. . . .) She was very *musical*,
too, and always drove about in a Victoria followed by two Dalmatians . . . of course you do,
dear . . . spotted dogs. And piebald horses, too,
now that I come to think of it, for I remember
Sir Timothy Tidmarshe always waiting there in
the morning to see it, and take his hat off . . .
piebald horses and died, oh years ago! before
you were born. She left very little money behind
her. I recall it quite well, for everybody was surprised; because, after all, she'd had a house and
garden, a carriage, and Dalmatians and everything . . . which niece can it be? That's the
point . . . there were two, if I remember. . . .
Oh? Is it Mrs. Shrubfield? I'll see her at once
then. Certainly. Ella, you had better run away
and write letters. Don't argue, dear. How am
I to know 'Who to'?"

CHAPTER VIII

THE NEW REIGN

*"It is only this last century that the crack appeared,
That the mark came on the ceiling, and the plaster
   broke,
That they came to knock the idols down,
And quickly put up others;
Like burglars at a shrine."*

MISS BRAMLEY found Newborough more
altered than she had expected; it seemed
larger and richer. There was a new sea wall,
and the magnificent public rose-garden, with a
few roses still in bloom . . . in bloom, actually,
in November. It made her feel quite as if she
was abroad—or rather what she imagined it must
feel like to be abroad. There was a subtle difference in the atmosphere of the place, though it
seemed very empty.

The truth was, had she realised it, that the
golden sun of Edwardian prosperity was mounting elsewhere to its meridian, and affecting life
even here. Manners were changing under its
genial warmth, which caressed, under certain conditions, the unjust no less than the just, and
heartily embraced the "lesser tribes without the
law," as long as they were not also without
money.

At the Court all were young, it was understood
(and, indeed, after Queen Victoria, nearly any

one was young) and all were gay. If the Court
was not really as young as it looked, at any rate
it only looked half its age. Queen Alexandra, it
was said, might pass for twenty-eight. There appeared now to be no border line between twenty-
five and seventy-five, and, in one of the phrases
of the day, "any one who was any one" was somewhere between those ages. The words "delicious," "heavenly," and "divine," and "too, too
weird" were to be heard for the first time on the
pouting, jutting lips of the middle-classes, while
the ringent Eastern Gentlemen from Brighton and
Bombay, Bagdad and Berlin, who now made
their first, rather clumsy though genial, bows, at
any European Court, skipped like young rams
and bounded—above all, bounded—like young
leopards. Finance had begun to come into its
own—and everybody else's—attended by the
caressing scents of henna and bath-salts, and to
the appropriate accompaniment of Puccini's
music, with its inevitable suggestion of constant
hot water and every modern convenience. For
the first time, strange accents, lisping in authoritative numbers, were making themselves heard
within the precincts of the House of Lords: lisps
and spluttering guttural sounds which had been
hitherto prudently confined to the purlieus of
Aldgate and pawnshops of Whitechapel. A
rodent-like scuffling and scampering could be
heard everywhere in London, as our guests
gnawed their way through into the West End.
For, to this Golden Age, there was, fittingly
enough, a golden key—Comfort! It was known
that King Edward "liked to be comfortable";
and the Wise Men of the East had grasped the

fact that it was their mission to make him so. Every Havana-rolled tobacco leaf, which they offered him, might be returned to them, they hoped, transformed by the Royal Hand into a Strawberry leaf. Since the days of Napoleon III, who inundated his country with "Syrian," "Armenian," and "Egyptian" Barons, the Race had known nothing like it, and there was a general rush to contribute to the "Barty Funds."

After all, there was nothing wrong in comfort, was there? Hoarse, glutinous and wheezing laughter at the primness and hard angles of the Victorian reign was to be heard resounding through the newly-built hotels now blossoming in London. Carpets were woven so thickly as to entrap the feet, arm-chairs were upholstered as for the harbouring of a hippopotamus.

But the welcome extravagance of the New Order was still ever so faintly reflected in these northern waters, for Newborough was, as always, rather behind the times, catching up a little self-consciously and with a loud panting. Even now, even here, however, certain modifications of life were visible, though the town had been as yet affected more indirectly than directly. A frothy sea of lace was receding for the first time for sixty years from the wanton legs of chair and table. The mantelshelf with all its fringed apparatus of red flannel globules and stalactites was delivered up to the lumber-room, while the chimneypiece beneath was now allowed once more to proclaim an unashamed nudity. The mansions of the richer and younger section of Newborough were beginning to be filled with soft mauve and green cushions. The apoplectic flush was be-

ginning to die away from the walls of the dining-room in which meals grew ever shorter and better. Every day the arm-chairs could almost be seen growing, like the Empire, larger and softer. The furnishing shops, which here, by some strange rules, always combined their decorating proclivities with the business of undertaking, now declared in their windows boldly flowering chintzes. With the advent of the motor-car, colour banished by the Age of Steam again inherited the land. For the steam engine had for half a century usurped the throne: a funnel, and not the effigy of Queen Victoria, should have been the minted token of her reign. In the next decade, with the artful help of the Borough Engineer, many changes would be effected in Newborough. Through his over-exertion, the entire town would be swept out of sight beneath a pink, an awful, avalanche of Dorothy Perkins roses. Everywhere "pergolas," supposedly Italian in design, and cement-edged ponds of goldfish, were to supplant the herring-patterned red roofs and huddled houses of the fishermen—houses that had preserved to an extraordinary degree the Rowlandsonian quality of the English eighteenth century—or were to drive out the wistful elegiac elegance of rustic summer-house, reeded pool and weeping willow which had hitherto been the feature of English public gardens. The character, prim or primitive, of the town was to wilt beneath a fallacious sub-tropical exoticism. Palm trees, however unwilling, were to be forced, at the point of the spade, to oust such trees as beech and sycamore, and were then to be coerced into unfolding their withered leaves on to the icy northern air;

cactuses, too, were to be made to exhibit in public
the suicidal tendencies brought out in them by
the East wind. Finally, there was an absolute
epidemic of Japanese rock-gardens.

On the other hand, the habit of life among the
majority of local old ladies, doctors, and clergymen, was to remain unaffected for a long time.
The upper rooms facing south in square, crescent
and terrace remained unaltered and apparently
unalterable, ever bathed in the sunset glow of Vic-
torianism. Within the limited space of her sick-
room, each invalid preserved inviolate a fragment
of the Victorian reign, though each portion varied
in epoch. Miss Waddington's bedroom, for
example, might have been an actual bit broken
off the Golden Jubilee; while the widow of the
Anglo-Indian Colonel, who lived next door, still
inhabited a room that belonged quite as plainly to
the now legendary periods of Indian Mutiny and
Crimean War.

Alas, as the brief Edwardian reign deepened
into an apoplectic flush, the richer and younger
part of the local life was being drawn more and
more to London. The old, comfortable doc-
trine—comfortable, because it endowed each believer in it with a small holding of duty which
he must cultivate, while the absolute necessity of
his doing so prevented him from ever feeling any
regrets—that it was necessary to do one duty in
that state of life to which it had pleased the Devil
to call one, was breaking down for ever. Whereas
in Victorian days if a man disliked living at Newborough he felt it all the more a compelling duty
to remain there, or as he would have put it, to
"reside" there, the young man felt, in similar cir-

cumstances, no such obligation. They just left,
without any regret or remorse. The large bow-
windowed stone houses were becoming derelict,
and wailing for bygone gentility was loud in every
room that faced south. For, even if members of
a younger generation visited the town in the summer, they seldom were possessed of stoicism sufficient to enable them there to pass the winter.
Thus interest was focused more intently upon
those who, in unconscious mutiny against their
period, came for the winter to this borealic borough. Besides, too, it was so "quiet" in the dead
months.

But, even if Newborough was a little quiet in
the winter, Miss Bramley did not dislike it on that
account. Llandriftlog had been quiet, too: she
was used to it. There was such a good piano in
the drawing-room, and, as the hotel was empty,
she could practise as much as she liked. Really
it was quite like being in one's own house! Now,
though, she almost wished she had not sold the
other piano. She could quite well have had it
put in her room. But you see, everything had
been so uncertain that it had seemed better at the
time to sell. . . . Still, the one in the drawing-
room was really good, and that was a comfort.
And, too, it was tuned regularly; for Mrs. de
Flouncey used to play it for her husband's dancing classes every Thursday . . . (she seemed a
nice woman, obliging, full of information, and
fond of music). You could always tell a Broad-
wood piano anywhere . . . the "timbre," she
supposed. Unusual, too, to find one in a hotel, at
any rate one in as good condition. But there it
was, the hotel was superior to most other hotels.

The hotel was, certainly, unlike other hotels; but it is useless to pretend that the eastern wave of luxury, which was now spending itself in London, had as yet broken over the interior of this, one of the first built hotels in England. Encaustic tiles make it echo, red flock papers make it dark. The rooms are too large, too well designed. With floating palm trees and ferns in them, they have, more than ever, the air of an empty aquarium waiting for new, half-human, half-marine specimens until even the round ottomans in the centre of the floor became so many closed-up red anemones on the tank bottom, the sofas and chairs loose rocks. Move these, and from under will crawl sideways some crustacean and armoured spinster, or a purple-faced monster of an old oceanic Colonel. When, however, the observer looks more closely, the greenery is too arid to justify such imagery; the leaves of palm and aspidistra are hard and withered, scratch the wall at any draught. Indeed the palm trees lumbering up in the corners of the rooms are so tall, their outspread fingers so bony, that they resemble rather the reconstructed extinct monsters at a Natural History Museum than anything in an aquarium.

The tiers of gallery, out of which open the rows of bedrooms, close round the hall and about the staircase. Opposite the foot of this, across the hall—or "lounge" as it had recently, in a fit of euphemism, been rechristened by the Management, is an oval-shaped ballroom ablaze with Saxe-Coburg cupids and gilt leafage; for though when this hotel was growing up into the air, the Consort already rested in his Mausoleum, the in-

fluence of his solid but fantastic taste is everywhere manifest.

Alas, apart from the ottomans and rock-like
sofas, most of the chairs and tables in the lounge
and elsewhere, are too flimsy, too temporary for
their setting. In a fever of modernity, the Management had spirited away much of the heavy,
original furniture and had mingled with what was
left a host of wicker chairs and tables. When, in
the winter, these wicker chairs are empty, unpro-
tected by the provincial visitors' overlapping flaps
of flesh, their unworthiness is very obvious.
Emptiness being a fruitful source of ghosts, the
creaking and moaning of vacant wicker haunts
lounge and sitting-room with impressions of the
ample bodies of vanished summer visitors.
Through these vast dark rooms and passages,
empty yet expectant as a dusty stage unused for
many years, move the figures, diminutive in scale
compared with their background, of Miss Collier-
Floodgaye, Miss Bramley, Elisa, the housemaid,
John the hall porter, and a few shadowy supers.
No one else moved through these dim, silent
places at such a season.

Still, Miss Bramley comforted herself that the
hotel being empty in the winter was a decided
advantage: for Cecilia would not be able to make
friends with strangers. Now Miss Fansharpe
would never have *dreamt* of making friends with
people she did not know. Never! But then one
must realise that Cecilia was . . . well, "different." Differently brought up, that must account
for it; and then, of course, every one had their
faults.

As Miss Collier-Floodgaye grew older, she had

seemed to Miss Bramley to become more and
more vague, more and more liable to confide in
strangers . . . a confidence very unexpected,
since she never trusted to any one, not even to
her Companion, the details of the early and
middle periods of her life. And she was becoming so boastful, that was the worst of it . . .
boastful, not at all ladylike; proud of her money
with the pride of one unused to it. She would
even talk to strangers about stocks and shares
. . . to *strangers* . . . stocks and shares . . .
you know . . . not quite the sort of thing to do.
No . . . could one even imagine Miss Fansharpe
doing such a thing? . . . and then, from whispered and intricate discussions of the life led by
the Royal Family (personally Miss Bramley
could still "not see much" in Queen Alexandra's
face) Miss Collier-Floodgaye would pass on to
discuss with "total strangers"—and a "total
stranger," it must be understood, was worse, infinitely worse, than an ordinary stranger, a sort
of super-Ishmael, disconnected *in toto* from the
rest of humanity—the lives of those fashionable
persons to whom, Miss Bramley in her own mind
was positive, Cecilia had never once spoken and
whom she had probably never even seen. Of
course, the old lady was so forgetful that it was
just within the bounds of credibility that she had
met them, and was, except at moments when their
names were recalled to her, oblivious of the fact.
Or it might be that at such instants she genuinely
imagined, and, for the duration of the talk
actually believed, that she was acquainted with
these illustrious immortals of the illustrated
weekly journals. It was, in fact, impossible to

arrive at any sure conclusion in the matter . . .
but, anyhow . . . to strangers, to *total* strangers
. . . very sad and deplorable.

At Newborough in the winter, however, there
were apparently but few persons to whom Miss
Collier-Floodgaye could impart these hypothetical encounters. Yet the tragedy of it, if only the
old lady had realised, was that there were so
many hundred invalids all round her, literally
pining away from curiosity and lack of gossip.
A thousand pairs of eyes, all facing south, were
fixed on this singular couple; yet no one had got
into communication with them, for there were
certain rules that had to be observed in this, as
in all other sports. Yet even Miss Waddington
and Mrs. Shrubfield were puzzled as to the best
method of prosecuting their campaign. It was
not the moment, for example, to call . . . or to
write . . . no, not yet: *dopo, peut-être.*

Despite the seeming difficulty of finding a confidante, Miss Collier-Floodgaye had achieved one.
Miss Bramley, to her disgust, actually found her
gossiping one day to the German housemaid.
Really too bad, and not at all the thing to do.
However perhaps for once, Miss Bramley said to
herself rather maliciously (for Miss Bramley's
character, now unchecked, was altering) Cecilia
has found some one to believe her. It was possible. Of course what the old lady really needed
was a hobby; the Companion felt sure of it.
Every one ought to have a hobby (invisible
blinkers to shut off human frailties such as illness and death—frailties which are always just
round the corner). Yes, a hobby. Miss Bramley's father had always said that "there was

nothing that took a woman out of herself like Rescue Work" . . . how true! . . . look at Miss Fansharpe . . . but then perhaps Cecilia was to old for it now . . . though, in a sense, it was a pursuit for the elderly. Or else she ought to read more. And it was so easy to get books; a splendid lending library close by, and another small one on the West Cliff. E. F. Benson, Robert Hichens, Marie Corelli, Hall Caine (Miss Collier-Floodgaye had been so fond of Marie Corelli's books—but she seemed to be getting "so bitter" now), and everything one could need . . . you know, really nice books . . . exciting too. And sometimes one could get the latest novel the very day it came out, which made a great difference. Much more interesting and *so* much cheaper than buying it. In fact, in the winter one could get almost any book one wanted. Poetry, too, if one cared for it. Certainly Cecilia ought to read more. But she was very nervous, and poetry seemed to make her worse—she ought not to read detective stories either—something light and cheerful was what she must get. Luckily Newborough was supposed to be good for the nerves, though at the same time bracing, ever so bracing.

CHAPTER IX

CANNON AND ANCHOR

"Theirs not to reason why,
Theirs but to do, and die."

IT was only necessary to observe Miss Collier-
Floodgaye's ascetic style and sombre mien for
an instant to know that, however correct had been
Miss Waddington's identification of Miss Bramley as niece of that lamented lady of musical and
Dalmatian memory, her diagnosis of Leeds in the
case of Miss Collier-Floodgaye was at fault. But
then, in spite of every effort compatible with dignity, Miss Waddington had not yet been able to
cast a practised eye over her. It is impossible for
a doctor to attribute symptoms to their right
cause, if himself has not examined the patient.
Yet Miss Waddington did not like to "hang
about" too much in front of the hotel, in her bath
chair: it looked unsporting, rather like taking a
shot at a sitting pheasant. It might even, by
lowering their estimate of the capacity and "fair
play" sense of their leader, impair the *morale* of
the storm troops under her command. Therefore,
though she could often borrow Mrs. Shrubfield's
carriage, or even go for a drive with her in a
direction expertly appraised as likely to yield good
sport, though she could pass the hotel door once
or even twice in the day, she could not wait about
in front of it. And so far in her raids she had

always drawn blank. If only she had been able
to see Miss Collier-Floodgaye and her Companion
leaving the hotel, she would no doubt have
reached a much surer conclusion as to the newcomer's origin.

For that old lady's tall, rather rugged frame no
more suitable setting could have been devised
than the appropriately austere background offered by the Superb Hotel. The building imparted to the scene a touch of grandeur. It
uprose from the town, dominating the entire prospect, in the manner of Landseer's "Monarch of
the Glen," its four domes, instead of antlers,
towering up into the glowering winter sky. Icy
little currents of air battered at it in vain throughout the dark months. Against the whole pack
of hunting winds, that snarled and howled so
hungrily, it stood at bay: for the giant building
was at this season the natural foe and destined
prey of every element.

One of the first hotels, as opposed to inns, attempted in England, it was built at a time when
the housing of large numbers of paying guests
under one roof was everywhere a new conception—so new, so startling, even, that the idea of
providing comfort for them need not enter at all
into the calculations of its creators. It was only
necessary, then, to build a hotel large enough to
house a great number of guests, for the daring
novelty of the thing to fill the place, and keep it
full. Space and richness of gilding were, as we
have seen, the objects desired within; so an impression of size and grandeur had been the exterior effects aimed at, and in a sense achieved.
This hotel looked as though it had been built for

the interment of grim, rich but still respectable manufacturers from the industrial cities. It lacked altogether that Louis Quinze atmosphere of the cosmopolitan caravansaries that now sprang up everywhere, even in ruined England, for the pleasure of fraudulent international financiers, and in order to flatter them with a feeling of security. For that purpose, too, each hotel of the sort must be indistinguishable from another; thus in London, Buenos Ayres, Cairo, Tokyo and Montreal, they are all the same.

The Superb Hotel, on the other hand, offers no comfort, spiritual, mental or bodily, but it is impossible to challenge a certain quality of stern, grandiose beauty. For the echoes of good building were still faintly ringing in the upper air when this hotel was created, nearly seventy years ago. Ruskin's arid but exotic teachings had not yet destroyed the old tradition. The Superb is obviously the work of an architect, as opposed to that of a commercial builder or latter-day luxury expert of the great hotel companies. It stands there, its two vast façades capable of holding out against the four winds, a rock, composed of yellow brick, in an undeniably rare tint, decorated with surface patterns in other bricks of equally unusual red and purple, crowned with a high slate roof and four barrel-like domes, the colour of cinders. No building could crown an important position more satisfactorily. Even the porch, in shape so akin to the fashionable bonnet of the period, even the mid-Victorian masks and statues that leer down so slyly—monocled satyrs in top hats and crinolined caryatides, possess an indisputable atmosphere. When it was built no

other social system was deemed possible, and so
it was intended like the Great Pyramid to stand
through all eternity, but an eternity that was to
differ in no respect from the present. Later generations may perhaps wonder at it as the Romans
of the Dark Ages marvelled at the Colosseum,
explaining it away as the creation of wizards and
strange gods. Like that enormous building, it
may, too, become the quarry out of which the
houses of a future Renaissance will be constructed. There is, in its erection, no trace of
small economies, no sign of plaster being used to
eke out the brick and stone, the tiles and marbles.
It is built on no foundation of sand: on the contrary, the roots of it are dug far into the solid
rock beneath, while the sea façade stretches down
boldly toward the crouching but rebellious ocean,
thus doubling on that side its already cyclopean
stature. Here it ends in a vast asphalt terrace,
each corner of which is marked by the flourish
of an almost feudal barbican. Upon this monstrous hub the entire system of the town's summer life revolves. Bath chairs, cabs, funiculars,
tramways, shops, public gardens, promenades,
crescents, terraces, the sands, the sea even, flutter
round it as coloured ribbons whirl round an electric fan. In the winter, the prospect, while it
lacks such gaiety, gains a compensating air of
proud desolation, and of great forces temporarily
held in check, similar to the respect all men must
feel before some mighty machinery, mills or fur-
nace, at rest.

On the entrance side out of which flowers that
enchanting but preposterous porch, the Superb
Hotel surveys an open space, and confronts across

it the incarnadined countenance of the Gentlemen's Club, in the bow window of which an enormous telescope, resembling a huge piece of artillery, appears to be aiming at it, though in reality
trained on the sea.   In the middle of this perpetual conflict is a circular green-baize garden, a
no man's land, necklaced by a single string of
black cabs.   Even in December and January the
cabs still wait there, expectant of altogether
legendary visitors, while from the green-painted
cab-stand, the emerald clasp to the necklace,
issues a cheerful odour of mingled oats and beer,
food for horses and men.   The baize circle is
protected by iron railings, and by a hedge of
scraggy, transparent shrubs, while in the centre
of it, deposited in state, on this green cushion, lie
those twin symbols of our civilisation, the very
regalia of the Modern World, a Cannon and an
Anchor.   These two symbols govern the world by
turns, force and faith, War and Peace, and at
the time of which we are writing, it was the
Cannon rather than the Anchor which attracted
the attention of the curious.   Now, perhaps, the
Anchor is the curiosity, of more interest to the
passers-by.

The Cannon was Crimean, and at it, in those
far-away days peered curiously the children, on
whom in a few years its brood were to batten.
No sooner had these children, gazing at it so intently, swinging and clambering on the railings,
become grown men than they would be exported
as fodder for this senseless god, who was to have
his greatest temple in the grey wastes just across
the ocean that they can hear sighing, singing or
roaring below.   And they will die, as they will

think, in defence of that other ancient symbol,
the Anchor. Faith will drive them on. At present, however, these heads, as they look at the
Crimean Cannon, are full of romantic ideas,
encouraged by the empty wind of Tennyson's
poetry, which they have been taught to recite in
the schoolroom, poems in which are inculcated the
doctrines of cringing, war-mongering and general
stupidity. "Theirs not to reason why," indeed!
They pay little enough attention to the Anchor.
But this imposing Anchor, like other symbols, is
not quite what it seems. Appropriately enough it
was once the anchor of a celebrated smuggler,
patriot and believer in private enterprise; so that,
all the time, the Cannon and the Anchor were
really in league. One was no more deceptive than
the other.

CHAPTER X

TREATS

THE two friends did not in the least feel the oppression of their surroundings. Though all Newborough soon knew them by sight, they were during their first winter acquainted with no one in the town. But neither of them felt the deprivation. Indeed this period of halcyon quiet, far removed from any material worries, and without disturbance of any kind, was probably the happiest period of Miss Bramley's adult life. The practice of her singing gave her great pleasure, and about this time she learnt several new songs. It may have been symptomatic that these were the "Indian Love Lyrics" of Amy Woodford Finden and Laurence Hope. The waves of Edwardian exoticism were perhaps beginning to break over her, to demoralise her. Certainly, Miss Fansharpe would never have encouraged her to sing them. But though she felt, somehow, that she would never learn to interpret them with the ease and understanding with which she was able to render Frank Lambert's songs, she could not conceal from herself that there was something very moving about them . . . something weird, queer and oriental. She would love to go to the East, really she would, with all its "Jams," jewels and jungles.

Nor were the "Indian Love Lyrics" the only signs of a progressive metamorphosis in Miss

Bramley. The dwarf tree was sloughing its old shape, was growing and loosening to an alarming extent, now that the rules, which had governed its growth, grew relaxed. This change was due, partly to Miss Collier-Floodgaye's assumption of equality with her Companion, and partly to that new sense of worldly security which supported Miss Bramley. With Miss Fansharpe, the Companion, however much deceived by the hints and promises of that old lady, had never felt secure. She had been constantly aware that she lived on the edge of that periodically active volcano, Miss Fansharpe's temper. In fact, it had been a life of perpetual tight-rope walking—she realised that now. And only those who have walked on a tight-rope can ever know the ecstasy of walking on solid ground.

Accordingly, in this ecstasy, she was transformed. If not less religious, she had at any rate become more mundane, fonder of the pleasures of that life which she had hitherto been taught to regard as a "miserable span." Mildred, for one, began to detect a new note in her sister's letters, and confided in Harold that their tone had become less spiritual. She prayed that Teresa might not deteriorate—or, as she said, in her new voice, "deteaheahriate." One could "nevah" tell. Only the elect, the very elect, could remain unspoilt by prosperity. It was a test.

Even (and this was most unexpected), even Miss Bramley's Evangelical views began to soften . . . she rather liked a little colour now . . . and, by a judicious compromise, the old lady and her Companion could now go to the same church (St. Peter's), Miss Collier-Floodgaye sacrificing

her incense on condition that Miss Bramley
swallowed the anthem.

Really, they were very happy. Newborough
was rather cold in the winter, but fortunately
neither of them minded the cold. Miss Collier-
Floodgaye, old as she was, could face the most
bitter weather without ill effect. It must have
been the fogs in London, they were sure, which
had given the old lady her asthma (this affliction was always referred to as a personal belonging—"my asthma," her "satham," "my friend's
satham"). The best of it was, the Companion
would remark, there was never a day, scarcely,
when it was not possible to go out. That, they
argued (for neither of them had ever left England) was what was so splendid about the English
climate. Life was regular, consisting in a varied
monotony. If the afternoon was "fine," which
did not so much indicate blue sky as the actual
absence or aftermath of snow, sleet or rain, the
two ladies, very warmly clad and veiled, would
usually promenade slowly up and down the long
hotel terrace. The extent of this asphalt stretch
even whittled down Miss Collier-Floodgaye's
large frame, till she and her Companion dwindled
to two flies walking on a window pane. Up and
down they paced, with a slightly broken rhythm,
due to the old lady's stiff knee and consequent
use of a cane as lever. The terrace was very
broad: the wall at its border high enough to prevent them seeing the foreground of the ocean.
To keep this in view, they must expose themselves
to winds that swept down upon the edge, and
whistled round the corner barbicans. Standing
by the wall they would, of course, watch the grey

backs of the waves, in their whale-like tumblings
and splashings, clumsily colliding with cement
walls, and sending over them every few seconds
an angry spout of white foam to ascend a hundred feet in the air.   But usually they kept close
to the shelter of the towering hotel, and from it
could see nothing save an infinite expanse of grey
cloud and grey atmosphere, endless grey backs
jostling themselves into an impenetrable distance
of spray and vapour.   When they reached the
end of the terrace, looking toward the Castle that
rode its hill as a man rides a horse, they could
see the red-tiled roofs of the fishermen's cottages
sweeping down in ribbed patterns to the level of
the grey monsters below.   As they turned slowly
round, a salt wind would circle down on them like
a hawk, and tear their faces, even through their
thick veils, with unexpectedly ferocious beak.
Sometimes from the open sea would descend a
wind, strong enough to pummel the breath out of
them, and impede their movements, as though it
were trying to bind their limbs, even as they
walked, with thongs of ice.   Too cold to stay
out for long, one lady would remark to the other:
besides, it was beginning to get dark, already.
And they would then turn back into the cavernous
obscurity of the hotel.   Still, they supposed, the
sea air was—must be—very good for them.   So
refreshing, you know.   Then, too, their bedrooms
did not face the sea, because of the wind at night:
no, their rooms looked out on to the Cannon and
Anchor.   Much more homely and quiet.   Still,
you see, it was necessary for them to get out, in
order to have a little real sea air.

Very gloomy the hotel seemed as they walked

back into it. Soon, though, Miss Bramley's voice
could be heard cooing, trilling in and out, rustling
among the solid gold flowers, the leaves and
branches of the upper air. The drawing-room
was so high and dark that it could have swallowed
up a whole flight of such bird-like voices. Softly
sung, demoded songs would flutter round the
fountains of clear but meaningless notes which
were their accompaniment, till the whole effect
was one of a moonlit mid-Victorian aviary with
running fountains, ferns and palms, with the
pallid sheen of water dripping through the darkness, and a flash of exotic brightness from the
captive birds as they flew past. The singing rose
and fell, caressing with dragging feathers the un-
fathomable height of the room, fluttering and
struggling round in the twilight.

Now the singer would pass on to other, newer
songs, and would evoke a penny-bazaar-oriental-
ism. Under cover of the darkness, too, she could
safely attempt those little professional tricks and
grimaces of which she had observed the use at
ballad concerts, but which she had so far lacked
the courage to bring out in open daylight. The
effects were carried out with brio, but the voice
was wearing, perhaps, a trifle thin.

Miss Collier-Floodgaye loved these half-hours
of music, and it was a great source of joy to her
Companion to feel that her gifts were appreciated. The old lady would lie there, with her
feet upon a sofa, listening, silent and stiff as a
felled tree. As the room grew yet darker, the
singing became bolder and more pure: the birds
were transformed into nightingales, and cascades
of silver notes tumbled transparently down from

the dark branches in which they were cradled.
But now tea was brought in, and the last song
died away in a golden glow. The waiter turned
on every light, and each leaf of the richly orna-
mented frieze and cornice weltered in a stiff,
stifling glory.

The two friends did not often go out in the
morning, for Miss Collier-Floodgaye took great
pleasure in late rising—a habit which made the
Companion wonder if she had not at some time
been under the necessity of getting up early every
day. But, of course, they had their special
"treats"—and every now and then it would occur
to Miss Collier-Floodgaye that there was *something* about the morning air which was to be
sought in vain at all other hours. She was sure
it must be good for one. Then she would dress,
and soon they would set off, very slowly, for the
Winter Gardens.

This pleasure resort was inappropriately
named, for between October and May hardly
any one entered it. It was a large stretch of
cliff tortured into terrace, garden and thicket,
and breaking out toward its base into an eruption
of buildings. For a short time in the summer it
blazed with bands, flowers and people, until the
general effect from the sea was of a hillside entirely covered with moving, mingling confetti.
But now, during these short grey days and long
black nights, it was entirely given over to the
uneasy, shivering ghosts of the summer. It was
the dusty, discarded chrysalis of a butterfly—infinitely used-up and empty. About all places of
this kind, which close for the winter, there is an
indescribable air of desolation: indeed, the knowl-

edge that they will open again in the spring adds
to the sense of calamity, rather than detracts
from it.　This identical feeling of "closed for the
winter" will be experienced by a visitor new to the
streets and houses of Pompeii.　That town, too,
is an empty chrysalis, a summer resort hermeti-
cally sealed by a volcano for a winter that has
already lasted nineteen centuries.　The untidiness
of it presupposes that it will shortly be reopened.
The trivialities of that distant moment have not
been swept away: bread is still left about in the
ovens, wine still in the amphora in the public
bars; the plaster and stucco show their cheapness
more surely.　Only a touch of paint here and there
is needed.　But if we thought that Pompeii would
shortly be put to rights and peopled again, how
infinitely more dreary it would seem.

So it was at the Winter Gardens; except that
here the North added a quality of devastation all
its own, for in the winter the whole place was
given over to be sacked and raped by the elements.　Those bluff rivals, the Gods of Sea and
Wind, took it for their own from humanity, used
it as a neutral ground on which they could meet
in joust and tourney, as once the Kings of France
and England disputed on the Field of the Cloth
of Gold.　Here Æolus and Neptune wrestled all
the winter long, boisterously unexhausted.

All the gates but one were closed.　Over this
it was obvious that the two competing Gods,
realising that the townspeople had a right of way
through their tournament-ground during the summer, had reached a compromise with mankind;
for they had installed in the lodge as custodian
a being that belonged in equal proportion to sea,

air and earth, part fish, part bird, part human. This fierce old white-whiskered crustacean, with a long beak, and prominent eyes that were, however, veiled by age and rage, resided in a minute barnacle of a lodge which had been attached to the bare rock. Miss Bramley, who always dreaded this moment in an otherwise delightful morning, gently touched the glass slide through which glared the ferocious guardian, and proffered, as the price of two tickets, a tremulous shilling. Unmollified by the little woman's terror, the crustacean thrust out a hard-shelled claw, clutched the shilling, meanwhile grinding his mandibles with rage, and then swiftly assuming his bird personality, tapped the bit of silver eagerly with his beak. He was always suspicious of winter visitors (what did they want here in the *winter?*) and it was his opinion that their object was to pass off on to him false coin. This appeared to be good, though, so he quickly threw out two pink tickets at the ladies and whirled round the turnstile, which he controlled from the interior of his lodge, with a clacking sound that was an excellent imitation of the cry of a corncrake. Startled by this, the visitors were caught in his remorseless, iron whirlpool, and deposited, safe but flurried, on an enormous terrace. The crustacean, smiling and obviously congratulating himself on the success of his manœuvre, then relapsed into his warm shell.

The long stone raft where the old lady and her Companion were now walking, was castellated at its edge as the waves, upon which it appeared to be floating. Further on, under the shelter of the cliff, rose a huge group of buildings, theatre, con-

cert-hall, and café, while on the near side of it
lay a thinly arcaded row of shops, all closed for
the winter. Though the windows were unshut-
tered, the doors were clamped and bolted, and on
them had already formed little crusts of salt and
deposits of rust. The windows still displayed
open boxes of cigarettes, first spoiled by the sun,
and now left here to be nibbled by brown damp,
or glass jars full of sweets oozing metallic colours,
coalescing into dreadful liquid rainbows. The
florist's shop, full of empty but rattling glass vases
was, perhaps, most ghastly of all. The light-
transmitting, bulging shapes were at first altogether invisible until their vibration called attention to this or that transparent vacuous form
hovering in the air, in the same way that only the
movement of a translucent jelly fish, which has
assumed for its own protection the look of the
surrounding sea, betrays its vague form floating in
the ocean. And then behind these sinister
spectres, and, apparently as a tribute to them,
could be perceived crosses and wreaths of damp,
but still dusty, everlasting flowers. Next to the
florist was the wide window of the chief hair-
dresser in the town; here again the door only was
shuttered while imprisoned behind their glass
walls several coquettishly mildewed wax ladies
were coyly grimacing. One or two of these were
cut off prematurely, like the effigy of the Sov-
ereign on coin or postage-stamp, but others did
not forbid a glimpse of alluring rotundities, for
the full figures of the last century were still in
vogue. It seemed as though these ladies had been
the victims, several years previously, of that
strange fate so often predicted for children by

their nurses: they must, surely, have been re-
hearsing these pouts and dimples, when suddenly
the wind had changed, and they had remained
ever since caught fast in the arch posture of the
moment. Wax figures, perhaps because they are
moulded and set in the very breath of an instant,
age more rapidly, more obviously, than anything
in the world. It is as possible to put a date to
them as it is to a fashion plate. And it added to
the mad indecency of the spectacle, that these
abandoned females, by their style of hairdressing
and of such drapery as they possessed beside the
natural shelter of their tresses, had obviously been
thus disporting themselves in the window for several years. One of these figures, at the time of
transmutation, had evidently just been about to
start for a fancy dress ball; for she exposed a
head of white powdered hair, and with a grace-
fully curved little finger indicated the position of
a crescent-shaped black patch, placed there for
the further emphasis of a dimple. This delicious
gesture was wasted on empty air. It was dreadful
to think of the poor silly remaining there all the
winter, while the ogre-mouthed winds howled
round her, and the sea thrust out at her its
threatening white claws. But, here, at last was
her justification, for Miss Collier-Floodgaye was
delighted with her, so pretty, she thought the arrangement, and fanciful. Indeed, both ladies
paused, examining everything in the window,
curls, old-fashioned ringlets, "transformations"
and fringes. It is odd to note that, though they
hardly ever looked in a shop window in London,
here they could seldom resist cataloguing with
their eyes every object in every shop window they

passed. Nor did the fact that these shops were
closed for the winter at all deprive them of this
pleasure. As they walked slowly along, they
could see, through the arches of the colonnades,
the waves leaping at the walls, and could hear the
thud they made landing safely on the terrace. Now
the shops were nearly finished; there was only
the bookshop to come, full of novels with damp-
stained backs, and a few old papers, lying about,
and the gigantic show case of the photographer—
or, as he preferred to be called, a "Camera-
Portraitist." Out of this glass sheet, local beauties leered briskly into the gloom: for these were
the days of the "Odol Smile" and mouths gleamed
white and curving as the new moon. So great was
the dental enthusiasm of the public, that had some
fortunate belle been endowed with a double row
of teeth, she would have been admired propor-
tionately. No such originality, however, was here
displayed, but still every tooth could be counted
by enthusiastic lovers of beauty. Usually the
photographs had a plain sepia background, but
in others still survived those enchanting two-
dimensional properties of the photographic studio,
oak-tree and rustic bench, caverns, torrents,
turrets, garden vases, bits of Venice, snow sledges
or Gothic ruins, while one lady even went so far
as to hold a book on her lap. Rather affected,
Miss Bramley thought, and tried to read the title.
To Miss Collier-Floodgaye these photographs
were of particular interest, for she was a great ad-
mirer of youth and beauty. They moved on again.
Now they passed the bar, the huge panels of its
many doors filled in with small squares of coloured glass which served both to obscure some-

what, from without, the interior scene of riotous
jollity, and, at the same time, to enhance, from
within, the brightness of a prospect which to those
gathered there, was already, on its own, assuming
an increasingly vivid and lively tint.   From this
vast, now empty, gilded saloon was still wafted
an odour of whisky, port and bad cigars, but instead of the roguish gold-toothed laughter of bar-
maids, there only issued forth in these winter
months the sound of the salt-lipped winds rattling
eager fingers among the empty bottles that still
littered the shelves.

Miss Collier-Floodgaye and Miss Bramley
moved on to the empty terrace, toward the band-
stand, which now harboured no music save that
of Æolus, trumpeting his victorious calls, perpetually blaring out till every trembling piece of
iron and wood danced to his triumph.   Above, as
far as the eye could see, stretched path and terrace.   On slanting surfaces of green grass could
be seen huge stars, ovals or circles of brown earth,
which seemed the freshly-dug, fantastic graves of
the strange monsters that must have inherited this
extraordinary, this dead world, but were, in reality, merely the beds destined for next year's
flowers.   In the hollows of the cliff-sides were
bosquets, now bare of leaves, through which the
Wind God wildly hunted a fallen twig, leaf, or
torn envelope.   The trees were thin, frightened;
they shrank back before so much violence.   A
lone tower, near by, lifted up its head three
storeys into the grey air.   This furnished a possible clue to the whole scene; otherwise the wide-
spread desolation, this parade of life brought suddenly to a standstill, was inexplicable.   This

tower, then, must have been the haunt of a wise, white-bearded astronomer, who, climbing up, high above this pleasure city, one evening—one evening when all the air breathed flowers, when the blossoms on the ground died away in the darkness only to come trembling out again with a new fervour in the deep blue pastures above—was appalled to read by the arrangement of them, the impendence over this strange terraced and green-sheltered town of an unavoidable doom. He had been able to warn the people in time for them to evade this disaster, but in the haste of their flight, they had only just had a moment in which to bolt their shop doors, and then to scuttle away as fast as they could. Only the two little figures below had remained, had survived. And even these were now hurrying off as fast as the limp of the elder one would allow them. But they had enjoyed their walk very much. So interesting, it had been, and gave one an idea what Newborough must be like in the summer.

.   .   .   .

On other, rarer, mornings—for this was a test by which the old lady could prove to herself how well she was feeling—she would pay a visit to the market, or to the harbour, at this season the only centres of activity in the town. The harbour cried a deep-toned masculine to the market's shrill but emphatic feminine. To compare them would be to measure a portrait of an Admiral by Holbein against one of Rubens' profuse females.

If the quays had not been so difficult to walk on, Miss Collier-Floodgaye would have taken a promenade there much more often, for both she and Miss Bramley loved the harbour and its busi-

ness. But the long jetties were unevenly paved,
slippery with fishy remnants, scaly as a whale's
back: further they were lumbered with boxes of
salt for herring-curing, barrels of sail-coloured
kippers, and mounds of white-stomached fish,
over which haggled—and sometimes swore—old
women, whose heads were enveloped in grey
woollen shawls, whose hands were like claws, from
their constant handling and cutting-open of fish.
As they ripped apart their silvery victims, throw-
ing on one side their entrails, a host of sea-gulls
would descend on them, fighting and uttering their
ferocious cries. The wind, too, had the cruel
beak of a gull (cruellest of all bird-masks) and
tore savagely at the tarpaulin faces of the fish-
wives, banged and buffeted the sails and rigging
of the ships at the quayside. The air was pungent
with salt, tar, sea-weed, kippers and coarse tobacco. The fishermen and sailors, in their blue
jerseys, many of them with rough red beards and
a gold ear-ring, lurched jauntily along the piers,
or lingered nonchalantly at the points where a
jetty met foreshore. Unlike the prosperous
tradesmen on the cliffs above, these men never
deigned to notice strangers. They called to each
other, and talked among themselves: but they
had seen so many things in their voyages, that
had a thousand howdahed elephants and a volcano
sprung up at the harbour side, they would not
have allowed themselves to indulge a landsman's
curiosity. Thus Miss Collier-Floodgaye and Miss
Bramley escaped their attention altogether. The
deep voices of the men barked out amid hammering and clanging, the whole merging into a din
that was the equivalent in sound of the harsh

odour of the air, while even the albatross wings of
the waves, as they struggled over the walls, beating at them with their white feathers, could not
for long muffle this uproar.

The market, though situate in another universe
of sight and sound from the harbour, was not
far from it in actual space. It was possible for
the old lady, even though she was lame, to visit
both in the same morning. But it was a pity to
cram into one day all the pleasures of life: besides, it was better to visit each of these places at
an early hour, when the scenes were more typical.
The market was open every day, but Wednesday
was the real market day, the best day on which
to go.

The market hall was a handsome stone building with a high glass roof, that multiplied every
sound beneath it. Here rusticity, as opposed to
the cosmopolitanism of the sailors, ran riot.
Under the hard light, which fell through the roof
as through a slab of ice, a stranger would be
speedily detected, and gimletted through and
through by the keen steel eyes of the countryside.

The stalls were arranged in four or five rows,
running back to back down the length of this
rectangular building. And hither, once every
week, came the country women, from distant
moor, hill or dale. To reach in good time this
stone temple it was necessary for them to leave
their farmsteads at four or five o'clock on a bleak,
black morning, jogging along the frozen ruts of
the road in carts that, like cornucopia, overflowed
with the stored autumn riches of the countryside.
For many a dark mile they jolted on, until the
grey light began to creep up, and, leaden though

it was, sufficed to kindle the inflammable red lanterns of hip and haw, and a hundred other berries
that now glowed warmly among the cobweb-
tangled and rimy twigs of hedge and thicket. The
flat lines of stone walls alternated with these
hedges, and repeated the rhythm given out by the
flat-topped hills, which cut off an interminable
perspective of grey thawing. But before this
greyness of the North, which sheds a light that
never favours unduly even the most sparkling object, but distributes impartially its realistic effects
over things dull and brilliant, had done justice to
everything it touched, the carts were already being unpiled outside the market. All this accumulated wealth was now poured into one vast
receptacle, and there ensued an ordered profusion
infinitely more impressive than the tumbled riches
of the carts. There were countless pyramids of
russet apples, polished till their shining red con-
vexities reflected, though distorting these expressionless discs in a thousand different ways, the
similar high coloured circles that formed the faces
of the country women. The apples filled the air
with a sweet, anæsthetic odour that mingled with
the stale, butterfly suggestion of cabbage leaves,
the warm sleepy smell of onions, and the scent
of damp mould, immediately calling up in the
mind the rotund tunes chased in vain by brass
bands at a flower show. But added to these ex-
halations were others strange to such functions.
There was the Southern, sharp smell of tanger-
ines, imported here from who knows what Southern palm-crested coast, and the woodland freshness of nuts, which lay in shallow baskets, in all
their primitive simplicity of shielding green

leaves. There were whole hillocks of pears that
repeated in their shape the pattern of an Indian
shawl, or the map of South America, bands of
earthy potatoes, wide baskets of onions gleaming
in purple and gold, and piles of severed cauli-
flower-heads peeping piteously out of their high
green collars. Near by, cream, butter and cheeses
of many sorts, exposed their various pearly or
silken surfaces, and there were baskets full of
the neat, prim faces of eggs. Honeycombs, in
which the fabulous industry of the worker-bees
had stored, not only the distilled scent of those
vast tracts of heather that sweep away from the
town, but also every memory they possessed of
summer days, were here for sale. Then there
were flowers, baskets of late camphor-scented
chrysanthemums that resembled huge spiders, or
early, ill-advised spring-blossoms, hyacinths like
blue or pink flames, or daffodils with their nodding canary heads pressed close together. Bulbs
could also be purchased, or flowers already budding, and brought here in their native mould.
Shallow baskets, lying on the ground, were full
of pink or red double daisies, nestling on tufts
of green, and still rooted in the earth from which
they had grown, so that they resembled a fragment torn out of the foreground of a picture by
Botticelli. Here surely, on these geometrical,
curling leaves and button-like flowers, the growth
of which permits the bare earth to show between,
a green though smiling beauty should have
pressed down a pallid, rhythmic foot. At one
stall, snowdrops sourly tinkled their ice-veined
sledgebells, while a few very domesticated primula
plants were on the point of donning their print

dresses for the spring. To add to this prospect of legendary plants, there were fowls alive and dead. Cocks and hens (as distinctively Chinese or Japanese as peacocks, that carry on their heads the proud, emerald diadem of their Shah, are Persian) imparted a fantastic oriental grace to this English solidity, gilding the air with the rococo flames of the combs. There were top-heavy, knock-kneed ducks and verdigris-beaked turkeys, most of them dead, and hanging from rails, with disembowelled hares, their noses fast in a child's tin pail. The rabbits, though, were alive hunching their fluffy arcs in wooden hutches, pressing back their furry ears, casting piteous looks from eyes placed in their profiles according to the conventions of Egyptian art. The scene had that quality of exuberant abundance, that blend of trailing flowers into dripping blood, that merging of feathery beauty into red, mangled flesh, that is only to be found in Flemish or Dutch still lives, in, for example, one of those enormous canvases by Snyders, formerly the adornment of so many dining-rooms in English country houses. Above this miraculous profusion darted, like shrill birds, the beaked voices of the country women, their bodies swaddled in layer after layer of winter clothing, till they looked ungainly as Esquimaux, waddling to show something to a customer, while all the time their intense greed for money was masked by faces red and smooth as those of dolls.

Besides these perishable treasures that have been described, there were more permanent objects for sale at counters round the walls of the market, steel knives and babies' rattles, china dishes and terra-cotta pots. The ladies would buy

artificial flowers because they looked so natural, for here it was possible for Miss Collier-Floodgaye and Miss Bramley to buy objects they did not in the least require, or really wish for, at half the price which they would have to pay elsewhere for objects they actually needed. Unable to resist such a feminine bargain, our two ladies would return to the hotel—being compelled, incidentally, to take an expensive cab on the way owing to the weight of their parcels—laden with a truly marvellous miscellany of purchases, all of which would shortly, owing to their uselessness, descend, like manna, in a grateful shower upon Elisa. To her they brought inestimable solace, though she never really had time to look at them.

After one of these infrequent morning excursions, Miss Collier-Floodgaye would rest all the afternoon, while Miss Bramley would practise her new songs below in the drawing-room. But these excitements were not the only ones. On certain afternoons, instead of "taking a turn" on the terrace they would walk through the streets, at this time of year often wrapped all day long in a plausible twilight. From time to time they would stop to gaze at some effort in window-dressing, some winter panorama, in which a cardboard Father Christmas, in a red dressing-gown with a white beard and his arms full of crackers, perspired lamentably over a gas-lit, mica snow-field. Newborough shops were so up-to-date, Miss Collier-Floodgaye thought. It was really wonderful how they *"got"* all the latest ideas. The two ladies moved slowly on through streets where countless pairs of eyes watched them,

where countless tongues prepared a report. Perhaps they would finish their small promenade by circling round one of the crescents. Within a few seconds the news of their approach would spread, as though by magic. Pale and, until now, listless forms would be rapidly propped up and cushioned like idols in cotton wool, to survey this interesting—no, more than interesting, historic—perambulation. The excitement seethed and foamed through the upper rooms. It was infectious and could penetrate any wall, sweep from room to room, from window to window, like the Black Death. Breaking out mildly in one upper chamber, that faced South, this plague could send its germs right through the walls of the next house, which was empty, and attack an old lady lying in bed two doors away. In a moment, frail and infirm as she was, this fresh victim would be at the window, and the virulent epidemic would have imparted its infection to old Miss Waddington, at the end of the Crescent. At last, she beheld them. . . . Goodness Gracious, so that was the woman! And Ella had said they were "quite ordinary." One simply couldn't trust the girl, that was what it amounted to. Could she never get anything right? So Louise Shrubfield had been right all the time. She had said, over and over again, in that affected way of hers, a *limp* and a malacca cane . . . something more than just *queer*, it seemed to Miss Waddington.

All round the Crescent, pale, old eyes sparkled with a delicious fire; while cheeks, hot as those of feverish children, were pressed close to the transparent ice of the window-panes. Queer . . . very queer, and not the sort of people, evidently,

upon whom one could call. A limp, you see. Besides, if one called—that is, if one was well enough to call—one would know everything, and then there would be no excitement. It would be as though a trout fisher were to catch the trout in the middle of tickling it. It would never do. Better, perhaps, wait to see what Miss Waddington decided.

Meanwhile the two friends were walking unconcernedly below. Miss Collier-Floodgaye noticed nothing unusual about the upper windows; while Miss Bramley, if for a moment she detected a gleaming eye, would preen herself, smooth out her little flounces, frills and lace edgings, and imagine a kind voice, in a fire-lit room saying "There goes that *attractive* niece of dear old Miss Titherley-Bramley. It's easy to see that *she's* well-bred. And such a lovely voice, she has, so they say . . ."

.   .   .   .

But, best of all treats, was that one heralded by Miss Collier-Floodgaye's announcement, early in the morning, that—what she needed was a "breath of fresh air" or "a blow"—though one might have imagined that the icy stiletto of the winter wind, stabbing through every crack, crevice and keyhole, would have sufficed to give her the necessary fillip. They would lunch rather early, at 12.45, and at about 2 would set out in a closed cab drawn by two horses, and drive up on to the moors that begin about five miles away from Newborough, and stretch away to Flitpool, and beyond Flitpool toward the ultimate icebergs of Thrule. When the two ladies had driven some ten miles, they would fade slowly into this strange

prospect, of undulating slopes and low table-
lands—so flat-topped and wide-based that it
seemed as though they were mountains, the top
of which had been sliced off with a knife, perhaps
because their Creator wished for a section, in
order to test His handiwork—which repeated
themselves for ever into swathing after swathing
of grey mist. In spite of the uncertain and hazy
distances into which this emptied itself, it was
nevertheless one of enormous width and remote
possibilities. However misty, the very mist, and
the lines that could just be distinguished through
it, proclaimed wide areas. The monotony of its
colour, which was in the winter an invariable
black alternating with brown, endowed this landscape with a rhythm elsewhere to be sought in
vain. In its reserve and apparent coldness, in its
occasional, well-hidden flashes of genius (as when
a green oasis of woods and bubbling streams is
wedged in a gulf between two of these angular
hills) and in the distant voice of the lonely grey
sea, leaping at high, brown cliffs, this prospect
at once declared itself much more truly the heart
of England than are the lush lanes of Devonshire,
or the dreary imitation deserts of the downs. The
wavering but flat lines were unbroken, save for
the glacial stones of vast dimensions, which
crouched like petrified, extinct monsters in the
mists, or where they were fractured by a hill, so
sudden in its rise that it seemed to have been
scooped out of an adjacent hollow with a spoon,
for convex and concave precisely corresponded.
Again there might be a group of three or four
burial mounds in the foreground, to repeat the
same rhythm in a minor key. In shape they

echoed exactly the flat-topped tables, and seemed in no whit more artificial. If these were the tombs of kings, then yonder hills must be the tomb of a God. These melancholy, monochromatic wastes by the sea were, indeed, studded with many such burial mounds—tombs of early kings, kings of unknown race—so that, at one time, they must have harboured a population much more numerous than that which they sheltered at present. Who they were, these early leaders, has never been discovered. Once in a while a local antiquary would disinter a huge gold necklace, or even a high crown of gold. The moors were still littered with their sharp flint implements. But these personal belongings and weapons helped rather to deepen, than to solve, the mystery. Gold crowns and delicate jewellery do not tally with such savage and inefficient instruments of death. For what dim and decaying race, for what lurking and now extinct animals, had these weapons been devised? Some enemy must, surely, have been skulking in these wide areas of land, in which comparative invisibility is so easy. It was impossible to answer these questions. No doubt the kings had come from over the ocean, across that pathway, which was so perilous to this land. They lay at rest now, in their enduring mounds, and once each year the earth that covers them would blaze out in the kingly mourning colour. Countless royal palls of this description have they witnessed, these deep-socketed eyes over which project such jutting ridges of bone. Once every year the entire earth, from sea to horizon, would be washed away beneath a flood of purple. Then, for a few weeks,

the landscape was transformed, all the values of mound and tableland altered out of recognition. But now it was again brown and bare, and the only sounds that bit into the intense quiet, which lurked just under the roaring wind, were the dead-world cries, such music as will survive after mankind has perished, of the sea-gulls as they swerved in on the wind. Few houses could be seen, and from these issued the aromatic smell of burning peat, while above them a blue ribbon of smoke was being whirled and knotted, and then dispersed into the air. The square grey houses, which broke this monotony so seldom, were blind and dumb: not an echo rose from them. And, as a final touch to this stretch of desolation, there stood a few black, leafless trees, frozen into impossible attitudes by the wind from the sea; trees that stretched their arms toward the grey sky and brown land, while the weight of their bodies was thrown forward, toward them, as if in flight. It seemed as though these grotesque, primeval shapes had once been giants, giants racing in terror from the on-coming rush of the ocean, which could still be seen behind them, dashing and hurling itself at the rocks; but the fury of the salt wind had been too much even for their strength, and they had been petrified into these monstrosities, still in the very action of their terror-stricken flight, but now able only to creak and groan like ghosts upon an empty wind.

Into this prospect the figure of Miss Collier-Floodgaye fitted with a singular consistency; she showed in stature, dress, countenance, the same gaunt and rugged characteristics. Out of some

such background as this, she must surely have
first emerged. But now she and her Companion
must turn back; they must not walk too far from
the cab, for fear of being lost. One might easily
lose one's way, they thought. Newborough was
out of sight, and there was only to be seen this
vast expanse of grey and brown, and on the other
side the great whalebacks of the jostling waves,
from here turned by the magic distance into a
cloud of grey-backed birds that fluffed and un-
furled their wings with a flash of whiteness. And
if the way was lost, one could shout for ever
without any answer being borne back, except the
scratching rustle of wind through dead heather.
So they drove on toward the warm and glassy
town, its lights already sprinkling the sea-shore
for miles round with a dusting of stars. It was
dark by the time they entered the town, and the
interiors of the outlying houses stood out brightly,
fern in foreground, piano and figure behind.
They passed the forge, diabolically flaming, and
filled with hammering black figures. Now they
were in the shopping streets, full of people. And
here they were at the hotel, already! Really it
took no time, getting back. But what a delightful
afternoon! The old lady declared she felt quite
a different person.

But the hotel looked dark and sombre. In a
few minutes, though, tea would be ready, and
after that Miss Bramley would sing once more.
Or perhaps both ladies would smoke a cigarette;
for Miss Bramley—another symptom—had lately
adopted this habit, though it would have made
Miss Fansharpe's bones rattle like castanets in
her grave, had she known. But then many ladies
at the Court smoke now, and one must realise

that Queen Victoria's reign was over. Miss
Collier-Floodgaye, indeed, had smoked for several
years; a cigarette perhaps being for her too the
symbol of deliverance from some unknown sub-
jugation. In any case, it suited her large, rather
masculine frame and her temperament, which
though nervous, was not fussy.

Then, quite soon, the two ladies must dress
for dinner. Dinner was at 7.30, and a rather
formal affair, alone in an enormous dining-room,
partitioned-off by screens, over which the winter
winds played a continual game of hide-and-seek.
There were several other tables, all laid as if a
host of visitors were expected, for, even thus
divided, the room was vast. Each table had a
lamp, with a red, railway-carriage shade on it,
which cast a hectic glow upon the faces of our
two heroines, and made their shawls and scarves
look even warmer than they were. The meal was
conducted to the accompaniment of a long menu
in French, which translated itself into the most
faded, woebegone English dishes. A little wine;
for wine, Dr. MacRacket (he had now, by means
of Miss Waddington's entente with the hall-
porter's wife over the red comforter, been installed
as Miss Collier-Floodgaye's medical adviser) had
assured them, acted as "a tonic on the system, but
only if taken in moderation;" but no coffee, of
course, for coffee keeps one awake. This nega-
tion, absence of coffee, brought dinner to a conclusion, and the ritual end of the performance
was always the same. Miss Collier-Floodgaye
would enquire, "Have we done?" and to this Miss
Bramley would intone back, "Shall we come?"
The two ladies would then rise from the table,
and go up to the empty drawing-room, where they

would smoke another cigarette, Miss Collier-Floodgaye would indulge in a solitary game of patience ("Miss Milligan" was the best, she thought) or play double-patience—or even "picquet," with her Companion. Miss Collier-Floodgaye loved cards. She wished she could play bridge. It must be such an exciting game. King Edward, they said, revelled in it. She wondered whether Queen Alexandra played or not? There was no knowing. She was told that quite a number of bridge-parties took place in the town (to whom, Miss Bramley wondered, had she been talking now? So infra dig.). Quite a lot. Even the wives of certain clergymen played, so they said. Miss Bramley was not sure that this was right: ought clergymen's wives to be quite so worldly? But Miss Collier-Floodgaye saw no harm in it, not nowadays. Things used to be different, of course.

After a game or two the ladies would mount up in the lift to their rooms on the first floor. Elisa the German housemaid came to see if they wanted anything. At this time of night she was usually in a better mood. Yes, she had filled their hot-water bottles; as hot as they could be: there had been a wreck just round the corner of Jaspar Bay, the lifeboat had put out but had been forced to come in again, and the washing would be back on Friday evening without fail.

As Miss Bramley got into bed, she thought what a nice day it had been. Cecilia was inconsiderate in some ways, but she was really fond of her. Somehow everything seemed more cheerful now than at Llandriftlog. In fact Miss Bramley was happy.

CHAPTER XI

"We, too, have spun our Sunday round
Of Church and Beef, and, after-sleep
In houses where obtrudes no sound
But breathing, regular and deep,
Till Sabbath sentiment, well fed,
Demands a visit to the dead."

MISS COLLIER-FLOODGAYE and Miss Bramley were delighted to be back in Newborough. They felt tired, *"run down,"* you know —after their summer in London. Then they had moved to Folkestone for August and September, but the change had done them little good. The place wasn't bracing, in the way that Newborough was bracing, and it had been so crowded and noisy, full of common *trippers*. They supposed all seaside towns were like that in the season. What a pity it was that such nice places should be spoilt.

But the winter at Newborough was very different, and Miss Bramley was sure that the quiet helped to rest Cecilia's mind. One must not forget that Cecilia was an old lady, and ought not to see too many people at her age. Her vagueness had grown to an alarming extent. All the same, tired or not tired, the moment Miss Bramley turned her back, the old lady would get into conversation with strangers, *total* strangers. Really if Miss Bramley had not been there herself to

see it, she would never have believed it possible—
such extraordinary people—and telling them
everything . . . money again, too. All Miss
Bramley hoped, was that the old lady would not
meet bad companions at Newborough. But how
could she, as they knew no one? And fancy
talking to people like that, to hearing the
"Indian Love Lyrics!"

At any rate, the old lady pretended to be
pleased at being back. They were thankful to
find themselves in their own room again. The
servants were so civil and accommodating, and
gave the two ladies quite a welcome. Miss Bramley had grown fond of Elisa (of course she was
a German and many people did not like Germans)
but she did her work well (it was wonderful how
the Germans worked, she had been told. That,
they said, was why they had shot ahead so
rapidly) and was quick, and didn't answer back.
Only on Sundays was she at all disobliging—put
out by her walk in the Cemetery, no doubt.

For every Sunday, in the winter, the Slave of
the Alarum Clock was given an afternoon off. If
the afternoon was fine—and in the North it must
be admitted that autumnal Sunday afternoons
have habit of cold blueness—she would walk in
the Cemetery. For this half-religious, half-
mundane joy, Elisa wore a special heliotrope-
coloured plush dress, with a high collar, which
she had brought with her from her native land,
twenty years before, and a large black hat. She
also carried a parasol, which, since she only used
it at the most once a week, she had never been
able to break in, never quite had time to tame,
and consequently carried when she walked, at a

great distance from herself, as though it were a
dangerous wild animal being led along at arm's
length on a chain. Her features, hair and complexion, all were arranged in a special Sunday
perspective, so that, as by a sundial, one could
by looking at them, even if waking out of sleep,
tell the exact hour of the exact afternoon. Unfortunately this ceremonial visit to the Dead had
the same effect upon Elisa that Sunday church-
going produces upon old ladies. The emotion
roused in her by the beauty of the scene, and
that state of eventual bliss for which the scene
stood sponsor, exacerbated her temper, which was
as yet but mortal. Hot-water-bottles that night
would be cold as ice, beds the next morning would
be dexterously given a semi-apple pie quality—
just not bad enough for visitors to be unable to
complain to the director—and rattling and banging would resound through room and corridor.

The scene in the Cemetery on a fine afternoon
afforded Elisa great pleasure. It was so pretty
and animated, full of nurses of the well-to-do, who
sauntered piously along, pushing perambulators,
and exchanging with one another the latest scandals. Then there were poorer families, the mother
on the left, the father on the right, and a chain
of children between them, holding hands. These
parties were more silent. But all of them were in
their best clothes. The men wore bowler hats,
and had given their moustaches an additional
heavenward trend for the Sabbath.

Beautifully kept it was, too, with a magnificent
flourish of chrysanthemums and china asters.
The geraniums were over now, the gardener said;
but all the same, with falling golden leaves, and

weeping willows still dripping their seaweed-like tresses over white marble angels, the place was at its best. It was touching to see how every Sunday, week after week, relatives would visit this or that grave to place a wreath on it. One woman, the Sexton confided to Elisa, had been up here every Sunday for thirty-three years, always with a nice bit of fern, a marguerite daisy, or a geranium. Some of the tombs were beautiful: vases and broken columns, weeping angels, Gothic lettering with a border of ivy in carved stone, vases, crosses and obelisks in Aberdeen granite—which the Sexton said, when one took everything together, one thing with another, probably made a better show for the money laid out than anything else—pretty colour, a beautiful polish (real finish that one couldn't mistake) and would last for ever. Real granite it was. In fact he often said to his wife, "Maria," he said, "if I should go first, nothing elaborate. Just a simple bit of Aberdeen," so that you could see that he meant it.

This place brought Elisa more closely into touch with the English people than anything else in the town. They were a difficult race to understand; but they had the same feeling for a cemetery that the Germans have—that one could say for them . . . the actual funerals might be better in Germany . . . better arranged, more orderly . . . but the cemeteries here were beautiful. This reminded her almost of the one at Potsdam. . . .

A few weeks before the return of Miss Collier-Floodgaye and her Companion to Newborough, Elisa had been walking, alone as usual, in the Cemetery. She had just paused to note the detail

of a rather pretty grave when such a nice woman came up and spoke to her, commenting on the tidiness of the tomb. It appeared that Miss Thompson (for such was the stranger's name) was parlourmaid to an old Miss Waddington, who lived in Ghoolingham Crescent. Elisa was much flattered; for though rigid in etiquette, and not, as a rule, caring to speak to any one without an introduction, she could see at once that Miss Thompson was a nice, respectable woman; and then, usually, those in "private service," those with old ladies like this Miss Waddington, were so stuck-up, gave themselves such airs, would not speak to hotel servants, despised them all. Though she had lived here many years now, Elisa had no friends in the town, except the Sexton, and him she knew merely in his professional capacity, as, for example, an amateur of Egyptian sculpture, who attends regularly the lectures of a celebrated Professor of Egyptology, is, perhaps, acquainted with that luminary. The relationship was merely one of master and pupil. It was a change to be taken a little notice of, Elisa reflected. Besides, Miss Thompson knew all about her, had seen her in the Cemetery for years. She even asked the hotel servant to tea one day. They would have shrimps, for a treat, she said, and Elisa must tell her all about Germany. Was the hotel full now, she asked? Who was staying in it? Was the funny old lady who had been there last year—with a Companion—coming back again? Oh! she was, was she, in another month's time? And then Miss Thompson had to go back to get tea ready. For her mistress was expecting a friend to tea, she said, a Mrs. Shrubfield.

"Rummy thing, that," said the Sexton to Elisa. "I've known Miss Thompson for years, and never known her to take a fancy to any one like that before. Stuck up, as a rule," he said, "haughty like." Elisa was still more impressed and flattered.

.   .   .   .

Elisa was pleased to see the two ladies. It was a Tuesday, and her Sunday evening temper had spun its course: she was able to sling a pallid smile of welcome across her features. Indeed, the return of Miss Collier-Floodgaye and Miss Bramley to Newborough was (though these ladies were not aware of it) an important event in the life of the town. The summer armistice was at an end. Mrs. Shrubfield had marched in triumph back to Newborough and, even now, she and Miss Waddington were perfecting their plans for a new offensive. Everything augured well—the battalions, in their rooms of Southern aspect, refreshed by rest, plentiful rations, and constant cups of hot tea, were enthusiastic and ready to rush on. As we have seen, contact with the enemy had already been established by Miss Waddington's scout. Further, it was rumoured in the town—though this may have been only an hallucination born of excitement—that the invisible Lady Tidmarshe had taken on human form for a while again, and had been seen, hovering, like the Angel of Mons, at the head of the troops, spurring them on to victory; that she had volunteered to lend the prestige of her precedence to the two Marshals, and to aid them with advice, that was the fruit of an experience, which, though now superannuated, had in its time been consid-

erable. Probably all these rumours were unfounded. Even the two Misses Finnis could not
be certain. Lady Tidmarshe did not mention
the matter to them, and they hardly liked to ask.
Sir Timóthy seemed more nervous than usual,
and Miss Tidmarshe could be heard practising in
her bedroom a new march of Sousa's on the banjo.

In any case, if such supernatural aid had been
afforded them, the two leaders made no confession
of it. Instead, they perfected a plan, the very
simplicity of which was to take one's breath away,
and prove more surely than anything else the
genius which made them worthy of the great trust
reposed in them. For some weeks both Mrs.
Shrubfield and Miss Waddington had assiduously
flattered and fawned upon Mrs. Haddocriss, wife
of Archdeacon Haddocriss; and, in connection
with rumours cited above, it may not have been
entirely without significance that during the same
period a footman in the Tidmarshe livery was
most certainly observed leaving a bunch of blue,
mildewed grapes—a bunch that appeared to have
made its escape from the fruit department and
to have passed several happy nights at the green-
grocer's, and, through a pardonable error, become
entangled at last among the vegetables, spending
joyous hours of play with cabbage and cauliflower.
This Message from Beyond the Barrier was
cradled in a green wicker basket.

Mrs. Haddocriss was a grim lady, with a long
backbone, and long teeth that would never quite
meet in the middle, but upon every separate one
of which was written a Scottish grit and determination. Her eye was cold, blue and charitable.
In all the town her chief aversion was to Mrs.

Floodgay, the wife of a cleric who rivalled her husband in influence. Now it suited Miss Waddington and Mrs Shrubfield—indeed it was necessary to them—that Mrs. Haddocriss and Mrs. Floodgay should be friends. With Mrs. Floodgay the two leaders had anticipated—and in fact had met with—no resistance to their plan, for they had always regarded her as their spy, their scout, their creature. But upon Mrs. Haddocriss they had been forced to lavish infinite time and care, tact and patience before they could cajole her into the requisite mood of amiability. Now, however, everything had been satisfactorily arranged, and the delicate plant of such a friendship began to expand and sprout its shrill green growth in the warm, fire-lit room of Miss Waddington.

Mrs. Haddocriss had called upon Miss Collier-Floodgaye just before that lady had left for London at the end of the spring. It had been part of her duty to do so, as Miss Collier-Floodgaye and Miss Bramley were regular attendants at her husband's church. An introduction to the old lady by Mrs. Haddocriss could scarcely, then, be regarded even by the most exacting critic, as an infringement of the rules of sport or warfare. The two Marshals were determined, therefore, that when a suitable occasion presented itself, Mrs. Haddocriss should introduce Mrs. Floodgay to Miss Collier-Floodgaye, the basis of this introduction being the similarity of their names, the omission of the "e." Once this presentation had been effected, the two ladies could dispense with the services of the grim and troublesome Mrs. Haddocriss, for they had little doubt but that Mrs. Floodgay would soon gain the confidence

of Miss Collier-Floodgaye. The latter was, they had heard, of a more talkative disposition than one would have expected, and Mrs. Floodgay was a "dear, insinuating little person." Thus, through their advance guard, they would be able in the most natural manner to meet Miss Collier-Floodgaye whenever it might be convenient for them to do so; and, in the meantime, the safety of their lines of communication would be guaranteed. They would be in receipt of the latest intelligence during all the winter, without the least danger of hitch or leakage.

Everything, of course, depended on the trustworthiness and loyalty to their cause of Mrs. Floodgay. But insubordination on the part of their agent had never even occurred to them as a possibility; while it was incredible that such a willing slave could wish to foster ambitions of her own.

The only question, therefore, that remained to be decided was, which moment to choose for the introduction. Mrs. Haddocriss had promised to do her share. After church, on Sunday, was perhaps the most favourable opportunity.

CHAPTER XII

NORTHERN CARNIVAL

THE monotony of winter life at the Hotel was not unbroken. Occasionally there would be a lapse into startling gaiety, a hunt ball, a hospital ball, a ball, even, in Aid of the Life-Boat. During their first winter at the Superb, Miss Collier-Floodgaye and Miss Bramley had taken no part in such subscriptive pleasures. But now the elder lady began to complain that her life here was dull, and also that the sound of these festivities wafted up to her room, kept her awake at night, so that she might just as well be sitting up. Miss Bramley thought it wiser to let her watch the scene. It was better to give way, or she might wish to spend the next winter in London, and begin her promiscuous conversations all over again. With Miss Bramley beside her at these balls, she could not get into much mischief.

What imparted an interest to these affairs was the participation in them of the "County." (It was, perhaps, her gradual apprehension of this fact which prompted Miss Collier-Floodgaye's desire to be present at them.) The county, with its three "Ridings," was the largest and richest in Great Britain, and still maintained a social life—infinitely more impenetrable than that in London—of its own—a social life that suggested the seventeenth century, but the seventeenth

century suffering from arrested mental development, elephantiasis and consumption, overgrown
yet undeveloped, hectic yet weakly. Newborough
was usually ignored by the County, which preferred to remain blue-nosed and frost-bitten in
its country houses, or immured in the grey,
cloistral recesses of the bleak northern capital.
But a charity fund of any kind offered a chance
to assert its social prestige, and accordingly it
would be gracious, and sweep down in hordes on
the Hotel. Otherwise it only consented to recognise Newborough during the annual cricket
festival, when it would descend, haughty beneath
panama hats and fringed parasols.

For one of these dances, the Hotel would suddenly, and for one night, be full of County
families. Doors would slam continuously, and
the vast, antediluvian lifts would become huge,
gilded cages from which rose without ceasing,
a senseless but never-ending exchange of chatter
and banter; up and down the cage would hum,
with the sound of an organ in a church; the
folding iron doors would rattle back and slam
again, and hoarse laughter and giggling would
fill the corridors. The young people were enjoying themselves. Pale cohorts of young ladies,
their dresses as much a part of the northern
capital as the stone is part of its dismal Minster,
would wanly entice a swarm of encrimsoned
young hunting squires. The high ceilings would
give shelter to whole flights of shrill giggles, or
would double the deep roll of bucolic laughter—
laughter at jokes which harked back in pattern,
and even in substance, to many a dead century;
while, released for a moment from the hereditary

duties of chaperonage, immense dowagers would, among themselves, give rein to a conversation so frank, full-blooded and scandalous that even an army mess-room would have shrunk back, surprised. In this society there was no faint breath of modern, smart æstheticism. In London, it is true, the fashionable world was beginning to take an interest in such things as furniture, house decoration, and the theatre; but to these people, though their houses were full of treasures, of furniture and pictures, accumulated by their more cultured ancestors, though an occasional wallpaper by William Morris may have sneaked, unnoticed, on to their walls, the possibility of such interest was inconceivable. To such a pitch had a century of modern public-school education with its organised games, petrified system of teaching and lack of all reality, reduced a once mentally vigorous and capable class. Other things, too, had affected the "County." Though its ranks were closely guarded, the snakes had long ago entered this Eden. There was now a counterfeit, as well as a genuine, "County"; and between the two were many gradations. The rich, loud, floridly handsome daughters of manufacturers from the fog-bound industrial cities or of shipowners from the murky ports, had penetrated into the "County," and to a certain extent permeated its spirit. They had adopted its standards, though adding a new and blatant vulgarity to its tone, while their brothers were, this being due again to the equalising and democratic tendencies of the public schools, indistinguishable from the genuine article in dulness, and only inferior to them, perhaps, in looks. The women, indeed, of

this new, wealthy community were soon to leave the County behind, socially, in the broader world of the cosmopolitan capitals, for they had more energy than the ordinary young girl of the now devitalised County families. To those of them who could remember a more humble beginning, or who were, at any rate, aware of one, their present existence must have appeared as a per- petual masquerade, and since pretence is always invigorating, this had endowed them with endur- ance and joy in life. To the same cause is to be attributed the increased vitality of the Jews, now that they have been allowed to discard their mediæval uniform, to adopt European dress and ape European manners. Their life is one round of pretence, of pretending to be Europeans, Chris- tians, Englishmen, English Gentlemen, Peers, and Viceroys. The ghetto has been stamped flat, and has become the scene of a perpetual carnival for its former inhabitants. Thus, too, these mercan- tile young ladies were provided with a never- ending scope for dressing up. This gave them their strong hold on life, though, at the same time, it removed them even further than the genuine section of the County from any sense of reality.

These febrile and frenetic attempts at gaiety on the part of a society so distinct from the life of Newborough, though so near it in actual geo- graphical space that its materialisation in the ball-room was almost as if the shades, that some believe to walk among us perpetually, were for an evening's pleasure endowed with visible sub- stance, produced a quite extraordinary effect upon the townspeople. Individuals, who could ill afford it, who were wont at other times to deny them-

selves the most reasonable pleasures from motives
of economy, would at once subscribe to such
dances, entering into these spendthrift amuse-
ments with great enjoyment and without the
faintest sense of remorse.   Even the Monstrous
Regiment would send delegates to these functions—delegates carefully picked for the proven
reliability of their evidence—in order to be informed, as soon as possible, of the latest happenings, of who was there, and how clothed.   Nor,
even, did the clergy, and most certainly not their
wives, perceive any reason why they should
abstain from such innocent diversions.   For days
beforehand, excitement would be mounting, ever
mounting;   Miss Collier-Floodgaye and Miss
Bramley would confess to each other, not without
pleasure, that the hotel was "quite noisy."   Borne
in on this spring-tide of joyous expectation, old
ladies, each one in a hooded bath-chair (for
already it would have started raining) that resembled a nautilus which had run up its sail,
would be cast up on the very steps of the Superb.
These old persons would demand from John the
most precise information, who had booked rooms,
which rooms and how much the guests would be
charged for them?   If the old ladies were debarred by ill-health from themselves taking part
in such researches, a niece or companion would
timidly act as proxy for them.   Meanwhile
aproned workmen would be carrying ladders that
caught in every cornice and chandelier, would be
clumsily opening and shutting doors, or treading
in heavily-nailed boots over tiled floors.   Soon
the aspidistras and withered plants in lounge,
ball-room and dining-room, were to be augmented

by whole oases of tall palm trees from the chief
local nursery garden. The platform, on which
the band was to play, the gilt decoration of the
ball-room, would become unrecognisable beneath
the binding green chains and cobwebs of smilax,
damply clinging as the hair of mermaids, while
the five-pointed red tinsel flames of numerous
poinsettias would crackle round the edge of the
ball-room like so many young bonfires. Then
(it was still raining) a tongue of scarlet carpet
would loll out of the slobbering porch of the
Superb, and an awning would pitch its striped
tent across the pavement outside. All these
details would be as well known, and known as
soon, to the invalid population as to Miss Collier-
Floodgaye and her Companion, who could survey
the operations from their centre.

When night—the night upon which so many
varied hopes were fixed—fell like a leaden pall
over the streets and squares of Newborough, even
then the preparations for the festivity were not
yet complete. But by eight o'clock the last work-
man had folded up his apron, put on his cap, and
departed. The detail, dead and dusty, of the
hotel interior was very conspicuous under a
dazzling illumination, and was further emphasised
by the flowers and evergreens, until it seemed as
though the face of a dead man peered through
the floral tributes at a lying-in-state. But this
intense, morbid vacancy, stillness and stiffness
only constituted the blackest hour before the
dawn. Soon the ball-room doors would be thrown
wide open.

Already a rain-drenched crowd of women,
among whom were sprinkled a few young men

in mackintoshes, jostled round the striped awning
outside the hotel. Such was—or, rather, could
be—the courage of the invalids, facing South,
that many of them, who did not run to a niece
or Companion, had, in order that they might be
in receipt of an immediate and accurate description of revel and revellers, dispensed with their
maids (and with the fear of burglary which this
sacrifice entailed) and had sent them to wait outside the Superb. They were to return, as soon as
the last guest had arrived, and there was to be
no dawdling.

The cabs began to lumber up first, vast black
leather, rumbling vehicles. Then would follow
the carriages, among them Mrs. Shrubfield's,
bearing in it that lady's temporarily captive
cousin, a skilled reporter. A few dapper motor-
cars would draw up, with an exquisitely smooth,
bedside manner, for these were the property of
the more daring and up-to-date doctors of the
town. All these vehicles would eject a torrent
of black-coated men, and an indistinguishable
mass of ladies, whose heads and shoulders were
swathed in sunset clouds of rose-pink and light-
blue tulle. At nine o'clock, rather late—for they
had been due at 8.30—but fresh from the railway
train and Leeds (there was a strong local super-
stition that a band from Leeds was the best band)
the musicians would enter the ball-room. Each
would unpack his instrument, inspect it carefully,
rap it with his bow or finger, and then on his own
account begin to play on it a particular refrain,
while these four or five popular tunes, coincident,
but refusing to mingle, imparted an air of quite
insane gaiety to the crowd gradually accumulating

outside in the hall. The obdurate and vacuous
strains, in which was repeated unconsciously the
motif of "County" and townspeople, and in which,
further, were implicit so many obsolete geometrical problems, in which one straight line unbend-
ingly refuses to meet another, ascended into the
upper air. But these subtle and haunting sug-
gestions of possible social difficulties in the future
quite failed to induce any idea at all in the minds
of that legion of girls, daughters of local doctors
and clergymen, which was beginning to assemble
in the hall and overflow into the "lounge." The
future revellers gathered together, then, in a
silence that apart from this uncanny, polyphonic
music, was only broken by an occasional, quite
inadvertent titter, which could gather force, speed
and substance as it ascended, served to embarrass
increasingly its owner and effectively aided the
silence. Another giggle would escape by stealth,
and the same process would be repeated. Each
giglot, as the sly laugh sped from her, was pledged
to everlasting silence. There would be much
pulling on, tugging, and smoothing out of white
kid gloves. Each girl held a programme of the
dance, printed in silver on a pale blue card, by the
rosy pencil attached to it with a blue silken string.
These swung and creaked ominously in the wind
at each opening or shutting of the door, and, to
those ladies whose dance lists were still unfilled
must have seemed so many corpses dangling on
a gallows. Dancing would begin with a waltz,
but until almost punctually an hour late, at nine-
thirty, the "County" burst in, chattering, and
pretending to be alone on its own property, the
abandon of the occasion was but fitfully felt.

Now, however, with the entry of these various too pale or too rubicund persons, the gaiety would start in earnest. The problem originally announced by the musicians, when each started a separate refrain, could be seen taking on actuality, though in a different form, for these two universes of "County" and seaside town would pass and dance through each other, would thus mingle momentarily but never become entangled or intertwined. Each dancing couple was a unit, a planet belonging to one of the two universes, which could move through the other one, but would yet never be of it.

The two friends sat in chairs against the wall opposite to the band, and, among the fluffily dressed dancers and chaperones, Miss Collier-Floodgaye struck a dignified discord by the sobriety, rich but sombre, of her appearance. Up in the gallery, over the huge doors they could detect Elisa's pale face and sandy hair. In her pleasure at the scene below, all her grievances had been forgotten, and a broad pleasant smile was rearranging her features. What she liked best were the waltzes! And indeed most of the dances were of this species, though after every cluster of three or four consecutive ones, there was inserted, for the sake of variety, an obsolete polka—pathetic moment when in a sudden spasm of Polish verve, the doctors' wives danced openly with their husbands (though they knew "it was not the thing to do") and bounced, flounced, hopped and skipped round the room to these almost incomprehensibly jerky rhythms of their youth. Then after about every eighth dance, would come the lancers, effete descendant of the

quadrille. The "County" arranged its own sets, and the elder ladies, sporting diamond stars or a tiara, would hurl their weight into these steps with a truly admirable zest, to clownish cries of "I do love to see the young people enjoying themselves." As a matter of accuracy, the younger section of the "County" was bored and disgusted by such displays of rustic grace, which, it felt, must rather damage the elect in the eyes of the townspeople, and had determined to reserve its romping for a later and more justifiable occasion.

Whatever the lancers may have been in its youth, it was now a most singular spectacle. In its accompanying music could already be detected an incipient death rattle, while the persons dancing it suddenly assumed the air of so many performing animals, for the rhythm of each step was precisely that of a poodle, with a stick in its mouth, crowned with a top hat, attempting to walk on its hind legs, or of a chestnut horse that had been taught to walk in time to the music of the *Haute École*. Miss Collier-Floodgaye never took part in the lancers, though it was a dance in which many old persons joined; she thought it a pretty sight, but, all the same, she preferred to watch a waltz, for, as she observed to her Companion, she considered a waltz the very poetry of motion.

In those days it was still a matter of inherited belief that the waltz was indispensable. There was, as yet, no sign of that syncopated rhythm which was in so short a time to conquer and drag captive the whole of the dancing world, and, incidentally, in its triumph to destroy the de Flounceys. If, indeed, any portent of the approaching

Negro Conquest of Europe was there to be remarked, it was to be sought less in the music
than in the dancing of the younger people.   In
one or two instances, their steps may have constituted the first-found footprint of Black Man
Friday on the Newborough Sands.   Generally
speaking, however, the dancing ranged from the
frenzied hopping of Dr. Sibmarshe (one of the
early pupils of the de Flounceys) through the
Viennese languor of Mrs. Sibmarshe, on to the
more gliding yet broken rhythms of a few rather
emancipated county families.

Now would come supper, an orgy of quails
and champagne—held in the provinces to be the
two symbols of metropolitan luxury—enhanced
by vivid ices and angry jellies of an indescribably
lost-world quality. These were further reinforced
by the symbol of England's gastronomic empery,
"trifle" or "tipsy-cake," a confection composed
of bits of old sponge cake that have been out
all night on bad port wine, and intensified by the
presence of a pretentious custard which, with good
fortune, might pass itself off as cream that had
taken the wrong turning. The tables groaned
under the weight of a hundred deleterious foods
prepared by the professional poisoner of the cater-
ing firm employed, while the chairs groaned
under the weight of the hundred superb dowagers
who courageously devoured these concoctions.
The tables at which sat the county families called
loudly to each other across the red glow of the
dining-room, now freed from its partitions and
fully illuminated, while the town tables were
either abashed or else defiantly lively. Ensued
more dancing and frequent suppers. Hunting

noises became incipient, and then epidemic;
while, finally (and this was, at once, for every
one the climax of the ball, and for many young
persons their opportunity of venting a special
rowdiness, which they had been saving up all
through the evening and had wisely refused to
squander on the lancers) there came the "Gallop."
In this romp, it was necessary for all those taking
part—and, indeed, expected of them—to behave
as roughly, and to shout as loudly, as possible.
Young and old joined in together. The weight of
the elder section of the "County" enabled it to
be rougher and louder than any other, but there
was considerable rivalry. A public-school atmosphere ran riot. The band, refreshed by champagne, played louder and louder, faster and
faster; they halloo'd and hooted with laughter.
But the laughter of the dancers, and above all,
the hunting noises, rose high above the efforts
of the band. Hair became crooked and more
crooked, dresses were torn, diamond stars were
awry. Feet trod on trains, and there were rend-
ing noises, perspiration flowed copiously, breathing grew louder and more stertorous, there was
much heaving and palpitation, and enjoyment
grew more rapturous and more general. The
sound of all this throbbing pulsation (for every
one felt sure, now, that the dance had been a
success) rose up and up in the air, and thundered
through the hall and corridors outside, the
clamour increased in volume by its rolling through
the empty corridors. Up and up it reached,
above the three tiers of rooms, to where, under
her dome, Elisa now lay asleep, though soon to
be woken by the brazen voice of her slave. It

stirred her, as she lay there, and she turned to wonder at the great roaring in the pine forests.

Such was the scene upon which the two friends gazed with sympathy; for they stayed till the very end; they had enjoyed it so much. And it had been just as they were going out to supper that Mrs. Haddocriss had stepped up to Miss Collier-Floodgaye, and had said to her, "I want you to know Mrs. Floodgay and her daughter. You ought to know one another for you must be related, the name is such a rare one. They spell it without an 'e' of course. But you must be relatives, really you must."

CHAPTER XIII

NO BIGGER THAN A MAN'S HAND

No bigger than a man's hand.

FROM the first moment of meeting them, Miss Collier-Floodgaye felt an inclination of friendship toward both mother and daughter; while they, for their part, were most attentive and kind to the old lady. Not for an instant did they deny the suggested kinship—indeed they welcomed the connection. And Miss Collier-Floodgaye was enchanted to acknowledge such charming relatives. During the last few years she had begun to comprehend fully what a deprivation to her was the lack of a family circle. She had tried to fill the void with Miss Bramley, but though fond of her Companion, indeed much attached to her, the friendship between them, she felt, could never be quite the same thing as that subsisting between relatives. It might be deeper, their friendship, but it could never be so *easy* as a family one. It may have been Miss Collier-Floodgaye's lack of relatives that enabled her to hold this opinion. At any rate, she felt that kin gave friendship a fair start, a place from which it was easy to kick-off. Besides, she had so great a need of affection, and of people to whom she could talk, that one friend was not sufficient for her. Her hope had been that Miss Bramley

would act as her impresario, that through her
Companion, she would gain more easily the confidence of others. But this hope had been frus-
trated by her Companion's firmness, by the very
intensity of Miss Bramley's feeling for her, which
made any other friendship attempted a cause for
apprehension, a thing to be checked at all cost.
With relatives, however, this jealousy on Miss
Bramley's part became at once indefensible.
Who but those that possess relatives have the
right to be suspicious of them?

Then, too, Miss Collier-Floodgaye had often
lamented that the name must die with her. It
was dreadful. And now, suddenly, she had found
a family that would hand on the banner of her
personality. Truly it was a remarkable coincidence, and they must be cousins, for not only
were their surnames the same—practically the
same—but the daughter's Christian name—was
Cécile, a variant of her own Cecilia. How very
strange! It quite cheered her to find this con-
firmation of their kinship. It entranced her to
discover a family related to her own—a ready-
made family circle. She accepted the theory that
the Floodgays were cousins of hers without any
desire to test unduly the evidence for such a
suggestion.

The only drawback to this impromptu and
advantageous arrangement was the behaviour
of Miss Bramley. "Tibbits," Miss Collier-Floodgaye noticed, was becoming cross and dictatorial—yes, dictatorial. Still, she was a good soul.
Yet the old lady was forced to confess that her
Companion lacked the *fascination* of her new
friends. And, really, it was too bad of "Tibbits"

to have been so off-hand . . . rude, almost . . .
with them.

It must be owned that Miss Bramley's manner
to the Floodgays was rather abrupt. She did not
like them. She had distrusted them at first sight.
And how could any one approve of their way with
the old lady? It was too familiar. After all,
it was their first meeting, the very first time they
had met her. "Cécile" and "Aunt Cecilia"
indeed! Why, Miss Bramley had never allowed
any one except her family, Miss Fansharpe and
Miss Collier-Floodgaye to call her Teresa.
Never—no one had ever suggested it: not even
suggested it! Then, too, she had heard Canon
Floodgay preach . . . and, well it might be old-
fashioned to her, but she liked a Clergyman TO BE
a Clergyman (you know, like the dear old Rector
at Llandriftlog . . . how he had got on! . . .
Dean of Malta now. She had always felt that he
was cut out for a distinguished career—in fact,
she might be wrong, but, in a cleric, she preferred
Affliction to Affectation) . . . to be a Clergyman.
To sum it up, the *Canon* was *Theatrical*. Yes,
that was the word: more like the stage than the
pulpit.

It was curious that as soon as Miss Bramley
saw the Floodgays she realised that they constituted a threat to her intimacy with the old lady.
And this intimacy she valued much more than
she knew. All her old prejudices, which dated
from her upbringing or from her captivity at
Llandriftlog, came rushing back to her. The
dwarf tree drew in its shoots, and uneasy, belated
blossomings, and relapsed into its previous harsh
but definite shape. She became again Low

Church and Puritanical; the only one of the new characteristics which remained with her was an outspoken severity. She was no longer timid.

Miss Bramley was therefore very frigid, very formal, in response to Mrs. Floodgay's overtures. When the Canon's wife remarked on the similarity of the names Cécile and Cecilia, pretending to see in it more than a mere coincidence, Miss Bramley replied firmly, "It certainly is *very* queer . . . but as a matter of fact my friend has no relatives living. Isn't that so, Cecilia dear? You have often told me."

Thus Miss Bramley, at her first meeting with them, was unwise enough to make her association with the Floodgays a rather difficult one; for her answer had made them feel that she regarded them as pushing. Cecilia had looked very uncomfortable, too: but then she should not encourage such people. What Miss Bramley liked—and she should tell Cecilia so—was RE-SERVE.

The next day the Floodgays called on them and Mrs. Floodgay invited her newly discovered relative to play bridge the following afternoon at St. Saviour's Rectory. Miss Bramley intervened at once, and before the old lady could reply, said, with great resolution, "Miss Collier-Floodgaye must not tire herself at her age; and, in any case, she has never played bridge, and does not know how to play it." Mrs. Floodgay countered gaily, by offering to teach her, remarking that it was never too late to learn, while, to Miss Bramley's consternation, the old lady accepted the offer! It really was "unlike her." She could not be quite herself, Miss Bramley felt, to-day. So

undignified. Could one imagine Miss Fansharpe doing such a thing? It was not that Miss Bramley minded Cecilia going—oh, no! it was not that—but it was her conviction that the wives of clergymen ought not to gamble. Surely it was their duty to Set an Example? . . . yes, Mrs. Floodgay ought to endeavour to set an example. That was it. She should not spend her time playing bridge: which was bad enough in itself: while it was even rumoured that she gambled. Low points, indeed. And without examining the testimony for this charge, Miss Bramley assumed, for her purposes, that it was true. She was sure it was true. "Low points" were written in every line of Mrs. Floodgay's face. Low points, indeed! Even low points accorded ill with High Church principles, she should imagine. Quite unpacified by her epigram, Miss Bramley proceeded to lash herself into a fury. Not very polite, she should have thought, to ask Miss Collier-Floodgaye to a party, and to omit inviting her friend, in that way. No, not the sort of thing a *Lady* would care to do. The matter could not rest where it was. Cecilia must not be made the prey of such people. No. Enquiries must be set afoot. There was something unusual . . . odd . . . almost (she hated to use the word) . . . DOUBTFUL about them. She wouldn't trust either Mrs. Floodgay or her daughter for an instant. She couldn't say why, but there it was. Write to Mildred as soon as possible: that was the best thing to do. Oh, the Archdeacon would be sure to know . . . bound to know something . . . very likely he would know the Floodgays . . . might have met them at a clerical garden party.

Why, she even remembered Harold saying one day, "As in every branch of life, I fear it must be admitted that there are all sorts in the Church. Yes, all sorts." She would write to Mildred at once then . . . besides she must, in any case, answer that last letter, now that she had heard from the Dean about Peregrine.

THE SUPERB HOTEL, NEWBOROUGH,
Nov. 29th, 1907.

MY DEAR MILDRED,

I am so pleased to have been of some little use to you in the matter of Malta. The Dean (who, you will remember, is my old friend, Dr. Broometoken) is delighted to have Peregrine as organist. But it appears that *Rooms* are at present difficult to find in the island. He has taken a lot of trouble, and, alas, these little things are made more difficult for him by his afflictions, which are, I am sorry to hear, increasing in severity. The *St. Vitus,* especially, causes him now the greatest agitation. Peregrine should, therefore, certainly write to thank him personally. After much looking about, the *dear* Old Dean has hit upon two rooms, from which the boy can choose. One is to be rented at twenty-five shillings a week from Two *unmarried* Ladies (Church of England) with a superb view (He writes) over the harbour and a new geyser; while the other apartment, at a shilling a week less, is kept by a Roman Catholic Couple, and has a *light* Continental breakfast thrown in. It is for Peregrine to choose. The Dean prefers *Not* to make the choice himself.

Now, dear Sister, I must ask your good offices in return. We attended the Hospital Ball here two nights ago, and *There* met a Mrs. Floodgay, the wife of Canon Floodgay. Could you ascertain for me what is thought of them? In these days one has to be careful whom one knows; she struck me

as . . . I do not like to say it . . . but . . . *fast!*
Perhaps Harold could find out from his Bishop?
Far be it from me to cast the first stone; but she
plays *Bridge*. They say, gambles, even, for low
points, while he is very High Church. There was
Trouble, I think, over a Tabernacle, while I have
heard him accused of incense, or even worse. Do
let me know what you hear.

For the rest, we have been full of our little
Trivial pleasures, Sales of Work and Concerts.
Have you, by the way, heard any of Guy d'Harde-
lot's music? They say it is a Woman. I have
tried over some of the songs lately, and though
rather unusual, I must admit they struck me as
full of *Melody*. I love melody, don't you, dear?—
in music, of course, I mean. Have you heard
further from Poor Minnie?

Yr. Affecte. sister,
TERESA BRAMLEY.

P.S.—The name is FLOODGAY (at St. Saviour's).
You won't forget, will you, dear? The weather
continues cold but bright.

A reply reached Miss Bramley two days later,
but unfortunately it contained very little definite
information.

THE RECTORY,
LANCASTER GATE,
LONDON, W.
Nov. 30th, 1907.

MY DEAR TERESA,

Your letter was most welcome. Harold and I are
indeed grateful to you for your enquiries at Malta.
It is, as you must conjecture, a sad grief for us.
But what can a Parent do? It is not for us to
question His ways. Besides, there appears to be a
strain of music in the family. It is no use looking
back.

It is the opinion of both Harold and myself that Peregrine should choose the room kept by the two Church of England ladies, though personally we regret the installation of the geyser. After what has happened, we feel that at all costs, Peregrine must avoid the canker of luxury.

Harold has been in communication with the Bishop about Canon Floodgay. It appears that he has the reputation of being eccentric and Theatrical. If he should hear more, I will let you know at once.

I am shocked to hear about Mrs. Floodgay. There appears to be a general Loosening in Modern Life. What queer times we live in, when a clean, healthy-minded game like "Ping-Pong" is driven out by a card-game of Oriental or even as some think of Negro origin (I often wonder to myself whether, if Peregrine had kept up his "Ping-Pong," as his Father advised, this would never have happened). As for gambling, you will no doubt remember what our Dear Old Father wrote in his New Year Message for 1884, in the Parish Magazine. I was looking it up only last week. Even to-day it reads so true, like a Clarion Call. In case you have forgotten it, let me recall it to you. "The prevalence of Gambling, which—with the exception of one vice . . . (I allude to *Drink,* though not when taken in Moderation) is the meanest of human vices, is most distressing." How clear the Message! People have lost the art of writing like that now, I think.

I heard from Australia a few days ago, and am glad to be able to give you good news of Poor Minnie. She is at last to be married, to a Mr. Eldred. The engagement, it seems, has been a distressingly long one: but it appears that he is a Delightful man, a Professor in Queenstown University, and a direct descendant of Ethelred the Unready. What a comfort to know that she will be provided for.

Do you still keep up your Croquet, I wonder? If so, I should like to send you for Christmas another little pig-skin pocket-book for your engagements. I designed the cover myself. Poppies and lilies. Some little time ago I took up Artistic leather work, and have had *Quite* a success with my Blotters. Besides, it is a most engrossing occupation. There is nothing like a hobby, is there? It takes the mind off things like nothing else.

Yr. affecte. sister,
MILDRED HANCOCK.

P.S. How fortunate you are to miss the fogs.

Alas! Archdeacon Hancock was never able to find out more about the Floodgays.

CHAPTER XIV

THE FLOODGAYS

I T must not be assumed that Mrs. Floodgay was
a "schemer." She was not. But she was
devoted to the interests of her daughter, and had
heard all about Miss Collier-Floodgaye's circumstances from Miss Waddington and Mrs. Shrubfield.

And the clergyman's wife, in the manner of the
whole race of mothers, had developed a vision,
a glorious vision of Cécile happily married, and
in enjoyment of a comfortable, even ample, income bequeathed her under romantic circumstances, by a lately discovered elderly relative,
the end of whose life Cécile had helped to
brighten. Nor must it be assumed from this that
Mrs. Floodgay was a doting mother. She was,
on the contrary sharp with Cécile, only too ready
to find fault. But, in spite of this, she wanted
to see her daughter comfortably potted-out from
the parent plant.

And then . . . the poor old lady's life must be
so lonely. Especially, as Mrs. Floodgay remarked
to Cécile, with a woman like Miss Bramley, who
does not seem very agreeable or kind to her, does
she? Dreadful, really, to have no relatives and
to be dependent on a Paid Companion. And far
too kind, probably, ever to turn away. For her
own part, Mrs. Floodgay would feel quite uneasy

to be left alone with a Paid Companion . . .
really frightened, you know, for terrible as it
might seem, those things do occur sometimes,
don't they?

With a touch of asperity, rather unusual in
her, outside her own family circle, Mrs. Floodgay
reflected on "that Class of Woman," which was
invariably, she understood, "scheming" and never
to be trusted. No really Nice Woman would
become a Paid Companion, would she? And even
if her father had been in the Church, it signified
very little. Anybody seemed to get into the
Church nowadays. Evidently Miss Bramley
wanted the poor old woman to lead a regular
hermit's life, seeing no one, going nowhere. But
Mrs. Floodgay meant to bring a touch of cheerfulness into this drab existence. Canon's wife
uppermost for the moment, she resolved to do
her duty, "Come what may." For, after all, it
was one's duty, wasn't it, to be kind . . . to
try to succour and be helpful . . . ? It would
be an awful thing to feel deserted in one's old
age. Awful. And that was precisely why Mrs.
Floodgay had offered to teach the old lady how
to play bridge.

The next afternoon saw Miss Collier-Floodgaye
at St. Saviour's Rectory, learning the game.
There could be no gainsaying the charm and attraction of her new relatives. Such an interesting
family, and so full of life. Cécile, in particular,
was a darling, pretty, bright and attentive. Young
people rarely had such beautiful manners nowadays. And her hair! Mrs. Floodgay told the
old lady, in confidence, that Cécile's hair was so
long that when it was let down, she could sit,

stand, or of necessary even jump on it. A girl like that would get on anywhere. Her hair was more than—what was it?—a crowning mercy? . . . no, a crowning glory. It was positively a career. Like one of those old Italian pictures, she was, exactly, with her masses of auburn hair and large hazel eyes. Such a pretty laugh she had, too; vivacious, in fact! (Here Miss Bramley, tired already of eulogies, interrupted to say that she knew that type, animated and with auburn hair . . . Miss Fansharpe's Home had been full of them.) And Mrs. Floodgay—May Floodgay—was so attractive, a sweet little woman and so artistic. Very lively, with a great sense of humour; almost roguish, indeed—not a bit like a clergyman's wife. Why, one could even comment on other clergymen's wives, in front of her; she wouldn't be in the least bit offended. Yet she never spoke ill of any one. Never. The only time that Miss Collier-Floodgaye ever heard her even approach such a thing, was when she solemnly warned the old lady against two women, a Miss Waddington and a friend of hers, who were, it appeared dangerous—but that was entirely in the old lady's interest—after all she knew so few people, and naturally May did not want her to make friends who might be harmful to her. And then how kind it was of May—for of course since they were related, they had at once come down to Christian name terms—to teach an old lady to play bridge. So kind. Willing to take so much trouble. Miss Collier-Floodgaye had always wanted to learn the game, always: and she picked it up quite easily; it seemed to come to her naturally, she thought—

though it needed a lot of *playing* . . . you know
. . . brains, not like other games.

. . . .

Miss Collier-Floodgaye would never cease from
such pæans, while Miss Bramley's dissent,
whether expressed by silence or in the spoken
word, only drove her to further orgies of enthusiasm, and to a closer friendship with the clergyman's family. She began to frequent the Rectory.
Her position there, as a theoretical cousin, gave
her a much needed background, filled in, as it
were, the gaps and hollows of her life, added
heights and depths to the prevailing flat surface
of her existence. It was so pleasant to share their
life with them. Aunt Cecilia, Cécile called her.
It made her feel thoroughly at home.

Now in her estimate of Cécile, the old lady was
not mistaken. The daughter seemed to contra-
dict in her own person all the theories of heredity.

At first one might have supposed that the fact
that her character appeared so faultless was
merely the result of a cunning foreshortening and
false-perspective, of her being shown in relief
against the background of her parents (for, with
persons or animals of the same species, it is
always the youngest who seems—and nearly
always is, in actuality—the nicest), or, again,
that the example of her family had served to
her as a conscious warning. But it was not so.
There was in the child an essential soundness,
probably transmitted to her from an entire generation over the heads of her parents. All her
affection, all her energy, which expressed itself
physically in the colour of her hair, was accumulating within her, in the same way that energy

is stored within a battery, to be expended one
day upon friends, and more especially upon husband and children; for had her parents only
realised it, Cécile was by her nature bound to
marry.   But at present she was young, young
with that combined grace and clumsiness which
belongs to a period of volcanic growth.   She
stood, as it were, almost hidden by the growing,
waving sentiments that she had sown, in the same
way that the figure of a man can be swallowed
up in a field of luxuriant August corn, lost to
sight in waving, golden intricacies, the green
shoots of which himself had nurtured.   That torment of constant watching and nagging which,
if inflicted upon a daughter by a mother, is often
informed   by   a   truly   diabolic   intuition—an
intuition, indeed, often so penetrating that it enables the parent to perceive clearly the existence
of predilections so secret and suppressed that they
are unknown to the child herself—Cécile endured
with a feminine fortitude, with that peculiar
bravery of women, whose instinct is ever to return
pleasure for pain.   Not for a moment would she
permit herself to realise that there was in her
heart for her parents anything but affection, and
over them she threw the enveloping cloak of her
own charity.   But that, thus, she gave more than
she received, rendered her peculiarly liable to
gusts of affection, made her touchingly responsive
to the kindness of Miss Collier-Floodgaye.   And
there soon grew up between them, even under
the threatening shadow of Miss Bramley, a silent
but genuine friendship.   Nothing that Cécile's
parents could do to make it appear sham, shallow
or false could in any way alter its quality: while,

on the other hand, Miss Collier-Floodgaye's consciousness of its sincerity helped Cécile's parents
to deceive the old lady more easily. When Miss
Bramley, for example, tried to demonstrate to
her friend the falsity of Mrs. Floodgay, the old
lady's sure knowledge of Cécile's character
strengthened her conviction of the corresponding
sincerity of the mother. Instinctively Cécile, for
her part, felt that Miss Bramley distrusted her;
which made her in return dislike Miss Bramley,
accept her parents' view of the Companion's
"scheming" nature, and become the champion of
the very couple that oppressed her.

And then the Canon, Miss Collier-Floodgaye
pondered, what a fascinating man! Amusing and
witty, yet, with it all, a man-of-the-world (it was
such a comfort to find a clergyman who was a
man of the world). You know, didn't disapprove
of everything. Original too. A great career in
front of him, Miss Collier-Floodgaye should
imagine, for he was still quite young . . . young
for a clergyman, that was. A Bishop one day,
probably. Of course some people abused him,
and said he ought to have been an actor; but
that was only their jealousy, and, besides, he was
so high-spirited. You could not expect him to
behave like other clergymen. Of course the
others did not care for him, because *his* church
was always full to overflowing, not a pew empty
in the whole church. Directly he mounted the
pulpit, he could do exactly what he liked with
his congregation: *anything* he liked . . . occasionally he may have been unwise—but, then,
he was so original. He should not, she supposed,
have attacked other of his "clergy-brethren"

from the rostrum, actually: and, no doubt, he ought not, strictly speaking, to have imitated them. She could quite see that. Still, he was only human, like other people, and he was such a wonderful mimic! What a humorous, clean-cut, clerical face he had, too, with its accentuated, incised lines, running from nostril to mouth, from mouth to chin. The eyes were light grey, with fair eyebrows and eyelashes (it was untrue to say, as his enemies said, that he had none) and his head was crowned with a mass of curling auburn hair, which had receded a little from the forehead. In his dalmatics, he looked most impressive: might have been made for them. And the church was so pretty; there could be no doubt of that. Miss Collier-Floodgaye even went so far in her enthusiasm for the Canon as to admire the representation of our Lord, which had been the cause of so much dissension in the flock.

It had long been felt by his brother ecclesiastics that Canon Floodgay's congregation would not "put up with his tricks for ever." It was cheap to behave like that. It might be true, as some said on his behalf, that the church was always full when he preached: but it was not, was it, with his own parishioners? Any priest, they opined, could attract such a congregation, as long as he did not object to making himself conspicuous or extraordinary. But a church was a holy edifice, and not a music-hall. Personally speaking, his brethren had a great aversion from self-advertisement, from tricks and trumpery of all sorts.

When, therefore, Canon Floodgay imported "the Thing," and hung it up in the church

(actually hung it up *in* the *church!*) his brethren were not surprised at the results. No; the vergers were Wise and not Foolish Vergers. After all, it was for them, and for the Church-Wardens, to guard the good name of their church, was it not? And so tawdry and bizarre.

Eventually, however, to the disappointment of some fellow-clerics and the fury of others, the affair was compromised, and the picture nailed up, outside in the porch. Yet, fancy! for the money he had spent on the object, he might have built another lych-gate! It was true that there was one there already, but one could not have too many, could one?

The whole business had created a very unfortunate impression. The Canon's thumbnail sketches of his confreres delivered from the pulpit, became ever more biting and incisive, while as a consequence, his church became each Sunday more crowded. The whole of the winter population of the West Cliff trundled across the bridge to St. Saviour's, decked out against the cold in every species of fur and feather. Every window that faced South sent its own contingent, while Mrs. Shrubfield and Miss Waddington, in close concert over other matters, drove there together. The wraith of Lady Tidmarshe was said to have been seen depositing her representatives, the Misses Finnis, at the lych-gate. The Canon's impersonations became still more life-like, still more frequent. The congregation seethed with excitement, and there were occasional bursts of involuntary applause. The St. Saviour's Parish Magazine, in which the gifts of Canon Floodgay were finding a new and withering outlet, was in

general demand and could be sold at a premium. This continued success still further envenomed the other clerics of the town. Bishops began to interfere—or, as was said, to intervene—and it was hinted that the Canon was anxious now to find a new living, and one that would give him more scope for his undoubted talents. Foreign Missions, his brother clergy thought, might offer him that larger field for activities for which a man of his energy must be looking. Life in New Guinea would be so interesting, they felt, to a *clever* man, and must hold so many opportunities for doing good . . . but Mrs. Floodgay decided that there was much more good to be done at home . . . there was so much bitterness, and such a want of charity in the town, that it was better to stay there and try to smooth things out and to brighten the lives of the inhabitants of Newborough. The Canon agreed with his wife.

CHAPTER XV

CHURCH INTERIOR

"While the Seraphs recline
On divans divine
In a smooth seventh heaven of polished pitch-pine."

SO the Canon remained where he was, and Miss
Collier-Floodgaye, for one, thoroughly enjoyed the services. At first Miss Bramley consented to go with her to one or two services there,
for she wished to ascertain the real state of affairs.
But soon the Companion intimated that in future,
if the old lady would consent to it, she should
attend divine service at St. Thomas's, where no
frippery was allowed to distract the attention of
the flock from true worship. Further, she insinuated that, with regard to St. Saviour's, she
preferred going to a theatre for that sort of entertainment. In fact, there was a time and place
for everything. Miss Collier-Floodgaye was
forced, therefore, to go to church by herself every
Sunday—an act which any other old lady with
a paid Companion would have considered as a
breach of unwritten contract, and one that would
entail for the younger lady the most severe re-
proofs and reproaches, the direst penalties. But
Miss Collier-Floodgaye was generous, and understood. Her Companion, she knew, was upset.
Indeed "Tibbits" was becoming quite irritable
and unlike herself. She would never now do
anything she was asked to do . . . wouldn't go

to St. Saviour's, wouldn't visit the Vicarage,
wouldn't sing for the Floodgays—not even for
their Parish Sales of Work! And she was so
fond of singing at Sales of Work, too, as a rule.
It was most annoying. Still, poor thing, it was
only her affection for her friend that made her
like that. So much, the old lady realised.

Now that the Companion was relapsing more
and more into her former severity of outline, she
found the service at St. Peter's too high for her
taste, and assisted at worship at St. Thomas's,
which was evangelical enough for even the most
rabid hater of ritual. But, Miss Collier-Floodgaye, for her part, hardly missed the presence of
Miss Bramley at Church as much as the Companion imagined. Up till now religion had meant
little to the old lady: she had always been rather
inclined, as we have seen, to evade regular church-
going, to cough and walk out before the Sermon,
or to "feel a cold coming on," and decide that it
was wiser to remain indoors. But now for the
first time, she suddenly felt the call of worship,
through a ritual that was rich enough to capture
her sombre yet emotional spirit. Never before
had she been able to combine the pleasures of
the World with the consolation of Spiritual Life.
She was as much moved by the Canon's rantings,
roarings, and distraught air as she was diverted
by his lightning, quick-change impersonations.
The anthems, too, were indisputably the best in
the town—nothing better in London, probably
(that came of having an *artistic* wife, Miss Collier-
Floodgaye thought) and the Organist was a real
musician, gave recitals, and played the March
from *Lohengrin,* so weird . . . (*Peer Gynt,* too)

while the voices of the choristers were beautiful
in the extreme. There was nothing so touching
as a boy's voice, nothing; and during the singing
of those strange mid-Victorian anthems, the
English reply to Grand Opera—in which the great
figures of Biblical history are made to masquerade before us in antimacassars instead of fig
leaves, in top hat and frock coat, in bonnet and
crinoline instead of their native Hebrew dress,
while the cairngorm takes the place of the Urim
and Thummin—little sensual thrills of religious
ecstasy passed through her gaunt and aged frame,
electrifying it, making it seem young once more.

The atmosphere of the church was personal.
The stained glass windows, with their series of
"Modern Saints," such as Florence Nightingale,
Father Damien, and General Gordon—the last
of whom was figured pursuing the heathen Chinee
in the sacred cause of opium with no weapon
in his hand but a cane, while round his head was
an irregular halo of thick white and green glass
that successfully, but quite unintentionally, communicated the idea to the initiated of a nimbus
of broken whisky bottles—were most pretty and
uncommon. The presence in this array of Father
Damien, a Catholic, served further to emphasise
the Canon's breadth of outlook. Then there was
a painted pulpit, very unusual in an English
church, while between Bodley-Gothic arches were
hung large, pre-Raphaelite-tainted Stations of the
Cross. The incense, the singing, the scarlet garments of the choir, the continuous bowing, and
turning to the right and left, which was here the
procedure, all produced for Miss Collier-Floodgaye a superb impression of worship. Indeed so

much did all this pageantry move the old lady that it was to the next Sunday morning service that she now looked forward as to the crowning pleasure of the week.

Every Sunday she would sit in her special pew, listening intently, and following with her eyes the dancing of the multi-coloured lights from the windows. As outside the winter clouds scudded like white ships across the sour blue of the Northern sky, these effects were shut off abruptly, or turned on again as suddenly. In the church, the warmth, the incense, the droning music, and fantastic dresses of the assembled, all closed in together to form a tropical haven. Large butterflies of green or purple light, fire-flies of blue or vermilion, hovered and trembled in the air, or fluttered listlessly over the faces and apparel of the congregation. Strange feather boas undulated through this jewelled obscurity, boas like the pythons that would exist in a forest created by the Futurists, so bright and iridescent their hues, or coiled themselves round the scraggy necks of elderly spinsters, while nearly every fur, which, when truly tenanted, had ever rustled through equatorial jungles or crackled over the uncharted ice of Polar seas, was represented in this exotic flock. Through this forest, over these bright flowers, the inquisitive butterflies roamed and loitered tremulously, while the hum and whirl of the organ supplied an appropriate, rather waspish music. The warm shrilling of these radiant insects rose and fell as they shimmered over the cold stone walls, or leapt gaily toward the pointed dimness of the roof. Occasionally, even, one of these little winged creatures would

alight on her sombre dress, or pause for an instant
on her gnarled and twisted hands, when, in response, the ruby eyes of her ring would flash back
a venomous fire at it. Then again, the butterflies
would dance over the wall and above the pulpit,
and the voices of the choir-boys, cherubs' voices
they seemed, would laughingly pursue them with
their golden nets, right up into the lingering
Gothic twilight of the arches. Then the light
would change and become menacing, as outside
a cloud obscured with its white patch the weak
eye of that aged Cyclops, the winter sun. In
the church, though, the darkness that ensued was
hot and ominous as that which heralded an equatorial storm, and the organ rolled out its thunder,
while all the creatures of dazzling wing, humming
birds, moths and fire-flies sought safety somewhere high up under the shelter of the wooden
beams, waiting their time to dart out again and
hover impertinently over the array of orchida-
ceous blossoms below.

It was strange to think that her Companion
should refuse to share this new, this intense
pleasure. But very different were the services
which Miss Bramley attended so regularly at St.
Thomas's. Outside that edifice was no array of
cabs or carriages: no social ostentation or mundane love of colour was here allowed to mock the
holy nature of the Sabbath. The congregation,
many of whom were over eighty, was usually
dressed in silks of black and grey, which rustled
and crinkled with a quiet but assertive dignity.
Indeed even a brown dress was regarded as
"rather loud." On the other hand, a certain
elaboration was felt to be fitting, and any amount

of ornaments, as long as they were not too large
or "flashy" could be worn. Bits of lace, bits of
jewellery, bits of ribbon, but all able only to call
attention to themselves by their quantity, plas-
tered the fronts of these churchgoers. The men
were more sallow, fewer, and less military than
those at St. Saviour's; if they ever feasted, it
would be tea and not whisky that passed their
blue and rather bumpy lips. The ladies, who, as
we have said, were elderly, were encased in
caskets of whale-bone; many a leviathan must
have spouted and wallowed in death agony to
prop up these sagging and withered forms. Umbrellas were innumerable, hats flat and feathery.
The church itself was simple, a few plain panels
of pitch pine, a daring but controlled outbreak of
German fumed oak, and for the rest, plain grey
Gothic stone: nothing more, no, nothing more—
except that there were two carved oak brackets
which displayed the numbers of the hymns, and
that a large brass bowl, of pious expression, supported a huge Bible from which the lessons were
read. The lessons for the day were indicated, the
only touch of colour, by a wide, red silk marker
with a heavy gold fringe.

But it must not be assumed from the presence
of the hymn-registering brackets referred to
above, that there was music in the church. There
was not. This was no place for *recitals* or anything of that sort, no concert room or stage for
theatrical display. The music, plain and church-
warden Gothic as the church itself, or as the lady
who was responsible for it, was contributed by
Dr. Limpsby's eldest daughter (Dr. Limpsby was
the vicar of the parish) assisted by an aunt.

There were no anthems, but the flock joined with
sibilant fervour in the hymns. Though the whole
service breathed Christian devotion, there was no
"show." The flock remained resolutely looking
to the North during the Creed, without bowing or
turning, or paying attention to idols. Little did
the weather outside affect the colour of the church
interior, where plain glass, with a greenish tinge
in it, interposed what appeared to be a never-
ending curtain of rain between mankind and the
certainty of the Wrath to Come. "Peace, perfect
Peace, in this Dark World of Sin," was the key-
note alike of the building and of the service that
it housed. But the peace, however impermanent,
was genteel and refined. The "Romans" were
the danger!

When church was over, Miss Bramley would
return home in that resolutely righteous bad
temper that marks the true churchgoer—a temper
that was certain to come into conflict later with
all the ghoulish furies that possessed Elisa after
her weekly visit to the Cemetery. No wonder,
then, that Miss Collier-Floodgaye tended to avoid
the Superb Hotel on Sundays.

For latterly a habit had sprung up that implied
a new intimacy between the old lady and Canon
Floodgay's family. As Miss Bramley no longer
accompanied her to church, Miss Collier-Floodgaye would go back with them to luncheon, on
such Sundays as the Canon was not away preach-
ing in other towns. This recurrent invitation gave
her the greatest pleasure; for not only was she
devoted to her theoretical relatives, but it added
to her sense of prestige to be seen walking back
with them to the Vicarage—was equivalent to be-

ing seen having supper with a celebrated actress after a triumphant first night. And, however fatigued the Canon might be by his histrionic exertions, luncheon was invariably gay and charming. Such wonderful spirits. And the family welcomed the presence of the old lady, for their little difficulties (and there were several of them) were, in honour of their new relative, suppressed. This censorship made the meal much pleasanter for themselves as well as for Miss Collier-Floodgaye, and this increased their liking for her. They felt instinctively, that life was less worrying when she was present. "She makes things go," the Canon would pronounce.

Previously, it must be owned, Sunday luncheon had been a rather depressing, even intimidating, affair. Cécile had formerly regarded it as the most unpleasant feature of each week. The development of the meal was stereotyped as well as perilous. Her father would be tired and irritable, and this state of exhaustion would supply Mrs. Floodgay with just the opportunity she needed for working off her own nervous irritability. If the special little darts and goads, manufactured for this very occasion during the week to which the Sunday luncheon put a pictorial finish—those little darts and goads with which she opened her attack—failed, in their objective or effectiveness, this redoubtable little toreador of a woman would revert to her weapon, the Canon's supposed fondness for his maidservants. This had been the cause and instrument of a thousand combats. In her most pathetic and unguarded moments, Mrs. Floodgay was wont to confide these suspicions to her friends, and they had consequently been

picked clean—or rather, dirty—like so many
bones, in every invalid room in Newborough.
(Poor little woman, so bright and pretty! So
often one failed to see the tragedy for the brave
and smiling manner that covered it.) The Canon
would rise to his defence in a towering temper,
while, at the same time, he referred to the unfortunate maids, against whom his wife was hurling these insinuations, as his "handmaidens."
This would drive Mrs. Floodgay into further
frenzies: she would deliver a furious onslaught
upon "irreligious and unseemly affectations."
The Canon would now take up the attack, and
would accuse his wife of extravagance—a charge
of which she was as innocent as was her husband
of the accusation which she had just brought
against him, for she had been forced all her life
to practise the most strict economy. Mrs. Floodgay would countercharge her husband with mean-
ness, and, just at the moment when each of them
had reached the climax of their ill-temper, they
would combine to turn on Cécile. A social failure,
that was what she was! With whom, they would
like to know, had she danced two nights before,
except with that awkward spotty son of Dr. Sibmarshe, and with the elderly mental-case who was
boarded out with Dr. MacRacket every winter?
Not much of a success. For what, her father wondered, had her parents given her so good an education, even at the cost of pinching themselves
(here to emphasise their point, they both pinched
her, and tugged at her blouse). For what had
they sent her to be "finished off" in Paris—for the
spotty son of Dr. Sibmarshe, and for the elderly
mental-case, boarded out every winter with Dr.

MacRacket, did she suppose? But it would always be the same, as long as she stood there, by the ball-room door, looking self-conscious and pulling her gloves on and off. She made nothing of herself—that was it. She ought to show off her accomplishments, play the piano occasionally, or do a scarf-dance, like the one she learnt in Paris. And then why didn't she do her hair differently? What was the use of having so much of it, if she did nothing with it? And with that, both parents would descend upon her, tweaking and pulling her hair in different directions.

Happily, however, during the winter months these evidences of family feeling were for Miss Collier-Floodgaye's sake hidden away: while Mrs. Floodgay even conquered temporarily her passion for confiding in others her stories of the Canon's apocryphal infidelities . . . stories which might easily have been detrimental to his career.

CHAPTER XVI

AVIS! AVIS! AVIS!

"O for a beaker full of the warm South,
Full of the true, the blushful Hippocrene,
With beaded bubbles winking at the brim,
And purple-stained mouth."

THINGS had not gone well lately with the two Marshals of the invalid army. In the defection of Mrs. Floodgay to the enemy, they had sustained a blow as unexpected as it was deadly, and one that might easily endanger their joint command. That such an instrument of their own making should turn against them, was an occurrence that had never even suggested itself to them, veterans though they were and accustomed to the calamitous changes of fortune. Even before this piece of treachery had overwhelmed them, they had felt the necessity of spectacular triumph in order to infuse the troops, who had followed them faithfully for a whole winter without being rewarded by any great victory, with a renewed confidence in their powers of leadership. Accordingly, they had laid their plans and had baited the trap with infinite care and patience. For weeks they had been forced to expend untold tact, flattery and charm upon that forbidding fortress, Mrs. Haddocriss. For several consecutive Sundays, moreover, Miss Waddington had been obliged to dispense with the services of Thompson, her parlourmaid, in order to gain a strategic

point; while her niece, Ella, had been commanded
to spend endless afternoons waiting outside the
Superb Hotel in the snow, or running through the
wet with a message to Mrs. Haddocriss.   Every
detail had been thought out, every device made
use of, when suddenly, just as they had achieved
their first signal triumph in the introduction of
Miss Collier-Floodgaye to Mrs. Floodgay, the
fruits of victory had been snatched away from
them by the hand of a traitor, and then, worse
still, proffered back to them in the form of Dead
Sea Fruit.   For not only had Mrs. Floodgay deserted to the foe in front of all the troops, but she
had then warned Miss Collier-Floodgaye against
Miss Waddington and Mrs. Shrubfield, filling her
with prejudice against them, without any suitable
fate, such as the earth opening to swallow her
up, overwhelming her.

It was not the way of such veterans to miti-
gate the bitterness of their defeat by an attempt
to belittle the extent of it.   They had been dealt
a crushing blow, one that had already immensely
damaged their prestige, and the example of which
might easily serve as an encouragement to further
mutinies.   And not a single grape from Lady Tidmarshe for a fortnight!   They realised to the full
their humiliation.   Moreover they felt that in
certain ways themselves were to blame for this
result of their labours.   This was the second
winter of their waiting on the Superb Mystery,
yet they were no nearer to any knowledge of its
essential constituent facts.   They had observed
the symptoms, but were still unable to diagnose
the disease.   Perhaps, they felt, they ought to
have pursued a more simple tactical system . . .

ought to have called on Miss Collier-Floodgaye in
the ordinary manner: but, then, that would have
been unsporting, equivalent to taming the fox
before hunting it (for deer, only, may be tamed
before being hunted). They ought never, of
course they ought not, to have trusted Mrs.
Floodgay, that monster of their own creation,
who was now poisoning the mind of their quarry
against them. But they had felt so sure of her,
because they had made her. Who, indeed, had
taken any notice of her at all until they had "taken
her up"? And now the impious creature had
turned upon her creators, in the same way that
the other monster called into being by Franken-
stein had turned upon him. It was dreadful!
But the fiend should not go unscathed through
Newborough. Already they had ignored her, cut
her in public: but if she thought that this was
the most dire punishment which her disaffection
would bring down upon her, she was mistaken.
Oh, yes, they knew a few little secrets . . . perhaps she had forgotten her lachrymose confi-
dences, horrid, whining little thing. Perhaps she
had forgotten telling them of her doubts and
fears about the Canon and his maidservants. . . .
Well, she should *see* . . . what if the Bishop—
the Bishop who was already not over-approving
of incense and tabernacles, should hear of these
little peccadilloes too? What, then? . . . the
penalty, if not death, would at least be *deporta-
tion!* Somehow they felt that a woman who was
so "artistic," always prattling nonsense about
Burne-Jones and Watts, would not feel quite at
home as the wife of a missionary among the
Headhunters of Borneo. But that was what it

would come to, if they had anything to do with
it. Just a little note to the Bishop, just a friendly
little chat, that was all that was necessary. . . .

Both ladies felt that they must once more
openly assert their leadership, frankly display
those qualities which entitled them to it. But,
just as they were relaying their plans, rebuilding
their stately façade, and in constant communication with the Superb Hotel through Thompson
and Elisa, another overwhelming disaster put
them out of action. Mrs. Shrubfield fell ill!

Not only was this a serious matter in itself—
for Miss Waddington realised that the Superb
Affair had now assumed such proportions that no
solitary expert, however keenly burnt the flame
of her genius, could deal with it—but the amount
of ill-natured and scandalous gossip which this
illness involved must of necessity damage still
further in the eyes of the troops the prestige of
the two great figures who led them. It was no use
being cross, Miss Waddington felt, with Louise.
She could not help it . . . there had been stories
of the same kind before . . . it was better not
to believe, not to notice, and never to refer to it,
otherwise their relationship in the future might
be difficult. But she should not have allowed
such a thing to occur, at *such* a moment . . .
however Miss Waddington would see Dr. Mac-
Racket and impress upon him in person how essential it was that the truth should be kept a
secret from others, while at the same time she
endeavoured to cajole him into confiding in herself the exact nature of the events that had taken
place. When Louise was better, Miss Waddington supposed it would be wiser to know nothing,

pretend to think it an ordinary attack of influenza. But Mrs. Floodgay should be made to pay for this too. It was as much her doing as if she had struck Louise down with her own hand.

The entire truth of the matter will probably never be known to the outside world, but the probability is that it follows somewhat in the lines of the very definite rumour which was current in the town. For some time, doubtless as a result of the prolonged mental stress which the campaign had imposed upon her, and in her grief at the desperate outcome of it, Mrs. Shrubfield had been in a queer state of health. Periods of profound and useless depression, followed swiftly upon fits of unnecessary and almost delirious hilarity, induced, so the lady insinuated, "by one of those deleterious 'toniques' which the doctor will order me." Perhaps the complaint was infectious, for the same symptoms, combined with a certain unsteadiness and discoloration of the face, were to be observed in both her coachman and footman; Miss Waddington peeping from her window, had herself caught sight of this presumably plague-stricken trio, crying and laughing as they rolled from side to side, for the pyramids had assumed mobility and were quaking like jellies. Soon afterward, Miss Waddington heard the front door bell ring, and this was followed by a rollicking hoot of raucous laughter, and then Thompson appeared, looking very disconcerted and put out, and bearing an empty bottle on a silver salver. To the neck of it was attached a label on which was written "with love et meilleurs sentiments, to Hester Waddington from Louise" while, within, as though a message from a drown-

ing man, was a piece of paper, on which was scrawled, *"Aqua, per piacere!"* It was, no doubt, a touching tribute, a gift in the same spirit as that which prompts a cat to place the corpse of a mouse on its master's doormat; but none the less irritating for that! Luckily Ella was out, and Miss Waddington commanded Thompson to tell no one of the afternoon's happenings. But, nevertheless, this gift was somewhat of a shock to the old lady.

Meanwhile, Mrs. Shrubfield's condition showed no improvement, and she had to be put to bed. Her restlessness increased to a point where her attendant relatives found it necessary to call in Dr. MacRacket. The physician entered her bedroom, and placed his top-hat on a table by the wide-open window, for it was one of those warm, rainy afternoons that occasionally intervene between wind and snow in the northern winters. The rocks could be heard cawing outside, and the air was sweet and mild. The branches of the trees, level with the window, seemed to hold in their outlines a fulness that already promised vernal budding. A shaft of wan sunlight rested on the hat, which stood like a funnel lined with white smoke on the table, palely illumined its white satin lining that enfolded a flesh-pink stethoscope as an open shell protects and sets off its fragile but roseate inhabitant. To the doctor this delicate contrivance was a symbol, the scientific equivalent of a Marshal's baton. All of a sudden—it is stated—Mrs. Shrubfield soared up from her bed, seized the top-hat and hurled it and its content out into space, to fall three stories, while in the same instant, she tore off every

lingering fragment of clothing, and announced publicly, with great sonority, and in the four chief international languages, her conviction that "Nobody loves Me." She then complained that the room was moving and sat down on the window-sill. Thus, it will be seen that never, in deepest depression or highest exhilaration, did the lingual gifts of this accomplished lady desert her.

At first the doctor was nonplussed. He should no doubt have remembered the notices posted up in foreign sleeping-cars, and have countered by replying,

IL EST DANGEREUX DE SE PENCHER EN DEHORS.

NICHT HINAUSLEHNEN.

E VIETATO SPORGERSI.

DO NOT LEAN OUT OF THE WINDOW WHILE THE TRAIN IS IN MOTION.

Instead, he said to her severely, "Mrs. Shrubfield, unless you consent to remain *indoors*, I must refuse to attend you in future." Even so, however, some minutes had passed before he could finally persuade his unruly, if unfortunate, patient to come away from her window-sill.

CHAPTER XVII

LADIES OF THE OLD SCHOOL

BY her one casual introduction at the Hospital Ball, Mrs. Haddocriss had profoundly affected the lives of five people, in not one of whom was she really at all interested. More especially had she been the instrument of transforming the lives of Miss Collier-Floodgaye and her Companion.

Miss Bramley had grown used, since she first came to live with the old lady, to a new liberty of action and utterance. She now expressed herself in conversation more freely than ever before. Previous habit to a certain extent prevailed against it, or controlled its method, but, nevertheless—though still effusive in manner, even when annoyed and irritable—she had become accustomed to making a more complete revelation of her feelings and opinions than had been possible in her life up till now. Indeed she was so foolish as to allow her irritability to get entangled with her effusiveness and to dilute her charm. The result, a poignant mingling of the pat and the scratch, made the carrying on of a conversation with her at this period of her companionship rather similar to the process of vaccination.

To Miss Fansharpe, Miss Bramley would never have ventured to suggest a preference, never have dared to admit a dislike: nor for an instant would

the Companion have presumed to comment on any friend of that lamented lady. But with Miss Collier-Floodgaye, even now that Miss Bramley's character was in many directions drawing in its new shoots and relapsing into its old growth, the Companion had not surrendered her newly acquired privilege of free speech. After all, she had to do everything for the old lady, and it was annoying, was it not, when a friend to whom one was devoted made a spectacle—yes, she regretted having to say it—but a spectacle of herself? Running after people of that sort (for nearly every day Miss Collier-Floodgaye would meet her new relatives and, if a day passed without her seeing them, would fret and become quite haggard). Undignified-and-all-that. She wasn't young enough, either, to sit there puffing at a cigarette and playing bridge all night long. Not that there was any harm in smoking a cigarette now and then . . . even for an old lady. But she was obviously in failing health, and ought not to neglect herself . . . becoming so absent-minded, too . . . of course there was nothing actually the matter with her except age . . . she ought to get out more into the open air, and lead a quieter life. And Miss Bramley sighed, though she did not know why. For now there were no more of those delightful drives up on to the moors, no more of those enjoyable walks through the Market or Winter Gardens. What use was there in the doctor coming to see her every day if she would not do what he told her? He could only impress upon her that she ought not to over-tire herself. Really . . . she was obstinate and pig-headed . . . yes, positively pig-headed . . .

and Miss Bramley's voice, as she practised a new song alone in the immense and over-gilded drawing-room, took on a new quality of pathos.

On the few occasions when she was obliged to visit the Floodgays everything was most awkward. All this "Aunt Cecilia" business got on her nerves: "Aunt Cecilia" this, "Aunt Cecilia" that, and "Aunt Cecilia" the other, or "Cécile, run upstairs and get your Aunt Cecilia's muff." And, to see a person of whom one was fond, playing the wrong cards continually, talking about people she didn't know, and being so boastful! "Duchess of Devonshire," indeed! Now Miss Fansharpe, no doubt, had had her faults, but she could never have behaved like that . . . never. And then, though Cecilia could leave her money to whom she chose (that was her own affair) she must *not* talk about it in front of people who were almost strangers. It was not a thing a lady could do. Actually in Miss Bramley's own presence, Cecilia had announced that she intended to leave a part of her fortune to the Floodgays. Not a thing a lady could do. "Naturally" (in front of her, remember!) "I have made Tibbits" (she ought to say "Miss Bramley" in the presence of people of that sort) "my heir. But I shall remember your kindness to me as well. It has made such a difference." Well, she was quite right there: it *had* made a difference. Oh, yes: Mrs. Floodgay may have thought that Miss Bramley had not seen her turn round at this, to count the people in the room and see if the old lady's promise had been properly witnessed by other "schemers" (and there were plenty of them) on whom they could rely. But fortunately

nothing escapes some people . . . a fine Canon's wife!

Another time Miss Bramley heard her friend saying, with quite a lot of people in the room, "Cécile, dear child, when you are going to be married, come to me: you must let your old aunt provide your dowry": and, as she patted the young girl, the snake-ring flashed its baleful, red eye at the Companion. Of course Mrs. Floodgay sat there, with a fond maternal look fixed on Cécile. But Miss Bramley, though she did not feel in the least sorry for the girl, could see the threatening glint in it, the uneasy suspicion that her fool of a daughter might not "play up." And the Canon, in Miss Bramley's opinion, was as bad as any of them.

Cecilia seemed to be getting her will on her mind. She was for ever mentioning it. She was always imploring her Companion to remind her that she must see her lawyer. "I am getting old now, Tibbits," she would say: "and I ought to get things into order. There are various little mementoes to arrange . . . of course the main will is all right, I think; but I ought to see him. Do jog my memory. It's not as good as it used to be." ("Then you shouldn't waste your time and strength playing bridge, dear.") "Do remind me to send for him."

Really, Miss Bramley felt, it was no affair of hers. She disapproved of the whole business. Certainly Cecilia had a perfect right to dispose of her own fortune—every one realised that; but, knowing her Companion's opinion of these new friends, it was inconsiderate of Cecilia to keep on mentioning her will in this way. It could only

mean that she was going to alter it, and leave
them something. Most inconsiderate. It was
not that she minded: but they did not deserve
it. Why, she had hardly known them for more
than a few days! And they were killing her (that
was what it amounted to) with all these bridge-
parties and tea-parties. A thoroughly bad influence. Directly the old lady could be kept
away from them, even for a day or two, she was
different (except that she fretted), more like herself. More like her *old* self. That was it,
exactly. To sum the whole matter up Mrs.
Floodgay was an intriguing kind of woman, a
regular "schemer."

One was fortunate, perhaps, in having other interests. And a scale took wing from her rather
wry mouth into the gloomy air above, fluttering
soft wings against the solid gold leaves and
flowers of the cornice. Luckily there were so
many interesting new songs coming out just now.
"Less than the dust," for example; and its
pseudo-oriental strains echoed dismally through
the vacant grandeur. Probably Cecilia wouldn't
be back till nearly seven. It was too bad. Even
Elisa had noticed the difference in her. So tired
and forgetful, and much more lame, she thought.
And Elisa did not notice things easily. She had
heard all about Mrs. Floodgay, it appeared, from
some parlour-maid who was a friend of hers. A
dangerous, scheming sort of woman, the parlourmaid had said. But Cecilia seemed to be infatuated, absolutely infatuated, with the whole
family.

Toward the end of the winter, though, Miss
Bramley made some delightful acquaintances of

her own: such charming, kindly, old-fashioned creatures. One evening a note (what beautiful writing) arrived by hand, from an old Miss Waddington.

"Dear Miss Bramley," the letter ran, "I understand that you are a niece of my old friend, Miss Titherley-Bramley, and so take the liberty of writing to you. I remember her so well, with her Dalmatians and black-and-white horses: and it would give me the greatest pleasure to make the acquaintance of her dear niece. Could you, perhaps, manage to *peep* in to tea on Thursday? If you could come rather early, at four o'clock or even at three-forty-five, we could have a quiet chat about old times. I fear my niece, Ella, will be out, but I have invited another old friend of your dear Aunt's to meet you— a Mrs. Shrubfield. She has been far from well lately—influenza and a carriage accident, or something of that sort—so you must forgive her if her manner is at all emotional. She has suffered dreadfully, and is given occasionally to short fits of crying or laughing. I trust, however, that by Thursday, she will have grown stronger, and in any case you are sure to find her a most cultivated, accomplished and agreeable companion, and as a rule, cheerful, even cheery in her conversation. If you can come, it will give Mrs. Shrubfield great pleasure to send her Victoria round for you to the hotel. But please do not mention her illness to her, as she is quite unaware of these seizures, and the knowledge of them would, I have no doubt, cause her intense distress. I fear you will find us rather quiet and old-fashioned. I must warn you that *neither* of *us* play *Bridge*. I hope you won't mind?

And now, dear Miss Bramley, may I ask a little favour? I hear that you have inherited a full share of your family's love of music. They say that you accompany yourself beautifully, and it would be

such a kindness if you would sing for a little to an
elderly invalid, who is obliged, alas! to live very
much cut-off from the world.

Sincerely yours,
HESTER WADDINGTON."

A charming letter, and so well worded.   So kind,
too, and friendly to offer to send round a carriage.
Real old-world courtesy.   Miss Collier-Floodgaye
was going out on the afternoon named to a bridge-
party at St. Saviour's Vicarage.   Miss Bramley,
therefore, decided to accept the invitation.   After
all, one must think of oneself *a little.* . . .

Tea was most enjoyable, really delightful.
Both the old ladies—for Mrs. Shrubfield was fortunately well enough to be there—appeared to be
interested (because of her Aunt, she supposed)
and overwhelmed her with questions; Miss Waddington, dear old person, seemed very frail, she
thought.   Mrs. Shrubfield, too, was charming and
remarkably well-informed, talked every language
as well as if it were her own.   It was all the nicer
of Mrs. Shrubfield to come, as she never *touched*
tea herself.   It didn't agree with her.   The doctor
had told her she ought never to let it pass her lips.
Jamais de la vie, he had said.   So that she was
here merely in order to meet Miss Bramley, and
do honour to an Aunt's niece.   Both ladies knew
all about Cecilia, too, but informed Miss Bramley
that they did not see much of Mrs. Floodgay . . .
no . . . peculiar . . . yes . . . yes . . . odd, almost
. . . and so materially-minded, didn't she think
so? . . . of course they ought not to say so to
Miss Bramley, for they knew she was a great
friend of Mrs. Floodgay's.   But it was difficult
not to say what they felt, for it seemed to them

already as if they had known her since she was
a child: and after all she was so young: and when
one was young one must be warned . . . and you
see, well they did not quite know how to put it,
but the Canon had an odd reputation . . . (all
the maids left, it was said) and Miss Bramley
ought not to be left alone in the room with him.
Not for a moment. It wasn't safe. They only
told her this because they knew she was always
at the Vicarage . . . what? not always there?
Not a great friend of Mrs. Floodgay's? How
extraordinary! Now wasn't that like people!
Fancy! . . . perhaps then the Floodgays were
friends of Miss Collier-Floodgaye's, was that it?
In spite of the similarity of their names, though,
they couldn't be related. Oh no, oh dear no!
for Mrs. Floodgay, though Miss Waddington
seldom saw her, had happened to call one day
before . . . yes, she was sure it was *before* . . .
she had *met* Miss Collier-Floodgaye, and had
definitely denied any such connection . . . it was
out of the question, she had said. Yes, Miss
Waddington supposed she must have asked her
if they were related . . . she could not remember
why. But she recalled quite distinctly Mrs.
Floodgay's answer. "No relation, absolutely no
relation at all, and you can say I said so." So it
was odd, wasn't it, that the girl, that queer girl
with the carroty hair, should now call the old lady
"Aunt Cecilia." Yes. As a matter of fact, Miss
Waddington was sorry for the Mother. Herself
was not in the least superstitious, but you know
what girls are, and Ella (dear, dear, she's out
now!) was always up to some mischief (once a
tomboy, always a tomboy)—well, she had gone

to the crystal-gazer—Madame de Kalbe—who
lived on the way down to the valley and sold jet
jewellery. In order to put her off the real scent,
Ella had given her part of Mrs. Floodgay's
broken bootlace, or something, which she had
found on the stairs. Mme. de Kalbe "went off"
at once into a trance, and what she saw was so
dreadful, that Miss Waddington hardly liked to
tell Miss Bramley. At first, she had seen a
clergyman having a quarrel with a Bishop, then
she had begun to scream and struggle, and had
apparently seen a missionary, his wife, and a
daughter (with *red* hair!) being killed and eaten
by cannibals . . . somewhere in Borneo or New
Guinea—or perhaps, both! And, you see, one
can't escape one's fate, can one? It was terrible.
But, of course, one mustn't let the rumour get
about. Oh, you'll promise, won't you, never to
tell any one? It might upset them. Such a
dreadful end for materially-minded people.

Having allowed these important facts to slip
out, just like that, the two old ladies asked Miss
Bramley to sing. It would be delicious. Do, oh,
do! How difficult it must be to accompany oneself. *Clara Butt* could not do it. It needs a real
musician, doesn't it? Oh, please do sing that
lovely . . . what is it . . . "Have you forgotten
love so soon, that night of June, that night of
June?" . . . no, no. "Could you remember love
so soon?" no, that's not quite it . . . "Have you
forgot that night of June, that Juny night, that
nighty June?"—no, "that night so soon?" wasn't
that it?

Fortunately Miss Bramley knew the song to
which they referred. She prepared to sit down at

the piano, first pushing back from it a little Indian embroidered cover, encrusted with minute
bits of circular mirror that winked, opening and
shutting diamond eyes, like so many devils.
Upon this diabolic drapery wavered, for the hard
pieces of looking-glass formed an uneven, unsteady surface, several silver vases, and a round,
bulging sky-blue pot, dented here and there into
unseemly dimples, and breaking into an edge of
blue foam at the top, from which sprang a surprised green fern shaped like a question-mark.
This fern was soft and crinkly as a green paper
ostrich feather, and crawling all over with black
insect-like seeds. Then there were photographs
in silver frames—amongst them a signed one of
Lady Ghoolingham in Coronation robes, balanc-
ing her coronet as a sea-lion balances a ball on the
tip of its nose, and at the same time (a domestic
touch, this) clasping an Aberdeen terrier to her
ample ermine. The gift of this photograph to
Miss Waddington had been the result of a sudden
political panic, for it had been sent round everywhere in a frantic, final effort to secure the representation of the borough for a rather unpopular,
though quite imbecile, Tory candidate.

The notes flickered up into the warm orange
air, and struck little rattling vibrations out of
every ornament on the piano, or beyond on the
small, littered tables that impeded movement, so
that one waded rather than walked through the
room. Now every object spoke and danced with
its own accent: and the marble clock on the
mantelpiece punctuated this sub-human chatter
with a suggestion of mockery, hooting out the
time in a clear, owlish voice. All these voices

could be detected through the tones of the singer, tones which, though they veiled them, yet called them into being, as they flitted hither and thither, caressing the ears of the two elder ladies as if they were not notes, but titillating items of gossip.

Mrs. Shrubfield was so entranced with the performance, that she asked Miss Bramley to sing a German song, and, overcome equally by the music and by her own familiarity with the words, conducted, more or less, with one foot, and joined in the chorus with the other. This established even more of an atmosphere between her and the singer. Miss Bramley left the house, quite bewitched by her two new friends, and promising that she would often return to sing for them. It was rather nice to have one's music appreciated. She had hardly sung at all lately. Cecilia never asked her to sing, now that she spent all her time in Mrs. Floodgay's drawing-room, or "Salon," as she thought it. Well, if what the fortune-teller had said was true, Mrs. Floodgay would have some funny-looking savages in her salon soon. What a relief it was to find two people who were clever without being affected or grasping, and so kind!

.   .   .   .

The truth of the matter was that the two Marshals had been in despair at the continual set-backs—to call them nothing more serious—inflicted upon them. As soon as she was better, Mrs. Shrubfield had agreed with Miss Waddington that something had to be—must be—done to retrieve both their reputations for leadership and their prestige generally. A letter to Miss Bramley was almost the only solution: for it was im-

perative to use that technique in which they excelled, and which was the residue left over from an infinite experience of this sort of affair, and, again, it was absolutely necessary to make use of that technique in an ostentatious manner, so that the rebellious ranks should observe, wonder at and applaud. Now this letter was a fine tactical manœuvre, for, sent at a moment when they judged, and rightly, that Miss Bramley was lonely, depressed and jealous, it placed them at once in her confidence by its assertion of long-standing family friendship, and gained them that trust at the very moment, when, owing to the sense of neglect under which she was smarting, she was most likely to confide: while, better still, their invitation to an early tea, coupled with the friendly offer of an open conveyance, served to parade their captive in broad daylight before the ranks, who lined the terraces, squares and crescents, infirm but at attention. Thus, too, the Emperors of Rome once dragged conquered monarchs through the streets of the Imperial City, after a victorious campaign, so that every citizen should be able to estimate for herself the martial prowess of his ruler. Mrs. Shrubfield and Miss Waddington had, however, with the added humanity of a later age, placed their captive inside, and not behind, their triumphant chariot.

· · · · · · ·

That night, alone at dinner with Miss Collier-Floodgaye, in the enormous red, cruciform dining-room (or, as the head-waiter called it, under special directions from the Management, "Sally Mangey") Miss Bramley imparted her information: the Floodgays had themselves denied the

relationship which they now claimed. But her news was of no avail. "You don't like them, 'Tibbits'—that's all it is,"—the old lady replied. She was always like that now, wouldn't hear anything against them. She must be infatuated—no, more than that, hypnotised by them.

And, indeed, the old lady loved the Floodgays, for among them she had discovered that which for so long she had tried to find—an interpreter: through the clergyman's wife she was enabled to enter upon other friendships, from which, through lack of social qualities, she would otherwise have been debarred. For the cleverness of Mrs. Floodgay was that of an impresario. She could present and interpret, explain and draw out. "I love my friends to make friends with one another," she was in the habit of saying. And once taught, Miss Collier-Floodgaye became a pupil of promise. Though an opsimath in friendship, she reflected credit upon her teachers.

Now this gift of interpretation, was one with which Miss Bramley had never been endowed: or perhaps the correct explanation of her lack of it was, that as a Companion, she was merely an instrument that had been fashioned by a more forcible will and personality for its own more perfect self-expression. To Miss Fansharpe she had been a nearly perfect Companion. But Miss Collier-Floodgaye, though her will, too, was much stronger than that of Miss Bramley, needed more than a recording instrument for her own personality: she needed an interpretative machine. She was afflicted with something in her character equivalent to a stammer in speech—something which prevented a simple, natural expression of

herself, and had to be cajoled, and aided tact-
fully: moreover her native kindliness allowed the
jealous disposition of her Companion to intervene,
like an impenetrable fog, between herself and any
new persons whom she might meet, and toward
whom she might feel an inclination of friendship.
But now the old lady was beginning to weave,
with the aid of Mrs. Floodgay, a life of her own
and independent of Miss Bramley's: though, for
all that, without her Companion to look after her,
she would not have been able to carry it on. She
was old now, and far from well.

   .   .   .   .

Of course when Miss Bramley met the Floodgays, she had to be polite . . . polite, but not
cordial.   Once or twice, even, she was forced,
more or less forced, to sing before them.   But
they were far from being the appreciative audience that one might have expected from all
Cecilia's chatter of their being "so artistic."   Instead of talking about her singing, and gathering
round her, as round a jockey who has just won a
race, when she had finished, they discussed instead the possibility of a flying visit from Melba
to the "Winter Gardens" during the coming summer.   Every seat was already booked up, they
said . . . after all, she had never set up to be a
Melba: but it isn't so much the voice or song, as
the way you sing it.   There was such a thing
as expression, wasn't there: and such a thing as
gratitude, as for that?
Really Cecilia's behaviour was scarcely fair.
Though Miss Bramley had consented, much
against her better judgment, she must say, to sing
at St. Saviour's Vicarage, yet the old lady would

never do anything in return, for her. She refused
to visit either Miss Waddington or Mrs. Shrubfield. Put against them by that scheming-
Canon's-wife, no doubt. After all, one could
hardly treat a Waddington quite like that, could
one? (Meanwhile Miss Waddington and Mrs.
Shrubfield were absolutely held-up. Here was
the train laid, and everything prepared: and the
rude old woman would not come. Really they
were beginning to wish they had never set eyes
on her—or, rather, heard of her. But *they* could
see through it. Mrs. Floodgay should pay for it,
bitterly, in the utmost ends of the earth.) Miss
Bramley reflected that the whole truth was that
now Miss Collier-Floodgaye really had no time in
which to do anything, for every spare moment she
spent with her "new relations." (Relations, indeed!) Infatuated and hypnotised, that was
what it was!

And these eternal, continual bridge-parties
were so bad for her: of course they were. A
strain, impossible for so old a lady to bear for
long. She hardly ever got out for a walk now:
and her lameness and stiffness were consequently
increasing. She would, for example, drive round
to St. Saviour's Vicarage in order to get there as
quickly as possible. And Miss Bramley would
not in the least have objected to going with her
as far as the door, so that the old lady might get
the benefit of walking in the fresh air. But no,
she must always drive round there in a closed
cab. And her conversation at dinner, after her
return from these parties, was not the same as it
used to be . . . vague . . . that was the word
for it. It consisted, almost entirely, of talk about

these bridge-parties, what Mrs. Floodgay had been doing, whom she had met there, or what the Canon had said, and irritating little stories illustrative of Cécile's affectionate nature. Her nerves were becoming affected, too. She had always been rather nervous, but now it was terrible: at night she was for ever turning on the light, or crying out.

The old lady adored these games of bridge. She would be drawn in a large, black cab through the empty black streets of the winter, where nested the scorpions of the East wind. These would be roused by the jolting of her cumbrous vehicle, and would sting her through every crevice. Then she would arrive, and hurry up the stairs, much more rapidly than many persons half her age and lacking her infirmities, for she loved the Floodgays.

CHAPTER XVIII

THE SALON

OF course, the Floodgays were not rich, but the house was quite charming, and the drawing-room unique—unlike any other drawing-room in Newborough. Simple it was, and rather empty, perhaps, and with incandescent gas greenly illuminating, instead of electric light. But that was always the way in a Vicarage: besides, it looked just like electric light, for the globes were turned downward in a last, but still hopeful, effort at dissimulation—for in our age (at once a symbol and a symptom of it) gas pretends to be electric light, while electric light is made to become atavistic, must pretend that it is a candle. Under this green, dim, yet pretentious light, objects could be seen palely loitering, as though they were those things half-animal and half-vegetable, which lurk so faintly in the depths of the ocean. The walls of the room were also green, softly and sadly green with a suggestion of moss in a country churchyard. This colour scheme had been decided on by Mrs. Floodgay, partly from the praiseworthy maternal desire "to make the most of Cécile's hair," and partly because it appeared to be the most suitable background for the display of her collection of framed engravings after Watts and Burne-Jones. Prominent among these, was that well-known representation of a rather dizzy lady, sitting blindfolded but still under the spell of an acute nausea, upon

226

a spinning globe, while at the same time, like
a true, free-born Englishwoman, she maintains a
"stiff upper lip," and resolutely insists upon finishing the piece which she is playing upon a harp
with broken strings.   This strangely moving,
allegorical scene is entitled "Hope."

The curtains of the drawing-room were green,
too, and for colour the hostess relied solely upon
flowers.   Always, even in the winter, a few daffodils—"daffies," as Mrs. Floodgay called them in
her pretty, sprightly way—added distinction to
the room.   What Miss Collier-Floodgaye especially appreciated about May was this—that she
was so lively and artistic, without being in the
least "stuck-up," or forcing her knowledge upon
you: could talk just like any one else when she
wished to.   But merely by placing one daffodil,
though—or a chrysanthemum—in an earthenware
jug or copper vase, she could get more effect out
of it than any other woman in Newborough could
obtain out of a whole box of flowers from the
South of France—that was the advantage of
being really "artistic."   Again, being original, as
well as artistic and economical, she would now
and then place some autumn foliage, red rose-
berries and blue, frost-bitten bramble in a large
vase that stood in the corner of the room.   Or
she would make a most effective use of "hon-
esty"—those withered white branches on which
crackle a number of round skeleton disks, that
seem the ghostly, minute and deformed progeny
of battledore and tennis-racquet—and "cape-
gooseberries" ("winter cherries" they are called
sometimes) which consist of a number of rusty
orange lanterns, that kindly obscure a shrivelled

red berry, like a dying flame, within. These preserved flowers constitute an eternal denial of the
possibility of spring, while, if they are moved,
they sound out a weird and creaking music, ex-
hale an asphyxiating dust.

Then, too, Miss Collier-Floodgaye admired the
manner in which the Canon and his wife had
kept up with things. May could always be depended upon to know what was going on, unlike
so many other clergymen's wives; and was "mon-
daine" (worldly was too harsh an adjective) as
well as artistic, and so bright and alive.

Her drawing-room was more than a drawing-
room. It was a meeting-place, you know, a
Salon—not that she looked down in the slightest
on those who were not so well informed, whose
tastes were dissimilar or not so advanced; but
that she managed to combine so many different
sorts of people—who could not have got on with
one another elsewhere. On the days when there
were bridge-parties, the drawing-room looked so
delightful, so different from other rooms, with its
three or four green-topped tables set out, with
shaded candles on them; while all the more interesting people in the town were sure to be there,
even if they only played for counters. Miss Collier-Floodgaye did not agree with the view that
clergymen's wives ought not to gamble (after all,
one must move with the times), but, in any case,
it was a very different matter if Mrs. Floodgay's
partner carried her . . . otherwise (one knew
what people were) there would probably be a lot
of unpleasant gossip . . . complaints, even, to
the Bishop.

.   .   .   .

Mr. J. St. Rollo Ramsden was undoubtedly the most cultured caryatide of all those that uplifted Mrs. Floodgay's salon. His dome-like brow formed a perfect support for such a ceiling. Short, fattish, with a pointed, rather blond, beard, it was his conviction that he looked like a picture of a cavalier by Vandyke, whereas he really more resembled a study of a dwarf in court dress by Velasquez. For he was always smartly garbed, with a pear-shaped pearl pin in his exquisitely knotted tie; and in his buttonhole there generally melted an ice-cream-pink and frilled carnation. Further he had all the over-importance of the undersized. He was usually to be seen moving his plump white hands, of which he was very proud, in explanatory but civilised gestures, or moving up and down on his finger a substantial signet ring, then the hall-mark of a University education. Though in his late middle-age, he still preserved the fresh complexion of one who has never been contradicted— for he was owner and headmaster of a flourishing private school on the West Cliff—and was famed for his lively reminiscences of Horace, Ovid, the Elder Pitt, Labouchère, and Mr. Joseph Chamberlain. By the other inmates of the Salon, not so well grounded, not so well acquainted with famous names, it was supposed that Mr. St. Rollo Ramsden and these great men had all been boys together; that the schoolmaster, though younger than many of them (than Colonel Spofforth for example) was by some inexplicable fatality the sole survivor from a Golden Age of history in which, still under the ægis of Queen Victoria, had flourished people as diverse as Napoleon and

Catullus, Galileo, Julius Cæsar, and Dr. Arnold.
Colonel Spofforth, the mutiny-veteran frequenter
of the Salon, was wont to say of him, with that
economy of vocabulary that ever distinguishes the
military man, "An entertaining fella and one
damnably-well-in-the-know, doncherno. I don't
know half the things that little fella knows, and
yet I'm twice the age of the little fella, doncherno."

As befitted a man-of-the-world, Mr. St. Rollo
Ramsden's interest was excited by a number of
matters, matters political, religious, theatrical,
sporting and artistic. In addition to the names
mentioned above, he was captivated by such persons and things as Virgil, Joan of Arc (he always
called her Jeanne d'Arc), Pompeii, Polar Expedi-
tions, Queen Elizabeth, St. Francis of Assisi,
Romney, St. Jerome, Henry Irving, the German
Emperor, the Japanese, Cricket Averages, the
Bishop of London, *Punch,* Ellen Terry, Rudyard
Kipling (how he understood boys . . . those
delicious "Jungle Stories"), Gilbert-and-Sullivan,
the Royal Academy, School songs, Cleopatra and
the Navy League. On these, and many other subjects, he was a perfect mine of useless information.

His school on the West Cliff consisted of sixty
boys between the age of nine and thirteen, all
wearing round red caps decorated with an in-
decipherable Gothic monogram in yellow wool,
and writing carefully censored letters home every
Sunday, and was conducted on the most modern
lines. Nearly every week there was a lantern
lecture on Flora in New Guinea, Wild Life in
Tierra del Fuego, the Scenery of the Holy Land

(this was delivered at pleasantly regular intervals by an old bearded clergyman like a white gorilla, with no roof to his mouth, and was a source of endless delight to the boys) on The Survival of Folk Dancing at Barnsley and Rotherham (with, in addition to the slides, illustrative steps and music supplied by two of the several daughters of another clergyman) and—and this was the most important of all—the Work of the Navy League. So great was Mr. St. Rollo Ramsden's enthusiasm for this latter object that the boys were forced to subscribe their pitiful pence to it, while such phrases as the "All Red Route," "the British Raj," and the "Police Force of the World" were seldom off his cherry-plump lips.

The school (St. Jerome's) had undoubtedly enriched him, and among his justifiable extravagances was a white-haired mother of over eighty (who in spite of her age, was very vigorous, interfered with the matrons, heard the boys their collects every Thursday, had as a young girl once shaken hands with Lord Beaconsfield at a garden party, and was the owner of a very creditable collection of old Debretts and Burke's *Landed Gentry*), Stamps, which helped to widen the mind, he said, geographically speaking, and the cultivation of mammoth inward-growing chrysanthemums. He boasted, too, special suits of clothes and appropriate liveries for golf, cricket, football, hockey, shooting, riding (but not hunting), bridge, winter-sports and the Town Council: while, in addition, he possessed several evening suits, and dinner jackets, a purple, silk-faced and frogged smoking-coat, a number of pipes in a rack, and a quantity of spats, studs,

sticks, umbrellas, boot-trees, tie-pins and shoot-
ing-sticks. The latter were a great joy to him,
for they imparted a subtle man-of-the-world,
sporting touch. Horticulturally speaking, he
made a good show of red geraniums, giant cal-
ceolarias, and sweet-peas, as well as the chrysanthemums which were his especial pride. At the
moment that we meet him, he was showing a
natural tendency toward rock-gardens; and all
sorts of horrible, hairy little plants, with almost
invisible flowers attached to them, were peeping
out from under boulders which were very rightly
attempting to crush them: but, like the Early
Christians, they flourished under oppression.
Summed up, in fact, the schoolmaster was a
courteous and cultivated English Gentleman, re-
grettably respectful to those above, painfully considerate in manner to those below him in station.

The unexpected facets of this protean personality were, perhaps, those gallant and religious.
He was a great lady's man, forever placing com-
pliments, full-blown as his favourite blossoms, at
the feet of old ladies: this, he did partly out of a
genuine admiration for them, partly out of Christian courtesy, a wish to assure them that their
charms survived, that they were still captivating
and desirable.

At one time Mrs. Shrubfield and Mr. St. Rollo
Ramsden had been great friends. The schoolmaster was as apt in classical allusion as was the
old lady versed in French "esprit" and German
"stimmung." At that period to hear Mrs. Shrubfield dealing out French, German and Italian
phrases with a scintillating coquetry while, in
swift return, Mr. St. Rollo Ramsden went snap

with a tag from Horace, or boldly declared no trumps with a line of Homer's, was to sip for the moment the best of both worlds, classic and modern. It was a battle of the wits, but a battle that betokened great affection. Indeed, it was more than suspected that the schoolmaster wished to share lawfully the considerable spoils of the monumental pyramid. Alas, it was not to be: mischief was made, and the friendship rapidly cooled down. Some people aver that when he went to call on her one day he found her black wig crowned too unsymmetrically with vine leaves, while her views on love proved to be too classical, even for such an enthusiast as himself. He thought of the boys' mothers . . . of the rollicking welcome which Mrs. Shrubfield might accord them . . . and fled.

As for the theological side of his character, he was not content with reading the lessons every Sunday in a challenging voice, but was prone to fits of religious emotion, liable to Solitary Vigils ih the School Chapel. Moreover, on one occasion a Vision was vouchsafed him. As we have stated, he had made quite a fortune out of his school; but it must be admitted that, in spite of this, the boys were not well-fed. A diet of stale, mildewed and musty bread, margarine, navy-blue beef from Australia, and equally patriotic mutton from New Zealand suet-and-treacle, suet-and-jam, suet-and-currants, suet-and-dripping, is never very exhilarating or—as for that—very healthy. Well, it appears that one evening he was communing alone in the Chapel on his knees, like a Christian Knight of old, when there was a sudden flash, as of a waterfall, and the figure of

Our Lord stood for an instant before Mr. St. Rollo Ramsden, and spoke the words, "FEED MY LAMBS." Then the glorious image faded out as rapidly as it had substantiated. In a mood of repentant ecstasy, the Headmaster confessed what had happened, standing up before his pupils the same evening. "Boys," he said—or rather "Boes"—for he was an adept at elocution— "there is not one of us who does not sometimes commit an error. I have a personal explanation to make to you. A wonderful experience has been maene this afternoon. . . ."

The narration of his adventure naturally interested his pupils, who were henceforth dragooned by the Matrons into eating, or filling their pockets with, twice the amount of suet that had nauseated them hitherto. Boys are notoriously irreverent, and one or two confided to their fellows that in their opinion it would have been more considerate on the part of the Holy Presence, if from His mouth had issued the mystic words, "Quality before Quantity," or if in fact He had come boldly forward and told the Headmaster to give them eatable food, and not so much of it.

For the rest, Mr. St. Rollo Ramsden was an accomplished versifier. His poems on such subjects as the Diamond Jubilee:

> "Lady, on thy diamond throne,
>   As each year succeeds another,
> May a humble subject own,
>   We come nearer, each to other,
> Empress, Queen, and Royal Mother."

and on the Coronation of King Edward, had been published in various journals. He was, in addi-

tion, a polished orator, and was seldom able to resist the chance of an appearance on any platform, however much he might disagree with the principles enunciated from it. This gave him a great reputation for courtesy and impartiality, and made him in constant request as a chairman. In the bouts of oratory to which he fell victim, his hands came in very useful. His elocution was perfectly studied; his periods were as beautifully rounded and groomed as his own person. His perorations were magnificent, and decorated with a thousand little blossoms culled from Virgil, Horace, Byron and Tennyson. In Newborough it was felt that he was an orator left over from another age, and to reproduce one of the Headmaster's favourite quotations, that "Take him all in all, we shall not look upon his like again": but, at the same time, it must be owned that it was one of the favourite, if more perilous, diversions of his pupils, to climb up the fire-escape to his window, and watch Mr. St. Rollo Ramsden, wearing the right clothes, practising his speech with appropriate gestures, in front of a large *console* mirror.

Colonel Spofforth was, perhaps, next in importance of the male caryatids that upheld the Salon, where it was understood that one would never take him for eighty-five. He was quite different from Mr. St. Rollo Ramsden but interesting and entertaining. His tale of Lucknow, of "tying the Dagos to the guns, and then firing them off, by Gad," was by now almost historical, while many of his later stories, such as that of, "The other day I tried to speak to the Missis on the Telephone, by Jove. Waited half an hour.

Ha-ha. Dammit if anything happens. Get-up
and go to the telephone again: have lunch: ha-ha.
Go back to the telephone. Still no reply. Queer
thing, I said, that—and confound it if I didn't
find I'd been asking for the wrong number the
whole time," were both historically and hysteri-
cally interesting to those who had been denied the
privilege of hearing them before.

The female caryatids varied in their attractions.
There was Mrs. Hunterly, known to her enemies
as the Fighting Temeraire, because of the vast
hats, like the sails and rigging of a ship, which
she invariably wore, and because of the tenacious
and savage disposition which she evinced across a
bridge-table. Tall, angular, and word-clipping, a
military rather than a nautical simile should have
been found for her. An intimidating red-brown
fire flashed from her fine, direct eyes, and she
had the hard, open-air complexion of one who
stays in England all the summer for winter-sports.
Her drawing-room was also a card resort, full of
spidery Chippendale chairs, like bicycle wheels,
and of bric-a-brac, which had crawled all over the
walls and was now starting on its conquest of the
ceiling. All these objects were set off by a yellow
wall-paper, which was supposed to be an artistic
touch of great daring.

Then there was Mrs. Masterton, who boasted
as many breasts as Diana of the Ephesians, all
encased in parma-violet silk, and masses of white
hair piled up prodigiously upon the top of her
head ("Just like a French Marquise," Mrs.
Floodgay used to say of her), while a touch of
more than usual distinction was sometimes added

to these gatherings by the presence of Mrs. Wilfred Toomany.

Mrs. Toomany, a thin, arid little woman, resembled a grilled bone. She wore a false curling
fringe over her forehead, and false pearl drop-
earrings, and had acquired an unrivalled social
prestige in Newborough by her profession of
friend to the fashionable dissolute. Herself debarred from immorality by appearance and inherited habit of mind, she had very cleverly made
a special line in titled drunkards and divorcees
(this, it must be remembered, at a time when they
were a much rarer article than now), and of any
people, rich or of good family, who were so dissolute and boring withal that no one else would
have anything to do with them. She was the
chief apostle of *"Tout comprendre, c'est tout
pardonner,"* and was for ever munching this
motto with unction, and oozing a rather odious
sympathy. That, from the point of view of her
profession, she showed genius is undoubted: for
many of the people whom she pursued, captured,
and upon whom she was now in constant attend-
ance, were snobs, in spite, or perhaps because, of
their having lost caste; and Mrs. Toomany was
not elegant either in appearance or manner: yet
once caught they never tried to escape her: while
her real gifts were still more demonstrated by the
fact that she could now be trusted to anticipate a
scandal, to become intimate with the perpetrators
of one, long before it had become a fact in time
or space. Thus she was able to travel in scandal
as along a fourth dimension: able at a glance to
detect its presence with equal ease whether lurk-

ing in the past, present or future: for it, she had
the trained snout that a pig develops for truffle-
hunting: more, she was an infallible indicator of
future corruption, an instrument so delicately
poised that the faintest heralding symptom of
moral decay was at once revealed to her. She
was ever at pains to champion the tediously disreputable, and the atmosphere of sympathetic
understanding which she exhaled was positively
suffocating. She would stay with these friends of
hers for months, and then, in the intervals of her
gilded scavengering, would relapse into the obscurity of her mother's residence on the West
Cliff. Her mother was intensely proud of her
daughter.

Mrs. Terringham-Jones, the wife of the rich
piano manufacturer, was often to be seen in the
Salon, too. Unfortunately, her husband was a
Radical. But Arthur (the Canon) was not at all
narrow-minded. Whether one liked it or not, he
said, one must recognise that a Liberal Government was in power, and might remain in office for
years. It was never wise for a clergyman to
quarrel with supporters of the Government. So,
in spite of her principles and those of her other
friends, Mrs. Floodgay defended and protected
the wealthy lady, and was in many ways useful
to her.

Occasionally there were sudden squalls over
the bridge-table; but, however severe, Mrs.
Hunterly would always be seen under full sail,
bearing and dealing out in return the most tremendous buffetings. All the ladies present would
push their chairs back from the table, stand up
and shout. Then Mr. St. Rollo Ramsden would

smile playfully, and put in a neat, swift, apt, classical allusion; Colonel Spofforth would remark that Hyderabad in '57 was nothing to it, by Jove; and the Canon would first peep slyly round the corner of the door, and then enter the room, smiling indulgently, and rubbing his hands together, "Ladies, ladies, I implore you!" he would say.

CHAPTER XIX

A LITTLE VISIT

I N the spring instead of going to London, as was
her custom, the old lady tried to stay on at
Newborough. But Miss Bramley was resolute
on this point, and contrived with the aid of Dr.
MacRacket to put an end to her manœuvres. It
would never do for her to remain at the Superb,
tiring herself out all the year round. Obviously
she would break up soon, if she were allowed to
do that sort of thing, do just as she liked.

As Miss Bramley had suspected, Miss Collier-
Floodgaye was on the verge of an illness, and
directly she reached London, she fell ill. It was
not until the actual strain she had imposed upon
herself had ceased, that she felt the full weight
of it. Fortunately, she recovered fairly quickly;
but, during the whole time, insisted on writing to
her new friends, though she had been told that
she must not read, nor write letters. And, what
was far worse for her, she imported the Floodgays, mother and daughter, to London for a whole
week. Miss Bramley supposed that one ought to
have been thankful that the Canon did not come
too. He was quite capable of it, she thought.

The visit was most awkward and difficult. It
began in this way. Mrs. Floodgay actually had
the effrontery to write to the old lady, deploring
the length of time that must elapse before herself
and "dear Cécile" would see her again. She went

240

on to say that "London must be so interesting,
and bright just now. It is many years since we
have stayed there." Of course the old lady was
delighted (naturally) and telegraphed at once to
ask them to stay. If Mrs. Floodgay had not
written in that manner, Miss Collier-Floodgaye
would never have thought of it. Practically, they
had invited themselves! A fine pair! Oh, if only
they had had to deal with Miss Fansharpe, what
an invitation they'd have got. But they could
do anything they liked with Cecilia, that was
what it amounted to.

Then, when they arrived, they behaved so
oddly. At first they made an attempt to be
friendly with Miss Bramley, to "get round her."
But she had no intention of being deceived by
people of that sort; nor could she approve of the
way in which they tried to drag out from her any
details she might know of Miss Collier-Floodgaye's early life. "I am sure you must know
more than I do, since you are related to her," the
Companion had replied with a rustling dignity.
Quite unabashed, Mrs. Floodgay even went so
far as to ask nibbling little questions about the
old lady's income! It was done quietly and
subtly: but was most unpleasant, all the same.
No, Miss Bramley felt that she could never like
them after that . . . never. It was useless for
her to try. She could never get on, she knew she
could not, with "scheming" women—you know,
regular "schemers," always on the lookout for
something. And in her opinion the girl was as
bad as any of them.

Then, behind the Companion's back, they ex-
torted new dresses out of the old lady: chose their

frocks and hats themselves, and left her to pay.
And, good gracious, what frocks and hats!
Hardly the things for the wife and daughter of
a clergyman.   Miss Bramley could not *imagine*
what *her* father would have done had he caught
Mildred or herself wearing one of them.   But
the Floodgays actually had the audacity to exhibit them in the Lounge.   She had actually seen
them sitting, in that green-latticed room, with
palms in every corner of it, under picture-hats!
There they were now, in fact!   Did you ever
know such a thing?   Really, she must write to
Miss Waddington about it.   How she wished now
that she had learnt to draw. . . .

It was too much for Miss Bramley, and she
went upstairs to write letters.   Indeed, during
the visit of the Floodgays she spent a great part
of the day in her rather box-like bedroom, reading the *Morning Telegraph,* or examining her belongings.   First she read about Keir Hardie.   The
brute wore a red tie in the House of Commons,
and had refused to go to the Royal Garden Party
at Windsor Castle after Ascot.   Then she passed
on to the scheme for self-government in South
Africa.   She agreed with the letter (to which
the Editor drew attention) signed "Angry Governess," demanding whether we were to "sacrifice
the first-fruits of a hard-earned victory" in order
to "hob-nob with scoundrels and traitors to their
country."   Too bad: this was what came of having the Radicals in power.   She felt quite thankful that (and here the muscle round her mouth
twitched convulsively) dear old Miss Fansharpe
had not lived to see the day.   She had, sweet old
lady, been such a patriot.   It would have broken

her heart. Now she paused in her political reflections, in order to turn round and examine the
silver hand-mirror, with the five bat-like cupids'
heads blistering out from it. A nice legacy——or
rather, memento that (for she had never felt any
ill-will toward her benefactress) and one that was
typical of her, because so thoughtful. She remembered that it had been given to her, you see,
by her Companion. And now all the details of
its original purchase came back to Miss Bramley.
She had bought it in Llandumfniff at the chief
jeweller's. "You won't find another one like it,"
he had said, "uncommon, artistic, and very good
value for the money." Miss Fansharpe had been
so pleased with it. Well, it certainly was a nice
thing. But there was no denying that Miss
Bramley had, she congratulated herself, quite a
lot of nice things. How pretty the scent-bottles
were (she ought to get some eau-de-Cologne or
something—lavender water, perhaps—to put in
them) and how dainty the filigree boxes! The
Indian ones were the daintiest, she thought. One
day she must try to find a silver-backed tortoise-
shell comb to go with the other objects. It
oughtn't really to be difficult to find. What a
difference it made having one's things round one.
And thank goodness! there was the bedspread.
She had been afraid that she had lost it. Of
course the housemaid must have moved it: that
would be it. But really she must try to look
after her things more. Where, for example, had
she put that bit of Franco-Prussian bread (apparently during the siege they had, actually, to
eat rats! How extraordinary having a war in
Europe, like that!)? It must be, with the

chasuble in the large black box, naturally that
was where it would be. Quite a historic relic
now! How the bread brought it all back—the
French Governess, whom her father always referred to as "Mamselle," with her upright bearing, her "taissez-vous's" and her shudders at the
mention of a German, the Sunday services with
dear Mamma (but how faint her image) playing
the organ, and the three-night visit from Lord
Liddlesfield when the cook let her eat candied
cherries and they had chocolate cake for tea and
tea sometimes under the cedar in the lawn—for
it was always summer unless it snowed, no rain
or dull days—and Mildred falling into the green
pond in her new dress with the red sash and
being made to go to bed and the old curate with
the stammer who always brought her a packet
of chocolates. And then poor Mamma disap-
peared, they were told that she had gone on a
long journey, were dressed in black, and sent for
a visit of several months to Aunt Georgie (Miss
Titherley-Bramley) at Newborough, donkey-
rides on the sands, she remembered, and hokey-
pokey on the foreshore and being ill afterwards,
and one day a Dalmatian snapped at her for
nothing and she was beaten! . . . well, it was
a long time ago now. Still, she must find that
bit of bread which was the talisman to that far-
away, eternal summer. And Miss Bramley spent
a blissful afternoon, oblivious of the Floodgays,
in rummaging through her large shiny black box.

·   ·   ·   ·   ·   ·

It cannot be said that, for her part, May Floodgay cared much for Miss Bramley, though she
and Cécile had at first made tentative attempts

at cordiality. But Mrs. Floodgay believed, somehow, in *first* impressions. One so often found
out afterwards that one's *first* impressions had
been right, she confessed to Cécile in front of
the enormous canvases by Watts in the Tate
Gallery (there was a *spiritually*-minded man for
you, all spirit and mists and hazes and visions
and dreams and auburn hair and goodness! and
yet not sensuous . . . if one might use the word,
like Burne-Jones) and hers had been that Miss
Bramley was . . . well, "a schemer." She didn't,
she couldn't like the woman. Cécile, to whom
Miss Bramley was horrid, agreed that the Companion was "funny," so jealous, and would never
leave one alone with Aunt Cecilia for an instant,
unless she was in "one of her moods," and then
she wouldn't come down at all. Surely if one
was a Paid Companion, said Mrs. Floodgay, one
ought not to pick and choose like that . . . and
always in correspondence with that detestable
old Miss Waddington . . . oh yes, at one time
she *had* been taken in by her . . . quite taken
in—but she was a wicked, dangerous old woman,
who spread dreadful stories about darling Daddy
(for Mrs. Floodgay was in saintly vein to-day).
But something terrible always happened to people
of that sort. However, to go back to Miss Bramley, surely it was wrong of her to refuse to come
down. If it were Mrs. Floodgay, she would *force*
her to come down. She would go up to the
woman's bedroom, and say to her, "There are
two alternatives. Either come down or pack up."
That was how she would put it. People ought
not to give way to temper. And, after all, they
had come all this distance to see Aunt Cecilia,

hadn't they? She might as well be kept under
lock and key as be looked after by Miss Bramley.
It was extraordinary that the old lady had put
up with it for so long. Mrs. Floodgay wouldn't,
not if it were her, not for a moment! . . . too,
too absurd, really laughable: for there could not
be anything wrong, could there in trying to
"brighten" the life of an elderly lady, and one,
at that, who was a relative . . . of course she
was a relative, or why should she say so? (Don't
be silly, Cécile.) In any case, as the Canon said,
it was not for us to question His ways. Perhaps
it was His way of Providing? Who knows? "He
moves in a mysterious way" as the dear old hymn
said. (Oh, look at that foot! How like Watts
to think of it.) What was there, *could* there be,
wrong in it? But then materially-minded people
were like that. Oh yes, that was materially-
minded-people-all-over. No, Mrs. Floodgay could
never get accustomed to that sort of atmosphere
. . . full of plans and scheming.

Never mind, Cécile: Aunt Cecilia was taking
them to see "Monsieur Beaucaire" that evening;
and the child had never seen Lewis Waller before.
She had missed him when he came to Newborough
(German Measles). So there was something to
look forward to: but she ought, perhaps, to lie
down before dinner. They were both longing
to see it . . . but, all the same, it would be quite
nice to get back to Newborough. . . .

Miss Bramley was certain that their visit had
harmed Miss Collier-Floodgaye, made her worse.
Her vagueness was increasing. It was quite
dreadful, her forgetfulness. Even now, after all
her fretting and worrying, she had not seen her

lawyer, either in Newborough or in London. Well, her Companion was certainly not going to remind her. It would only make her own memory worse, if she became dependent, in this way, on the memory of another. As it was, Miss Bramley was always having to put her in mind of things. She must learn to remember things for herself.

. . . .

As the summer wore on, the old lady appeared to improve somewhat in health. It was easy to understand why: Miss Bramley knew *quite* well why it was. It was simple enough—that she had not been tiring herself so much, and had not been bothered by other people. Yet not for one moment would Miss Collier-Floodgaye consider her Companion's suggestion that the winter should be spent at Torquay instead of Newborough. No, she was longing, evidently, to get back again to that life for which she was so eminently unsuited. Indeed, when Torquay was first proposed, Cecilia became quite angry: one of the few occasions in all these six or seven years that Miss Bramley had seen her get cross. In fact, far from any thought of giving up her winters at Newborough, the old lady insisted on going there at the beginning of September, two months earlier than usual, so as to take Cécile to the Cricket Festival. It was most inconvenient, the hotel would be full, and Miss Bramley did not even know whether they would be able to have their usual rooms. At her age, too . . . but then she was so dreadfully obstinate, like a child, and nothing could be done with her in such moods.

The Companion had dreaded the long train

journey, but the old lady stood it remarkably well. She would not go into the restaurant car, because of her lameness and the jolting, so they made quite a picnic in their carriage. Each had a "station-luncheon basket" (now extinct) with two hard-boiled eggs, the whites of which had turned black out of perversity, an Eton-blue leg of chicken which tasted of tunnels, a "luncheon-roll," with butter, and cheese fresh from the mouse-trap, and one hard, shiny Cézannesque apple: and, after it, the waiter brought them some coffee from the restaurant car.

Soon they had to change carriages at the northern capital. Ebur Station was grimly fortified, with a hundred round loop-holes of grey sky, and two gigantic arches to support them. The old lady, leaning on the arm of her Companion, limped slowly along the interminable platforms, up-and-down under the shadow of the smoky branches thrown out by the avenues of trains and funnels. Ghastly shrieks and whistlings, melancholy hootings, sounded out continually, the voices, perhaps of some grim, grimy race of harpies, who chatter unmolested up in that black foliage, unseen as the brobdingnagian eagles which are said to hover above the tops of the dense, sun-slashed jungles in Africa. No attention was paid to these supernatural cries by the bustling porters, banging luggage, by the fussing women, accompanied by their maids, or by the self-important gentlemen, who, all smiles, were now leaving Ebur after some committee-meeting which, though no one else was aware of its existence, it had long been their settled con-

viction, was of national, almost European, importance.

. . . .

After all, they were fortunate enough to find themselves in their old rooms at the Superb, with Elisa, more faded and flaxen than ever, to wait upon them. Even Miss Bramley, who had begun to hate Newborough, was pleased at first to find herself there again, and John, the hall porter, though he had much to do, exuded a special first-night geniality. The hotel was very full, and yet more guests were expected for the Cricket Festival. The whole place seemed different, crowded like this: and a band was playing in the hall; Germans, she supposed. The weather was held, authoritatively, to be "promising." What a blessing for the town, the manager said to them, if they could have a spell of fine weather. It was, undoubtedly, promising.

At nine o'clock, though, the Floodgays called. It really was too bad of them to come so late, after the old lady had been tired-out by the journey, and keep her up talking like that. Miss Bramley left them, went upstairs, and banged her bedroom door, so that it resounded high above the chatter of the guests.

CHAPTER XX

THERE is much of truth contained in the cynical saying, attributed to the Duke of Wellington, that the Battle of Waterloo was won upon the playing-fields of Eton. The very same quality of heroism which intelligent boys prove in the course of learning to endure the spectacle of school-matches, in the process of becoming accustomed to ennui, does one day undoubtedly help them in the battlefield, does teach them to undergo unflinchingly the greater boredom of watching and participating in a larger, more evil, and quite as unnecessary stupidity. A boy who learns to like cricket, will learn to like anything: while, if forced when very young to play it against his better judgment, he will mind nothing so much in adult life. Indeed, after being at an English private and public school, the remainder of life, however hard, seems a holiday: and even the War came to many a boy leaving school as a relief rather than a catastrophe.

Other games, it may be, have their advantages over cricket. Football, for example, has one which is inestimable—that, at the worst, it can only last for an hour and a half as against the ennui of the full three days which a cricket match may entail: while, too, an expert though unwilling player, can, with the aid of the leather strips and lumps thoughtfully provided on the soles and

heels of boots sacred for this waste of time, mete
out severe punishment to those chiefly responsible
for the game, probably without being detected,
or, if discovered, without being held guilty of
anything more heinous than an exaggerated enthusiasm. Golf, again, acts in the same way as
does a grouse-moor—interns all those addicted
to it. A golf course outside a big town serves
an excellent purpose in that it segregates, as
though in a concentration camp, all the idle and
idiot well-to-do, while the over-exertion of the
game itself causes them to die some ten or fifteen
years earlier than they would by nature, thus
acting as a sort of fifteen per cent. life-tax on
stupidity. While alive, it not only removes them
for the whole day from the sight of those who
have work to do, or leisure which they know how
to spend profitably, but causes them to don volun-
tarily a baggy and chequered uniform, which
proclaims them for what they are, at half a mile
or so off, and thus enables the sane man to escape
them. Similarly, a grouse-moor, like a magic
carpet, whisks away its devotees to one of the
bleakest, most misty and appropriate places in
the northern hemisphere, and there imprisons
them, to the sound of bagpipes, throughout their
most dangerous months.

But cricket has its own peculiar merits as a
training school for manhood. It is the very
cumulative strain of boredom which this game
imposes that constitutes its superiority. Any
game, too, which, by laying down fixed rules,
teaches boys not to think for themselves, will
be of help to them in their mature years; while,
should these years coincide with a period of war,

the lesson will be of inestimable value. Curiously
enough, though schoolmasters inculcate the doc-
trine that an inter-school match is a thing of
vital importance to the schools taking part in it,
that defeat to a team is equivalent to the loss of
a battle by an army, yet certain rules are laid
down; and the boy, who, believing these protestations of his teachers, sought genuinely to
help his side by the invention and use of some
ingenious mechanism, by the breaking of some
old rule, or establishment of some new one, would
quickly be disillusioned, called to order by the
umpire, lowered in the esteem of his comrades,
and perhaps afterwards disgraced publicly. Had
Nelson, for example, won a cricket match instead
of the Battle of Copenhagen, by regarding the
umpire through a telescope applied to his blind
eye, how much would his fame have suffered.
But, fortunately for the English, Nelson was
never at school—or if, as some say, he was,
quickly ran away from it—for there can be no
doubt, we fear, that his action was hardly "playing the game." Things have progressed since
then, for no General (we do not speak of Ad-
mirals, for they have a tradition of eccentricity:
and it may be here worth while to enquire to
what extent the superiority of the officers of the
English fleet over the officers of the English army
is due to the fact that they do not go to public
schools) on any side during either the Boer, or
Late Great Bore, Wars even thought of winning
a battle. No, the behaviour of all parties was
correct and decorous in the extreme. In the end,
the European War was won by *never* winning a
battle, by vast mutual slaughter, and intolerable

ennui. The only relief is that, owing to their
inefficiency and slowness, it is unnecessary and
almost impossible to remember the names of the
"leaders," except as a warning.

It is at cricket, then, that the schoolboy first
learns the oft-repeated, dreary lesson that all
men must march in time with the pace of the
slowest among them. Thus the intelligent boy
is made father to the stupid man.

At Newborough, however, the watching of
cricket was no mere training. It was the fulfil-
ment of an ancient savage rite. To the local
young girl, whether of town or County (for the
County participated in these observances) going
to the Cricket Festival was equivalent to taking
part in the initiation-rites that herald adult life
to the young male in certain African tribes. It
was the event of the year, for the aged and experienced as much as for the tiro. And Miss
Collier-Floodgaye was determined—and Mrs.
Floodgay had been determined that Miss Collier-
Floodgaye should be determined—that herself
should initiate Cécile into these semi-sexual
mysteries.

The green, flat lawn was hemmed in by tall,
flat inquisitive houses; yellow, angular houses
which rolled hundreds of blood-shot eyes back
at the sun when it glanced at them. This circular
ground was further surrounded by a wall of
yellow brick peculiar to cricket-rings, and this
wall was lined on the inside with square wooden
pens for the towns-people. In certain spots these
stands had a line of deck-chairs in front of them;
seats, these, for the local patricians. At two
points, only, was this circular symmetry broken,

where rose the Cricket Pavilion, part Swiss chalet, part Neolithic-Lake-Dwelling, above which in fine weather floated a silken banner of blue sea, and opposite, where swelled the canvas Tabernacle of Lord and Lady Ghoolingham. Between these two cynosures there was a continual show of intimacy and interfluctuation, which would be described by critics, if such a thing were to be observed in literary circles, as "an orgy of mutual admiration." From the Pavilion issued forth for their imbecile sham-battle the strangely armoured demigods of professional cricket—demigods, covered, as though they were soft-shelled crustaceans, with soft, white armour, pipe-clayed brasslets, gauntlets, greaves, vambraces, cod-pieces, and crowned, perhaps as a mark of their arrested mental development, with those round caps that usually cling to the heads of schoolboys—while within the Tabernacle opposite moved figures yet more august and gigantic, the vast forms of the Gods themselves, who preside over, though they do not take part in, this ceremony of initiation, this scene—who were, indeed, originally responsible, for the founding of this modern, more humane Stonehenge, where the mind is sacrificed alive instead of the body. Even the County stood in awe of these figures that moved so dimly. And it is symbolic that though the home of the demigods was as it seemed permanent and immovable, that of the Gods was temporary and mutable.

Behind and rather at the side of the Tabernacle crouched a smaller and deprecating tent, that of the local President. For though the festival was in reality entirely under the sway of the almost fabulous Lord and Lady Ghoolingham,

yet, in order to impart the necessary appearance
of democratic independence and good-fellow-
ship (jolly-good-sportsman-and-all-that-and-not-
a-bit-stuck-up-either) they encouraged the election of a president from the town. But no
one paid much attention to him, except at the
luncheon interval, and he was left to worry out
for himself those questions of local precedence
with which he was perpetually concerned. It was
upon the other tent that the eyes of the town-
noblesse were fixed, fastened in a state of snob-
bery so ecstatic that the gazers were, after a time,
mesmerised, rendered almost semi-conscious.

Usually the Festival consisted of three
matches; the first was an inter-county match,
the second an international match, and then, at
the end, took place that delightful old English
institution titled "Gentlemen *v.* Players." By
long custom certain days were more fashionable
than others, and it was the second day of the
first match which Miss Collier-Floodgaye had
chosen for the initiation of Cécile. Miss Bramley
had refused her friend's invitation to go with her,
so there were just the three of them, May Floodgay, Cécile, and the old lady. They had very
good deck-chairs; could see everything. And
. . . they were near the Tent. What a lot of
panama-hats there were, already, though the
game had not even begun! Evidently the Ghoolinghams could not have arrived yet (the deck-
chairs remained intent on one another, ignored
the hoarse, paper-unwrapping crowds in their
pens: pretended not to see the caps for the
panama hats). All the same one could not help
noticing the bananas. A horrid smell, on a hot

day, like pine-apple drops. Miss Collier-Flood-gaye wished people wouldn't sell so common a fruit as bananas, to her mind it spoilt everything: but Cécile liked it, thought it part of the fun, the crowd, the shouting, the paper, the bananas and everything.

Suddenly the occupants of the deck-chairs were struck dumb, paralysed though still able to move their eyes as if not looking, for—heralded by a particularly hoarse voice shouting "Good old Ghooly"—the Gods and Goddesses were descending on to the stage. They walked slowly toward the Tent, talking to each other, smiling a little too graciously, or if unsure whether they knew those persons they were at present passing, smiled in such a way that it would not commit them if they were unacquainted, might be taken as an apology, implying "I am so sorry, was that your foot?" or "did I tread on your dress?" while, on the other hand, if they were acquainted, the curve of the mouth, though vague, was so sympathetic, they felt, that not even old friends would feel unrecognised or wounded. It was very hard to recognise every one; and by this method nobody would be offended.

What a shame to go on shouting "Bananas," in that way at such a moment, reflected Miss Collier-Floodgaye: "two a penny" indeed. That must be the Duchess of Dunston over there, with the pretty young face and white hair. A sweet face, she called it. White hair always suited a young face, she didn't know why. And that swarthy-looking woman in bright yellow must be Violet Catling, the famous beauty, who was so "smart"—and fast, they said, and bad-tempered.

How daring to wear a colour like that, one could not help admiring her for it, could one? (Why couldn't they stop shouting bananas?) So swarthy, she looked, like a common gipsy. Fine eyes, though. How "society" must be altering, that she could go about as she did; though the Queen would not receive her, they said. But the Queen was kind and broad-minded; if it had been Queen Victoria . . . ! Lord Ghoolingham looked such a real sportsman and she—she was, well not handsome exactly, but regal-looking, you know.

The informal procession was now entering the Tabernacle, which swiftly swallowed up its own, so that the figures of the Immortals could be but dimly seen within, moving through the heart of the purple heat and darkness.

Soon the Neolithic chalet began to evacuate its tenants, spherical forms in white: for cricketers were already beginning to get old and fat. "The youngsters were not shaping as they should," in fact, it was said, "Was golf the cause, or what was it?"

At first the game was very silent, except for the drawing-room conversation of bat and ball; this wooden small-talk would proceed for some time, and then, suddenly, one of the talkers would snub the other, and away would run the fat white mice over the flat green baize. The banana-vendor was silent (why couldn't she have kept quiet before?) and weird women-enthusiasts, possibly the wives of the cricketers—epicene, tweed-clad figures, crowned with large straw-hats, wearing sensible-brown-shoes with flapping and fantastic leather tongues lolling out of them, and,

exhibiting, tucked into their coats, men's ties, blazoned in dreadful stripes that held for them some hidden significance—leant forward, watching with a flushed and strained inanity, or occasionally allowed it to be seen by a smile, glance, or exclamation, that they had duly followed some esoteric subtlety of form or style. The men were even less emotional. They sat there rigidly, smoking, occasionally tapping their pipes as a woodpecker taps its beak, against the wooden rail in front of them. One wondered if this was their way of communicating with their mates, some form of expression superseded in mankind by speech. But their round, clear eyes held in them no meaning that they could possibly wish to convey to any one. Now and again there might be a flutter of excitement at some peculiarly imbecile sally, such as when a batsman allowed himself to be caught out, or the umpire decreed, in another case, the mystic "L.B.W." Even the wooden contingent in the deck-chairs would then vibrate for a moment while in the stands behind them there would be a seething of hats and handkerchiefs; but these outbursts were rare.

It was fine, really fine, and the air danced over the hot ground. The dry chatter of bat and ball, the humming of sun and grass, the fluttering of aerial forms (for the air could be seen dancing and shrilling over the green spaces) and above the roof of the pavilion the glittering of the northern sea, which threw golden rings of light into the air from each wave crest, as jugglers throw rings into the air on a stage; all were soothing and cheering, Miss Collier-Floodgaye thought: good for the nerves. How warm, quiet,

yet droning, it was. Gradually, for the old
woman, the green expanse and its railings melted,
and changed shape, but into another scene of the
same sort. She was now far away, back—before
the days of her untethering prosperity—back at
other cricket matches, for her father had been
Captain of the Eleven in a large, northern village.
Hot days had then lulled her, while old ramose
trees fanned her with their green feathers. Captain of the Eleven, and much looked up to, he
had been. But people must never know: very
respected locally, of course; but timber-mer-
chants always are looked up to, she did not quite
know why. Then her father had died, and soon
there were no relations. Her brother had been
found shot, shot through the head. And she had
been so fond of him. How could he have done
it? He had never even mentioned the thought
of such a thing; but he had always been strange,
like her mother, dead so long ago, strange and
full of fancies. People were for ever following
him, he said. Wherever he moved in the countryside, there was a stirring after him, and branches
rustled slowly, slyly, and he could feel faces peer-
ing at him through fluttering branches: and there
were footfalls, he had said, footfalls on the stairs,
and sombre figures grimacing at him in dark
corners. But she could understand it, for though
she was not like her mother—in fact the very
image of her father—yet when she had been very
young, or when she was unwell, she, too, was
afraid of whispering leaves and crouching
shadows. There he was found, lying face down,
half buried in bracken, with a shot through his
head. "Temporarily Insane," they had found

him; but she could not judge him so. Yet it was
a cruel thing for him to leave her like that, to
all the talk of the village, and the loneliness in
the middle of all this talk was unimaginable. She
could not even go to church without being stared
at. She had realised that, unless she were prepared for a similar end, she must get away from
the talk, and from people who reminded her,
whose very kindness reminded her, of the past.
And she was rich now, so she could get away.
After all she had no relations left, except some
very distant cousins. She did not dislike them:
indeed they were too kind, but she had felt then
that she must get away, leave the place, forget
everything and become ordinary. She had sold
all her property, kept nothing in her possession
that could recall the past—except, only, that
snake-ring with the ruby eyes, which her brother
had been wearing at the time of his death—that
brother she had loved so dearly. The ring was
unlike others, and it was typical of him to have
worn it, for his taste was personal. In fact she
supposed, he had been "artistic."

Yes, she had felt then that she must leave the
place, and become ordinary: for that was her
chance of safety. Even at that time she had
been no longer young, and when you were old it
was easier to forget: indeed, she forgot easily,
now, forgot everything. And when she moved,
how lonely she had been, worse than ever before
and getting older. Now, though, she was better:
tired, it was true, ever so tired: but she was in
the light and the heat and with friends. There
must be nothing queer about her, however, or
they would not like her, and she would be left

lonely again. The humming of sun and grass,
the cicada sounds of bat and ball were soothing,
while the occasional waves of applause were calm-
ing as waves rolling over you. How quiet and
warm it was. Gradually the green field melted
away, and she was lying in a gently-rocking boat,
sailing away from a dark, huge forest of dead
timber, in which sombre shadows moved, sailing
away, away into the light over the blue waves.

"Cécile, your Aunt Cecilia is asleep, I'm
afraid," said Mrs. Floodgay tartly, and, by her
phrasing of the sentence, immediately threw the
onus of hypothetical relationship to a public-
snorer upon her daughter. It would never do,
with Lady Ghoolingham near by. If there was
a thing Mrs. Floodgay hated, it was to see some
one nodding like that, asleep in daylight; the
sudden totter and fall of the head, and then the
somnolent efforts at deportment, irritated her.
Cécile must nudge her aunt; that was all that
could be done. Nudge her and say—yes, it was
better to say—"Did you see that stroke, Aunt
Cecilia?" On reflection, perhaps better not say
stroke. It might alarm an old lady waking up.
Instead, try saying, "Did you see that hit, Aunt
Cecilia?" No, not like that, so that every one
could see, but softly, quietly. Really she must
know by this time how to do a thing of that
sort. One couldn't be made to look ridiculous.
What man would ever think of proposing
to a girl-who-did-not-know-how-to-nudge-an-aunt-
who-happened-to-have-fallen-asleep-and-say-
"Look-at-that-hit-Aunt-Cecilia," she should like
to know? After all—men weren't all fools, were
they? . . . that was better now. But of course

there was that horrid old Mrs. Shrubfield watching. (She would be! Usually at this time of
year she was pretending to be away. Horrid old
mischief-maker, like a large black-beetle, in her
sequined garments. All Mrs. Floodgay hoped
was that she wouldn't make a scene after the
luncheon interval. It was shocking to see a
woman in that state.)

Indeed Mrs. Shrubfield could be heard wheezing internationally into the distance. *"Eccola!*
Regardez ça, liebeham," she was saying to Ella,
Miss Waddington's niece who was serving as
aide-de-camp.

Of course she'd seen it all. Fortunately, however, the old lady was awake again now. But,
naturally Mrs. Shrubfield would make a story of
it: that went without saying.

"Yes, dear, it will be luncheon soon," and Mrs.
Floodgay was again smiling and twittering
sweetly. She put the old lady in mind of a pretty
bird, so soft and kind: a robin or a chaffinch or
something. And Cécile looked ever so charming
with her white filmy dress and soft hat trimmed
with red poppies: not too fashionable for a young
girl, or too "showy." (How clever the French
were—even when they settled in an English
town—and neat with their fingers). Her hair
looked quite lovely to-day. What a business it
must be brushing it! The old lady would dearly
love to see Cécile married—to a nice man. She
was extremely attached to the girl and would
like to know that she was happily settled. There
must be one condition, however. The husband
would have to call himself Floodgaye—or, it
might be better if he adopted Floodgay-Collier-

Floodgaye. It sounded well and the name *could* not be allowed to die. Well, she ought to marry soon, with hair like that. And Miss Collier-Floodgaye felt delighted with herself, her relatives, and, above all, pleased that she had bought Cécile that dress. But she was tired, very tired.

Now came the luncheon interval. The deck-chairs ejected their tenants, who walked about the corner of the ground in front of the Tabernacle, greeting one another. Mingled in this mysterious moment, Gods, demigods and mortals. The heat waved its banners just above the grass and sent streamers curling into the air, winding round the legs of the promenaders like serpents. Miss Collier-Floodgaye leant on the arm of the young girl, and slowly limped up and down through the crowd. So that was it! The yellow dress that the famous Miss Violet Catling was wearing, was one of those new "Directoire" gowns she had read about. More daring, much more daring, than she had supposed. Bright yellow and slit up to the knee. What would people put on next, she wondered . . . and a large picture hat.

Generally speaking, the Goddesses were wearing white, mauve, or yellow; for these were the fashionable colours of the year. The Gods were tall, ox-eyed, pink and moustached as prawns. Lord and Lady Ghoolingham were talking to the cricketers and to their wives. Why, Lady Ghoolingham was asking herself, why because one is married to a famous cricketer, why, because one is a woman who wears tweed, brown leather shoes, and a striped tie, need one shout like that to show one is pleased and at one's ease?

The part of the crowd which belonged to the
town and its neighbourhood was self-conscious, for
this was a great day—London, as well as local,
papers had installed their reporters here for the
occasion; moreover, Illustrated Society Papers, as
well as ordinary London papers, had despatched
their representatives to this famous field.

Mrs. Floodgay stopped every now and then
to speak to a friend, to lots of friends. Mrs. Sibmarshe whispered to her confidentially. Mr. St.
Rollo Ramsden, his beard freshly-trimmed, wearing a gorgeous uniform appropriate to the occasion, and carrying a shooting-stick, so that he
could sit down whenever the spirit seized him,
was here; for he loved Newborough so much,
he said, that he could never make up his mind
to leave it, even during the holidays. His brown
shoes were perfection, having the exact requisite
shade of mahogany, not too new, nor too far
disintegrated, while in his tie he wore a small
ruby and diamond cricket-bat. Did Mrs. Floodgay remember, he wondered, what Ovid had
written, when he was living in exile, near the
Black Sea? . . . rather a jolly little thing, he
thought . . . Mrs. Floodgay could see that
dreadful, little deaf old man, Mr. Bradbourne,
skulking in the opposite corner. No doubt he
was in one of the common stands, so as to avoid
seeing any old friend who might know him. He
would come to a bad end, she felt sure, an
old horror. Then there were the Terringham-
Joneses; and really Colonel Spofforth was a
marvellous old man, over eighty-five, now, and
walking about like quite a young man, though
strongly reminded by the day of Lucknow in '56.

"There we sat, by Jove, in the Club," he said,
"absolutely unable to move, doncherno. Punkah-
wallah, black chap, doncherno, suddenly dropped
the punkah and ran away, you know. 'Where's
that damned nigger?' I cried. What, what. Just
then the . . ." Mrs. Toomany, more arid than
ever, and dressed in a tone of charred ember
which suggested that the grilled bone had now
been burnt quite black, was engaged in her professional researches. But this sort of truffle-
hunting was fatiguing, and her promenade had
been on the whole, a disappointment. Violet
Catling "shaped well," she thought, the German
Prince had a "sympathetic" face, and Lady Carrie
Conyers showed distinct promise, she felt. Still
she would not care to prognosticate. Everybody
seemed so dull and respectable: there was hardly
a person she knew. Then Mrs. Floodgay spoke
to the two little Misses Finnis, sent there as
delegates, she supposed, by some one: probably
that old woman with white hair and prominent
teeth who lived on the West Cliff—half-mad, they
said, always playing with a doll, but rich and
very inquisitive: must know everything that was
going on. Or perhaps Lady Tidmarshe had sent
them. Miss Pansy Finnis was wearing the same
blue serge dress, in which we met her in the
winter some three years before, the skirt stretched
over the hips and short legs, assuming the shape
of a thimble, but her hat had broken into a
pathetic summer trimming of blue cornflowers.
Miss Penelope, shorter still, was sporting a rather
gay cast-off dress which she had been given by
that queenly woman, Mrs. Terringham-Jones. It
was a nobly embroidered affair, and above al'

this richesse showed a badly nourished face, in which were to be detected a hundred shades of blue and purple, the weals inflicted by genteel poverty. The sisters were deprecating, sad and amiable to a degree. They smiled and laughed, but their eyes were always rolling round uneasily as though in search of some crust, for almost to that level had they by now been reduced. People did not appear to want piano lessons, or writing lessons, or anything now. The commoner you were, the more money you had.

All that the young people cared about now were these "cinemas" or whatever you call them. It made one feel quite ill to see the sort of people who listened to the Band in the Winter Gardens. You never saw such *frights*. Really it was quite a treat, Mrs. Floodgay, to come here and see such a nice-looking lot of people. It reminded one of the old days, when everybody came to New-borough . . . but Mrs. Floodgay was eyeing the crowd, for she was never sure that she liked Miss Pansy; a crafty look, she had: perhaps more "shifty" than crafty . . . At this precise moment, Mrs. Floodgay caught sight of that mystic figure, who only materialised here once every year, that apparition who heralded the gathering of the Great World, known as the "Passing-Pageant Boy." This Boy, who had long been a grown man, was the representative of the famous illustrated journal. He had intended (he once confided to Mrs. Sibmarshe) to "go in" for the Church, but had felt instead the call of the World. He was thirty-five years of age, and took himself most seriously, still wearing, how-ever, an Eton collar and jacket, in order, as he

said, "to further his literary career." To match
his collar, eyebrows and mouth were all turned
down, while the nose receded from the rest of
his features with a great look of surprise at the
triumph it had achieved in this little act of
mutiny.

Mrs. Floodgay greeted him and fell into a
reverie. She could see it all. "Among those
noticed by our representative was Mrs. Floodgay,
wife of the celebrated North Country Canon,
looking very piquante in a veiled charmeuse of
the new tone in mauve; with her, and she has
inherited a full share of her mother's looks, was
her attractive daughter, Miss Cécile Floodgay.
The latter was wearing such a pretty hat,
trimmed with red poppies à la Parisienne." Or,
better still, it might be one of those social false
perspectives, in which she and her daughter might
figure, "Snapped at the Newborough Cricket
Festival. Reading from left to right, Mrs. Floodgay, Miss Cécile Floodgay and friend. Behind
can be seen, marked with a cross, the Duchess
of Dunston and Lady Carrie Conyers."

It would help Cécile. It would be in all the
papers, London and local. Up and down paced
the throng expectantly, and Mrs. Floodgay was
not the only day-dreamer among them.

The Ghoolinghams were within the Tabernacle,
entertaining the demigods to luncheon. The
party enjoyed itself immensely and exchanged
comments on local dresses and manners. The
President was also giving a luncheon party, in
the cringing tent huddled up behind the Tabernacle. To this celebration Mrs. Floodgay had
been invited to bring her daughter and her friend.

It was very hot, and such a fight took place to get the slab of tepid, scaly salmon, edged by warm cucumber. The whole tent perspired over the hot and trampled grass. Hired waiters with mutton-chop whiskers, and red-noses, quaking with age, handed a trembling plate here and there, their faces streaming. The guests, too, were swollen and purple with the heat. It was hot, oh so hot; and Miss Collier-Floodgaye began to lose herself again. This time she was walking in a green maze, under a burning sun. She could not find her way out of it, anywhere:—and then, suddenly, everything stopped—

They had to lead her out, and drive her back to the hotel. Miss Bramley, fortunately, was in. Oh, no; she was not a bit surprised; the old lady should not be allowed to do such things, which, naturally, were too much of a strain for any one of her age. Real friends (for Miss Bramley felt that for once she could say what she felt) would not encourage her to take them to tiring functions. No . . . it might be only a fainting-fit, of course. She seemed better now.

CHAPTER XXI

WINTER

The tree's small corinths
Were hard as jacinths,
For it is winter and cold winds sigh . . .
No nightingale
In her farthingale
Of bunchèd leaves lets her singing die.

HOWEVER, Miss Bramley thought it better to send for Dr. MacRacket. He hurried down to the hotel in the brougham, drawn by two Velasquez horses, to which he still remained faithful, and sped up to the lift with that portentous look of important preoccupation, which was one of his professional assets. With him he bore the assorted insignia of his calling: top hat, two stethoscopes (one shaped like a small wooden trumpet, while the other was a replica of that pink meteor which we saw hurtling to its doom in the street below), and a black shiny bag full of instruments. These he placed on the table as though they were so many fetishes, accompanying his movements with varying degrees of ceremonial. He now apologised to the two ladies in case he had kept them waiting. The truth was, turning to Miss Bramley, that he had been called in to see a friend of hers, Mrs. Shrubfield. Nothing serious, fortunately: only she was very excitable, and seemed to have been upset by the cricket festival, or the luncheon, or something of that sort. Oh, yes, very cultured and sympa-

thetic. Then he applied one of the stethoscopes
to his patient: fastened his ear to the trumpet
end, and commanded her to echo after him the
mystic spell "99." He then, as doctors sometimes
do, lapsed strangely into common sense, and told
Miss Collier-Floodgaye plainly that she ought not
to exert herself at her age, ought not to go out
so much among people, ought not lead so
furiously exhausting a life. On the other hand
she should go out more in the fresh air, a little
walk every day, not far enough to tire herself,
or a drive up on to the moors. That was the
thing: if, of course, the weather permitted. Naturally he did not want her to walk through the
rain. If she followed his advice, she would soon
be well. But she must stay in bed a few days,
in order to rest.

When Miss Collier-Floodgaye got up again,
she found that summer and autumn had both
spent themselves in a thunderstorm, and that
winter reigned cruelly in their stead. Needless
to say, she was determined to neglect the Doctor's orders; or perhaps she had already forgotten
them. For she was, Miss Bramley noticed, much
more absent-minded and visibly more infirm, but
still so obstinate that one could do nothing with
her. She refused to walk, refused to exercise her
knee, would not go out for drives.

Moreover the Floodgays were the first to observe the change in her. No longer did they ask
her to play bridge at their parties, for her game
was too erratic. They pretended (oh! Miss
Bramley could see through it!) to be solicitous
about the old lady's health, afraid that large
parties would fatigue her, and would only per-

suade her to play when there would be few people present. This altered attitude on the part of her "relatives," though they disguised it as much as they could, tended to retard rather than to aid Miss Collier-Floodgaye's recovery, for it fretted her continually. Nor was it any less tiring for her, because Mrs. Floodgay since she had stopped asking her so much to the Vicarage, was now, in order to disguise this falling off in hospitality, always "looking-in" with Cécile about luncheon-time, "dropping-in" to tea, and, indeed, positively pestering the old lady. And it was not so much playing bridge as seeing people which tired her. And she always returned from the Vicarage over-tired, even if there had been no one there except the family.

Her obstinacy was as great as ever, perhaps greater, Miss Bramley thought. When, for example, there was a ball at the Superb, she would buy tickets for it, make Cécile and her mother dine with her on the night in question, and, as often as not, would sit up till two in the morning. Nothing that any one could say would dissuade her from doing this, though it was a habit that no one of her age could form with impunity. It was *too* bad of the Floodgays allowing her to do it, of course; but just what one would expect of them. It was useless, the Companion realised, for her to speak to them directly about it: but she insinuated, and allowed her feelings to appear in her manner. It was very obvious that such festivities absolutely exhausted the old lady, and it was Miss Bramley's belief that the Canon's family could see it too.

·　·　·　·　·　·　·　·

This winter Miss Bramley saw as much as possible of Mrs. Shrubfield and Miss Waddington. Their friendship was a great solace to her. The two Marshals of the Monstrous Regiment were, indeed, most gracious and through them the latest news was sifted, passing through their perfected mechanism to nourish many a frail old form facing South. Alas, owing to the duration and rigour of the military operations, one or two of the veterans had fallen out of the ranks, and had been buried with full military honours. But the two leaders were determined "to see it through," resolute as ever in their determination to prosecute the campaign with every resource at their disposal, and to bring it to a victorious conclusion. Miss Waddington had suppressed with the utmost vigour her asthmatic tendencies. The doctor was delighted with the progress she had made, and it was obvious that she was now capable of an endurance and effort which would have been impossible to her a few winters previously. "Isn't Aunt Hester wonderful?" her niece would quaver weakly. While, however much in her own house Mrs. Shrubfield might indulge her leanings toward rollicking jollity or lachrymose despair, yet she never allowed these alternating moods of optimism and pessimism to be witnessed by the rank and file, never came to the battlefield except with an undimmed eye and an unclouded judgment. After the Cricket Festival, it is true, she had been unwell for some days, for the spectacular success which she had achieved by actually being the witness of the fainting—or as she considered it, the seizure—of Miss Collier-Floodgaye, and of the consequent,

obvious discomfiture of that odious little Mrs.
Floodgay, when she had seen fixed upon her the
Marshal's acute and sparkling eye, had unduly
excited Mrs. Shrubfield. Miss Waddington, for
one, was not inclined to blame her for it. It
was all the fault of that stupid girl, Ella. Why
had the silly creature supposed that Miss Waddington had sent her there with Mrs. Shrubfield?
Was it necessary to explain everything to her in
black-and-white? (Black-and-White, indeed, had
been the cause of the trouble.) Could she really
have supposed at her age that it was a treat,
organised specially for her, and that Mrs. Shrubfield was acting as her chaperone? Really it
made one despair of the Girls-of-To-day. A
curious feature of the friendship between these
ladies was, that though Mrs. Shrubfield was
nearly always present at tea with Miss Waddington, Mrs. Shrubfield never asked her back in
return. She never drank tea, she said, it was
bad for the nerves: and her nerves, *Carissima,*
were not what they had been. Ah, *La Vita, c'est
difficile;* not all beer and skittles . . . as the
servants say.

But by Miss Waddington, Miss Bramley was
constantly invited to tea. Indeed an unusual
amount of entertaining, for so quiet a house, took
place both above and below stairs; for Elisa, too,
was a favourite and indulged guest beneath, and,
so great the impression she had made on Miss
Thompson, that she was several times allowed
to see Miss Waddington for a few minutes. For
these occasions Miss Waddington would relapse
into bed, and would give a remarkable impersonation of a dear, but rather weak-minded old lady,

entirely ruled by her parlourmaid. Miss Thompson, however, had warned the simple Elisa with
great solemnity *never* to speak of these visits to
Miss Bramley, who might be jealous: for Miss
Waddington, she added, received the Companion
so differently. Elisa was delighted by these signs
of being held in an especial esteem, an esteem to
which she was not accustomed, and kept her
silence, though she answered any questions that
the delicate old lady tremolo'd at her with the
greatest readiness, and all the accuracy which
was possible. It had been Miss Thompson's
friendship with Elisa, indeed, that had enabled
Mrs. Shrubfield to bring off her coup in the
cricket ground.

Miss Bramley, though she was aware of Elisa's
friendship with Miss Waddington's parlourmaid,
was ignorant of its extent and fervour: nor was
she even informed of her friend's rather unbecoming condescension to the housemaid. It
would have pained her, for she was so fond of
Miss Waddington and of Mrs. Shrubfield: for
they made a great show of intimacy with her.
They laid more and more stress upon their former
friendship with her aunt, until, to listen to them,
one would have imagined that the two ladies had
never for an instant been separated from the
owner of the Dalmatians, and that the mere name
of Bramley acted as *open sesame* to their affections. It was really touching, the Companion
thought, to notice the subtle ways in which they
were always trying to help her. It was obvious
that they would go through fire-and-water for
her. What an advantage it was to belong to a
family, a well-known family (that was where

Cecilia lost so much. That was what was lacking). Just because of her aunt they were for ever trying to make things easier for her. They never lost interest in her. For example, they never allowed an opportunity to pass of advising her—in the nicest way possible, of course—to end the intimacy between Miss Collier-Floodgaye and the Canon's family. Nothing but ill would come of it, they averred. After all . . . one had heard stories, Mrs. Floodgay herself was responsible for the information. Even the housemaids, she had said: no woman it appeared was safe: and then you could not get away from it, incense was incense; and bridge-parties, whether Mrs. Floodgay gambled or not (they would not discuss that: that was not the point) were bridge-parties. No good would come of it, that was certain. And last time that Ella had been to Mme. de Kalbe—you know, the Clairvoyante—the forecast had been worse. Even the cannibals were not safe now, it appeared . . . though, of course, they would eat them in the end. But think of the scandal, and of the poor Bishop responsible for sending them there. Mme. de Kalbe had fainted, so great was the shock. Of course, one could not believe everything that fortune-tellers told one; but still it was queer: described them exactly, Ella had said.

Incidentally, Miss Waddington did not often encourage Ella to be present at these intimate tea-parties. It was the old lady's opinion that "there was no one like Ella for getting in the way." And Miss Bramley did not "take to" the niece: the reason being, though she was not aware of it, that she harboured a great distrust toward un-

paid, hereditary Companions. She resented them.
They did not know their business, and were, to
her unconscious mind, taking the bread out of the
mouths of other girls. She felt, then, the contempt and hatred of the professional in any
branch of art for the amateur. She did not
realise that to be a niece is as much a profession
as any other. But as we have said before this
is never realised by any one outside the bargain
of mother and daughter, aunt and niece.

No, the two Marshals kept Miss Bramley to
themselves, and discussed with her the best
methods of breaking Mrs. Floodgay's influence
over her supposed relative. They renewed their
offers of personal assistance: if necessary, either
of them was willing herself to interview Miss
Collier-Floodgaye and inform her of the sort of
people into whose hands she had fallen (after all,
it was the Canon's own wife who had told them
the stories!). But since Cecilia was so pig-
headed, and refused to call on them, or receive
them, what was to be done? The worst of it was
that Miss Bramley could not tell them this, for
it sounded so rude and might cause offence: so
she had to invent excuses for Cecilia. But the
two leaders did not need to be told. They could
see, they knew, the evil influence at work. That
was why that nasty, carroty-haired girl looked
so sly . . . but just let her wait. . . .

Miss Bramley's frequent meetings with her two
friends, the gay little familiar tea-parties, even
their appreciation of her singing, failed to comfort her. For she was a Paid Companion and
expected to be treated as one, not to be given
this endless liberty in which she had nothing par-

ticular to do. She would not probably have
minded being bullied, being played-with and tor-
mented as by Miss Fansharpe . . . but for the
company of unpaid and amateur Companions to
be preferred, openly preferred, to that of the professional, salaried graduate in the art of friendship, constitutes an insult of the deadliest order,
though not recognised as such by the rest of the
world; and one that is utterly degrading to the
Companion, must in the end entirely destroy her
self-respect. Really, it almost made Miss Bramley hate her employer: all the more, because she
was genuinely attached to her. And she did not
hate her the whole time; when she was ill, she was
as fond of her as ever. Now people insist on
treating love and hatred as though they were
totally unconnected, instead of being symptoms
of the same disease, in the same way that alternating subnormal temperature and high fever
may be tokens of an identical illness. Indeed,
love and hatred, apart from those that are the
result of purely physical attractions, are nearly
always based on an excessive understanding of
one person by another, who is therefore rendered
peculiarly sensitive to the kindness or unkindness
that their conduct implies. And Miss Bramley
possessed a real intuition into Miss Collier-
Floodgaye's character. Naturally the Companion
would never even admit to herself that at moments she hated the old lady, for it would have
seemed a thing utterly inconceivable—or inad-
missible, which was to her the same thing. Love
and hatred were manifestations of a passion that
had entered so little into Miss Bramley's life,
that she was very far from comprehending them.

If any one had suggested to her that she hated Cecilia, hated her for one moment even, she would have been profoundly shocked, deeply indignant; but at times, she did undoubtedly feel, beneath the upper layers of her consciousness, a desire to get even with the old lady and, beyond that, to wreak a fit revenge upon the Floodgays. Apart from these emotions, she was sorry for Cecilia, often very sorry for her. But the old lady's continual if clumsy consideration for her, and wish not to injure her feelings, only aggravated the Companion further, only made the slighting of her worse and to herself more obvious.

Miss Bramley felt, instinctively, for she had never reasoned it out, that her life was now hollow, deceptive as a hollow tree. Cecilia never asked her as she used to accompany her on any outings. Gone were those halcyon days of only two years before, when the winter sun was always rosily shining, pecking at one's face warmly as a robin nestling (really Miss Bramley thought, the climate seemed to have changed. So much colder, the sea and wind always roaring) when they had such delightful walks in the Winter-Gardens; no longer did they spend delicious hours "poking about" in the market, or strolling through the peat-scented moors, inhaling the acute air. Cecilia hardly ever asked her to sing, except sometimes, when she was dull, not going out after dinner to the Vicarage: then of course, she could be made use of. Not that she minded that, but simply a PAID Companion, that was what she had become (alas, in reality, it was exactly what she was not, and what she wished to

be) . . . All these unnecessary people. Before
Cecilia had met them, how different she had been:
and Miss Bramley sighed bitterly, and if her eyes
had been used to tears, these would have flowed
and have comforted her. As it was, the best thing
to do was to order a nice cup of hot tea. But if
she ever rang the bell, Elisa would be sure to
grumble. It was not that the housemaid did not
like her; it was a matter of principle. But what,
Miss Bramley reflected, was the use of hanging
up a printed notice, with "Ring once for the
waiter; twice for the chambermaid" on it, if
Elisa insisted on answering if you rang once?
It was scarcely fair: and then the maid would
look sulky for the rest of the day; while since,
beside Miss Waddington and Mrs. Shrubfield, she
was practically the only person to whom Miss
Bramley could talk, this was very annoying and
awkward. And, usually, Miss Bramley had been
told, Germans were so willing. . . .

Really Cecilia ought *not* to be out to-day. Besides it was rather hard to have to sit by oneself
in a hotel on a day like this. One could practise
one's songs, of course; but then every artist likes
to have an audience. The drawing-room was too
large and dark to be in by oneself for long: and
dismal, looking over so rough and threatening an
ocean. The sound of sea and wind rushing and
jostling rose up too sharply at the large windows.
It quite got on one's nerves. For far down below
the waves were hollowing out every kind of crevice, vault, cave, coffin and cavern, every place
imaginable on which to secrete bleaching bones,
every form of tube and hollow instrument, upon
which the wind could play an accompanying and

awful music. The prospect was full of the aerial
commotion caused by all this labour, full of white
foam, the steam given off by this titanic and terrible machinery. The vast, grey, undulating
backs rolled sideways against cement walls, rocks,
cliffs and precipices, acting as inspired and living
hammers. These monsters pushed and heaved
against each other, and then with an added force
rammed at the obstacles interposed between
themselves and humanity, meeting them with an
unimaginable dull and forceful thudding, while,
in the very act of clashing with them, they uplifted feline white claws by which to grab hold
of the hated, hard objects obstructing them. Still
dully roaring, they clambered up with unexpectedly lithe and sinuous movement. For a moment
they clung tenaciously, held their own; then, unable at present to lift up the whole, enormous
weight of their bodies, fell back gurgling and
snarling to recruit themselves for another leaping
attack.

All this sound and movement made Miss Bramley nervous and irritable, made it impossible for
her to sing, or concentrate upon anything but
Cecilia's behaviour. Nor was she a person who
could, by natural charm, manufacture her injured
feelings into a fresh claim on the affection of the
offender. On the contrary, trials and sorrows of
this sort merely served to harden the shell of her,
making her disagreeable, sourly disagreeable
through her mask of effusive sweetness.

Thus it was only by degrees that Miss Collier-
Floodgaye, through her ineffective, rather masculine perceptions, realised these slow accumula-
tions of jealousy. In vain she would try to soothe

her Companion, saying "Tibbits, if I did not care for you more than for any of my other friends (other friends, indeed!) is it likely that I should make you my heir? I am only leaving small sums of money or mementoes, such as my little bits of jewellery, to other people: but, meanwhile, do remind me to send for my lawyer."

This gradual sensing on the part of the old lady, of the fact that her Companion was suffering, followed by clumsy attempts to placate and reassure her, only embittered Miss Bramley the more. Really she could not see why she should remind Cecilia about a lawyer, simply in order that the old lady might make a fool of herself by leaving things to people like the Floodgays: after all, if the old lady would only learn to behave sensibly, would stop running after High Church Clergymen and their families, she would be able to remember things for herself. And if people encouraged her to ruin her health and wear out her memory, it was only fitting that they should learn by experience that such conduct would not pay in the end. But Miss Collier-Floodgaye continued: "You must jog my memory about the lawyer. Don't forget to remind me to see my solicitor": these and like phrases were often addressed to Miss Bramley. At other times she would pet and pat her Companion. But no display of affection could now convince Miss Bramley. She possessed insight into her friend's character, as well as jealousy: and, in spite of her annoyance, was genuinely concerned about her. There could be little doubt that the old lady was growing weaker, more absent-minded and weaker, every day: while the very vigour of the effort

which she made to disguise this growing vagueness from the Floodgays, only aided and facili-
tated the disintegration. Miss Bramley realised
the state of her friend's health, and fretted over
it: was, indeed, perhaps the only person, except
Elisa, who grasped fully the seriousness of it, for
the Floodgays and the frequenters of their Salon
saw merely an old lady who was growing older—
they did not understand the steep angle of the
decline.

Elisa in a dumb, flaxen way (though the flax
was now being transformed by the passage of
years into white cotton) had become attached to
the old lady, and to the considerable donations
which her presence in the hotel during the winter
months signified. Not that for a moment the
housemaid stopped grumbling (for what was the
use of a little money and a half-day off if one was
treated like a brute beast and had no one to walk
out with, or to keep one company, nobody to talk
to except Miss Thompson and the Sexton?), but,
at the same time, she was willing in the intervals
of her lamentations to take counsel with Miss
Bramley about the old lady, to aid her with the
indirect advice of Miss Thompson, who, in her
turn, was but a mask for Miss Waddington, and
to try to think out what could be done.

Miss Collier-Floodgaye slept so badly now
that, her Companion decided, after consultation
with Elisa, to move into the same bedroom as the
old lady; nor did she encounter from her any of
the objections to this plan which she had expected; which in a way made things no better,
for it amounted to a tacit admission by the old
lady of the gravity of her sufferings. All these

mutterings in the darkness, these sighings and turnings were, it seemed to the Companion, the tokens of a fatal return to childhood. Occasionally the old woman's deep voice would toll out sentences, fragments of conversation, though penetrated by no meaning which the Companion could distinguish: yet in these emotional phrases were recurrent the same words, the same names. This muffled crying-out, these appeals to persons unknown to her, persons who had probably passed long ago into oblivion, except in the memory of this lonely, old woman, this hovering of an enfeebled mind upon scenes enacted so long ago, made the Companion excessively uneasy. Her sleep was soon invaded by the same microbe of restlessness, and she would lie there for hours listening. For in this dwelling upon days that were past, there was something deeply disturbing, as though one were to hear an old harp, lying dusty and untouched in a lumber-room, suddenly give out again its golden and liquid music. It was terrible, Miss Bramley felt, to see some one, of whom, in spite of everything, one was fond, sliding down the few final years in the space of so many days.

But Dr. MacRacket, cheerful and sensible, did not take an alarmist view of Miss Collier-Floodgaye's health: he insisted that she was, as he phrased it, "sound in heart and limb." The change in her was temporary, she would grow stronger again. "Leave it to me, Miss Bramley. Don't fret. Everything will come right," he would prophesy in his buoyant way. And, in any case, in a seaside town where many old ladies and gentlemen remain in complete dispossession

of their faculties until well on into their tenth decade, the doctor was not inclined to treat the question of mind or memory too gravely. After all, her eyesight was as good as ever . . . and with a little regular exercise: and she should try "Plasmon" biscuits—they are wonderful: and then look at old Mr. Woodly-Cateham on the West Cliff, ninety-two and every tooth in his head—or Mrs. Kinderbull, look at her for example! Oh, no, no, no. It would be all right, quite all right, he assured her.

The optimism of Doctor MacRacket did not persuade Miss Bramley to alter her view of the situation. She was very uneasy: and the most difficult feature of it was that while Miss Collier-Floodgaye's health had grown obviously worse, while her mind was loosening every day, her resolution of character, her obstinacy, in fact, remained unaltered, and, apparently, unalterable. She still insisted on driving round to St. Saviour's Vicarage every day: insisted on going to Mrs. Floodgay's bridge-parties, when she was invited, insisted above all, on attending Morning Service every Sunday, whatever atrocities the weather might perpetrate, and on further tiring herself by lunching with the Floodgays after it. Any battle entered upon with the old lady on these habits of hers, merely succeeded in making her angry, thus injuring her health, without affecting her determination to do as she wanted.

While her character remained otherwise unaffected, her religious fervour was growing. It is probable that Miss Collier-Floodgaye was never now so happy as when she was in church. The music droned right through her, bringing ex-

quisite sensations to her tired nerves: the lights danced round her with a joyous rhythm, the incense brought back to her the sunlit gardens of her youth. She was strangely moved, her sombre spirit was calmed and cheered: while the prestige of the Floodgays was still further enhanced, for it was through them that she had learnt to appreciate this final and most abiding pleasure.

After many weeks, Miss Bramley contrived to wring out of her one concession. Ground down by perpetual fret, Miss Collier-Floodgaye promised that she would walk for half an hour, every "fine" day, round the plot of grass in front of the hotel. This place was the most sheltered from the wind.

CHAPTER XXII

EVERY afternoon at three-thirty down the
steps of the hotel, out from under the
bonnet-like porch, would issue forth, well-
armoured against the cold, grey air, Miss Collier-
Floodgaye and Miss Bramley. The elder lady
would lean heavily on a stick, and be buttressed
upon the other side by the wispy figure of her
Companion. Thin as ever, Miss Bramley had
now allowed her dress to cut clean away from
Rectory conventions. It showed an intensified
tendency to break into small waves of lace, diminutive eddies and whirls of jewellery, which
suited ill so sallow, defined yet meagre an appearance. Her fixed smile, invented originally to
overspread the little nervous tic, the contraction
of the muscles round the mouth, that must be
considered as the memorial which Miss Fansharpe had erected to herself during her own lifetime—a memorial, too, on which it had been
necessary for that dear old person to spend incessant care and infinite time—had become
habitual, though it was now contradicted by a
pained yet defiant expression in the eyes.

Miss Collier-Floodgaye, however, admitted of
no relaxation in her dress. She was sombre,
gaunt and outlined as ever. So bony had she become, indeed, that just as Bernini shows us
Daphne on the very verge of being transformed

into a green luxuriance, so the old lady appeared
to have been arrested at the exact moment of
sprouting into antlers at every extremity.
Daphne's hands, Daphne's feet seemed to have
been caught on the point of budding into delicious
little curls of spring foliage; thus, too, Miss Collier-Floodgaye's extremities always suggested
that they were about to unfold creakingly into
similar ramifications of horn. It may be that the
bones were already wishing to assert independence, plotting to be rid of the flesh, impatient to
start on their long and solitary vigil.

The two contrasted figures would painfully
emerge out of the hotel, disentangling themselves
slowly from the clustered and overwhelming detail. Their procedure was always the same, fixed
by formal, invariable rule. First they would
pause for an instant at the bottom of the steps;
then, looking carefully round, they would lumber
across the road, past the comfortable-smelling
cab-shelter, past the cabmen—who were standing
about in extinct green liveries decorated with tar-
nished brass buttons, and battered, rakish top-
hats, stamping their feet to keep them warm,
thrashing their arms across their bodies, and
blowing long trails of dragon-breath upon the
air—greeting these amiably as they went by.
The Companion would now scrape a clumsy key
in its rusty lock, and they would pass through the
angry-sounding gate into this green heart of the
town. Heavily they would revolve round it, on
an asphalt path, the black and white marking of
which always revived in Miss Bramley's subconscious mind an impression of her aunt's Dalmatians and thus made her think, though herself

could not imagine why, of Miss Titherley-Bramley.   As they circled laboriously, two winter-
vistas would be revealed to them, for the whole
space in front of the hotel resolved itself into a
long, narrow rectangle, of which the vast bulk
of the hotel, looming up over them, formed one
of the wide lines.   The other, opposite, was taken
up by a row of houses, its chief feature the purple
flushed façade of the "Gentlemen's Club," from
which seemed to rise a stertorous palpitation, a
sound of hurrying and harrying.   The small sides
of the rectangle were formed by the vistas framed
in between these two lines of building.   One prospect disclosed a side canal of shiny, blue-grey
road, on which, in the foreground, floated two
weighty islets, supporting lamp-posts, and further
embellished by the presence of numerous vestigial
guardians, absurd little phallic pillars of polished
Aberdeen granite.   These, by their present uselessness, yet serve, as do so many relics, for testimony to past glories, evoked the roaring 'six-
ties, the stentorian 'seventies, when "Champagne
Charlie" was the folksong of the decade, when
Newborough had been a centre of the social
world, when lamp-post climbing was considered a
suitable midnight diversion for any self-respect-
ing young masher, and when the municipal authorities had striven to guard these highly deco-
rative lamp-posts, which were their particular
darlings, by hemming them in with appropriate
stumbling-blocks.   That, at least, seems the
reasonable explanation.   But now such glories
were past, and the only purpose for which these
little pillars could suffice, was that over them the
loitering errand-boy could practise perpetually his

favourite game of leap-frog, to the neglect of
basket and patron.

Beyond this broad canal, with its pair of heavy,
formalised rafts, showed an Italian-Comedy perspective of three streets, full of shops and hurrying little figures, or women pushing perambulators, and pausing to gaze in at the windows with
feminine rapacity. Toward the end of their walk,
the ladies would see the arch-magician of the
town in black coat and bowler hat, walking
straight down one pavement of the middle perspective and back along the other, touching the
lamps with a long wand, whereupon in each glass
flickered a green flame.

The narrow side of the rectangle disclosed distant grey cliffs and hammering sea. The old
battle between static and dynamic was once more
to be seen clearly in action: while as if to sum up
that ancient, fierce feud, in the centre of the circle
round which the two ladies revolved, were the
twin symbols, Cannon and Anchor. Down below
the rolling, wallowing monsters were lashing the
cliffs. Sometimes the immense creatures would
be crowned with sparkling diadems of foam as
they flailed the rocks; or, again, they were
washed, roaring on to the beach, there to dissolve
into an instantaneous death, as in the atmosphere
of this world would a creature from another
planet be, before you could see it, disrupted
utterly. In a moment these bellowing giants had
been transformed into a receding avalanche of
snow that would slowly sizzle backward over the
pebbles, to be reorganised into various other on-
coming bodies.

On the backs of the cliffs across the ravine,

above this ceaseless game of thrust and parry, the white houses of the West Cliff, rubbed by the last, frayed edges of winter sunshine, could be seen gleaming and golden as the gorgeous howdahs that elephants carry at a durbar.

Round and round the green circle the two ladies would walk, eyed from the porch by John, the hall-porter, round those symbols, Crimean Cannon and Pirate Anchor. From the houses on the other side, too, a close watch would be kept on them by the representatives of Miss Waddington and Mrs. Shrubfield. Even opera-glasses, even a telescope, were not unknown as the instruments of this intense scrutiny.

The old lady's spirits seemed very low, and she hardly spoke to Miss Bramley at all during their walk.

CHAPTER XXIII

TEA

INSTEAD of resting after this exercise, the old lady would insist, more often than not, on lumbering round in a cab to have tea with the Floodgays. There was no stopping her when she was in these moods: but it infuriated Miss Bramley, because really it was difficult to have much patience with a friend who continued obstinately to wear herself out for such people. Look at Miss Waddington! Now, there was a case in point. She must be older than Cecilia, much older: but she was too sensible, too well-brought-up (perhaps that was it) to fatigue herself running after comparative strangers (in a sense, a comparative stranger was regarded by Miss Bramley as being even more of a double-dyed stranger than a total stranger, for in addition to the Ishmael-quality common to both, there was, somehow or other, in the word "comparative" an implication of dubiety) and ought to last many years longer, dear old lady.

It was at this hour, deserted after her walk, that the Companion, unless invited to tea by Miss Waddington, felt more solitary than at any other time in the day: for tea was the only ritual to which she did not present a protestant attitude. Tea, to Miss Bramley, meant infinitely more than a mere beverage: it was a synonym for an hour of sprightly conversation and agreeable

camaraderie: while to be forced for ever to have
tea by herself was to her the very proof of being
outcast from the worlds of fire-lit rooms and
friendship.

Thus one afternoon the desolate Miss Bramley
was sitting alone in the "lounge," trying to steel
her will before ringing the bell to order a lonely,
an early tea. She could not make her mind up
to it. Seated, as she was, in that echoing, shadowy room, her mind wandered down the long
avenue of pleasant trees that lay behind her, a
diminishing perspective of summer fêtes-cham-
pêtres or of brightly-lit interiors, with the flickering cockscombs of the flames mirroring themselves in china cups and china bowls, while the
clear silver music of spoon clinking against cup
mingled with the refined hum of well-bred voices,
not too loud, nor too deprecatingly soft. Even
scented shade of the cedar, the seed of which had
been brought from Lebanon by some fervent
former incumbent, had been charming and gay:
after Mildred's marriage, herself had been allowed to pour out the tea and preside. The
curates had always helped to make things "go,"
and it had been so pretty, with the beds of flowers
and evergreens. Then, best of all, followed the
drawing-room at Llandriftlog, with its hissing,
silver kettle straddling prodigiously over a flame,
a flame so hallowed that it was never allowed to
be annihilated by such rude processes as blowing
from puffed-out cheeks. As, formerly, in various
countries, the criminal of illustrious birth was,
when at last the dreadful hour of earthly expia-
tion struck, suspended from a silken cord, lest the
common hangman's hempen rope should sully his

nobility, thus here too, when the time came for
the sacred flame to be quenched, a special im-
plement, shaped like a trumpet and wrought of
silver, was provided for its stately extinction.
Down this, which seemed the pipe of some fairy
music inaudible to the grosser senses of mankind,
Miss Bramley had been allowed to practise: on
it, indeed, at one time, she had attained to a considerable degree of virtuosity, so that when people
were present she would be sent for, from her
corner, to perform. "Where is Teresa?" Miss
Fansharpe used to demand, "Ask her to come
here and blow it out for us." There had been
so many little touches of that sort about Miss
Fansharpe's teas, bowls of hot water, over the
steam of which were balanced plates of scones—
those special, little "soda" scones which had been
provided for the enticement and delectation of
Dr. Broometoken, and all sorts of small cakes and
biscuits, things unusual, and refined and "out-of-
the-common." After she had left Llandriftlog
there had been some nice teas at Mildred's, often
with a Fuller's walnut-cake, while the thin,
tinkling treble of teaspoons harmonised with the
distant, more manly music of "ping-pong." And
there had been many enjoyable teas at the Badminton, very lively, in the "Palm Lounge," with
little tartlets made of tinned cherries, very French
and prettily made, and people going in and out.
Lately, too, had come all those delightful intimate tea-parties at Miss Waddington's. How she
wished she was going there to-day; but she did
not like to go there too often, unless definitely
invited: for Miss Waddington asked her constantly, and she did not wish to appear "push-

ing" . . . why even the teas which Cecilia and
herself used to have in the drawing-room—before
the old lady had met the Floodgays—had been
pleasurable.   The tea was good, and there had
been tea-cakes: and, until it was ready, she
usually asked Miss Bramley to sing. She remembered it all so well, because it was before tea one
day that she had sung for the first time, "Because
God Made Thee Mine," and Cecilia had made her
repeat it twice, she had liked it so much . . . and
here . . . now . . . she was alone in an empty
room, for Cecilia (it was no use pretending to
oneself that it was not so) *preferred* to sit there
at St. Saviour's Vicarage, boasting of her money,
boasting, like a badly-brought-up child, of her
money, and being humbugged—for that was what
it came to—by that sly, simpering girl with the
red hair, and by her disagreeable, scheming, and
"*fast*" mother.

As Miss Bramley pondered on these past
scenes, and compared them with the present,
which she was still unable to face, for to-day,
really, she could hardly bear to order her solitary
tea, a page-boy came in, bearing on a salver a
card, the alternate corners of which were turned
up and down. On this she read the name of Mrs.
Shrubfield, while written below, in a rather shaky
hand, was "*Ma chérie,* would you care to come
for a drive, *pour passer le temps,* with your
'*molta vecchia*' friend? Then we might have tea
somewhere?—L.S."

How odd her coming round like this, for she
never called at the hotel as a rule because she
did not know Miss Collier-Floodgaye, Miss
Bramley imagined. But how thoughtful and kind

of the old lady to "look her up" like this. "Tell
Mrs. Shrubfield that Miss Bramley will be delighted," she said to the page, and hurried upstairs to get her things on. Soon she was ready,
and going down the steps toward the carriage.
The hood of the Victoria was up, for it was a
cold, dank evening and Mrs. Shrubfield leant
out with a true, if rather unsteady, old-world
courtesy, to receive her young friend, for such
she invariably termed her. Thus framed, between hood and box, the pyramid presented an
imposing spectacle. So great was Mrs. Shrubfield's pleasure at seeing Miss Bramley, that
from her eye it was obvious that she was suspended half-way between tears and laughter.
The jet of it was softened by a pendent tear.
Miss Bramley got in, and they drove off at a
considerable pace. Mrs. Shrubfield had come
out, she said, because she had not been feeling
very well, and had thought that a drive might
do her good. It had struck her suddenly, why
not call at the Superb for that little *darling,* Miss
Bramley, and take her for an outing. She was
not feeling at all well, shaken you know, and very
tired, very tired indeed. Her speech was sibilant
and indistinct, Miss Bramley noticed: from weak-
ness, no doubt. Mrs. Shrubfield was inclined to
attribute this unfortunate state of feebleness in
which she found herself partly to those dreadful
"tonics" ("Never take tonichs, they're absholutely
fatal," she said, "Tonichsh only make you tired,
O SHO tired"), and partly to the fact that she
had foolishly indulged in a claw of lobster for
lunch. Lobster always had that effect on her.
Curious. It was silly of her to take it. And

(hélas!) she was getting old: washn't whatch she ush'be." A little air was the thing, she had said to herself: and the coachman (had been with her years) had wanted little-air too, you know, lill'air: not feeling quite the thing, he had said to her. Perhaps he had eaten lobster too (and here Mrs. Shrubfield in sudden, spasmodic recovery, laughed loud and long). No doubt that was it: lobshter, you know what seaside towns are!

He seemed a very fast driver, Miss Bramley thought. And the carriage rocked so. She did not like to say anything, but she could not help wondering whether the motion of the carriage was not connected with Mrs. Shrubfield being unwell. However, in spite of feeling tired, she was so genial and pleasant. Even now, though, she complained of not getting enough air: notwithstanding the fact that the carriage appeared to be positively whizzing through square and crescent (they must be very good horses to go like that, but Miss Bramley could not see quite in which direction they were going, as the hood was up)—and would send her guardian wild-beast spinning like a roulette-ball round her neck in the effort to disentangle tooth from toe, and so gain more ventilation. The horses drew up, all at once, with such a jar that the footman nearly fell off the box (he was not feeling well either, apparently. Miss Bramley began to feel quite worried about them. She hoped so much that they had not *all* been poisoned) and there they were . . . at Miss Waddington's. What a surprise, for Mrs. Shrubfield had never mentioned where they were going for tea. · Indeed she seemed somewhat startled too, at first—she had

not expected to be there shoshun, she said. She
got out, saying, "Here we are," with her usual
dignity of bearing; and it was just tea-time. So
much nicer than sitting in the Superb with no one
to talk to. They rang the bell (Mrs. Shrubfield
did it herself, and waved the footman away: but
it was difficult to find the bell at once in the dark.
Where wash-it?) several times, but for some time
nobody answered it. Then Ella came running to
the door. "I am so sorry to have kept you waiting, but I've only just come in. I can't imagine
where Thompson is. But of course Aunt Hester
will see both of you—she is never out to you.
Let me straighten your bonnet, dear (to Mrs.
Shrubfield). There, that's better!" And she led
them upstairs. Ella threw open the door; there
sat Miss Waddington, and with her, to Miss
Bramley's intense astonishment, were (and actually *sitting down*) Thompson the parlourmaid
and . . . Elisa! . . .

For a moment, Miss Bramley felt that she was
going to faint, it seemed so unreal and dreamlike.
Surely it was not quite the thing for a Waddington to do, to have servants to tea in that familiar
manner? What could she want with Elisa? And
it was so queer that Elisa should never have mentioned it. Why, Miss Bramley was almost sure
that the German maid had told her she was going
to tea with the Sexton at the Cemetery. It was
extraordinary. . . .

But the effect of the scene that greeted Miss
Bramley was as nothing compared with the result
of that lady's entry upon Miss Waddington,
whose fragile old face (just like a piece of carved
ivory, Miss Bramley used to think) was now

suffused with colour, contorted with varying emotions. The master-eye was swift as ever in diagnosis: she took in the situation at a glance.
Louise was having another of her "bouts" evidently, and it was all that fool-of-a-girl again.
But this time, it was too much. Obviously it was
not safe to leave the creature by herself for a
moment. The idiot should pack up to-night, and
leave to-morrow morning: and Miss Waddington
would alter her will as soon as the lawyer could
get down to see her.

Meanwhile it was difficult to know what to say.
Fortunately Thompson could be relied upon. By
this time she had already dragged Elisa, still
placidly greeting Miss Bramley, out of the room.
Mrs. Shrubfield was sobered by her consciousness of the enormity for which she was responsible, and remained for the moment silent but
gasping, as if having come to the surface after a
dip into ice-cold water. Miss Waddington could
therefore concentrate on the two most important
points—how best to disguise from Miss Bramley
the actual nature of Mrs. Shrubfield's illness, and
how best to account to the Companion for the
visit upon which she had intruded. It would
never do to leave it unexplained. That would
only make her think of it the more.

Miss Waddington was determined to restore
order. The first thing to do was to look pleasant
again, as if nothing had happened. The only
drawback was that then Ella might think her aunt
was pleased with her. Never mind, the fool
would quickly be undeceived after the departure
of the guests.

Oh, Miss Waddington was so pleased to see

them. What a delicious, unexpected visit! And
some fresh tea was coming up in a minute.
Thompson was just getting it. "Louise, dear,"
she said to Mrs. Shrubfield, "you must break your
rules for once, and have tea. It will freshen you
up. You look depressed." Indeed, a startled,
tearful expression was fixed in the eyes of that
lady. Thompson, relapsed into the perfect parlour-maid, brought in the tea, and the hostess
began to explain.

How curious to think that Elisa was the maid
who looked after Miss Bramley. What a strange
coincidence (here Mrs. Shrubfield, seeing that she
must help, with a supreme effort, overcame her
feelings and remarked in a voice, which harboured
a fat tear of remorse, "Doesn't it only show how
small the world is!"—too tired to talk for herself,
she wisely acted the part of Greek chorus).
Really, it was extraordinary ("the sort of thing
one reads about," Mrs. Shrubfield added) extraordinary—why, Miss Waddington had known
the girl for years—she was interested in Mission
Work ("nothing like Misshun Work," Mrs.
Shrubfield thought, but Miss Waddington flashed
a glance that signalled silence on her) of all sorts,
and especially in some of the bigger German
cities. One of her German friends had written
to her, asking her to "keep an eye" on the girl.
And Miss Waddington felt one could not do
enough for foreigners in a strange land. They
must feel so alone, so deserted (dear old thing,
Miss Bramley thought, how charitable she was!)
so she often asked the poor thing to tea, just to
show her that one person regarded her as a
human being like herself: and, she had found it

better ("mush better") to have Thompson there
too. It put the foreigner more at her ease; but
Miss Waddington had always told Elisa not to
mention her, for she hated these little actions
of hers to get about. If these little actions one
did were once to become public property, one
would be prevented from doing any more; because people would say (here the tragic chorus,
unable to repress itself any more, joined in with,
"You know what people are") that one did them
simply to gain applause (sweet old lady, that was
just like her! the Companion reflected). And
Miss Waddington had to admit that she thought
the girl was really grateful to her and understood
("Oh, yesh, she undershtood"). Why the very
fact that she had never mentioned her to Miss
Bramley, went to prove it. A good girl, in her
way. "But, perhaps, my dear," she concluded,
to Miss Bramley, "perhaps you had better not
say anything to her about it. It may embarrass
her. Promise me, dear."

Really Miss Waddington was a wonderful old
lady. Her consideration for others continually
came as a surprise to one, Miss Bramley reflected.
Mrs. Shrubfield seemed very quiet; she hoped so
much that she was feeling better. As a matter
of fact, by an intense effort of will, Miss Waddington was still holding the unusually jovial lady
in check. Her expression had changed; admiration now mingled in it with repentance. But, if
still rather overcome, she meant to atone to some
little extent for her misdemeanours.

Miss Bramley had to return to the Superb in
order to dress for dinner. She rose to go. Miss
Waddington commanded Mrs. Shrubfield not to

move. "You're too tired, dear. Stay where you are for the present. Deah Teresa (this was the first time she had called Miss Bramley by her Christian name) will understand"—by which she really meant that under the circumstances she hoped Miss Bramley would *not* understand.

Now was Mrs. Shrubfield's moment of triumph. She must do something that would show her normal, sober grasp of foreign languages, and, by installing her still more surely in the Companion's favour, would blind that lady to all little oddities of manner. She did not get up. Instead, she enunciated clearly, but not without effort, "Teresa, *Liebchen,* may I 'tutoyer' you, as well?" Miss Bramley walked out into the dark night, where wind and sea could be heard in their perpetual tourney, more than ever enchanted with her two friends. Dear old ladies! And she looked up at the lighted windows with a gust of emotion.

Up there in the fire-gilded room an affecting scene was taking place. The knowledge that through her failing she had nearly brought their plans to naught, hurled away with her own hand the Cup of Victory, the intensity of the exertion she had made, on realising this, to retrieve the position, and to support her fellow-leader, had been too much for Mrs. Shrubfield. The tears which she had long held back were flowing. Indeed this was the only time in their acquaintance that Mrs. Shrubfield ever mentioned "it" to Miss Waddington. "Forgive me, Hester," she choked, "if I have been at all foolish. But I have been so tired out by the whole affair, that I simply had to take something to keep my strength up. And,

you see, if one's not used to it . . . I wish I'd
never seen that horrid lame, old woman: and that
little beast Mrs. Floodgay is blackening our characters everywhere. It'll be the death of me." So
moved was she at this instant, that for perhaps
the only time in her life, her lingual gifts deserted
her. "It will be the death of me," she repeated.
"I have a good mind to leave Newborough for
ever, and find a little *'ventre-a-terre'* in London."

CHAPTER XXIV

THE POOL

MISS BRAMLEY had begun to shrink from the long black nights. She was sure that her friend's health was worse, but this the doctor would not admit. The Companion dreaded the sighs, the strugglings, of the old woman in her sleep. These turnings and groanings must have communicated to her their infection, for she was not, in this sense, inherently at all nervous: but now she was filled with apprehension, startled by any sound, however obvious its explanation. It was disturbing to lie there listening, in the lulls that occasionally intervened between the bellowing of the gales outside, to the broken murmuring and deep susurration of the old lady in her sleep. It was not natural. With whom was she conversing in the dark, wintry recesses of her mind, what was it she feared, the image of something that had occurred at her life's beginning or the shadow of that which was yet to come to pass, the only sure event that was still left before her, an event of which she would only be able to trace the prognostic shadow, never to grasp the reality by which it was projected? There were times, indeed, when Miss Bramley felt that she could not go on like this, could not stand it any longer. The days, burdened by loneliness, the nights with their load of fear, were becoming unsupportable. How she wished that she had a little money put away,

a little money of her *own,* so that she could live somewhere quietly, near Mildred. Why she might even go out to Malta for a winter, to see Peregrine; the Broometokens would be there. It would be nice to see them again. Of course, though, even if she were suddenly to find herself rich, she could never leave Cecilia, trying as she was, in her present state. Still, there were times . . .

Life revolved regularly enough. Tea and bridge; church and luncheon on Sunday; the walk in the afternoon: tea and bridge again; dinners, complaints of failing memory, and troubled nights that opened out like a telescope.

As for Cecilia's memory, Miss Bramley was determined to aid it no longer. It was bad for her, taught her to depend too much on others. Certainly she was not going to remind the old lady about seeing the lawyer. Surely, as she was always asking to be reminded, she could remember to do it for herself? But that was Cecilia all over. She could always call things to mind, when it was useless, too early or too late. And she only wanted to see the solicitor in order "to make things easier" for the Floodgays (the Companion could hear in her own mind, at this moment the girl saying "Aunt Cecilia," in her silly, ingratiating manner). Well, Miss Bramley was resolved not to interfere, one side or the other. It was no concern of hers: but she was not going out of her way to favour the plans of a scheming woman like Mrs. Floodgay. No, if Cecilia wished to do that sort of thing, she must remember it for herself. Miss Bramley was willing to do anything else for her, but not that.

If Miss Collier-Floodgaye showed a tendency
in any direction, it was toward tiring herself still
further. She was inclined to sit up later now, and
would seize on any plea for postponing the hour
of attempted slumber. Dinner in the hotel was
at 7.30, and when the old lady had first come to
Newborough, she had been in the habit of retiring
to rest at ten. But this winter, even if there was
no excuse for sitting up, even if she was alone
with her Companion—with whom, now that her
aged mind was always and entirely occupied with
the Floodgays, she found conversation difficult—
in a vast room that stood dark, empty and deserted, it was usually well past eleven o'clock before Miss Bramley could persuade her to go to
bed. The Companion considered that a long
night, restful or unrestful, was necessary to the
health of any one, especially if that person were
old and failing; but Miss Collier-Floodgaye was
content with little sleep, for, with a surer judgment, she perhaps realised that just as bed is the
most common scaffold for men's execution, so
slumber is the most venomous foe of the elderly.
Indeed it is very noticeable that the old favour
late hours and early rising, usually attributing
this to the fact that they require less sleep than
the young. But, in all probability, it is that they
are aware, without thinking it out, that directly
the controlling will slumbers, old age can seize on
the body, attempting to assassinate it as it lies
there helpless. How often do we hear of fortunate people who died in their sleep; a peaceful
end, it is said! Yet who is to know the agony
of terror which may have engulfed them in their
last moments of dreaming, and, which, since they

never woke from it, was to them the reality? The
hideous nightmare from which we awake is yet
sufficient to impregnate the whole day that
follows with the blue-black poisonous tint of
nightshade, though we know it to be but a fantasy
spun out by the unconscious mind, that lumber-
room of acquired and inherited memories. But
to those that die under the spell of such a storm
of horror, the dream is the actuality. They die
writhing under the tortures of the Inquisition,
stabbed by a murderer, falling down a precipice,
or entangled in some catastrophe so involved, in
the grip of a fear so intense, that the waking
mind cannot conceive it, as truly as if these experiences had befallen them in fact. Perhaps
Miss Collier-Floodgaye knew that the night was
waiting to catch her, to swallow her up for ever.

The old lady seemed bent, however, on
fatiguing herself in every possible way. She was
resolute on participating in any gaiety or attempt
at gaiety that was being planned. This may have
been the result of an effort to prove to herself
that she was still young, or it may have been due
to a belief that so long as she behaved in a normal
manner, not refraining from ordinary pleasures,
no such unique or final a thing as death could
overcome her. Thus, too, Bess of Hardwick is
stated to have believed that she would never die
while she continued to have new houses built for
her, for building had been her life's interest.
And, in truth, it was not until there came a hard
frost which prevented the laying of bricks, that
the venerable lady passed away.

As all else in Miss Collier-Floodgaye weak-
ened, her religious fervour increased. Once or

twice a week even, she would now attend Morning Service at St. Saviour's on a week day, while she never failed to be in her pew every Sunday: and it tired her as much as anything, for she allowed it to draw so much vitality away from her. But the flowers (how well May arranged them!) the warmth, the colour, the incense, the crowd, the music, all mingled in an atmosphere that was exciting to her. The coloured lights would flicker hither and thither, the colours would change, shift, graduate, in tone as the organ sounded out, rose up majestically toward the roof that redoubled the volume of it, till her senses were caught in all these combining strands that joined together, almost invisibly, the silken intricacies of a spiritual cobweb that entangled her reason. The voices of the singing boys became the actual, welcoming roulades of the angels, while the rolling thunder of the accompanying music was transformed into the authentic, awe-inspiring accents of the Supreme Being. Her spirit was excessively troubled. Heaven and Hell took on a new and comprehensible significance. Heaven was a ritual and emotive affair, compounded of colour and music, such as this service, but transcendent and eternal, Hell a black, never-ending night of fear and torture.

．　　．　　．　　．　　．　　．　　．

Shortly before Christmas there was a ball in aid of the Life-Boat. It was a local festivity. The County refused to take any interest in it, for they could not spare a moment from the varying massacres of the season. But though this abstention may have detracted from the social in-

terest it is not so certain that it did not promote the gaiety of the occasion. The townspeople displayed an abandon, the secret of which, having been instilled in most of them as children by Mr. de Flouncey, whose *joie-de-vivre*, as we have seen, was derived from a long line of hypothetic French noblemen, could be regarded as Continental by adoption.

Of course Miss Collier-Floodgaye had taken tickets for Cécile and her mother, and, long before the dance had started, was waiting for them in the hall; an inappropriate enough figure she looked, among the accumulating crowd of revellers, all at present silent, pulling on and off their gloves but looking as pleasant as tense expectation would allow them.

Miss Bramley had refused to attend this function. She could not express how much she disapproved of the whole proceeding. If Cecilia was determined to shatter what little health remained to her, she, at any rate, refused to take any responsibility in the matter. She was not going to tell Mrs. Floodgay what she thought of it, for that would be undignified, "playing into their hands"; instead she would allow her outraged feelings to be reflected in her manner, which she had contrived as a mirror for them. But Miss Bramley was really worried about her friend. When she had left her standing in the hall, her anger had evaporated, leaving only a residue of intense concern. The Companion, therefore, made up her mind to watch the dance from the gallery for a while. There she found Elisa, so immersed in the scene of revelry below that she had lost her gift of loquacious lamentation, and

had relapsed into that other self, the dumb, flaxen automaton.

Looking down, Miss Bramley could see the girl, dressed in green, of course (that hair, again) pulling at her glove, swinging her programme from its attached pencil. And there, sitting against the wall, were Cecilia and Mrs. Floodgay. The music throbbed out, drumming round the ceiling like a swarm of bees. The couples began to revolve, as though a bed of multicoloured flowers had determined to arrange itself in new patterns. One or two tired and fading blossoms drooped at the side, pushed against the border of the more vigorous flowers.

Cecilia looked absolutely worn out, Miss Bramley thought, so weary and sombre. It was ridiculous for her to pretend that she enjoyed it. She ought not to be sitting there, tiring herself by talking through all that noise. Nothing could be worse for her. Mrs. Floodgay, evidently, was not even listening to her stories. She just sat there, tapping a white shoe in time, more or less, to the music, and piercing her daughter with a reproachfully bright and benignant eye. Not a clumsy movement, not an awkward word on Cécile's part was lost upon Mrs. Floodgay (but she should not speak to the child about it while Aunt Cecilia was there. She should wait till afterward.)

Miss Bramley felt angry again. It disgusted her to see her friend sitting there, talking, talking, talking. It was no use fretting—she was obviously determined to stay there all night. Miss Bramley could see that. Really she must be very strong after all. Supper at her age! The truth of it was that she must have a wonderful consti-

tution, and it was silly of one to worry oneself about her.

Not until past two o'clock did Miss Collier-Floodgaye come upstairs to bed. Miss Bramley had been waiting for her many an hour, for, in spite of her decision not to worry, she had been unable to obtain a moment's rest, gnawed as she was by the iron tooth of jealousy, torn by the steel claws of anxiety. There she lay, listening for the ascending, comforting chant of the lift. Many times it disappointed her. It seemed to her that she had never known it used so much, even during the biggest dances, at this time of night. And after each of its chantings, she hoped to hear the well-known footfall, accompanied by the tapping stick. So often did the lift deceive her by its cheerfulness that, by the time the footstep was heard, she had reached the stage, so well-known to expectant lovers, where, when she heard the long-awaited step, herself refused to believe in its authenticity. At last the door opened; the light was switched on, and the old lady entered.

Miss Bramley was intensely relieved; for, she did not know why, but she understood now that, under the superficial feelings of annoyance and irritation, she had been really alarmed about her friend all the evening. Well, it taught one not to be anxious, for Cecilia seemed perfectly all right. Another time, she should just go to sleep, without fretting. At the same time, Miss Bramley could not help feeling that people who behave in a manner contrary to all sane laws, ought to be made to suffer for it. After all, if herself stayed up to supper, though only half the old

lady's age, she would not feel any the better for it. But, in spite of her appearance of "failing," the old lady seemed to be able to do anything she liked with impunity. And, before going to bed, she began about the lawyer again. "Would Tibbits remind her in the morning?" "If you did not tire yourself like this, dear, you would have no need to ask me to remind you," the Companion retorted, quite overcome by her irritation.

But in the night, the old lady appeared to be frightened. The faintest sound in the darkness (and any dark room is full of those inexplicable little rustlings and crepitations of which what we call silence is composed) would startle her. As soon as Miss Bramley had obtained a moment's sleep, the old lady would wake her up. "What's that? Do you hear it?" she would cry. After all, there was nothing to be afraid of: and if she behaved like other people of her age, she would not be visited by such dumb and eyeless terrors.

At last Miss Bramley was permitted to lose her way in a real stretch of slumber. In the fantastic place and period where she found herself, Mrs. Floodgay had somehow or other become Companion to Miss Fansharpe, and the Colonel— Colonel Fansharpe of whom Miss Bramley had not thought for many years—had come on a long visit to his aunt. And Cécile had been engaged as a housemaid, but Miss Fansharpe did not trust her and wished to have her placed in her Home, while, at the same time, she was busily occupied in playing her old game of cat-and-mouse with Mrs. Floodgay. And dear old Dr. Broometoken was there, and they were all going out to Malta to stay with him. Then Dr.

Broometoken said how delightfu' it would be to
bathe . . . yes, bathe . . . and as they plunged
into the embracing ocean, it became a still-water
pool, overhung by long green branches. She was
nearly at the bottom of a deep, calm pool, filled
with wan water-flowers and coral rocks, when a
sound, an ever so faint sound, called her up
through the various layers of consciousness. She
was swimming up and up, through the green
waters to the dim daylight at the top of the pond.
Would she come to the surface in time, for some
one was drowning? She could hear the strangled
gurgling of the sinking body. She must hurry
to rescue it. Daylight filtered with more strength
into the green abysses. She was near the top
now, must rescue: and, as she gained the surface,
she was saying to herself, "I told you so, I told
you so."

The grey light was creeping stealthily into the
bedroom. It was nearly eight o'clock. Elisa
would be here in a few moments now . . . but
there it was again, that sound of choking that
she had heard. Miss Bramley switched on the
light.

.   .   .   .

Yes, it was a seizure, Dr. MacRacket said. Of
course she might recover the use of her limbs.
We would know in a day or two. Oh, yes, it
was inevitable. He would send a very good
nurse, a nice woman, capable and cheerful. Miss
Bramley must take care of *herself*, too, he added.
Everything would be all right. Leave it to him.
Quite all right. Nothing would be gained by
taking a pessimistic view. One must look on the
bright side. Nothing to be done really, at

present, except send round the nurse. Had she
tried to speak at all? No, not much?

. . . .

The day, like the night that had heralded it,
grew longer and longer. The winter gales could
be heard cracking their knouts at each window,
attacking the hotel as though they were determined to overpower and sack it, while through
all this furious galloping could yet be detected
the more remote sound of the sea battering at
rock and cliff. The cold light, which was the
very colour of the sea, penetrated painfully into
the hotel bedroom, where, upon her bed, the old
lady lay rigid and prone as a tree uprooted by
the gale. During most of the day, Miss Bramley
thought, she was insensible. The face had set
in tragic lines, and when for a few seconds each
hour or two the spirit was dragged back through
interminable tunnels into the worn-out vessel that
had contained it, the eyes flashed again with their
brave, accustomed fire. But something, they
made it evident, was on the old lady's mind.
This occasional life, flickering through the eyes,
made still more painful in contrast the surrounding deadness. As a sparking-plug attempts to
fire an engine, so the eyes appeared to be engaged
in an attempt, as it were, to infuse with life the
stricken body. At less frequent intervals it
seemed that the eyes were momentarily successful in the task they had undertaken, for from the
mouth struggled a few sounds that bore a mimick-
ing relation to human words: thus might an ape,
perhaps, essay speech. During these few instants
the eyes of the old woman assumed a look of
remote but utter sadness, almost of despair; con-

tained an appeal that came from the distance
of another planet. Then, utterly exhausted by
the violence of this effort, the darkness of approaching night closed round her again. The
nurse could make little of these simian sounds
that died on the old woman's blue cold lips. But
she wanted something, of that she was sure.
Before the end, very possibly, she would be able
to speak. It was often like that: they spoke
just before the end came. It couldn't go on for
long. She was sinking, the nurse was convinced.

It seemed that these words were comprehended
by the felled figure in the bed, for the eyes became insistent, begged and implored help, while
for several minutes the meaningless sounds bub-
bled up and foamed out of the slack lips. The
nurse wondered what it could be?

But Miss Bramley could interpret these
strangled utterances; Miss Bramley knew what
the eyes entreated. The old lady, ill as she was,
dying perhaps, was still fretting herself about
seeing the lawyer. That was what it was. Well,
the Companion, for one, was not going to help
her. She loved Cecilia in her shrunken and
dwarfish heart, but would not aid her, in this
matter, though she would have done anything
else in the world for the old woman. After all,
it was the Floodgays who were answerable for
the terrible punishment inflicted on the gaunt,
motionless body, and Miss Bramley would be
party to no scheme that would benefit them; do
nothing that could be to their advantage, nothing!
Why even now they were besieging the hotel;
never a half-hour went by, but a card was brought
up, and on it—in Mrs. Floodgay's writing, of

course—"How is Aunt Cecilia? Can we see her
for an instant?" or "How is Aunt Cecilia? Does
she want anything?" It was really disgraceful
to continue pestering and scheming at a time like
this. They were responsible, entirely and absolutely responsible, for the old lady's plight, and
Miss Bramley was not going to stretch out her
little finger to help them.

The stiff figure in the bed made a renewed
effort, struggled again with her words: more
fiercely she fought with them. The sombre eyes,
gazing from so far away, took on a more tragic
glow; for she was now aware that her Companion had grasped the meaning which she was
attempting so painfully to frame. She felt no
anger with her, knowing that it was affection,
and no mere material greed, that prompted Miss
Bramley's refusal to interpret what she understood. No, it was anguish, intolerable sorrow,
that burnt from under these deep sockets. If
only she could make "Tibbits" understand, give
way, in time: for she realised that little time was
left. But once more her enemy, the night, carried
her off in his powerful, black arms, and the
swollen tongue was still.

She lay quite quiet now, the bony ridges and
furrows of her face very clearly marked. "No,
tell Mrs. Floodgay that I can't see her," Miss
Bramley was saying outside the door to John the
porter. Every moment they were coming round
to the hotel—that is, if they ever quitted it! So
inconsiderate. And it stirred the old lady up
again. Evidently they did not mind what happened. How different was the tone of Mrs.
Floodgay's note from that of Mrs. Shrubfield's.

"*Ma chère Teresa, Povera ragazza,* I have come round to see if there is anything I can do for you? Miss Waddington is with me. You have only to say the word. Yr. sincere old friend, L. S.

P.S. Mrs. Floodgay is here in the hall. That queer, red-haired girl of hers is crying, extraordinarily upset. It is, surely, hardly the time to make scenes of that sort. We have taken no notice of either of them."

What dear old creatures they were! But how had they heard, Miss Bramley wondered. However, that was like them! They were ever on the watch to help; to try, in their quiet way, to do good.

And, indeed, it was surprising how the news of Miss Collier-Floodgaye's illness had spread. In every room facing South the news of the end of it (for such invalid veterans were not deceived by Dr. MacRacket's optimism) was awaited with interest, though with equanimity. (Another name, then, was to be struck off the list!) The sight of Mrs. Shrubfield's carriage, displaying in its open shell the two aged but indomitable leaders, kindled emotion in the ranks, and caused a thrill of loyalty and enthusiasm to course through their knotted veins. If it had been correct on such an occasion, if, indeed, their asthmatic lungs had permitted of it, they would from their upper windows have greeted the dauntless Marshals with a hearty and united shout of encouragement and loyal approval.

. . . . . .

When Dr. MacRacket called again in the evening, Miss Collier-Floodgaye was unconscious, did not stir. Night had imprisoned her. The

doctor advised Miss Bramley to wait up with the old lady. The nurse, too, must stay in the room.

Miss Bramley, meanwhile, dismissed the last appeal of the Floodgays. No, she could not see them: and they could not see "Aunt Cecilia." Miss Collier-Floodgaye could see no one, she added. The night passed tardily to the watchers.

CHAPTER XXV

THE LAST POST

THERE was no sound, no movement. The dying woman lay there unmoving, apparently unthinking. But who is to know what processes were taking place in that remote mind, buried deep in the night, what memories of childhood were reviving with a strange, if flickering, intensity on that dark screen? There was present, undoubtedly, the ever strengthening motif of religion. The rainbow-winged butterflies hovered and danced again over the stone walls, through the warm, droning air. The voices pursued them yet more swiftly, trying to secure the fragile, beating sails in their nets, while the host of cherubs that swept after them through the upper dimness clapped their golden wings in leaping, swallow-like flight.

Toward six o'clock in the morning, the expected change set in. The old woman opened her eyes and tried to speak: her brain was alive once more. Perhaps the inanimation of the rest of her body served to give the eyes a more than normal share of life, enabled them to flame with a concentrated intensity. In their dark, cavernous recesses they smouldered fiercely, and the fear in them had deepened into terror. During these few moments, the look of appeal, of entreaty, became doubly vehement; they spoke, indeed, with infinitely more ease than the tongue,

which, in its piteous struggle was tapping out
idiot-tunes against the palate. Not for an instant
did these terrible eyes leave Miss Bramley. As
she moved, they followed her, within the limits
imposed upon them by the immobility of the
neck, trunk and limbs. The Companion, it may
be, felt a little inclined to move out of their range,
to busy herself with the trivial paraphernalia
of illness, of pillows, eau-de-cologne and medi-
cine: but they met her anew as she moved within
their orbit. Yet they exercised a fascination over
her. She could not for long look away. Now
with the final, supreme effort of a mighty frame
and a strong will, the old woman contrived to
utter a deep, warning moan—a sound which,
though it lacked words, possessed the old
authentic and authoritative note, the personal
music of her voice—and with a shuddering of
the entire form, moved her right hand in the
gesture of signing a paper.

The nurse wondered what the patient wanted,
as the old woman relapsed into night. It must
be the last return of vigour, she thought. So
often they do something like that. But, just as
the old woman was travelling away from the
light, dragged down those endless black tunnels
and corridors, something again touched in her
a chord of memory. Her hearing, possibly, had
become more acute, as the fire in the eyes had
burnt more brightly, from this same restriction
of energy. Except for the tumult of the invading
army of winds, and the distant clamour of the
turning tide, the darkness was very silent; but,
now, a bell could be heard clacking out, high up
under the dome. She opened her eyes. How she

longed to speak in that same iron voice, loud
and strong enough to make any meaning understood, any command obeyed: and, because time
had long since ceased to have any significance
for her, the metallic music occupied an indefinite
period, a stretch that rivalled the whole length
of her lifetime. Still the bell racketed on. If
only she could make herself heard as clearly;
but the words stuck, stuck far down and would
not creep out from the guttural hiding-places,
while the iron voice upstairs was distinct and
determined. Gradually this persistent music
draped itself in her mind with a new beauty.
She found herself back again in the long tunnel,
and now there shone at the end of it, that for
the first time she could see, an immense glory.
The music, ever deeper and more magnificent,
reached her, it seemed, from this burning majesty
which she was so tirelessly approaching. As she
strode on, for her lameness had left her, the
gorgeous butterflies flew in front of her, the pursuing choir of angels rode the air level with her.
The iron voice, which betrayed itself through
their singing, at the end of the tunnel, was the
voice of the Great Judge. She was going toward
it. Now they were trying to drag her back, and
she would then find herself once more lying there
unable to move. They were trying to pull her
back down that immeasurable corridor, but she
would not turn. She must go on toward the
Voice, march forward to the music; meet the
Glory. She had left them, and silence and darkness received her.

・　　・　　・　　・　　・　　・　　・

But the bell shrilled on. It had only been

ringing for a second or two. **The tin-tongue**
rattled through the silence of the empty building;
so loudly it racketed that, surely, it must have
pierced through the layers of cloud, at this season
stretched like blankets, one over another endlessly, and must now echo through the ultimate
blue imbecility above. But this lining was in
the winter a thing utterly incredible; while the
grey blankets above and beneath yet invited
slumber, warm deep slumber. But on and on it
cackled, this idiot tongue, trying to inform the
sleeper of its monotonous, invariable message,
slave to a slave, machine to a machine. It seemed
fearful, though, of betraying its trust. Six
o'clock, six o'clock, six o'clock, it hammered and
ranted. The sleeper could calculate precisely,
through long experience, the last moment of this
alarum. She swung back swiftly from her wanderings in the pine-forests of Germany, lumbered
out of bed into the frozen air, switched on the
light, tumbled into her tousled, rumpled clothes,
and reset (as later she must reset her clock) her
features into their daily, customary perspective.
It grew colder and colder. Angrily she shook
her body, turned out the light and creaked
blunderingly out of the room.

Now she was wading through the familiar stillness, a silence infringed by a thousand crepuscular crepitations of the hotel corridors. As she
advanced, these minute, crackling vibrations were
lost in the cascades of sound which her clumsy
feet unloosed to dash up against tiled walls. Soon
it would be light, she supposed. But before dawn
came, there were the grates and the fires to do,
and the boilers and the stoves, and the floors

and the stairs; and the grates and the fires and the boilers, the stoves and the floors, the stairs and the grates and the fires; and her mind wandered without ceasing on this Housemaid's Miserere. It brought a sense of comfort, this expression of hardships. She would feel better by and by. She must light the fires.

First the flames were born in a faint blue flicker, and then, swiftly growing lusty, purred and coquetted at her from their iron cages. The rhythm of their lithe and feline movements woke the reflections that had been slumbering in their nests, high among the overwhelming gold frondage of cornice and capital, which had been overgrown in a breath by the bronze forest of the darkness. Directly the light was turned off, the jungle overgrew all this splendour; but now all the richness was revealed, and the fire woke all these little reflections up in the branches, making them stir and preen themselves, and peep out of their dark, high nests as a wild creature, moving through a forest at night, would wake all the young birds, set them quivering and twittering.

Now it would grow warmer, she thought. But, as she drew aside the heavy plush curtains, and threw the shutters back, immediately the cold twilight poked and scratched at the window-panes with its sharp black claws, then moaned like a hunted animal that craves shelter. Blue frost flowers could be seen expanding and contracting on the glass, and the cruel wind squeezed through every crevice and conducted a paper chase high up into the grey air of the open space outside, above the Cannon and Anchor, whirling its quarry

over and round them, while within the grates the
flames for a moment shrank back, became sensitive plants that closed, opened and closed, their
red petals.   The floors next; and, after that,
would they want tea, she wondered?   The old
lady was ill (oh, she'd seen it coming on, of course
she had.   Why she'd told as much to Miss
Thompson a fortnight ago), too ill for tea, she
expected.   Only one cup of tea, that would mean,
to make: but there was as much trouble making
one cup as two.

CHAPTER XXVI

SITUATION REQUIRED

IT was a few days after the funeral. Miss
Bramley had been caught so fast in all the
intricacies of business, with which the recently
dead yet contrive to entangle the living, that,
fortunately, she had been given little time for
reflection. Really, if the whole day was occupied, there was no time in which to think about
oneself, and by nightfall one was so fatigued (it
could only be called *dead-tired*) that sleep hurled
itself down on one like a boulder, knocked one
senseless till the morning. Still, she felt it: it
was a break. And she had such a headache
(neuralgia, probably) that she felt inclined to
cry. Into the passage outside, through the half-
open door, was wafted that combined odour of
old leather, dead railway journeys, scented soap
and camphor, which denotes invariably that packing is in progress somewhere in the vicinity. Indeed the shiny black trunk revealed its canvas
lining, with only a few, precious things carefully
stowed away at the bottom. There! the chasuble
was neatly folded up, wrapped in tissue-paper,
and placed within. It tired one's back, though,
leaning down and lifting things. Now there were
the two scent-bottles (one had to be careful with
glass) and the piece of 1870 bread in its casket:
better put that at the bottom, too, she thought.
It was wiser, perhaps, to wrap up each photo-

graph separately in tissue-paper, and then they could not get spoiled. After all it was no use having nice things unless one looked after them properly. The frame was so fragile, wonderful work! The silver-backed brushes must be put in their wash-leather covers: but what was the best way of packing the silver boxes, the filigree box? Porters were so rough, bumped things about without giving a thought to their value. All they considered was to get the thing done quickly (she was so tired that, really, she felt she could drop!). There! that was folded up nicely, too . . . of course she did not mind, but nevertheless it had been a blow—not that it had been Poor Cecilia's fault . . . no, it was the Floodgays that were responsible. The only comfort she could find was the fact that, at any rate, it had not benefited them. . . .

Miss Bramley had been authorised to arrange the service—Archdeacon Haddocriss had officiated—for a funeral was no place for Acting and Affectation. She had seen the solicitor afterwards—a typical lawyer with gold pince-nez and a special, official black-banded top hat for the funerals of his clients—and he had spoken to her very nicely, a cultivated man. "It is dreadful to talk, so soon after the dear old lady's death of such things as testamentary depositions," he had said, "but I should like to assure you that you have not been forgotten."

"Quite so."

"I ought not, perhaps, properly speaking, to tell you any more, but," he added, "I think it may be of comfort, as showing my client's fondness for you, to know that there was an unsigned

will in your favour. She was very forgetful, and
omitted to sign it. But you may rest assured
that you will be treated with due generosity. In
fact the next-of-kin, to whom the property passes,
has already empowered me to give you any one
piece of jewellery which you may choose as a
memento of the deceased lady."

.Miss Bramley said "Quite," again, for it was
difficult for her to find another answer. So that
was why Cecilia was always asking to be reminded about seeing the lawyer: that was why
the dying woman had striven to talk, why she
had looked at her in that intent, imploring way.

·   ·   ·   ·   ·   ·   ·

Miss Bramley had chosen a gold ring, with a
curious design of two intercoiled serpents with
ruby eyes. It reminded her of Cecilia, who had
always worn it, and was very pretty in itself,
she thought. She hoped it was not too "showy"
for a Companion. The worst of it was that she
was no longer as young as she had been (there
was no use in disguising it, that was why she
was so tired) and, though it seemed silly that
it should do so, for, of course, one had much
more experience, this undoubtedly made it more
difficult to find a situation. She must not forget
to buy the *Times*, when she went to the station.
It was far and away the best paper in which to
look.

It was odd, too, she thought, that she had not
heard again from Mrs. Shrubfield or dear old
Miss Waddington, very strange: for they had
been so kind before the funeral; both of them
had asked her to stay for as long as she liked,
placed their houses, practically, at her disposal.

But when she had called two days after the
funeral, Miss Waddington had been unwell. She
must write to them, as there was not time in
which to see them: they might know of something that would suit her. They had so many
friends.

Here we may say that, as a matter of fact, on
the afternoon on which Miss Bramley had called,
the two Marshals were having tea at St. Saviour's
Vicarage with Mrs. Floodgay. They had not
spoken to that lady for two years, but after hearing that Miss Collier-Floodgaye's estate had
passed to an unknown, distant cousin, they had
felt that she was adequately punished for her
offences against them. They had chanced to
meet her in the street, the day after the funeral,
and there had ensued (for the two old ladies
were so impulsive) a lightning reconciliation.
"Really," Miss Waddington observed to Mrs.
Floodgay, "that little daughter of yours is getting
so pretty . . . such lovely hair." At tea, the
next day, they had confessed that they had found
Miss Bramley's singing "attractive" (they were
so *devoted* to music) but she had seemed to them
rather . . . well . . . you know . . . rather materially-minded. . . .

. . . .

Miss Bramley was ready to leave. The vast,
black-canvas trunk was already placed on the
top of a cab, of which it might have been the
very bud or offspring, so much did it resemble
its parent in shape and colouring. Just as she
was passing through the hall on her way to the
door, an elderly military-looking man stepped up
to speak to her. It was Colonel Fansharpe

What an extraordinary coincidence: for she had been dreaming of him only the other night—just before Cecilia's death—and she had not seen him, or thought about him, for years!   In fact she had not seen him since that snowy day on which she had driven away from Llandriftlog. He was most kind and affable.   There was a lot of good in him really.

Colonel Fansharpe had been much struck by the coincidence of seeing her, too.   "Fancy seeing her here!" he remarked to Mrs. Fansharpe (Ivy) afterwards.   "She must be damned well off, that woman, to stay in an hotel like this;   *I* can't afford it for long . . . she's feathered her nest pretty well, that's evident.   A scheming sort of woman, I'm afraid, my dear."

Elisa saw Miss Bramley into her cab.   She was quite sorry to see her go.   And soon Miss Bramley was slowly jolting past the green plot, with its Cannon and Anchor, past the bow-windowed seaside houses, past the terraces and crescents. The sea flicked a white arm above the walls at her for the last time, and she was in the station, buying the *Times*.   "Situations Vacant," she read, "Gentlewoman wishes young Companion, artistic and refined. . . ."

.   .   .   .

EPILOGUE

THE Cannon was once more to assert its supremacy over the Anchor, which had held power for a century. During that period the triumph of this latter symbol had appeared, to most people, absolute and eternal. For a hundred years sudden misfortunes, violent death or dispersal of property, had been considered as things irregular, almost indecent, over which it was better modestly to draw a veil. Thus the subsequent adventures of various persons in this narrative are of interest to others, because so utterly unforeseen by themselves. Viewed from the crow's-nest of any of the ten previous decades, the events which were soon to overwhelm the inhabitants of this calm, rather stagnant town were so startling, that their sensations can only have been comparable to those experienced by the Roman Legion which, secure in the knowledge that the subterranean fires of their mountain were extinct, happened to be caught encamped in the crater of Vesuvius at the moment of its first historic eruption. To the people of Newborough, History had seemed dead as the flames of the volcano to the Legionaries. Indeed the corpse of the Dear Departed, who in her life-time had shown so many kindnesses to this country, had long been interred, her memory kept alive only by such ageing and recurrent ritual as that with which children, here and there, still celebrate

Guy Fawkes Day, or, at intervals, by the rarer, more dignified observance of Jubilee or Coronation. But now the old harridan was to rush out of her prim, neatly-kept grave, and sweep down without reason on this unoffending place. Further, she intended to insist that those who had mourned her should now play the principal part in a fresh funeral, that the audience should become participant in the performance—a nightmare drama that, for all we know, may not yet have been brought to its culminative, last act, and of which the present time may serve merely as a more or less quiet ten minutes interval.

Some six years after our story ends, the "Great War" broke out. To this occurrence no one in Newborough was at first inclined to pay much attention. For a few days it was feared by those retired Majors of the Auxiliary Forces, to whom war always remains an interesting possibility, that, as a Liberal Government was in power, we might not be able to "join in the fun." This conceivable restraint on our part would, they agreed, damage fearfully our reputation for good sense and sportsmanship. One could always depend on the Conservatives, if there was a war in progress in any part of the world—or even if there was not—to plunge into it, or, at any rate, to become entangled. For a day or two suspense hung like a purple thunder cloud over the Gentlemen's Club, where flushed and fuming sat ex-military officers and superannuated captains in Yeomanry and Volunteers, in front of Gargantuan whiskies-and-sodas, swelling visibly as they made known their intention, by facial expression as much as vocally, their intense de-

termination to "do their bit," "keep a stiff upper
lip," and "see it through." Fortunately there
were no tragedies, for the Liberal Government
soon proved that in the hour of need it was everything that a Conservative could wish.

The War began everywhere rather quietly.
The Regular Army, though by nature pacific,
as are all regular forces, had long been prepared
for *a* war—but, as usual, not for the one that
substantiated. This ideal European conflict,
which the military authorities, with their accustomed foresight had seen coming, and to which,
in spite of all the evidence tending to disprove
its identity, they remained loyal during the opening months of the campaign, was one built on
the model of the Boer War, but larger and
shorter; it was only to last three weeks, and
was, in fact, to be a sort of prolonged Gentleman
v. Players cricket match. The author, if he may
be allowed a personal confession, joined the army
two years before the War broke out; and well
remembers the talk of war which was prevalent
during 1913 and the first few months of 1914;
his memory retains the private prophecies of
Generals that a European War was coming.
(Every one must be ready for it. The shape of
the men's toecaps must be improved, and the
right hand man in the last left rank but one
had the last button but one on his tunic slightly
loose,) and their expressions of gratitude to the
Providence which guarded Britain that we should
have been vouchsafed the experience of a victorious Boer War some years earlier as a training,
a full-dress military exercise, a transcendent re-
hearsal of the coming conflict. The German

army, meanwhile, had been for forty years plod-
dingly preparing for the war of 1870, while the
Russian Command was feverishly completing its
lack of arrangements for the Crimean Campaign;
for all armies, unless directed by a genius, foresee
and prepare for a war that is over—and never
for the one that is coming.

The embarkation and departure of the First
Expeditionary Force from England caused little
emotion in Newborough, where the passage by
night, in specially constructed shuttered trains,
of a mythical host of heavily bearded Cossacks,
was much more eagerly discussed. Mrs. Shrubfield, who knew a little Russian, had distinctly
heard a dark, bearded figure pitifully demanding
vodka in the night, in his native tongue: one of
Mrs. Toomany's favourite divorcees had met
them at King's Cross when they arrived, and
Mrs. Sibmarshe's sister had seen them at Ebur
Station. Perhaps more attention would have
been paid to the departure of the English troops,
had the news of it not been so carefully censored
and hidden. It was hardly until fighting began,
that the English understood that their troops were
in France.

And, by that time, a kindly Government had
provided the country with that cry, which would
have moved Napoleon to despair: "Business as
Usual"; and a great peace descended on all the
people of Newborough, all except upon those few
who had relatives fighting across the water. It
was feared that the lodging-house keepers would
suffer, for the town was rather empty of visitors.
Otherwise life remained at present unaffected.
The only alteration noticeable was the increased

excitement of reading the newspapers. On the other hand, several leading persons answered the call for economy by giving up newspapers for the duration of the War. To these, life became increasingly halcyon. In the local sheets which Miss Waddington was in the habit of perusing, the lists of names, with the rhythm of which she lulled her nerves, was no longer that of stall-holders at charity bazaar or hospital ball, but of their young male relatives lying dead in France or Flanders. Otherwise life was normal, there had been wars before, and this one would not— could not—last for long.

. . . .

It was a dull morning in the first December of the "Great War," and Miss Waddington, then in her eighty-seventh year, was sitting propped up in bed at 8.30, before a creditable breakfast of tea, toast, poached eggs and marmalade. The local newspaper was by her side. So Mrs. Sib-marshe's son had been killed! Well, one could never have foreseen that. But here her attention was drawn away by the intruding damp coldness of the morning—a rather unusual morning for the time of year, it seemed to her; though foggy and cold, there was for once no sound of em-battled wind and wave. It was chilly, the old lady observed, distinctly chilly in spite of the fire, and she was just asking for an extra shawl (the light blue one in shell-stitch) when, quite with-out warning, death darted at her from the sea, and Miss Waddington, and her bedroom with her, was pulverised, fading with a swift, raucous whistling and crashing into the murky air. It was as though she had never existed. But so

loud was the raging steel voice that Mr. Paul
Bradbourne, right at the other end of the town,
heard a sound for the first time in forty-four
years. He was certain that he had heard something, while in guarantee of it, he had felt an
accompanying tremor, the stamping of an angry
metal giant. His jaw fell open; he was puzzled.
He rushed to question his housekeeper . . . but
he was never to reach a sure conclusion as to
whether his senses had deceived him, for the next
moment he, too, was disintegrated, and the passing of Miss Waddington from life was most surely
the last sound that ever reached him.

Within a few seconds the Superb Hotel stood
like a gigantic honeycombed rock, full of gaping
caves formerly the dwelling, it was obvious, of
some race of splendour-loving troglodytes, for
these caverns blazed with the most extraordinary
relics of past grandeur, gold and scarlet and solid
bronze. As one watched, fresh caves were opened
up, each one with a deep roar, as though a
ferocious, titanic guardian within were about to
spring out and avenge the insult. The four domes
puffed lightly into the air like bubbles. Shattered
wood cracked and sagged at terrible angles.
Next, the attacking ogre snatched away the bow-
window of the Gentlemen's Club, but the telescope could still be seen pointing out of the
wreckage as if it were a dismantled machine-gun.
The hour was so early, that fortunately at the
time no one was in the room to be injured. In
all this desolation, only the Cannon and Anchor
remained placid and undisturbed on their green
cushion. Almost simultaneously the Cricket
Pavilion melted into dust and greyness, and the

Cemetery was outraged by those ghoulish, giant hands. Elisa's friend, the Sexton, was killed—a fantastic death, for he was first given time to see the tombstones, eternal "Aberdeen" as much as plain ivy-bordered stone, hurled tumbling and whirling through the air, while white marble angels fluttered up into the mist to vanish, allowing the skulls of the lean skeletons beneath to leer hungrily from rusty coffins. The Cemetery happened to shield the Power-Station, and that no doubt was the objective.

The worst was now over: but meanwhile many of the squares, crescents and terraces that faced South had been transformed into the likeness of excavated cities, and many were those shaken survivors who wished that, in defiance of both custom and medical advice, they had faced North. The inland trains were crowded for several days. And Mr. St. Rollo Ramsden, calm and cherry-lipped as ever, was surprised on arriving at St. Saviour's Vicarage in order to enquire after the safety of Mrs. Floodgay, to observe in the hall mirror that he was wearing a tie, without its usual appendage, the collar! He hurried back through the stricken streets, nervously clutching his neck; for even, in adversity, Newborough eyes were sharp in their scrutiny, and when one was a public man, one had to be careful . . . these stories do so much harm.

. . . .

Now it may appear from the account above that Destiny had finished with Miss Waddington. But such was most certainly not the case. Her end did not constitute the annihilation that might have been imagined, indeed it was only

after her forcible and unexpected end that the
frail form of Miss Waddington impinged upon
History, and then upon Art. Her doom was not
confined to herself, but, in this comparable to
an octopus, after the preliminary fog of ink dis-
charged by the journalists, had enveloped it, was
to fasten its tentacles on to thousands of young
men, sucking and dragging them down to the
depths where they would be devoured. For some
reason or other the fate of this particular old
woman was seized on as an aid to recruiting.
The country blazed with placards, on which was
printed in staring, red letters:

REMEMBER NEWBOROUGH AND
HESTER WADDINGTON

Her age was the chief attraction emphasised, but,
in addition she was described as "a rare and
gracious presence, and an inspiration to the poor
and needy." Little stories, illustrative of her
dauntless courage and indomitable patriotism
were related in every newspaper. Her niece, it
was written, had on one occasion tried to hide
from her a paper containing a Roll of Honour,
in which was announced the slaughter of a
cousin; but the old lady, like the Spartans of old,
had insisted on reading it through, indeed over
and over again, merely remarking, "He is not
the first Waddington to pay the penalty"—a comment with which the niece may have agreed.
Then there was the yet more moving tale related
by a friend who had begun to read aloud to her—
for her eyesight was failing—an account of the
Retreat from Mons. The dear old lady had
proudly interrupted—interrupted in words, which,

though she knew it not, were afterwards to become famous. "Do not read it to me," she said, "it is painful and unnecessary. *I* am content to know that our lads are doing their duty." But later she was found, with her old eyes glued close to the journal, draining in privacy the last dregs of a bitter cup.

Bishops preached sermons on her fidelity, and the Prime Minister made a touching reference to her in his famous oration at a Guildhall Banquet.

"The Allies," he said, "are not fighting for trade, territory, or an indemnity. They do not demand an inch of enemy ground, they will refuse to receive, when the time comes—as come it must—even one bar of gold; but, speaking as an old servant, however unworthy, of my country (hrump, hrump; and after coughing, he surveyed the rosy faces round him), I say, I say again, and I reiterate, that we will not replace the sabre in its holster, nor the musket in its scabbard— until Russia has been requited, France rewarded, and Belgium and Servia avenged and recompensed—and more than recompensed—for the outrages committed upon them, or our reputation for justice will be forfeit, and the name of Hester Waddington will be indelibly inscribed upon the shield of a Nation's Shame—nay, more—of an Empire's Infamy."

The propaganda was effective. Thousands of young men, out of horror at the atrocious death inflicted upon this defenceless old woman, as she sat up in bed before a typically English breakfast, besieged the recruiting-stations, subsequently to be dealt out a variant of her own fate,

but on the more remote fields of France and
Flanders, Mesopotamia and Turkey. Thus at the
moment of her cruelly sudden atomisation, Miss
Waddington entered the sphere of History, and
remained as she had always been, a leader. Now
it was that she was to make her first curtsey in
the world of Art.

By this time the interest in Miss Waddington,
instead of being merely a thing foistered on the
public by the journalists and recruiting-authori-
ties in league, had become genuine. The public
had become attached to this new heroine, and
raised, quite on its own initiative, a considerable
sum of money to celebrate her likeness in marble.
After having made so much use of the missing
corpse of the old lady, it was impossible for the
Government to refuse to support any effort for
her further glorification. Consequently, her
statue (erected in a style of which, had she been
alive, she would have disapproved so vehemently
as to raise unfounded suspicions in the mind as
to its possible merits) now stands as a centre of
provincial pilgrimage in Trafalgar Square. As
a matter of fact this representation, if such it
can be called, of the old lady, is not the work
as might at first be imagined, of a young Servian
sculptor demented by the horrors of the invasion,
and subsequently interned for the duration of the
War in a Berlin studio, but of an almost crippled
Academician, several years senior in age to Miss
Waddington. How this little, old bent man
achieved such an energetic group remains a
miracle! He had, however, manifestly decided
"to keep up with the times," and in spite of a
vicious hatred for everything good in the modern

movement (while, for example, he always lends
the prestige of his name to the periodic demands
for the removal or mutilation of any new Work
of Art, such as Epstein's "Rima," which happens,
by some mischance, to find itself jostled among
the vile mob of London statues) had, with true
academic eclecticism, adopted all the tricks of the
advance-guards, and added them to all the laid-
aside tricks of every other movement in history.
The whole conception, however, is simple and
affected, and bears no resemblance to the old
lady in figure or countenance. It is also extremely allegorical, for allegory is very remunera-
tive to the sculptor, if costly to those subscribing.
It is impossible to ask much for "a plain likeness," but throw in a figure or two of Liberty
and Justice, and you can at once sextuple your
demand by an artistic process of compound
multiplication.

.The group shows Miss Waddington, a rather
unrobed, muscular giantess of ample bosom and
straining neck, holding up a large male baby of
doubtful symbolism in one hand, and a Bible, or
bank-book, or something, in the other. Behind
her the lachrymose figures of Justice and Liberty proffer a shawl, like a fishing net; while the
octogenarian maiden lady's naked feet are entangled with crosses, cupids, anchors, lifebuoys,
shell-cases and banners. The pedestal is quite
plain save for the inscription:

HESTER WADDINGTON

PRO PATRIA

"I AM CONTENT TO KNOW THAT OUR LADS
ARE DOING THEIR DUTY."

Her niece, Ella, survives her, but is in a home, suffering from shock. She does not realise that Aunt Hester is dead, and is for ever answering her imaginary calls, and looking for her in corners.

Mrs. Shrubfield barely tided over the War. She came through the actual experience with colours flying, and had left Newborough, for ever, two days after the sea had once more quickened it with history, and had taken up residence in London. She was immensely interested in the fate and renown which the War had brought her old ally, and was often seen in front of the Waddington Memorial with a pensive tear suspended in the corner of her jet twinkling eye. Herself indulged in an orgy of sock-knitting, gave up the use of all German words and the consumption of all non-alcoholic liquors for the period of the conflict: further she did canteen work, and stood for hours behind a bar, serving out drinks to others, in spite of her own need, after the example of Sir Philip Sydney. Alas, after participating largely in the celebrations that inaugurated the Great Peace, when it came at last as a fitting reward for the "Great War," she expired suddenly from Spanish Influenza—or "La Grippe," as, even in her last moments, she preferred to call it—a suitably cosmopolitan illness, but one which was the direct result of the conflict: so that she perished as much a victim of hostilities as any man who fell in battle.

Elisa was arrested and interned in August, 1914. But, after the calamity at Newborough, she rested under the most grave suspicion. Not only had she been employed for many years in

the Superb Hotel, which had been so devastated, but it was now recalled that she had often been detected mooning about, in an apparently quite purposeless way (as it was then thought, by the inhabitants in their good-natured folly) or trying to enter into conversation with the Sexton. And, before she had been arrested, she had been caught turning on the light after dark in one of the hotel rooms which faced the ocean: what was more, the window was uncurtained. At the time, she said her action was due to force of habit, but it was easy, now, to understand to whom she had been signalling in the grey wastes. Nothing, however, could be proved against her, and she was therefore allowed to remain, though, naturally, under special surveillance in one of those civilian concentration camps, where, since prisoners were so indulgently treated, she was doubtless happy.

Though Mr. St. Rollo Ramsden came through the Bombardment personally unscathed, he was to know sorrow. He gave his white-haired and aged mother to the cause. After the ordeal at Newborough, though uninjured, she felt that it was fairer on her children to move to London, and went on a prolonged visit to a niece living at Hampstead. There, one dark night, a bomb fell, and poor old Mrs. Ramsden paid the Supreme Sacrifice. His mother's tragic end must have acted as an incitement to renewed patriotic effort, for the energy of Mr. St. Rollo Ramsden during those dreadful years acknowledged no limitations. In the inland town, to which as Headmaster, as guardian of his pupils, he had thought it wiser temporarily to remove his boys,

he achieved endless useful work for his country.
His gift of eloquence made him in demand at
every local recruiting meeting. He sat on a
Tribunal, and was tireless in ferreting-out consci-
entious objectors. Generally speaking, he set
an example. This was no moment for self-
indulgence, and in a true spirit of sacrifice, he
unhesitatingly cut down by half the rations of
the boys under his care. In addition, meat was
allowed only once a week, and himself gave up
more sugar, and believed more spy-stories, than
any one in the neighbourhood. He was deservedly
popular in his new abode, and it was with great
regret that the townspeople saw him leave them,
when the Great Peace came, to move his school
back to its original, salubrious habitat. Many of
his former pupils, though, lay dead in Europe and
Asia; and he caused two beautiful tablets to be
erected in the School Chapel—one to his mother,
the other to the Old Boys. Indeed it may be
said that the Headmaster's Valediction to the
Fallen, at the unveiling of these Memorials, will
long be remembered by those present at the ceremony. His reputation as an orator was still
further enhanced, and it is understood that he
nurses new ambitions—that, in fact, he would
be willing to seek election to Parliament in order
to help ward off the Red Menace. But the town
is not so Conservative as it was before the War.
The Ghoolingham influence, for example, is no
longer there to help the candidate. Up till 1914,
in spite of the predatory budgets which were so
often denounced, that influence was still para-
mount, as it had been for three centuries: but
Lord Ghoolingham died in 1915, and both his

sons were killed serving their country, which, in grateful recognition of their services, mulcted each corpse in enormous death duties, and completed the ruin of the family. The title is extinct, the land and houses have been sold.

Mrs. Toomany, on the other hand, gained rather than lost by her war experience. She contrived to attach herself to a rather disreputable woman of good family, who ran a canteen in France. She vastly enjoyed the work, and later reaped the golden harvest which she had helped to sow—that great crop of gilded divorce cases which is the one clear result of the War.

Cécile Floodgay married a young officer in the Artillery, who was stationed at Newborough Barracks, a year or two before hostilities broke out. They had very little money but were extremely happy . . . he was buried alive by the fall of a shell when with his battery near Ypres, and his widow survives him solely because of her love for her young son, and her belief in spiritualism. The child is said to bear the strongest resemblance to his maternal grandfather, the present Bishop of Gothland, and is already an accomplished mimic.

Sir Timothy Tidmarshe died shortly after King Edward's death. His august relict, recovered from her surprise at the discovery of that ruby and diamond tiara which was found under some clothes, at the bottom of a chest of drawers, continued to live in Newborough. But the bombardment brought her growing invisibility to an unlooked-for climax. Her sons, however, though all good, indeed distinguished soldiers, by the

strange fortunes of war, outlived her, and still quarrel fiercely among themselves to this day.

It is better to omit the full recitation of these things, of how, as an indirect consequence of the War, little Miss Penelope Finnis was forced to starve herself to a genteel death—for all the rich tradesmen of the town had moved inland, so that there were no girls to instruct in the arts of young ladyhood—while Miss Pansy, left alone, was driven into an asylum; of how Dr. MacRacket died of smallpox in Mesopotamia, and poor Mr. de Flouncey's only son was burnt to death in a falling aeroplane. About these things there is such a lack of proportion. The penalties are too severe to be credited. That such things, too, should happen to the descendants of fallen angels is undignified: indeed the position is somewhat improved if, instead, the view is adopted that this is a forged genealogy, and that the genuine pedigree of man is an ascent from the chattering, swarming tribes of simians, ever inquisitive, ever examining and inventing, whose only fall was from a tree-top, in the course of a voyage of perilous but splendid discovery and that the only bad ape is the stagnant, incurious ape.

Before the Bombardment

By

Osbert Sitwell

"Is it Winter the Huntsman
Who gallops through his iron glades,
Cracking his cruel whip
To the gathering shades?"

NEW YORK
GEORGE H. DORAN COMPANY

BEFORE THE BOMBARDMENT

OSBERT SITWELL